Then Time Stands Still

by

Mary Georgina de Grey

Then Time Stands Still

Cover Art by *Teddi Black*

The Wild Rose Press, Inc.
PO Box 708
Adams Basin, NY 14410-0708
Visit us at www.thewildrosepress.com

Publishing History
First Edition, 2024
Trade Paperback ISBN 978-1-5092-5749-2
Digital ISBN 978-1-5092-5750-8

Published in the United States of America

Dedication

To Trish—sister, friend, and reader. Thank you for your support and insightful comments.

Chapter 1

Staring into the mirror in the museum cloakroom, Amancia pulled a face. The interview was this afternoon. When she sat before the members of the panel, they would surely notice the bruise on her chin that she hadn't managed to conceal. There was nothing she could do about it, but it was important they see she was a strong, confident woman who'd achieved much and was ready to take on more. Would they? She peered closer at the image and pressed her hands to her cheeks. Or would they read in her eyes that she'd lost her way?

She stood upright, suddenly disgusted with herself, and turned away. Somewhere in her heart was a dream that was dying, and she had to change things before it was too late.

Since the curator's post had come up at the beginning of June, she'd been looking at a lot of things differently. Maybe, if they appointed her, it would be the first step to realizing her long-held ambitions. She pushed her shoulders back before despair took hold. What right did she have to feel so despondent? But of course, it wasn't just work that was bothering her.

She washed and dried her hands, left the cloakroom, and went to unlock the doors at the front of the building.

It was busier each morning, a steady climb back to

pre-covid numbers, and when she glanced at the clock a little while later, it was already eleven. A couple of hours had passed, and she'd had no time to think of anything other than dealing with the public. But suddenly, the lofty front hall was empty. Coffee was cooling in a cup on the desk, and now she raised it to her lips and took a sip, the bitterness reminding her why she'd left it there so long. But it was good to have the unexpected moment of quiet, though it wouldn't last. She often worked at the front desk and was always run off her feet.

Smoothing her hair, she pushed the escaping strands back into her ponytail and tried not to think about who might be on that interviewing panel. But for the moment, there was work to do, and first, she should check if anyone was keeping an eye on the Egyptian section. The exhibition was very popular this year, with the Tutankhamun anniversary, and those artifacts were among the most vulnerable of their collections. A few of them had been lent especially for this important time, but last week, a girl had climbed into a sarcophagus and lain down like a mummy, so her friend could take a photo. She'd shown no shame. "Look, I haven't done any harm, have I? We just wanted to take a picture."

No harm? Amancia had tried to hide her anger but made it clear that what they'd done was unacceptable, talked them through the reasons. Then she insisted they erase the photo, but it was already out on social media. Remembering the conversation, she sighed in frustration; they still hadn't understood that the lack of respect was a violation as bad as any physical damage.

She waved at the guard, Richard Woodhead, retired city planning officer and stalwart of the volunteer team, and then entered the Roman rooms, which revealed an elderly lady staring down at a case of glass bottles and tiny, clay oil lamps. She didn't look as if she had criminal damage in mind. Satisfied there were no problems, Amancia turned back. As she crossed the main entrance hall, a tall figure was ascending the steps outside. The man pushed open the glass-paneled door, and they arrived at the reception desk together.

She slipped quickly behind. "Good morning."

The mere sight of him lifted this day out of the ordinary. His broad shoulders filled the soft brown leather jacket, and jet-black hair curled around the collar, a little longer than she was used to. And the fact there was no gel on it was a definite plus. Smiling, she waited for him to speak.

"I believe you have a Roman section here. I have only one hour, but I would like to look."

The English was a little stilted, almost perfect, but she'd swear there was something different there in the vowel sounds.

"Yes, of course." She selected a leaflet, spread it over the desk so that it read correctly from his point of view, and pointed out where the main exhibits were. "You go through this door to your left and follow through as it shows here. Each section is numbered. I'd take you around myself, but unfortunately, we're short-staffed today, so I can't leave my post."

Where had that come from?

Of course, escorting visitors around the displays wasn't normal practice. But she would've enjoyed playing tour guide to this man.

He looked up, his head slightly angled to one side, and gave her a lazy smile, light glinting in his hazel eyes. "Something I would very much have appreciated. But there's no need, thank you. I can follow this excellent map."

Velvet with traces of gravel in it; how did some men do that? She'd thrilled a little as he spoke. How important the voice was to the way you viewed a person. She could happily stand here listening and daydreaming, allowing the sounds to carry her far away from the reality of a wet Monday in Bristol. And an impending interview. But it seemed he was keen to make the most of his short visit, and he turned away. High-pitched voices were swelling in volume outside the main entrance, but Amancia ignored them, as she watched him stride across the expansive space, and enjoyed the tug of attraction. Wondered if he felt it, too.

She glanced at her watch: one minute to twelve. When the clock in the tower began its ponderous striking of the hour, and the lugubrious notes reverberated around the building, a young woman in a smart grey skirt suit ushered into the hall a line of excited eight-year-olds wearing scarlet blazers. Amancia welcomed the teacher and picked up the phone to speak to her colleague. "Katie? Could you come through? They've just arrived."

As the children exited toward the Tutankhamun exhibition, the door opened again, and a couple walked toward her desk. The pre-lunch rush had begun.

Chapter 2

"Hello, boss!" Tim said, the following day.

A lot of things could change in twenty-four hours, but Amancia hadn't yet been told the result of the interview. What would she do if she didn't get the post?

"Don't. I haven't got the job yet, and I probably won't, not with my luck."

She smiled and patted the man's arm, the darker skin of her hand contrasting sharply with his lily-white complexion, which was rust-spotted with freckles. The elderly technician seemed to live behind the scenes and would probably shrivel up if he ever ventured into the sun. But he was always rooting for her cause, and he was good at what he did, so she valued his opinion.

"Whether you get it or not, you really know your stuff—and you care. I've seen how you handle things. You're the best person for it, streets ahead of the competition." He grinned. "Just my thoughts."

"Oh, you mean Sarah?" She was dejected by this mention of her rival. "I'd like to think so."

Amancia pulled her black curls once more into a ponytail. She needed to be in the foyer, ready to interact with the visitors, but her mind was still on the interview of the day before. Her archaeology degree made her a natural choice for the curator's job that had come up for the Roman section of the museum, but Sarah Bane, who'd arrived just a few months earlier, was always telling people how good she was, and they seemed to believe her. Amancia's application had been in on the first day—and so had Sarah's. She didn't have a good feeling about the way it had gone.

It wouldn't be so bad if Sarah had done anything to deserve their admiration. But she hadn't, or at least, nothing that any of her colleagues had seen; she did a lot of talking, true, but there was little of substance.

"She doesn't even like the Roman period," Amancia muttered, thinking back to their last conversation.

When they'd talked about the direction the museum was taking, Sarah had made a point of telling her that. "It's old-fashioned, Amancia. Modern museums need to look at quite different things."

And now she was suddenly willing to take on Ancient Rome. Or was she a genius who was going to pull it all apart and create something totally different?

Amancia had agreed. "It is old-fashioned, but that should mean focusing on innovation in presentation, in the visitor experience. I said that at the meeting last week. It should not be about removing a section that people are still interested in."

Sarah hadn't responded to that, apparently not convinced. So, why had she applied for the post?

They'd never got on, although Amancia tried to stay cool around her. That said, it was hard to remain professional when the other person cut corners and belittled what you did. But it wasn't personal, not really. Her whole attitude suggested a woman who wanted to ascend the career ladder as rapidly as possible, and it was entirely Amancia's fault if she couldn't match up. It didn't make things feel any better that she appeared to be succeeding. Sarah was plausible, provided you weren't a colleague blocking her on the way to the top.

For Amancia, it was all about the Romans; that was her passion. Granted, a bit of stone might appear to be boring, but as far as she was concerned, each object was the opening of a story. The post was perfect for her.

She accepted that she'd probably already lost the opportunity, but she wasn't going to moan about it and sound like a victim. She pushed back her shoulders, a determined frown on her face: nobody could be allowed to think that of her.

****

Yesterday, anything had seemed possible, but this afternoon, all her hopes had been demolished. The director, David Belling, had tried to console her when he told her of Sarah's appointment.

"Look, Amancia, I voted for you." At least, he was meeting her eyes, so perhaps it was true. "But there were three other people involved. Nothing I could do. And everyone recognizes how good you are with people. A lot was made of that."

Disappointment almost crushed her. A lump grew in her throat, and tears pricked at the back of her eyes. She hadn't realized how much she'd wanted this. But she couldn't see the point of giving way to her feelings. With an effort, she swallowed and said quietly, "I'm not in public relations, David. I have a doctorate in archaeology, and it's being wasted." She hesitated, but she needed to know. "What do you think I did wrong?"

He said nothing for a moment, considering.

"Sarah told us what she would do for us. You talked mainly about what you had done. I guess it's as

7

simple as that. She told us about an immersive experience—computer-aided pictures, music, and speech that would greet the visitor in the first room and make them feel they were in Ancient Rome."

Ah, yes, that was what she, Amancia, had suggested a few days earlier at a meeting. One of the panel members had even been present. Had he forgotten whose idea it was? She felt a surge of anger that they were incapable of seeing through the woman. And that they apparently didn't appreciate the enthusiasm and expertise that Amancia brought every day to her work.

She was quiet for a minute, taking in his words.

"Thanks for letting me know, David." She paused for a moment, forcing herself to think it through. "It's time for me to go. I'll hand in my notice later today."

He tried to change her mind, but she was adamant.

It'd been useful information he'd given her, although hard to hear. But she'd learned something. Wheeling around, she left the room. She felt dizzy after the step she'd taken. Now she was forced into action. All she had to do was find a new post.

It was her own fault she was still working at the museum. As the eldest of five girls, the youngest not yet ten, she'd felt the weight of responsibility when her father had died from cancer. Mum had really needed her then. Made to feel indispensable, she'd stuck close to home. The museum had been hiring, and she'd applied, but things had moved on.

And of course, that wasn't the only problem.

Anyway, it was a good thing she didn't have to face people this afternoon, because she wasn't up to it. First, she checked her contract and wrote her letter of resignation. Only two weeks' notice was necessary.

That alone showed how little her job was valued. She went down to sort through new acquisitions. As she turned her phone back on, a fleeting image of the guy who'd enquired about the Roman section the previous day entered her mind, reminding her there was a world beyond the museum, but the ping of a text snagged her attention: James, wanting to know how it'd gone. She texted back.

—*Didn't get it.*—

After a moment, she added a grumpy, rueful face.

—*Oh, poor thing. Meet this evening?*—

She didn't want to; he'd be too satisfied with the result and wouldn't be able to hide it. He didn't take competition well and was happy for Amancia to continue as she was. He'd even suggested she shouldn't bother applying. "Why take on all that extra responsibility," he'd said, "when I'm earning enough for both of us?" She sighed deeply. He really didn't get it, and his words suggested a longer-term relationship than she had in mind. They weren't living together, and she didn't intend to live with him. Not after what had happened.

—*Tomorrow, James. Can't make it tnt.*—

—*Not free. Tonight if you can manage it.*—

No, the relationship he envisaged really didn't appeal. She grimaced. It wasn't only the job that had to change. So, yes, they should meet, and she would end it. Her heart fluttered at the idea of the confrontation. What had happened to her that she'd become so nervous? Anyway, it would have to be late because Lizzie would call.

—*Okay. About 9:30. Where?*—

—*Crying Wolf.* —

Around the corner from his place on Cotham Hill. Convenient for him, less so for her. But it didn't matter anymore. Frustration was building, and she needed a few changes in her life—starting with James.

The basement of the museum was dark and airless, and the musty smell of antiquity rose to meet her nostrils as she went through the doorway. Bequeathed items, boxed and stored, awaited decisions as to their future. Someone's treasured glass vase or piece of jewelry didn't necessarily fit with an existing collection, but it could be the start of something entirely new and exciting.

Setting the box aside, Amancia sat down on an orange plastic chair next to a three-foot section of fluted stone column and ran her lilac-gloved fingers over it, tracing the carving at the head. It came from a Roman villa, twenty miles away from the city, a surprise discovery, unearthed long after everything else had been excavated and carted away. As always, contact with these precious objects made her feel better, keying in to some deeply felt need. While she worked, she thought hard about how to solve her problem.

There were quite a few changes she could make, and first she would pursue the job she really wanted. She'd hate to leave all this behind, but she was going to. She stared blankly at the opposite wall. Now that the decision had been taken, it really wouldn't be all that difficult. Shot through with a tiny element of fear, her mood immediately lifted.

The phone vibrated again in Amancia's pocket. Quickly, she opened the text: Lizzie responding to her disappointing news.

—*Want to meet tnt for a drink?*—

—Thx. Where?—
—Old Mortuary at 6?—
—Yeah. TTYL x—

It would be good this evening to download a little of the frustration. And she'd tell her that she'd handed in her notice. But she had to get through the remains of the afternoon, and it wasn't yet three o'clock.

Chapter 3

The Old Mortuary had only recently sprung into being, in the way city bars and restaurants did. It was as dark as its name suggested, and wafts of aftershave overlaid the old stone building's lingering stink of damp and other things she'd rather not think about.

A good-humored group pushed and shoved around the bar, creating a barrier between Amancia and the rest of the room. Glasses clinked and people shouted across the space, the volume rising. She stood on tiptoes, trying to see over heads. Lizzie was ensconced in a secluded corner. She looked comfortable as she sipped from a tall glass. It would be her usual weak gin and tonic with no ice. Disgusting stuff, as far away from a real G&T as you could possibly get. Beside an open packet of crisps, a glass of red wine stood on the table, waiting for Amancia.

She warmed at the sight of her oldest friend. They'd been at primary school together, and although they'd studied at opposite ends of the country, the friendship had continued right through university. But five years ago, they'd both returned to Bristol, and here Lizzie was, to provide the support that friendship demanded. Just seeing her made Amancia feel better, stiffening her backbone. Despite the rubbish day she'd had, she found herself grinning.

Sliding onto the rough wooden chair, she pointed

to the wine. "Not sure about this, Lizzie. I might get seriously into it, the way things are going."

The other woman laughed. "I did feel for you for a couple of minutes, when you texted me the result."

"Only a couple of minutes?" What did she mean? Surely this was the one person she could count on for support.

"Well, I decided it's for the best."

"What? I thought you were my friend."

"I am. You can stop being sorry for yourself because I've got some good news." She paused dramatically, watching Amancia's face. "Hope you really are prepared to leave your job at the museum—like right now."

"How did you know what I'd decided?"

"I didn't, but I knew you had to come to that decision sooner or later, and I think it's the right move." Amancia began to protest, but Lizzie wasn't having it. "I'm only judging from what you've been saying recently, and it's clear you're not appreciated—or not enough." She grasped her friend's hand and pulled it to her, turning it to reveal the dark stain on the inside of the wrist. Her eyes flicked to Amancia's chin and back to the wrist. "Not appreciated—and not only by the museum."

"What? Oh, this? I dropped a stone exhibit, tried to grab it before it hit the floor, and this was the result." Her laugh sounded artificial to her own ears and wouldn't have convinced a stranger, let alone her best friend.

"Don't lie to me, Amancia. He did this, didn't he?" She gently touched the almost invisible bruise on her friend's jaw. "And when did this happen?"

13

Tears gathered at the corners of her eyes. "Three days ago. I...I couldn't believe it, but he's under terrible pressure just now, and I know I annoyed him. It was such a silly argument. Please, Lizzie, can we not talk about this for the moment? I've had a tough day, and I'm meeting him later. That's more than enough."

Lizzie gave her a long, hard look. "The way I see it, you're too good at the work you're doing, much too useful, so they never really wanted you to do anything else." She loved all the gossip and the amusing stories from the museum that Amancia provided, and it appeared she hadn't forgotten a single thing. "You pretty much keep the public side running on your own...yes, you do. I've seen you in action." She waved down Amancia's protest. "And you're very good."

Yeah, she did like dealing with the public, although she couldn't deny she got irritated with the visitors at times. But it wasn't what she wanted to focus on. And it didn't use her knowledge and training.

"I think it's time you moved on."

"Oh, yeah? And how am I going to live?" said Amancia, forgetting she'd already said she was leaving.

"Come on, Amancia. You never used to be like this. I remember when you were at uni, you'd come back for the holidays, and you'd done all sorts of stuff. You were always encouraging the rest of us, and you never let any of the gang give up." She looked into her friend's eyes. "You wouldn't allow anything to defeat you then."

"Well, a few things changed."

"And they can change again." Lizzie scrutinized Amancia's face. "You can't carry everyone's problems all the time. Your mum's coping well now, and the girls are settled. This is a good moment to try something new." She stopped, letting her words sink in, and then added, "Because I think you've got stuck, Mancie, darling. Get out there, girl, and grab a life for yourself."

Amancia was silent for a long moment, recognizing the truth. At the beginning, after Dad's death, she'd been the mainstay of the family, but there really wasn't the same need for her anymore.

"I'm not certain Mum could…"

"Are you sure you're not just staying because you…er…need to feel needed?"

"Don't push it, Lizzie."

"Anyway, haven't you just said you've told David you're going?"

Amancia shoved her curls behind her ears. It took some effort to smile, but she managed it. Then the hair fell forward again. She should have tied it back. Maybe she'd cut it, straighten it. That would be a real change. Yeah, but how horrible that would be.

"Okay, you're right. I decided it's time to leave. I have to stay two weeks. He knows I'm ready to go."

"Well, that's the first step, and I've found the perfect job for you."

"What? What have you got?"

Lizzie folded her arms below her ample bosom and produced a coy, little smile. "Think dusty sites. Think Roman remains. Think Spain."

"How could you possibly…?"

"You forget, I find things out before everyone else." Lizzie smoothed down her streaked blond hair, preening a little. She looked very pleased with herself. As PA to a professor at the university, she made it her business to know what was happening, and she was

15

very good at unearthing valuable little nuggets of information. If Lizzie said she had something, then it would be worth following up.

"I was talking to Maddie in admin," she continued, "and she was about to insert an advert for…" She fell silent, looking across the room. "Tell you in a minute." She raised her drink to her lips. "Let's keep this to ourselves, shall we?"

Amancia swirled the ruby-colored wine around in her glass, took a gulp, and let the mellow liquid go slowly down. It was good. She needed it after her big disappointment.

Lizzie watched as a colleague waved at them, before heading deeper into the bar. Only when he moved off in the opposite direction with a pint in each hand, did she complete her sentence. "So, it's an advert for an archaeologist in Spain, on a Roman site. Unexpected maternity leave. You'd head up the team."

"You're kidding," said Amancia.

"Nope. I said to Maddie I had the perfect person with the right qualifications for the job, and she's given me twenty-four hours because she knows that will be so much easier than going through the process from scratch, for everyone concerned. And quicker. They've got some bod over here at the moment who can represent the university in Spain, but he's on a tight timetable, gone up to London this afternoon, and he'll be back midmorning tomorrow, in time for the interview, so it has to be done right away. It's a joint project, you see, so they need a Spanish presence."

"Lizzie, I can hardly believe what you're saying."

"Believe it, girl. I thought you could prepare this evening, remind yourself of the good things you've achieved, so you can tell them about it, and see the prof tomorrow. I'll arrange it."

"How can you? They'll want to interview."

"You, yes, but not a whole string of people. It's too urgent because they're already out there and about to lose a key member of the team. Looks like they'll have to shut things down if there's no one available. A lot of young people are involved, health and safety, the university's responsibility, nah-n-nah, all of that. I'm telling you, if they can find someone in this way, they'll go with it. All you have to do is your impressive best. Like I said, he's going back to Spain tomorrow evening, so it must be done quickly."

"And you think this might work?"

"I do. You have to go for it."

Amancia gave her friend a hug, and they talked for a while longer. She forced herself to stay cool, recalling the disappointment when she didn't get the curator's job; she had to keep everything under control, no getting carried away this time.

"Another?" asked Lizzie.

"No, I'm meeting James."

"I thought after…you were…well, not—"

"Exactly. I'm giving *him* notice as well. I'm not as hopeless as you think."

"Ah, I don't think that at all—but it is about time. You can do much better than James."

"Really?" She shuddered. That she could even ask proved just how low her self-esteem was. "Anyway, I must go. You're a good friend, Lizzie, the best."

"Oh, I meant to say, you have to be able to speak Spanish."

"Claro. No es un problema."

17

It was, actually, quite a big problem. Years had gone by since she'd done the oral exam at school, which was the last time she'd spoken Spanish, but she'd always been prepared to have a go, especially at speaking, which accounted for the A grade that had so surprised her when the results came out. She grinned; it was great, the way Lizzie had thrown that in at the last minute.

She leaned across the table to deposit a kiss on her friend's plump cheek. "Thank you, Lizzie. Can you get some information to me?"

"All in your inbox already."

Chapter 4

The morning was nearly done. Each time she thought about the coming interview at the university, a surge of adrenaline flashed through her. She had to get this post. This was her opportunity, and it could be a step toward so many other things. Better not make a mess of it this time.

She was on her way out, halfway across the museum foyer, when Katie called to her. "Amancia, can you have a quick word with Mr. Edwards here? He needs you to tell him about the History Now scheme. I don't have the details."

If they appointed her, History-bloody-Now would most definitely be in the past.

Ten minutes later, she was hurrying down the steps to the road as the crossing lights turned red. She waited, fuming. She really couldn't be late for this. The green man appeared, and she sped across in the too-tight shoes. Ah, there was a board showing the campus plan. Okay, fourth floor at the end of that wing. She was in the right area.

The job should be interesting but hard work. Of course, everyone had to pull their weight on a dig. As a student, she'd sometimes felt like a slave, back aching and dehydrated, and it could get boring, chipping away at earth that held nothing at all, except…earth. She'd be terrified all the time that she might damage something she'd discovered, because she was too keen or too clumsy. But what a high it was when she'd made a find!

She entered the building and scrawled a signature at the desk. Bad timing again—both lifts were heading upward. Diverting to her right, she pushed through the double doors and sprinted up the stairs.

Would they realize she'd have to be paid? It wasn't obvious how that side of things worked, since it was usually university staff who were involved, but she couldn't work just for the love of it.

"Just go and do it," Mum had said when she'd let her know that she was applying for a job in Spain. "Never mind the money!"

Could there have even been a hint of relief in her mother's voice? Had Mum been worrying about her, stuck in the museum, feeling guilty about holding her back? She didn't like that thought.

But this was a joint English and Spanish effort, so where would they get the funding? Having worked all the morning, she'd had no time to research.

Just after one o'clock, Amancia took a few calming breaths and entered the corridor in which Professor Miller had his office. She'd made some effort to dress smartly, and a glance at her reflection in the mirror at the far end showed her choices hit the right note for the time of year—kind of business-like but feminine and attractive. The shoes were now pinching, so she was probably going to regret the unaccustomed torture of high heels. Worth it though.

A grey-haired woman of about fifty sat at a desk just inside the entrance to the offices.

"Dr. Harding?" she asked with a smile. "Take a seat for a moment, would you."

She went to a door on the far side of the room and disappeared inside. There was a low murmur of voices, and a few moments later, she reappeared. "Come through, Dr. Harding."

The professor walked toward her and shook hands. Rotund, with a ring of wispy, white hair around his balding head, he was about the same age as his secretary and half a head shorter than Amancia's five foot ten. With a kindly smile, he said, "It's good to meet you, Dr. Harding."

"Thank you for inviting me for an interview." She spoke calmly. Inside, she was shaking.

"I'm only an observer here, as we already know quite a lot about you. Of course, we wanted to meet you, but from our department's point of view, this is a formality. However, we're working jointly with the Spanish university, which means you're now going to be interviewed by their representative, Señor Max Dominguez Serrano."

Amancia blinked at the mouthful, but then remembered it was the way Spanish surnames worked, with first the father's and then the mother's family name. It was good to know she was halfway there, as far as the interview was concerned. All she had to do was convince the Spaniard, when he arrived, that she was worth taking a risk on. That was all. Easy.

There was a short cough. Startled, she turned. The visiting academic was already in the room, standing at the window behind her. God, this was surreal. It was the visitor at the museum who'd asked about the Roman section. With a quick glance out the window, he abandoned his contemplation of the street four floors below and came across, holding out his hand to shake.

"Buenas tardes, Doctora Harding."

She gulped, forcing herself to smile confidently, to show she wasn't at all put out by this greeting, which she managed to return with a passable accent. But if he expected to interview her in Spanish, he was going to be disappointed. And before that became an issue, she had to take the initiative.

Forcing herself to relax, she adjusted her black-framed glasses. She didn't need them, but they were a great accessory for an occasion like this, giving her an academic look. "You'll have to forgive me," she said in English. "I haven't spoken Spanish in ten years. It'll take a while for it to come back."

So not today, right.

A faint, rather supercilious smile crossed his face. "Touché!"

He'd seen through her.

He didn't look like any academic Amancia had ever seen. Today, he wore a suit that fitted him so well, it could have been sculpted in place by someone with the talent of a Michelangelo or a Cellini. The longish face, topped with thick, black curling hair, had perfect proportions, and the stubble on his jaw was clearly the real thing, rather than a carefully cultivated fashion statement; this man had to shave twice a day. He didn't look that old, either, for a full professor, maybe only midthirties.

She smiled at him. She'd bet all his classes had a high female contingent. At age nineteen, with a teacher who looked like this, she'd have been one of the first to arrive at his lectures—every time. With the benefit of experience, she wasn't so easily taken in by looks—well, not that much. Anyway, he was too pretty for her taste. But then he turned his head and revealed an ugly scar that ran down the side of his left eye and past his ear. How had he got that?

He indicated she should sit and waited before lowering himself into the chair behind the desk. Ten out of ten—maybe nine and a half, given the scar—for looks. And probably the same for arrogance.

However, this interview mattered, and she needed to concentrate; he was here on behalf of the Spanish university to assess her suitability for the work. That meant she'd better listen and ignore everything else, even though her pulse was racing, and she felt short of breath. It was hardly surprising, considering just how important this was to her.

She turned a little to one side. He was too disturbing, and she really couldn't look at him the whole time—though she'd remember to make eye contact occasionally, or he'd think there was something underhanded about her. She settled down and gave her full attention to his questions. And David Belling's words were at the forefront of her mind; this time, she'd tell them what they'd get if they employed her and make sure they realized there wasn't anyone else who could offer the same. She was going to get this post, short-term or not.

****

The Salamander was one of the many new bars on the Gloucester Road that had opened since lockdown. Desperate after months at home, people flocked to these places in the heart of this zany, young city, particularly if there was room to sit outside.

It was great the way bars and restaurants had colonized parts of the pavement and even the roads, creating an almost Mediterranean feel, in a place that could, on occasion, be as cold as Norway. The Salamander wasn't one of them, being squashed on the side that had the narrow pavements. They'd put out two minuscule tables pressed up against the wall, with a couple of chairs each, but those were occupied. When she entered, she hurried toward the one free space on the far side of the room. At least the door at the back of the bar was open and a gentle breeze was blowing through. She pulled out her purse and left her huge shoulder bag on the table to ensure the seats didn't get taken. Then she went to the bar and ordered.

There was Lizzie now, entering from the street side, and was that someone with her? Her heart sank at the idea of having to talk to anyone else. But there were people in the way. Maybe they weren't together.

"Well done!" Her friend slid onto her seat and picked up the gin concoction to take a sip. "I knew you'd get it."

"I'm so grateful, Lizzie. I'd never have got a look in if you hadn't told me about the advert."

"And they've agreed to pay you, I understand?"

"Not what I'm earning at the moment, but I pointed out I didn't have the luxury of doing the job for the pleasure it would give me, so yes, they've agreed to a miserable sum which I'm not disclosing. Although, knowing you, you already have the details."

Lizzie frowned.

"I'm not into digging around in my friends' personal details, despite what you might think." She studied Amancia's face for a moment or two. "I do think you've done the right thing, Mancie."

Amancia smiled. She was enjoying the sense of

triumph at having succeeded, but she couldn't quite ignore a growing tension at the thought of what she'd be doing after this moment of relaxation. As usual, their conversation followed a dozen different paths, but she was going to have to confront James later in the evening. In the end, she'd put him off the previous day, so she could prepare for the interview, and miraculously, he'd found the time to meet today after all. But even that one day of delay was making it more difficult. She hated how easily she could weaken.

A fresh start meant ditching a relationship that had felt like an obligation for a long time and had become toxic, so she wasn't looking forward to seeing him. Not only would she be telling him she was leaving the country, but also that they were finished. It had to be done, and the sooner, the better. She stood up.

"I have a few things to do, Lizzie, and not much time, so I'm off now."

"Let me know your departure time, and I'll drive you to the airport."

"No need. I've bought a ticket for the airport bus. It's time for me to take charge—of me!"

Then her new life would begin. She grinned, knowing Lizzie would get it. They'd shared so many things over the years, and if anyone understood Amancia, it was her.

"Right then. Congratulations! Maybe I'll see you out there."

"Out where?"

"Spain, of course. Zaragoza," she said, heavy on the Zs.

"Tharagotha they say in Spain. It's a 'th' sound."

"Whatever."

Lizzie raised her glass and drank to her friend's future.

Chapter 5

Later that evening, Amancia turned onto Cotham Hill and headed downward. Her strides grew shorter, and she slowed on reaching the point where the street flattened out. Finally, she stopped, psyching herself up for the discussion they were going to have. It was so much more difficult than she'd have believed possible, even though she'd told him she needed time to herself. Time away. Even though she was leaving the country.

The area around the pub was noisy. It was still light and very warm, and people sat at the outside tables or stood drinking and talking in small groups. Two men headed toward the entrance, and she moved away from the door, still trying to find courage. The coward that she was just wanted to leave and say nothing, but she couldn't do it. How could she disrespect him like that when he'd loved her? When she'd loved him? And maybe still did?

No, she didn't love him anymore, she was sure of that now, but they'd been together for nearly two years and had shared so many experiences. She couldn't just wipe that out.

She put her hand on the door but still hesitated. She must face him…just so long as she remembered that they'd given her the post in Spain. Looking back at the interview, she thought she'd done a very good job of acting a role—that of a confident, professional young woman whom anyone would choose.

But that was wrong. It was no role; that had been the real Amancia, daring once more to be herself.

In case she weakened, she reminded herself that James had done this to her, gradually convincing her she wasn't quite top-notch, not the high-flyer everyone had said. The logical part of her mind told her it was his insecurity that had created the unwholesome dynamic in their relationship. And that it was time for her to do something about it. She'd let things ride for far too long, making everything so much more difficult now.

At last, feeling slightly sick, she pushed open the door of Crying Wolf and stepped inside. Bursts of laughter mingled with the clack-thud of the pool balls, and the smell of stale beer hit her. A few tables were occupied, one or two people eating, plates piled high with fries, and not a lettuce leaf in sight. But this was a drinking hole, not a place for fine dining.

The bartender, a middle-aged man with glasses and a good smile, looked up as she approached. It was the owner, a retired policeman, whom she now recognized, and seeing him reassured her that this was the right place to have the conversation.

"Tonic water on ice with lemon, please."

She'd had her quota of alcohol this evening and wanted to be on top of things.

No sign of James. It was one of the ways he liked to keep her on her toes—setting an exact time and then oversailing by half an hour or so.

At the beginning she'd thought this erratic timekeeping was because he worked so hard, had deadlines to meet, and this fitted with her idea of a successful journalist, so she'd never minded. She'd even been a little proud to be with someone like that. Now she recognized it as more calculating. She picked up her drink. That corner table at the back facing the entrance would be good. She'd see him the moment he arrived, and for some reason, that was important.

Her mouth had gone dry, and she took several large gulps, forgetting the drink was gassy, and a moment later, an uncomfortable bubble lodged halfway down her gullet. She was breathing too fast, just needed to calm down, but before she could do so, the door opened, and James walked in. He spotted her and gave her a little smile. Her heartbeat accelerated, and she wanted to run, but she forced herself to smile in return. He waved and went to order at the bar.

Now, he was heading in her direction, a good-looking man with everything going for him, seemingly attentive and at ease. A couple of heads turned to follow his progress toward her. Few women would reject the opportunity to spend time with him.

"Hi," he said softly, hovering over her. He had a beer in one hand and a red wine for her in the other, and he placed both on the table. "Oh, you've got something already. The wine'll do you more good." He plucked up her glass of water.

"Leave that, James. I'm thirsty."

Reluctantly, he plonked it down next to the wine, and the glass clanked hard on the tabletop.

"Had a good day?" He leaned across and kissed her. She didn't want him to do it. It increased the difficulty of saying what she had to say, but reluctant to antagonize him, she didn't pull back, keeping her response to the bare minimum. Though the heat rose up her neck and covered her face, there was no point in being angry. She took a few deep breaths.

"Yes, it's been a really good day. James, I got the job in Spain, and I'll be leaving in two weeks. Remember what I said about needing time to myself? It's been a hard decision to—"

"What's been a hard decision?"

"The decision to leave. I think…no, I know we have to split up."

"What are you talking about? We belong together."

"James, we've had some good times, some great times, but I have to move on."

"Who is it? Who's trying to steal you from me?"

Heads turned in their direction. She couldn't believe he was shouting at her, here in public. She kept her voice low. "There's no one. You knew I was going for the interview." She paused and then added, "Well, they appointed me."

"Someone's put you up to this."

"I told you there's no one. It's about taking the opportunity to develop my career, about me being the way I want to be."

"Well, I can tell you, you'll be desperate to get back here at the end—if you even last that long." The tone was threatening, but he was speaking quietly again. "It's just some summer fill-in, isn't it? Because they can't find anyone. Is it worth going to such lengths for that?"

Amancia breathed deeply and slowly to calm her trembling. This was like talking to a wall because nothing she said seemed to get through to him.

Now, his voice took on a persuasive note. "Look, why don't you tell them you've changed your mind? We'll go on holiday together, a couple of weeks in

Rhodes, maybe? I'll clear a space in my schedule—it's time I had a holiday as well. Sun and ruins, something for both of us. We can relax. And the museum will take you back afterwards, I'm sure of that."

"I'm going to Spain. They wanted me because I'm the right person, I'm well qualified, and I—"

"Can you hear yourself?" The sound level now rose several decibels. "The right person? Well qualified? Have you any idea where you'd be without me by your side?" He grabbed her chin, forcing her face round so she had no option but to look directly at him. His fingers dug into her skin. "Well, have you?"

Amancia wrenched herself backward and leapt to her feet. Her breathing had gone awry, and she was gulping for air as she swept up her jacket and bag.

"I'm not taking this, James. It's time for you to let go." She was trapped between the table and the corner, blocked by his chair. "Now, get out of my way."

He pushed her, and she slammed down onto the seat, hitting her elbow on the chairback, and agonizing pain shot up the back of her arm.

"You listen to me. You—"

"You need to leave, sir."

Unnoticed by either of them, the barman had come to their table.

"Eff off. I'm talking to my girlfriend."

"And I'm talking to you. You're shouting and disturbing my customers."

Red in the face, James stood up and grabbed Amancia's bruised arm, increasing the agony. "Right, we're leaving. Come on. We'll talk somewhere else."

"No, I—"

"The young lady stays. You go, or I'm banning

you. I've already called the police, and I suggest you leave before they arrive."

"How dare you tell me what to do?"

A vein throbbing at his temple, he glared at the older man as if about to take him on, but the guy was solid muscle, and James was no fighter, she knew, not when faced with someone like this. Somehow, the man's calm made him more formidable. James turned to Amancia.

"Don't imagine I'm letting you go. You'll be hearing from me."

He swung around and stormed out. The rest of the room had fallen silent, other customers entranced by the drama. Now they returned to their own conversations.

Tears were streaming down Amancia's face. She rubbed at them ineffectually with a paper napkin but couldn't stop the flow.

"Don't worry, miss. Just you sit there. I'm calling a taxi for you."

"You're very kind, but I'll be all right in a moment. I can walk."

"No, he might be waiting outside."

"Oh, I don't know what you must think. He's not usually like that. He's not dangerous."

"Maybe not, but if you were my daughter being treated like that, I'd not be letting you out of my sight. Have you got somewhere to go?"

"Yes, we don't live together. I will be all right."

****

In the end, something of what the barman had said stuck in her mind and she went back to her mum's. The whole story would not be told this evening, but there was always a bed there for her, and Mum would listen to whatever she disclosed and make sensible comments.

"You look washed out, Amancia. I suspect you've been working too hard." She poured a cup of tea for them both.

"I'm exhausted with these interviews, and we're especially busy at the museum this week as well. Is it okay if I stay the night?"

"Of course you can. You know that. And you'll be able to tell me about the job."

An hour later, she'd talked about the things she felt she could share with her mother and was feeling much better. Her phone buzzed.

—I've been trying to make you hear, to let me in. Can you open the door.—

—No, I'm not at the flat.—

There was a long pause, and then she could see the little dots, indicating he was texting.

—I'm sorry, darling, if I've upset you, but you always take things so personally. Can we meet?—

Amancia stared at the screen. Take things personally? He talked as if nothing serious had happened. Was he incapable of seeing how his own behavior looked to others? Tempted at first to ignore him, she decided no harm would come from underlining the fact she was going, that she hadn't changed her mind.

—No. I have too much to do before I leave.—

This time, there was no reply. She put her phone away, but a few minutes later, it buzzed again.

—Okay, let's give each other space, and I'll see you before you go.—

It sounded as if he now accepted that she would go to Spain. That was good, but they wouldn't be seeing each other. After all, she hadn't told him exactly when she was leaving, nor would she. She thought for a moment about erasing his name from her phone, but it seemed cruel. She couldn't bring herself to do it.

Chapter 6

Two weeks later, Amancia stepped down from the vehicle into an improvised car park and dabbed again at her forehead. Sweat dripped down the back of her neck, and the dampness under her breasts was unpleasant, but she'd have to get used to it. Still, it was good to be in the open air. She took a couple of deep breaths and inhaled the smell of dry clay.

Once her appointment had been confirmed, things had happened quickly, and the moment of elation had been followed by furious activity so that she could be ready in time. She'd worked full time at the museum, right until the last minute.

The two-hour flight had dropped her into a different world, an alternative universe. It would have been great to look around Zaragoza, with those gorgeous towers and spires, and she'd caught a glimpse of the remains of the Roman walls. It'd been a bit of a blur, with no time to absorb details, but her appetite had been whetted. There'd be plenty of opportunity later.

She wiped her brow again, the tissue starting to disintegrate. It had been a cool fourteen degrees at Bristol airport that morning, like most of the previous week. This temperature was at a whole different level. A woman in her early forties with fading blonde hair tied back in a tail approached. This would be Rosalyn, whom she'd be replacing. As the woman reached the car park, she pulled a large white handkerchief from her pocket and dabbed at her face. Even from a distance, the mottled red of her cheeks showed up. Finally, the poor thing would be able to go home.

"Thank God you've come!" she said, shaking Amancia's hand briskly. She glanced at her watch. "Look, I'm going to give you all the information you need, and then I'm off. Not a moment later than four thirty, okay, Dominic?"

The student who'd driven Amancia from the airport nodded.

"I'll be here from four."

"I didn't realize you'd be leaving this afternoon," said Amancia, panicking a little. "I thought we'd have a couple of days to go over things."

"Sorry—my plane leaves at seven," Rosalyn said firmly. "This is the whirlwind tour."

It was. When reading the briefing notes they'd emailed her, she hadn't taken in that the dig site was literally in a vineyard. Large sturdy plants grew in serried rows stretching out to the horizon. Halfway down one of them, the minuscule figure of a man was tying branches to a post, and another was working a row farther away. So not all vines grew low to the ground; these ones reached the man's shoulder. She turned away, and Rosalyn said, "I'll show you the huts."

Her room was the first of a dozen, in a long, wooden structure built to accommodate harvest workers come the autumn. They entered. A couple of suitcases and a carrier bag were stacked neatly on the bed.

"I thought I'd be in a tent."

"This is slightly better, but only just."

Amancia had to turn sideways to get past the chair to the top end of the bed, to place her things on the only bit of floor space available, but the tiny room was a luxury compared to the setup she'd expected. Rosalyn pointed out the door to a shower room shared with the person who had the next room. All mod cons in this vineyard. Amancia grinned, conjuring up memories of a long-ago summer spent picking grapes in France.

Their minds filled with dreams of a degree in archaeology, Amancia and a friend had been lured to an area full of Roman ruins, most of which had been nothing more than well-excavated foundations. They'd slept in barns and washed under a cold tap in the farmyard. But at the age of seventeen, that hadn't seemed such a penance and had prepared them for many of the digs that followed.

"The next room along is Pete's."

Peter, she remembered, was also a supervisor.

"I'm surprised he didn't take over from you."

"Pete is very good at what he does. We needed someone else because it's not the same role. And it's better to have two people with different areas of expertise." She sat down heavily on the bed. "Open that door and have a look at the shower. It works, and you can lock both doors."

It was adequate. Amancia stepped out backward and closed the door, and Rosalyn sprang to her feet again. "Come on, I want to walk you over the site and then show you the store where the records are kept."

She pointed out the kitchen building as they left the dormitory complex, and they approached an area where two people were working.

"They've mostly finished by lunchtime, but on a

cooler day like today, some enthusiasts work on."

A cooler day…the woman had to be joking.

The land was flat here, but hills and mountains rose to the north. Her study of the site plan during the flight had shown an abrupt drop down to the river. They walked on, and it came into view a moment later. She approached the edge carefully to peer down the cliff at the water below. The swollen river was yellow and muddy, with strong currents. "You've had storms?"

"Not right here, but there were violent storms up in the mountains two days ago, and torrential rainfall. This is the runoff. No rain has fallen here for weeks. You can see the land is bone dry."

The site was open, vulnerable, and that river edge worried her. They would have to protect their excavation if storms were likely. After all, the area was known for it. Hadn't the Romans eventually abandoned their port in Zaragoza because of flooding?

"How was this site discovered?"

"The landowner had one of his workmen clearing the brush here on the riverside. They told us the vineyard had been neglected, and no one had bothered with this part for years. But since he took over the property, he's gradually reclaiming it for farming use."

The fields fell away into the distance. The area closest to the site was recently ploughed, and ancient, gnarled vines had been cut low. Even from a distance, long green shoots were visible.

"The farmhand used a chain and a tractor to pull out a couple of bushes. Fortunately, from our point of view, he chose the best method to do it because the bush came straight out of the earth doing no damage to what lay underneath. If he'd used a mechanical shovel, it could have been another story."

"Lucky for us."

"Definitely. It left a gaping hole, and inside were some pieces of pottery—and a single coin. If it hadn't been for the coin, I guess he might have ignored the find and assumed it was more recent rubbish. But people always react to coins."

"It's surprising he didn't just pocket it. It happens."

"Yes, it does. Anyway, he told the owner, who recognized the find was possibly significant and consulted people at the university. That was several months ago."

It was the way these things happened, like the guys with their metal detectors, hoping to find the odd coin and discovering a hoard of Viking gold. There were many stories like that, particularly in Britain. It was often farmers who uncovered artifacts, but cumbersome farm machinery could do a lot of damage before people realized what it was that they were looking at.

"So how did Bristol get involved?"

"We have an informal partnership with the new Zaragoza university for other areas of study, and they know we have the post-grad archaeology course, so they approached us."

"Nice!"

"Yes. Of course, I didn't know I was pregnant when it was set up—or even that I'd be affected like this by the heat, but I have been so ill." She'd been huffing loudly as they picked their way at speed over the dry, stony ground. "You're not from Bristol University, I take it? I haven't seen you around."

"No, I was at Durham. But my home is in Bristol."

Rosalyn's face had gone a deeper shade of puce.

They were about to walk the grids, but maybe she didn't have to put the poor woman under such stress.

"Look, you could just take me to the store to show me how it's been set up, explain how the admin works. Surely Peter can do the rest."

The look of relief on her face was enough to show Amancia she'd made the right call. The woman paused for a moment, taking deep breaths, before setting off again toward a large, free-standing building, a wooden structure, about twenty feet by twelve.

Inside, Amancia scanned her surroundings, curious to know how they'd managed the recording and administration. They would have been keeping a daily log, of course, because that was standard practice on digs, including those days when nothing of significance was found. And even the smallest objects would go into the store, where someone would clean and bag them, adding the relevant data, like location, date, and proximity to other finds.

Rows of demountable shelving had been erected, and large, clear plastic crates occupied half of them. Other, smaller boxes were laid out on the tables which ran down the center of the room. A female student was sitting with a container open in front of her, writing a label which she proceeded to attach to the lid.

She looked up, and Rosalyn said, "Let me introduce Maya, who's part of the Bristol contingent. Maya's writing her doctoral thesis on the analysis of materials—ceramics, metals, and glass, but with a particular focus on kitchenware, cookware—Roman cookware, of course."

The girl smiled and said, "Hi, Dr. Harding. I'm not sure I'm in the right place for kitchen cookware, but it was the dig experience I needed."

"I'll look forward to hearing about it."

This site was impressive and organized. Wires ran around the walls. "I see you have electricity."

"Yes, and internet."

No important site could run efficiently without work done on computers. She'd assumed everything would be carted up to the university in the city for that, but having the means to deal with everything right here was excellent. Evidence, clearly documented, was essential in the race to claim the next big discovery, and doing it on-site made it so much easier.

"The owner had a powerline put in last year, and this building is a common room for the workers at harvest time. We arranged a linkup with the university."

Everything was meticulously cleaned and labeled. Two computers stood on tables at the left-hand wall, with a couple of filing cabinets between them. Rosalyn clearly knew what she was doing and made sure her team did, too.

"The university here supplied the equipment. Logging is carried out by everyone, and I usually do spot checks to ensure nothing's been forgotten." Rosalyn took another moment to wipe away sweat. "At least, I started out that way, but you'll need to bring it all up to speed."

Amancia stored this information away. She'd kept up with what was happening in archaeology, tried to understand new techniques and approaches. Last summer, to James's annoyance, she'd done a couple of courses. "You're so selfish, Amancia," he'd said. "Using up our precious holiday time. What about us being together?" She'd felt guilty, although he'd backed out of a trip to Italy earlier in the year for work reasons. Now her efforts would pay off. It was good that things looked familiar, but courses were not the same as recent experience in the field.

"What happens when you've got a body of material, maybe from a particular layer?"

Rosalind shot her an approving glance. "It stays here until we assess its importance. We're trying to build a picture, so it's good to have everything to hand. Like this." She pointed to a tray with a clear lid, divided into tiny pockets in which could be seen fragments of pottery. "It's taken all week to find the parts of this pot. Now we should be able to reconstruct enough to get a clear idea of the original. We'll put the pieces in a box here, and then it'll be rebuilt. It's not something we'd normally do ourselves, but some of the students are keen to learn. This is the most exciting object to date."

Amancia knew how a find like that felt.

Rosalyn was looking a little worried. "Look, you're going to find things that are wrong. I've not been functioning well, but they're a good crew, and with Pete's help, you'll be able to put everything right."

Was there something that could derail the project? One of her first tasks must be to go through the computer records and contact the university office to see how they thought it was going.

"Don't worry. You need to get home and ensure you're well for the baby. What about valuable items?"

"I wish there were some! We'd send anything like that straight up to the university."

"Have you had any trouble with people stealing from the site?"

"Well…not so far, although there was an intruder

the other night. We're meeting with the locals soon, to explain what we're doing here and get them on our side, so they feel protective about it."

"It looks as if you have the evidence to be sure this is a significant Roman site." She'd follow up on the intruder with Peter later. "It's a fantastic start. I can't wait to get involved."

Rosalyn smiled and handed over the passwords for the computer, opening a couple of files to show how things were set up. The system wasn't difficult, but she'd have to go through it again in her own time.

"It's the summer break now, so our contacts at the university are a couple of student volunteers, Donna and Ángel. They take turns to be in the office every afternoon between two and four, on weekdays, and there's an emergency number for the weekends which we're encouraged not to use. All the useful contact details are here, including the site owner's telephone number. He likes to be informed of what's going on."

Landowners could be a pain in the neck, particularly if they thought they knew a lot about the find. Some wanted to be involved—there was a certain romantic interest attached to archaeological finds. If it was on your land, you would take an interest. She'd make a point of meeting him as soon as possible.

What a relief that Rosalyn had been organized. It'd be great to get straight down to the site investigation.

"Let me introduce you to Pete now, and then I'll have to go."

They walked across the hard, sand-colored earth to an area where several tents had been erected. The sun was searing, and the dry air carried a scent of herbs and something else she couldn't quite pinpoint, although up here, nothing grew beyond a few scrappy bushes. Maybe it came from the vines.

"There aren't enough huts for everyone, so many of the students are camping, mostly in pairs, and that large tent sleeps three of the boys. They've come from Winchester, full of enthusiasm. The problem has been holding them back."

"I'm pleased to have a room with a bed. I've done my share of camping on digs."

"Haven't we all. Anyway, the students don't seem to mind, and it's also good to have people right on-site most of the time, as a precaution."

"Against your intruder?"

"Yes. A couple of them came back from the city late the other evening and found someone crouching by the door to the store. It looked as if he was picking the lock. Ran off, of course."

That didn't sound good. "Find out who it was?"

"No. We reported it, but we haven't heard anything yet. We've been looking at ways in which we can improve the security."

Who might be interested in getting in there? Perhaps they didn't realize that items with potential monetary value would be sent straight to the university. Far from being put off by these revelations, Amancia's curiosity was piqued.

Up here, she felt removed from the everyday but struggled to identify what was tugging at her consciousness. It was too quiet, that was it: the constant buzz of the big city was completely absent.

Chapter 7

"Great to meet you, Amancia," Peter said a few minutes later. He was tall and thin, fifty-ish, with floppy, grey-blond hair, that was starting to thin on the top, and a friendly expression. They shook hands.

"Pete, can you walk Amancia around the site? We've been to the store, and I've given her all the necessary information."

"Of course. You off now, Rosalyn?"

"Yes, and I'm sorry to have let you down."

"No problem. You couldn't stay. Take care."

He gave her a hug, and then he and Amancia stood with their backs to the river as Rosalyn walked away. As the minibus drove out of the car park, Peter said, "You up for this now? We can leave it until morning, if you prefer."

The site looked empty. It was tidy, no tools lying around. Small areas of excavation were covered with blue plastic sheets.

"I'm fine. Let's have a walk around."

"Okay, the area is divided into six grids, each broken up into squares. The guys from the university came with their gear before we arrived and surveyed it all." As he spoke, he was leading her around the first of the squares. "Ángel in the office created duplicates of this layout on the computer, which means finds can be entered rapidly and mapped with accuracy."

Amancia listened. Things had changed a lot over the years. Archaeologists learned from the proximity of one object to another. The rush to snatch an artifact out of the ground and run off with it, an approach which had characterized many excavations in the early part of the previous century, had given way to a painstaking, forensic approach. Anyone running a site had a responsibility to ensure people were recording the material correctly, and every detail was important.

She wouldn't risk making mistakes, which happened when tired people left the task until the next day and then forgot. Most students on digs were enthusiasts who quickly learned the importance of the smallest details. She followed him, wiping her brow.

"Okay, that's good. How far down have you got?"

"In places, about two feet, but we've gone farther down along the riverside, and we've just uncovered the top of a construction." The tumbling water swung back into view as they approached. At this point, it pushed its way through a narrow canyon, foaming white, booming and roaring as it went on its way. "We made a real find on this edge, these large stone blocks here, so progress has been quicker recently, as we only need to remove a shallow layer of earth and debris to uncover them."

Amancia's pulse picked up. It wasn't just a Roman rubbish tip. Not that a rubbish tip couldn't produce some amazing finds. But discovering something that had been constructed was brilliant news. And it supported a major hypothesis that there'd been Roman ports along the river Ebro besides the one at Zaragoza.

"Could this be one of the ports the archaeologists talked about when excavating upriver?"

"They've not found anything since, but it fits."

The idea was based on evidence provided by the finds made years before in the city. This could certainly be a smaller version of the port situated near the Forum, an extraordinarily rich site, excavated in the 1980s.

"Finding those blocks must have been exciting."

"It was. When we first arrived and had a look around, Rosalyn suggested there could have been a port here, and she insisted on working on that assumption. Turned out to be spot on."

"Poor woman! She must hate to leave this behind."

Amancia's general knowledge of the area, and the Roman era in Spain was extensive. Zaragoza had been a trading hub. Anything here was going to be of interest.

"I'm trying to build a picture of how it worked."

"Yes, goods would have come in from the surrounding countryside. There'd have been a steady tonnage going down to the boats at the jetties. They'd have sent everything to the big cities on the coast, and onward, maybe to Ostia, the old port of Rome."

This was exciting. There was the detritus inevitable when many people worked in an area like a port, which would give some rich possibilities.

They walked farther. The river formed a gorge and left a large, quiet pool where it turned abruptly to the left and hurtled down toward the sea. Was it possible the domain on which they stood had once contained a substantial Roman villa? Why else would you create a port just here? She looked at the low, tree-capped hill half a mile away, which sat in the center of the vineyard. "What's over there?"

"The landowner's house."

That's what she'd hoped. What else could have led to the building of a port, with stone buildings?

"A port here would be smaller than Zaragoza," she said, following through on her thought. "Perhaps this domain belonged to a rich merchant, the descendant of Roman nobility or a pensioned-off army general."

"Yes. Anyone of lesser importance, and it just wouldn't have happened."

What would the current house be like, nearly seventeen hundred years after the Romans left the region? Maybe the people who'd lived there stayed. One thing was certain: it wouldn't be the same building.

"Have you had contact with the Zaragoza professor?" she asked, wondering how likely it was she'd bump into him. "I'll need to talk things through." Her heart was beating a little faster than usual at the thought, as she remembered the excitement of their meeting in Bristol. Should she even try to meet in person? Maybe it wasn't such a good idea.

"None at all," said Peter. "We've mostly spoken to the site owner, and he's been helpful. I've met the professor, but he's in Chile already, or about to go."

That was disappointing.

Peter led her closer to the trenches, but suddenly, her legs began to tremble, and she longed to sit down. It was going to take time to acclimatize.

"We often have to finish early because it gets too hot," said Peter, confirming her fears, "so we make a start around five thirty in the morning with coffee, before it gets light."

"That sounds like a good idea. What time does the sun come up?"

"Half past six. But it's often over twenty degrees by that time. And the other day, it was twenty-seven at midnight. It'll take you a while to be comfortable with it. Breakfast around eight, and we work until the sun gets too much to bear, one o'clock at the latest."

As they came away from the last grid, her phone buzzed in her pocket. It would have to wait.

"Okay, that's all clear. How often have you been meeting up as a team?"

"It could have been more often. I've held a couple of meetings on Rosalyn's behalf, but none this week."

It was Thursday. Several days without a meeting.

"Could you get everyone together this evening to introduce me? Say at seven, to give people a chance to pick up food first?"

"No problem. I'll make sure everyone knows what's happening."

The glare had subsided, but there was no change in the temperature. With only the kitchen left to see, the enticing prospect of a cold drink loomed up. A couple of chairs stood in a deeply shaded area outside the building, and she slumped down. Perfect.

"Have you eaten today?"

"No. Could you show me how things work in the kitchen?"

"Yes, but why don't we leave that meeting until breakfast? Let's go into Santa Maria de la Montaña." He glanced down at his watch. "It's only a short distance away, and the van will be back soon. That'll give us a chance to go over things. Do you like pork and beans? They do a really good *fabada*."

"I can't think of anything I'd like better."

Chapter 8

Amancia stared at her little travel clock the following morning, certain she must have set the wrong time. A minute after five. She dragged herself upright.

She'd enjoyed the meal with Peter at a restaurant that was also a bar and a grocery store, and people could fuel up their car as well. They'd eaten simple food under an awning, with a distant view of Pyrenean peaks. Bougainvillea, a bright magenta plant that sprawled over the walls and trellis of the arbor, filled the air with its heavy scent and made her dizzy. She'd begun to relax in Peter's undemanding company. Her fatigue came from weeks of tension and then the rush of activity just before her departure.

"What's going on here?"

From where they sat, the street sloped down, and quite suddenly, it was filled with men dressed in black trousers and voluminous white shirts with a yellow cummerbund. The women wore black, but their hats were elaborate with silk ribbons and flowers piled high.

"Oh, it's their saint's day. I'd forgotten about this."

The group paced toward them, carrying a litter with a large statue of what looked like the Virgin Mary. Progress was slow, the beat kept by drummers dressed in black. Gradually, other people joined the procession, and children ran alongside. Amancia watched with fascination as they passed the restaurant, heading up to the church which was perched above the town.

She glanced at her watch. "It's late. Is that usual for something like this?"

"I guess it is here. As you can see, everyone takes part." He swallowed down the last of his wine. "Do you want to follow? We could stand at the back of the church and see what goes on."

****

Filled with the singing and the bright colors, and the serious expressions of the participants, she'd returned to the dig site relatively early. She'd missed a call from James, who'd texted —*Really missing you, darling. Don't forget to call.*—

Did he not get it, that she'd left him, that it was all finished? She didn't answer. It would encourage him.

Now she had to get back in the zone, that space in her head where she existed when out in the field, where time stood still, and everything was dictated by the rhythm a dig imposed.

Still unfamiliar with the space, she stumbled out of bed in the dark and entered the shower. The pressure was good, and a couple of minutes under the cool spray was enough to set her up for the day. She returned to her room, remembering to lock the door. Before she picked out a T-shirt, she applied a layer of sun cream to her neck and arms. The cheap pairs of shorts she'd brought would be great later, but she wouldn't wear those until she'd acclimatized a bit. Instead, she donned thin cotton trousers.

With her hair twisted up under a white bucket hat, Amancia crossed the rough square of beaten earth to the kitchen. Her first day. Breakfast was still a long way off, but if she was going to function properly, coffee was essential.

The place was deserted. She filled a saucepan and set it on the stove, found a plunger pot and the ground coffee she'd noticed on their tour. She was pouring the hot water when she heard movement behind her.

"*Buenos días.*" A young woman had come in. "*Me llamo Elena. ¿Eres Amancia?*"

"*Sí. Eso es. ¿Quieres un café?*"

She'd understood the greeting and managed a simple reply, offered coffee. That was a start.

"Good to meet you, Elena."

The girl tried some tentative English, and they stood talking either side of the stove. It was hard to walk up to people you didn't know and start a conversation. She gave the impression she was super-confident, but it wasn't true. Confidence was the armor she put on when she didn't know people. But initial impressions always mattered so, finishing her coffee, she steeled herself to do a tour of the site.

She spoke to various people, and unsurprisingly, it was easier than she'd thought it would be. She asked the occasional question and let them talk about what they were doing. It was a relief that everyone appeared to understand the basic tenet of "do as little damage as possible." Of course, any intervention on a site did damage. You just had to take care.

Back in the kitchen a couple of hours later, people were diving into various cereal bags, pouring coffee or orange juice. The smell of toasting bread filled the air, and her stomach rumbled. She couldn't wait to get her hands on a couple of pieces.

"Help yourself to whatever you want," said Peter, arriving a moment later. "Everyone makes their own breakfast. The cook comes at twelve to prepare lunch and leaves cold dishes for the evening meal at six."

"Right, thanks, Peter." She set a slice of bread to toast. "I'm going to talk to them, as I said."

A few minutes later, she wiped her mouth and headed to the front of the serving bar. People were eating, and there was a good buzz of conversation, which died down when they noticed her waiting.

"I think I've managed to speak to you all. If not, please come up afterward and tell me who you are."

She'd worried about this moment, but it was good she'd made the effort to do the rounds because they now felt like her team. She'd keep it short, make sure everyone knew her and how she wanted things done.

"So, any find, anything at all," she was saying five minutes later, "and you get Peter or me before you dig farther, is that clear?" She smiled. They seemed a good crowd, very keen, and she was looking forward to working with them. "And finally, I want a meeting at eight each morning, with everyone reporting back, even if there were no finds the previous day."

This was new, and people turned to one another, registering the fact.

"Not finding anything is important to know and could lead us to relocating some of the dig areas around the site earlier, so that we don't waste time. And we can share in the success of those who do uncover something, right?" There was a murmur of agreement. "Okay, let's get to work."

People started clearing away. It'd gone better than she'd imagined, and for the first time, she allowed herself to think it would be all right. The kitchen emptied. It was great the way they scurried off, full of enthusiasm. There couldn't be many professions where people started work at half past five in the morning in the dark, with no breakfast, and couldn't wait to get back to it three hours later.

****

Amancia went to Rosalyn's grid overlooking the river. Her grid now. Given the two big blocks of stone that had already been found, neatly situated opposite one another, this promised to be an interesting area. Only the top couple of inches of stone were visible, so there must be a proper construction beneath the current ground level. If there really had been a small port here, they'd soon be uncovering more of these blocks, forming a bulwark against the cliff, holding back the earth and creating a pathway to the water.

She paced around, tracking back from the edge a few yards to where steps might have started. There must be steps. How else could they have got goods down to the jetty to load the boats? Logic and geometry would help decide on possible places to dig. She'd get more people working here, close to the river.

"Rosalyn was obsessed with finding steps," said Peter, coming over.

"Well, that's what I'm thinking." They approached the cliff edge again. "It's not difficult to see how it would have been done." It would help if she got to know the site. "I'm sorry if it's boring for you, Peter, but I need you to tell me everything you know about the dig if I'm going to get up to speed and make sensible decisions. I haven't had time to read up on everything. Do we know what happened along this stretch of the river? Is there any documented history?"

"There's quite a bit of information. It wouldn't

surprise me to learn that all this was more visible a few hundred years ago, but no one would've been interested at the time. And you only need a few storms to silt it up. The river has changed for other reasons, as well."

"Talk me through it."

He gave her a good overview, and then said, "A lot of modern-day activity like the building of the dam and hydroelectric system upriver will have had an effect. There've been two major storms in three years, especially the one the year before last, and there's nothing to say we won't get another big one this year. The Ebro flooded last year, but it's my belief it carried away a lot of earth, so the layer covering any stonework is probably very thin at this point."

She nodded. "Meaning if there's anything to find, we'll soon get down to it?"

"Exactly."

Once again, they were looking down on the water, with views upriver to Zaragoza, and to the right, where the river headed in spate down to Lleida and the coast.

"You can see how it takes a new direction just here. When the pressure built up, there was such a mass of water forcing its way through, that it would've changed a lot of things. Of course, no one paid attention until the discovery was made, so it's not documented."

"I need to talk to the owner of the land. He must have information. There seems to be nothing on file."

"Yes, we can organize that, and I should have mentioned there's a meeting in a few days, over in the village. We both need to be there."

"Okay. Rosalyn said something about it."

A shout from behind made them both turn around. "Hey, Pete, can you come and look?"

It was Chris with the ponytail. It would take a while before she could put a name to everyone, but he stood out because of his hairstyle.

"Got to go. And remind me to tell you about the inspection later."

"What inspection?"

"Government body. It oversees historic buildings."

Chapter 9

"Good morning, *señorita.* Have you had any thoughts about the site?"

Amancia's heart leapt. She recognized that voice, that lovely way he spoke that made her feel shivery inside; the delivery was unique to him and reached right into her, stirring up unfamiliar feelings. For the last three days, she'd been speculating as to when they were likely to meet up again. Now, her heart began to thud, driving the breath from her lungs. How come he was here? He was supposed to be in Chile, giving people the benefit of his superior knowledge or something.

Taking her time, she stepped back and looked up. "Lots of thoughts, actually, but I'm not sure there's anything I want to share at the moment. I need to test my theory first."

Now she could see him, the Spanish professor who'd interviewed her in Bristol, every inch of him just about as sexy as you could imagine. She swallowed. He was standing on the edge of the trench, looking at her from a long way up. With a challenging expression—or was that her imagination? Whatever, he dominated the scene, and she didn't like it.

"*¡Muy bien!* It's good to hear you have theories."

Sarcastic as well. Hmm. But he was an academic. He'd appreciate that she needed to gather information and formulate theories, so that she didn't waste time.

Her pulse was galloping along, and she huffed in a couple of breaths as if she needed extra oxygen for some reason. The thing was, she couldn't blame it on being nervous about the interview and desperate to be appointed. That was all in the past now. She'd got the post, and she was still nervous and desperate about something. Which was unacceptable. She would not allow this man to interfere with…with anything.

There was no getting away from it; he was just a great-looking guy with a sort of magnetism. Yes, that's what it was. Some squirrelly part of her brain was trying to work out how to get closer to him and prolong the moment.

She'd better say something, or she'd look an idiot, so she smiled. "Of course I have theories."

He continued to look down into the excavation, not taking his eyes off her. This was completely wrong. Hadn't she decided she didn't want any complications? The important thing was the work she was doing, mainly because if she did things in the right way, it would contribute to a reference and could lead to a university teaching post. She'd been offered this extraordinary chance, and with him as the supervising academic, she would do well to keep their relationship cool and professional.

"I came to see how you're finding things here," he continued. "I see you've got straight down to work."

Already, since coming to Spain, she'd felt the old Amancia re-emerging—fierce and abrasive when necessary. Cool and arrogant if it got her what she wanted. Maybe getting away from James was good for her. She could cope with this.

"My colleague left everything running smoothly,

so I've no reason not to."

Her phone buzzed as she was speaking. Whoever was calling, it couldn't be that important.

It was her third day of work, and there was already a different shape to the site, one she'd imposed to match her findings and the direction she wanted the dig to take. They had made progress.

"I'm lucky she was so organized."

"Is there anything I can help with?"

Staring upward and adjusting her sunglasses which conveniently masked her expression, she stopped to think for a moment. It allowed her an uninterrupted view of him, which was enjoyable, but it didn't do much to lower the pulse rate.

"Maybe there is. Is that the main estate house, over there among the trees?"

"Yes, that's right."

"Do you think you could organize for me to talk to the owners? Could you persuade them for me?"

She gave him a wide smile and raised a questioning eyebrow, in a flirtatious but "it doesn't mean anything" kind of way, and then wished she hadn't. The corners of his eyes crinkled up.

"I certainly can. As it happens, I've come with an invitation to dinner there for this evening."

"That's great! Thanks for arranging it. I'm impressed you realized it would be important."

"No problem. What time would suit you?"

"What about seven?"

"Seven's fine. I'll pick you up."

"No, thanks. I'd like to walk, but thank you."

She'd forgotten how demanding the first couple of days on-site could be, and every muscle now ached.

Walking would be good to smooth out the kinks, but she wanted the chance to look at the terrain, was determined to walk down that putative Roman road she'd been thinking about. It'd be mad to believe she'd find anything definitive in the fading evening light, but the experience would be worthwhile.

"So that's arranged. Excuse me. I have to go. *¡Hasta luego!*"

He turned away, and it was as if the warmth had gone out of the sun, although it was shining as before. She shook her head. Fantastic. She had an invitation.

He was walking along the cliff edge to the car park, and she took in for the first time what he was wearing: jeans and a rough blue shirt, boots, a wide hat. Not very professorial. But, of course, it was the summer break. Perhaps he wasn't going into the university today.

Mopping sweat from her face, Amancia sat down on the edge of the excavation and stared around. He was here, right here, and she was going to see him this evening. She'd been so busy, she'd managed not to think about their meeting in Bristol more than about ten times a day, but this revived everything she'd felt, and that complicated matters. All she wanted to do was get on with her job.

She stood up. There'd been a call, hadn't there? And a glance at her phone showed it was James: —*I know you're busy, honey. Just want to know if you're okay. xx*—

She had to get him off her back.

—*I'm fine. Need to get things organized here at work. Sorry.*—

As she returned to her digging, James slipped from her mind, and it was Max who occupied her thoughts.

He'd said he'd see her later, so he'd be there this evening. Her heart gave a little flutter. Then, she frowned. Why should it possibly matter to her?

As Max strode away, Peter appeared, and Amancia forced her attention back onto the present.

"Have they found something?"

"Another piece of pottery—and something else. It looks good. Come and see."

She held up her hand, and he leaned down to grasp it and haul her out of her hole in the ground. It was time to install a ladder.

"Let's see what they've got."

The pottery pieces were nice, with one larger, diamond-shaped shard on which there was a faint design in black. It was maybe a marker of sorts, written by a hauler, the sort of thing used to identify the provenance of goods. They'd have to find a few more pieces, in order to work it out, but it was nothing special. It was the "something else" that interested Amancia: a big, flat stone with a faint, chiseled line showing, where the student had knocked away some of the dirt. She looked back to her grid and then off toward the hidden house. It was perfectly placed.

"You're thinking it's part of a road?" said Peter following her gaze.

"I'm wondering. But I could so easily be wrong."

****

What a first-class, prize idiot he was! He didn't have time for this emotional stuff in his life. There were plenty of women who were unproblematic, happy to have a light-hearted, practical relationship. Why was he trying to make things more difficult?

He attempted to shut down these thoughts and keep

his mind on driving, but Amancia's image, the essence of her, filled his head. He tried to shrug it away. He was already late, and Sofía needed his support now.

Max liked intelligent, independent women with ideas of their own. Of course, it wasn't just talk; he enjoyed the things they could do together as well, but he didn't want the complications of a relationship. There were plenty of females who felt like him, but he'd known instantly that, despite the slightly flirty manner, Amancia wasn't one of them. There was a serious streak there. Which made her entirely unsuitable as anything but a work colleague.

So why could he not get her out of his mind?

Amancia wouldn't be interested in anything too casual, unlike a lot of younger women. With those amazing looks, she'd have had plenty of experience fending off all sorts of men, who no doubt hungered for her in exactly the way he was doing right now. She probably wasn't interested in a relationship at all, but if she were, it would be something more long-term. More mature, with commitment. There was no way he was getting into anything like that, so he'd better forget it.

He sighed deeply. It was time to stop thinking about her and concentrate on getting into Zaragoza. He glanced at his watch. With less than ten minutes to make it, he sped up. Damn, what had he been thinking about, going to the site like that? If he didn't reach his destination in the next few minutes, he'd be letting his cousin down. He could've easily sent one of the men to deliver the dinner invitation, instead of acting like a pathetic messenger boy. Juan would've taken it up there for him. That was common sense.

But it wasn't common sense that'd been guiding

him. No, he'd needed to see her again, so he could prove to himself that she'd had no effect on him whatsoever, that it was all in his imagination. A fine way that had turned out! His instincts had been totally right the first time. Of course they had, and intelligent thinking wasn't getting a look in. He clapped his hand down on the steering wheel, and the vehicle bucked.

Naturally, she was just as attractive and tantalizing as he'd remembered. More so. And now he felt an unaccustomed confusion of emotions. He'd tamped down emotion years before and functioned perfectly well without. Why stir all this up now?

Max gave another huge sigh as he negotiated a difficult bend. Everything was unsatisfactory.

And why had he felt he had to play games with her? Not letting on that he was the owner of the land was stupid. This was his home, so how was he going to explain things? It wouldn't have been difficult to mention it at the start, but now, it was going to be embarrassing. He'd set a trap for himself, and the fallout would be entirely due to his own stupidity.

Anger made him swing the wheel of his truck too hard as he turned through the narrow gateway into the drive of his cousin's house, and he just missed the fir tree on the left, coming to an abrupt halt. It shocked him. Children lived here, members of his family, and behaving like a spoiled brat was inexcusable. It proved how stupid and dangerous this obsession was. He pushed all thoughts of Amancia to the back of his mind.

Sofía was already waiting at the front door, baby on one arm, and three-year-old Marisol clinging on to the other. He took a couple of deep breaths and climbed out, hoping she hadn't noticed his bad driving. He needed to sort himself out, and the sooner, the better. But for the moment, it was Sofía who mattered.

"*Gracias, primo*," she said, giving him a kiss and a brilliant smile as she handed over the baby. "You've saved my life. Show him where everything is, Marisol."

She ran to her car, and then she was gone.

A soft little hand slipped into his. "Are you staying to lunch, Tío Max?"

He wasn't really her uncle, but it made no difference to their relationship.

"Only if you invite me!"

Sometimes, the child's trusting innocence touched him so deeply, he wanted to cry. His mouth twisted in a rueful expression; there must be some part of him that was unsullied by what had happened in Ukraine. Her sweetness contrasted sharply with the ugliness he'd experienced out there. His tour of duty with the UN Peacekeepers had come to a sudden stop three years ago, and he'd gone through rehabilitation and come out the other side.

But some things don't go away. Physically, he coped, but what had happened there had permeated his life and was now a part of him. And then Putin, the Russian president, had sent in tanks at the beginning of 2022, and it made it seem as if everything the UN had accomplished there had been for nothing. He'd stopped walking and stared unseeingly at the sky, a prickling at the back of his eyes.

There was a tug at his hand. "Come on, Tío Max. Are you coming inside?"

Even before he was injured, he'd known he'd had enough of the army, but he'd stuck with it. Duty. There weren't that many Spaniards involved in the initiative, and it'd been up to him to show he could play his part.

Now he hoisted the baby up more comfortably and smiled down at the little girl, giving her hand a squeeze. He needed contact with this side of life to remind him why it all mattered.

Max was familiar with Sofía's house from long experience. She and Ricardo were probably his closest friends, after Andrés. He let the child lead him around, show him once again where her favorite toys could be found, and then she took him into the kitchen where Sofía had left a prepared meal in the fridge.

"Did *Mamá* really say you could have that?" he asked, eyeing the chocolate cake she said was for her.

"No, but she didn't say I couldn't have it. You can decide, Tío Max."

That was completely honest, and he'd probably still let her have her way, in the end. This young lady was far too advanced for her age, already winding him around her little finger.

"I'm not saying anything until you've eaten what's on your plate."

She pouted but sat at the table and began to eat, while Max placed the baby, Luisa, in a highchair. Last time, all the food had ended up on the floor when he'd tried to feed her. He held on to the dish and began the laborious task of getting some of it into her mouth.

"You have to eat as well, Tío Max."

"Not today, *pequeña*. I'm having mine later. We have a visitor, *tía Consuela y yo*."

"Who is it?"

"A *señora* who's working at the dig."

"What's a dig?"

His explanation and all her questions about what

65

they were doing there carried them right through to his cousin's return.

"I'm so sorry to have put that on you, Max, but Dolores let me down at the last minute. It wouldn't impress anyone if I failed to turn up at a job interview and the excuse was that I'd had to look after my children. And this really was a one-off with Dolores. I know it won't happen again."

"Well, if it does, you know I'll always try to help. It's a pleasure anyway with these two. Did it go well?"

"Yes, they've appointed me. It's only one day a week, but they're prepared to let the role grow, when I can manage it. I'm so happy, Max."

"And I'm very happy for you. My cousin, the lawyer," he added, dropping a kiss on her cheek. "But I have to get back—we've a visitor this evening. Marisol's been interrogating me, so I'm sure she'll tell you all about it."

"It's the lady from the ex...exvacation."

"Excavation."

"Rosalyn's replacement? You met her in Bristol, didn't you?" Sofía's eyes were bright with curiosity.

Had he given something away when he'd talked about her? Shown in some way that his interest went beyond merely finding the right person to run the site? He could do without Sofía taking an interest. Her first priority, after the children and Ricardo, of course, appeared to be finding him someone suitable to settle down with, and he knew how relentless she could be.

But it wasn't going to happen anytime soon. Not ever. He was a mess, no two ways about it. How could he inflict himself on any woman? On any decent woman who was looking for a proper relationship? The short answer was that he couldn't.

"Get Ricardo to give me a ring when his current shift pattern at the hospital finishes, and we'll go out together to celebrate your new job."

The young doctor seemed to work all hours, but he must be due some time off soon. He kissed his cousin and patted the little ones on the head, before hurrying out to the big truck he used for getting around the farm. He drove very carefully through the gate.

Chapter 10

Parking the image of Max at the back of her mind, Amancia studied the terrain several hours later. Excitement flooded in. The old Roman villa had to have been on that hill, the perfect site, defendable even. The building wasn't even half a mile away, but all she saw from the dig was the tree-covered hilltop.

"Are you going for a walk, Amancia?" Maya was hurrying to catch up with her. "Can I join you?"

"Please do, but you'll have to come back on your own. I'm on my way to the house to meet the owner."

They walked along for a while in companionable silence. Freed of the obligation to make conversation, Amancia was interrogating her surroundings. If that was where the original Roman villa had been, then this was exactly where the owner would have created a port to carry his produce down to the coast. Finally, she said, "I'm looking for traces of a road between the site and the house, so keep your eyes open."

"You'd think you'd find some slabs of stone, even after all this time."

"Not all Roman roads were paved, remember. It would depend on whether the volume of activity between the house and the river was enough to warrant that much effort. Even getting the construction materials up here might not have been worthwhile."

"I suppose this whole area may have been forested,

making wood the more logical material."

"It's just a theory at the moment."

"What if you can't find any evidence?"

Amancia stopped to look around. "It won't matter. There's still a big house up there, and we know there was a structure by the river. We must wait for evidence to emerge. I'll have to leave you here, Maya. Thanks for the company."

Well protected from the glare by her old, cracked sunglasses and a large, floppy hat, she strode on toward that enticing hill with its top obscured by trees. It was still light, and although the sun was sinking to the horizon, it remained hot.

She entered a grove between rows of vines. Finally, the heat was becoming more bearable, something to be enjoyed rather than endured. These vines were tall, reaching above her shoulders, and the wide view had disappeared.

Her phone again. With a sinking heart, she took it from her bag and saw the text message.

—*Been thinking about you, darling. Worried about how you can manage on your own.*— The words were followed by a couple of faces wreathed in pink hearts. —*Tell me what you've been doing today.*—

Although she'd seen immediately who it was, the realization of how far she'd moved away from her ex and his possessiveness shocked her, and resentment flared up. She had to put a stop to this.

—*James, it's finished*— she wrote. —*We're finished. Please don't text anymore.*—

She hated to be cruel, but why couldn't he just leave her alone?

Heart still thudding, she continued her walk.

Excited by the possibilities in front of her, she gradually put him from her mind. This wonderful place called to her with an insistent voice and drew her in. On her own, here in the fields, she teetered on a thin line between the past and the present. All her best dig experiences had been like this. She longed to see the house.

Curious, she bent down and raked her fingers through dry soil, searching for irrigation pipes for the very healthy-looking vines, but she saw none. How did these plants survive without water? Pulling her bag into a more comfortable position, she lengthened her stride, her trainers crunching rhythmically on hot stones.

So, where was the road she'd so vividly imagined, with the carts of amphorae that contained olives and oil and wine? Where were the sacks of grain? Where the wagons, piled high with goods, drawn by bullocks? She scanned the horizon as if at any minute they would appear. Had slaves run alongside with shouts and sticks and whips, urging the heavy beasts to get a move on? She strained to hear them, but there was nothing. And there was no sign of a road.

The soil must have been turned thousands of times since CE350, when the Roman army had departed from this region of Spain. Whatever they'd left behind would have been crushed and broken and returned to the earth. It was unlikely there'd be anything remaining of the original structure. But that didn't mean it hadn't been there. She wasn't going to abandon her theory of a road linking the house with the riverside quite yet. They had to keep digging. She would find the evidence.

The chirping of crickets grew noisier as she walked. She made out a variety of calls, from a pretty fluting to a definite rattle. The creatures must settle all over the place, even on the vines, though she couldn't see any. She wiped her face. It was still too hot.

Her pace slowed as the track rose, and she stopped once to look around. She'd gained height, and the surrounding fields swung back into view. The long rows of vines now appeared to radiate out from the hill. A glance back at the dig was enough to show that her logic was sound—it was a straight line from the house to the river. She envisaged the possibilities: they'd already uncovered the top of a wall, and the next thing they'd find would be the steps leading down to the water's edge. She tramped on.

How harsh this region was, burned dry by the sun, quite different from the idea of Spain that was held by so many people at home, who experienced only the holiday life along the coast. This dramatic country, with its swathes of ochre, umber, gold, and dark red, felt big and uninhabited. And if she ignored the mountains, it wasn't tourist beautiful. She gazed on it, and it made her want something deeper than she'd yet known, filled her with a raw emotion she couldn't define.

She liked being here. She loved being here.

An insect buzzed insistently around her head, and she flicked it away. Now, she climbed a rocky trail that passed through a barrier of trees and brought her to an opening between boulders, blocked by bushes and saplings. Sixteen hundred and fifty years ago, had this been the beginning of the road that led from the house to the riverside? The tumbled stones might reward some study, perhaps reveal the hand of the stone cutter.

She picked her way through. On the other side, a rutted lane passed close to some large, well-kept farm buildings that looked new. The air was heavy with the smell of fruit, suggesting this was where the winemaking took place. She scrambled down and followed the lane up to her right.

Ahead, a solid, two-story stone house slowly came into view, larger and much taller than the average farmhouse. Its poor state of repair contrasted sharply with the barns. The upkeep of a place like this must cost a fortune. Before she was born, Amancia's parents had bought a big, old house in St. Paul's in Bristol.

"We managed to get it for very little because of the riots in the eighties," her father had said one day. A few unsavory happenings had made sure St. Paul's was a no-go area in the city for a long time. That had changed, of course. She knew about hungry, old houses and the way in which they could devour every penny you had, because at her father's death, she'd helped with the mortgage repayments. That was partly what had kept her in Bristol.

Holidays abroad were impossible once that money left her account, so she'd relished this opportunity to come to Spain. She smiled. It was hardly tourism, but she loved seeing an alternative Spain.

She came out onto a wide, graveled space at the front of the building. Silence reigned here, broken only by the buzz of bees hovering over large pots containing dark red roses. A couple of cars were parked over to one side, and a low wall encircled a shady forecourt. It separated the space from an area of woodland. Amancia sat down on a bench by an iron gate and dug out her leather evening pumps, dropping the dusty trainers into her bag.

Where was everyone? She looked over at the facade of the house and studied it minutely. The building was stuccoed and had a skirt of stone, a sort of plinth rising to about three feet all round. It could indeed be built on the foundations of a Roman villa. But "could" was the operative word; there was nothing to back up the theory. It had the right general shape, but Roman villas came in many different configurations and sizes. If there had been one here, it would have been bigger than this, she guessed. She would have to ask a few questions, and hopefully, the owners would have something helpful to tell her.

Finally getting to her feet, she walked over to a paved area under a massive stone canopy, four-square and held up by solid pillars. Here, repairs had been started, and the tall double doors were varnished to a high black gloss. They stood open, allowing her to see inside. A young man was crossing the immense tiled hall, and when she rang the old-fashioned bellpull, he changed direction and headed toward her.

"Please take a seat," he said as he ushered her in and indicated a row of painted ladder-back chairs with green tapestry seats. "I'm sorry, but there's something I must do immediately. I promise to return in a moment."

"Thank you."

It was cooler inside. She walked around, looking at the lofty ceiling, and breathed in the lavender scent of polish. Two floor-to-ceiling windows filled the space to either side of the front door, the double-height hall occupying the central portion of the house. The imposing internal space was almost baroque, with dark, carved-wood paneling, a dramatic contrast to the simple lines of the unpretentious exterior. Faced with this unexpected grandeur, Amancia huffed in a breath and wondered what the evening was going to be like.

The floor was paved with black-and-white tiles, each three feet square, and a long, black table with bulbous, curling legs had been placed in the middle of the room. Doors led off from three walls, one open and leading onto the stairs. It was a beautiful space, but a closer look revealed cracks in some of the floor tiles and missing pieces of cornice.

After the initial impression, Amancia wasn't really paying attention. She was agitated and excited, the imminent meeting with Max filling her mind. This pleased and disturbed her equally. Until their encounter that morning, she'd concentrated on ensuring the work on-site started well, but this evening, things were different. It worried her because she found him deeply attractive. How stupid that was when the relationship with James was still so close, and simple common sense told her she needed time on her own.

She had to decide how things would be in the future, not something that could be achieved by tumbling out of one relationship straight into another. James was controlling, and she needed time to adjust, to find her true self. It was all happening too quickly.

More than a little troubled by the intensity of these thoughts, she wandered farther and was drawn to a double row of portraits that occupied the wall high up, opposite the entrance, but before she had chance to study them more closely, a vehicle entered the parking area, sending gravel flying, and she whirled around as it came to a stop. A dusty green truck appeared in front of the windows, the driver invisible as he leaned into the vehicle. She faced the door.

Max and the young man arrived in the hall at the same time.

"I was just going to take the *señorita* to your *mamá*," the latter said to Max, and turning to Amancia, he added in English, "I'm sorry I had to leave you, but there was a small emergency."

His mother! Had she really understood that correctly?

"No problem. I've been enjoying this beautiful building," she said, indicating the room around them and then smiling sweetly at them both.

"It's all right, Fer. I'll take over now. I assume you've sorted the problem out?"

That's right, send him away. She rather wanted to have Max to herself, even though it wasn't good for her. The best things very often weren't. However, she mustn't forget the purpose of her visit. She'd come to find out about the house.

Chapter 11

They looked at each other. He covered the distance between them in two strides and held out his hand, welcoming her. He was big, very male, very exciting. They shook hands, and she was short of breath, her heart thumping, so that it was all she could do to smile, and for a moment, speaking was out of the question.

Despite his apparent confidence, a trace of anxiety showed in his eyes. "You've uncovered my secret."

"What were you trying to hide from me? The fact that you live with your mother? That's hardly a crime."

"No, but I couldn't resist it when I realized you thought I was a professor at the university, so I let it ride, and by the time I saw how stupid that was…well, it was too late to do anything about it. I'm sorry. Will you forgive me?"

His grin was engaging.

"There's nothing to forgive."

"But the invitation did come from my mother. I'm just a simple farmer. She doesn't get out much, and she's very keen to entertain you, so I'm pleased that you accepted."

"You're not a professor at all?"

"No, the professor is my friend, Andrés, who's stuck in Chile."

Ah, that explained why she'd been finding it difficult to imagine him behind a desk or lecturing to a group of students; he was a farmer, an outdoors type. There was something about the way he moved, a look in his eyes that was fiercer, keener than you'd expect from an academic. He'd seen things that they might only ever read about in books. She was startled by this insight into someone she'd first viewed as a typical arrogant male, and her curiosity was aroused.

"So how does a farmer end up representing the university at an interview in Bristol?"

"I'm a wine producer, as you can see. I had to be in London for a meeting with other wine producers, so Andrés asked me to do the interview in his place."

"Being stuck in Chile."

"Exactly. I'm sorry. It was juvenile of me."

Hardly a simple farmer, then. But he looked so contrite, she couldn't resist a smile. And she'd liked the affectionate way he spoke of his mother.

"No harm done."

They walked to the double doors beneath the portraits, and she tried to catch a glimpse, but it was already gloomy in the lofty hall. If she took the time to study them, she'd probably find faces that looked like his, the features inherited from a long line of ancestors. He was certainly attractive, but he came from another world, cool and sophisticated, so different from her own. But now they were coming into a large sitting room. A strong, resiny smell of burning wood greeted them as they entered. A dark-haired woman sat in a wheelchair close to the source of heat, a massive stone fireplace, in which a log glowed in a small fire basket. He introduced them to each other.

"*Encantada, señorita.*"

"*Amancia, señora. Me llamo Amancia.*"

"Thank you so much for coming to see me, Amancia. I felt sure you'd want to know something about the estate."

"Very much so. I'd just asked Max if he could arrange a visit when he gave me your invitation."

Even saying his name gave her a sharp jolt of pleasure. But this was his mother, so she would tread carefully. Mothers were sensitive to such things, especially when very fond of their sons. Maybe the *señora* wouldn't be happy about him associating with a girl of Amancia's...provenance. That was the expression. Art and wine concerned themselves with provenance, didn't they, so that word should please the grape grower. And then she hated the thought she'd just had because he'd given her no reason to be so cynical. But experience had taught her to be like that.

Far too many men got excited by her appearance and left her with the feeling that they didn't actually see her, just her outer carapace. When she let people in, she got hurt, so she had to appear tough. Probably, she should have taken up modeling, like her Somali friend, Hani. Then at least, the photographers would simply appreciate her looks for what they were, a tool to be used by the designers and not a challenge they had to overcome. But she wasn't interested in such things. Even way back, "scholarly approach" was a phrase that had appeared on her school report. Parading in front of the cameras was never going to provide a career path.

Max was pulling out a chair away from the heat of the fire. She couldn't read him. On first meeting, she'd caught the look of appreciation she got from most men. Later he'd teased her a bit, but she sensed a barrier, behind which his real feelings were hidden.

"I'm sorry about the fire, but I don't get enough exercise to keep the blood flowing properly in my veins, so I feel the cold."

It was hot, but she said, "It's no problem."

There was a tray of bottles and glasses on a small table beside her hostess. Only when she'd fixed drinks for them, did she turn to her son. "Can you say to Catalina we'll be ready in about fifteen minutes, *querido*?" She reached across and patted Amancia's arm. "I want to talk to my guest."

How hard for her to be confined to a wheelchair.

Max left the room, and they began to talk.

The woman's face revealed pain and suffering. Perhaps she'd been involved in a car accident, which had resulted in her being unable to walk, and which continued to cause her pain. Or did she have one of those degenerative diseases, one of the big, unfair things that could happen in life? But this didn't take away from her attractiveness or the warmth of her smile. How similar the son was to his mother.

"What can I tell you to help your investigation?" she asked in English.

****

Max wheeled his mother through to the dining room. During the meal, he hardly spoke, apparently content to listen to the women interacting. That was good. She concentrated on learning everything she could. She had a lot of questions about the land, about the house, about any history they might know, which kept everything moving at a good pace. Consuela was obviously enjoying the conversation as much as she was. It was a pleasure talking to this intelligent woman, who had an encyclopedic knowledge of the area and was sharing it in an interesting way.

Amancia was transported from the dust of the dig, with its basic level of amenities and community living, to this civilized house with entertaining company and good food. It was a perfect evening, and the time passed too quickly. Just perfect.

Except for her host.

All that time, she was hyper-aware of him, and his nearness seared her, like a furnace she'd got too close to. It was perilous, threatening, and she should run away as fast as she could, but instead, she wanted to be still closer. He was sitting across the table from her, and whenever she looked up, it was to meet his lambent gaze. She did this as the thought occurred and again found his eyes on her, a smile crinkling in the corners.

She'd come out to dinner. It was meant to be social and informative, and she was forced to deal with these unexpected emotions. As though again she'd forgotten to breathe, she had to drag oxygen into her lungs. If she touched him—and she wanted to touch him—her hand would come away burned, even if she couldn't see that was the case.

She didn't know how or when this had come about. One minute, she was indulging in a little mild flirtation, appreciating a good-looking man, and the next, she had to cope with a torrent of unfamiliar feelings. She'd never felt like this with James or any previous boyfriends. And this man wasn't a boyfriend. For the first time, she'd seen through the outer layer, and that changed things.

It wasn't fair. How was she going to sort out her life if she allowed him anywhere near her?

The food was simple but delicious, and the wine

was heavenly. In quite different ways, her hosts stimulated her. She wanted to prolong the whole thing, but she couldn't relax because of the sense that she was heading into danger. Eventually, it was time to go. These few hours had felt so short.

"Max and I will go through the things we've talked about," his mother said when Amancia had thanked her. "I'll email you anything which could help. And you're welcome to come back and look in the basement."

"Thank you, I'd like to do that."

"We've never really given a thought to the origins of the estate, but maybe my husband did before he died. I'll check to see if he left any notes."

****

As they came out through the front door, Amancia said, "I need to change my shoes. It's impossible to walk in these."

"It's impossible to walk, full stop, at this time of the night, and on your own. I won't let you. It's too dangerous, so—"

"You won't *let* me!" she said. "There's no way you can *stop* me, *señor*. Let me tell you—"

"Sorry, sorry! I apologize. Please, I didn't mean to imply anything, but…"

She took a deep breath. "I'm sorry, too." Shame warmed her cheeks. She really shouldn't have said that. "I overreacted. It's just that I don't like people telling me what I can and can't do."

His mouth curved in a smile. "I can see that."

He placed a hand on her arm to steer her toward his truck, and the light touch seemed to puncture her skin, sending her blood fizzing around the rest of her body. Even when he took it away a second later, she could feel its imprint. Although the sun had long gone down, all its heat had returned with that single gesture.

"I'm sorry," he said again. "I didn't express that well. I am only concerned for your safety, Amancia. How can I let you walk off into the night? It's dangerous. Ploughed land is deceptive to walk on, and you could easily twist an ankle. But I understand also there's been an intruder. I won't…I, er…I can't risk it."

She was really tempted to fire back at him, but what he said made sense. There was no point in putting herself in danger. He wasn't James, so why was she so suspicious of his motives?

"Okay, I understand. So, what do you propose?"

Her voice sounded cool again, under control, just as she wanted. It would be great if he just walked back with her. That would take care of several problems at once. But if he did so, she'd be in even more danger. And the threat wouldn't come from him, but from her own feelings and actions. All those opportunities on a walk had her imagination running wild: if he so much as laid a finger on her arm again, she…She felt sick.

God, that is just so much nonsense, you foolish woman! Have you gone completely mad?

She didn't recognize herself. Anyway, he wasn't going to do anything like that. He was controlled, interested in her only insofar as her actions might affect his business. Accidents could be bad news. He didn't find her interesting, and perhaps it would be better if things stayed like that. No, she certainly didn't want him to walk with her. Definitely not.

It was time to get a grip on things, and it was a relief to find he had a sense of suitable behavior for the occasion, because clearly, she didn't. She flushed and was grateful he couldn't read the thoughts passing through her mind.

But now he'd stopped at the truck and was answering her question. "I'll drive you."

Part of her felt deeply disappointed at these words.

Chapter 12

Amancia made no sound after fastening the seat belt and behaved quite unlike the animated guest who'd sat across the table from him, just a few minutes earlier. Now she leaned away into the corner of the vehicle and looked out of the window. She must be tired. There was no doubt the temperature had remained high this evening, and it could be exhausting.

Or maybe she didn't want to talk to him.

There was a spark of attraction between them. Hell, he knew there was on his side, more than a spark, more like a raging fire. And that was just when he was thinking about her, which had been most of the time over the last few days. Longer than that. It'd been ever since he'd met her in Bristol.

And this morning, he'd peered down into that hole where she'd been digging, out there by the river. The moment she'd looked up at him was an image that stayed imprinted on his mind. It would have been good to know what she was thinking, but the dark glasses had hidden her eyes. His heart rate had speeded up, a purely visceral reaction that was totally unexpected. He'd teased her to hide his shock.

That distinctive look she had was exotic and exciting: high cheekbones and very dark eyes, startling against the golden skin. There had to be an interesting heritage there, but he couldn't work out what it might be. Whatever it was, she was lovely. Being this close, with his senses stimulated by her perfume, was something else again. It was no longer enough to think about her. He wanted to reach out and pull her into his arms, kiss her luscious lips, bury his face in that gorgeous hair. He gave a shudder and forced himself not to look at her. He should concentrate on driving.

The thing was, he had too much going on to waste time on something like this. This was a make-or-break year for the vineyard. He'd put all his money into the business and was now looking at the possibility of having to sell assets to pay for unforeseen developments. The contingency fund wasn't big enough and was disappearing fast.

He slowed as a pothole appeared on the right. It meant long hours, not just of physical work but other things like marketing. Get it wrong, and he'd be left behind. He was leaving tomorrow for Madrid, for a series of meetings with restaurants and wine shops. There was no time for a new relationship. It wasn't as if he didn't have someone already.

Max heaved a huge sigh. Amancia glanced at him, but he said nothing, and she turned away again, as if the contemplation of the dark trees flashing by was infinitely more interesting than looking at him.

He wanted to stop thinking about the whole situation, but each time he pushed the thoughts away, they came back. It was exhausting. There wasn't a single moment with her here by his side when he could relax. And there had been something…well, he'd thought just for a moment, that maybe she'd felt the same way. And that was good—and bad.

She certainly seemed withdrawn now. He was so

out of the habit of getting close to a warm, passionate woman, that he could no longer trust his ability to understand what any woman was thinking and feeling. Vala was extraordinary. But "ordinary" was not the right word to describe Amancia, who in no way resembled his lover. Amancia was also extraordinary, but in quite a different fashion, beautiful, exciting, clever, stimulating. Wonderful.

His mind was wandering, and he quickly brought his attention back to the road. It was unlit, so he slowed down. It would be ironic if he crashed the car after what he'd said about danger.

But the teasing problem would not leave him. He glanced at her. Incapable of understanding her sudden withdrawal, he decided he'd done something to put her off. He straightened up and gripped the wheel, steering around another pothole, and made a mental note to repair the track. Amancia stayed rigid by the window, as if she couldn't wait to get out of the vehicle.

It didn't matter. There would be no relationship between them. It was much better this way, no chance of him making a fool of himself. They could keep things on a friendly basis when they happened to meet, and now that his mother had satisfied her curiosity about the new site director, he had no need to arrange anything else. No need to go anywhere near her at all.

His mother—he couldn't help thinking there was some hidden agenda there. She wasn't just some poor, debilitated person in a wheelchair, whatever an outsider might think. True, she could hardly get around without the wheels, but that didn't make her negligible. On the contrary. But whatever she was thinking…well, that had no importance. He would not permit his mother to interfere in his affairs.

Max concentrated on making his way toward the faint glow marking the entrance to the dig. His mood darkened as the future rolled out in front of him, a desolate terrain topped by a louring sky which the sun could not penetrate. So what? He could see that was the way it had to be.

"We're here already."

It was the first time she'd spoken, and it didn't sound particularly friendly.

The tents on the site, with the entrances facing inward, huddled together like a collection of wigwams in an old western. No one was about. He brought the vehicle to a halt, and silence fell. Now, she was picking up that enormous handbag.

"Thanks for the lift, Max, and for dinner, of course. It's been a wonderful evening. I loved meeting your mother and learned a great deal. Please thank her."

He could hear the sincerity in her voice, and he stretched out his hand, an involuntary movement, but she had the door open already, and she stepped down.

"No need to get out. Thanks again for a lovely evening. See you around."

She slammed the door.

So that's the way she was playing it. He was damned if he knew what he'd done, but she was making it easy for him. He wound down the window.

"*Sí.* I'm in Madrid for a few days on business, but let me know if you need help with anything—just email or call me. Maybe I can smooth the path with the local council if any problem comes up, things like that. I'm glad you enjoyed it."

"*Gracias. Buenas noches.*"

"*Buenas noches. Hasta luego.*"

Formal. Excessively polite, which was just as well—and there'd be no *luego*, no later on. He'd already decided.

Chapter 13

Quietly, Max let in the clutch and drove away from the sleeping campers. The evening had been wonderful. She'd been sitting there opposite him, at his table, in his mother's house, all that gorgeous hair released from the ponytail she'd had it tied up in when he'd seen her before, her eyes dark, enigmatic pools—when she deigned to look in his direction. But it had also been a nightmare, because he'd struggled every moment to appear normal and unaffected by her presence, fought not to let on to either his mother or Amancia just how devastating her effect was.

He slowed as two students on bicycles came wobbling toward him around the potholes, their lights bobbing up and down in the intense darkness.

His mother was probably just as keen as Sofía to find him a suitable partner, so that didn't help, although maybe she was a little more subtle. But neither of them understood his reservations. There'd been plenty of sympathy when he'd first returned from Ukraine, but that had soon faded into exasperation.

He looked down at his watch. Still only ten o'clock. The night was young. The thought brought no pleasant sense of expectation.

It had only made things more difficult, seeing her up close, the pleasure quickly outweighed by the amount of frustration he felt at being stuck in a situation he'd had no desire for and no hand in creating. Somehow, he had to work out how to get back the equilibrium he'd enjoyed before she'd arrived, before he'd even met her, back in Bristol.

Stopping the SUV at the side of the road just before the crossroads, he pulled out his phone and scrolled through the contacts. Even as he waited for her to answer, he was asking himself if he should be doing this. If he even wanted to. But before he could rethink it, she picked up, and he said, "*¿Vala? ¿Querida, eres libre?*"

When she replied, there was that soft laugh and the silken and seductive voice at the other end of the line. It always raised a flicker of excitement, though not tonight.

"Depends on what you're proposing, *mi amor.*"

"Well, we could start with a drink at that little bar at the back of your place."

"We could. I like that word, 'start.' What else do you have in mind?"

"How about we discuss that when we meet. Half an hour?"

"*Perfecto.* See you then."

Vala was a mad, sexy little elf of Icelandic origin, with spikey, white-blonde hair and the morals of a gutter cat. And that was before she'd snorted a couple of lines. He left the coke to her; drugs were something he associated with recovering from the mess a Russian bomb had made of him in the East, not with recreation.

Always exciting to be around, she'd helped him pass many an hour demonstrating her undoubted prowess in bed, always a bed in some anonymous hotel room. He never took her back to his home.

Insatiable was the word that sprang to mind when he thought of their time together. She'd been wonderful, and frankly, he'd learned a lot over the last couple of years, which was quite an admission for a man of his age and experience. But maybe this was the moment for their trysts to come to an end, for her to return to the husband she'd always led him to believe existed. Not that there'd ever been any proof. Or maybe, she could find another man; who was to say she didn't already have one?

It had disturbed him after the call that he could barely summon the enthusiasm to meet her. And it didn't get any better. After the second beer, he still hadn't made a move to leave the bar.

"What's wrong, Max? You're no fun at all this evening."

"I have to go, Valita. I'm not feeling well." Hopefully, she wouldn't make a fuss because he really wasn't in the mood for it. "I need to go home," he repeated, acid rising to his throat.

She reached across and stroked his cheek, running her fingers lightly along his scar, her green gaze penetrating as she tried to work him out.

"I hope that's the real reason, *mi amor*. I truly don't believe I have a rival in bed, and you always seemed to appreciate that before. I thought we were well matched."

"I truly don't believe you have, either."

Not as far as her skills were concerned. That was one of the many things he appreciated about her.

"So, why do I feel I'm losing you, Max?"

He stared at her for a long moment, trying to formulate a reply. Then, he looked down. "I'm not myself, Vala. I think I'm ill. Sorry."

He leaned forward, dropped a light kiss onto her full, red-painted lips, and then gently pulled away. *"Hasta la próxima, querida."*

Even as he turned his back on her, he knew this was probably the last time he'd see her. Suddenly, he wondered what on earth he'd been doing all these months, though that was unfair; she'd provided him with something he'd needed beyond the sex, but how could he have believed this shallow relationship was enough? When he reached the door, a man crossed the floor and slipped onto the stool next to her. A woman like Vala would never want for company. Not male company, anyway.

Chapter 14

Amancia's first thought the following morning was that Max was not going to be around for at least a week and…that was good. She could get on with her work. She stood under a cold shower, attempting to wash away the feverish dreams that had occupied the night.

Another text from James greeted her as she stepped back into her room. She stabbed at the button, forced herself to read it.

—*I'm worried about how you're coping. I've always supported you, Amancia. You know that.*—

—*Coping just fine—but it's nothing to do with you anymore.*—

It was good she had to prepare for the meeting that evening, because it didn't give much time to think about what James was doing with his constant texts, what a problem they were becoming. She hated the way any communication from him destroyed her good humor for half of the day.

She did allow herself to think about Max.

****

The meeting in the old stone building, some sort of community center, was breaking up. A few people had already left, and others were hurrying off to their evening meal. They'd been interested and had asked a lot of questions that all of the team had a part in answering. The locals were waking up to the fact that an important Roman site could put their village on the map. Of course, a few people wouldn't want that, and it was why the university had thought the charm offensive was necessary. But there'd been no animosity.

A woman came up to Amancia and introduced herself and her son. Carlos was pale, rake-thin, and looked about sixteen.

"Can you accept a volunteer?" she demanded. "Go on, tell her what you told me."

"I want to help on the site," he said in heavily accented English, clearly embarrassed by his mother's pushiness. "Can I do that?"

"Er…I don't see why not, in principle." Amancia had to be careful. She didn't know the law in Spain and wasn't going to put herself in a situation she couldn't get out of. But extra help wouldn't be a bad thing.

"Look, tell me what you know about archaeology, why you want to do this, and I'll make enquiries tomorrow."

"I know quite a lot. I've been ill with months and months of treatments and time in bed, almost two years, so I've done a lot of studying, mainly English and archaeology. There wasn't much else I could do."

How awful at that age. But most kids wouldn't have chosen studying as a way to occupy the time. It suggested there was something special about him.

"He's still not strong," his mother said. "But he's getting better, and he's a clever boy."

"¡Mamá!"

"I'm saying he could be helpful to you. And we aren't asking for him to be paid."

That was a good thing because there wasn't any money. "Okay. I'll check and let you know."

As they exchanged contact details, Carlos dropped his worried frown and smiled. *"Gracias, señora. Es muy importante para mí."*

"Email me and tell me why you want to do this. I have to know you have the basics and won't be a liability," she said, giving him the address. "I can't look after you." She hurried away to catch up with Peter.

"I can't see a good reason for saying no," she told him, "except that I have no idea how the university might react." When they got back on-site, Amancia and Peter went into the storeroom and turned on the computer. Seconds later, quite a long email came in. She scanned it briefly and said, "He must have written this before going to the meeting. The fact that he prepared like that tells us quite a lot about him."

She sat down to read.

"It looks as if he spent most of the time that he was ill on archaeology. He seems clever, so he probably knows almost as much as some of our students. What do you think—take him on?"

Peter finished reading over her shoulder. "It's up to you, Amancia. You could email the professor and tell him what you're doing, though you'll be lucky to hear from him. We've had no news of him for a week. His secretary says he's in some mountains above Santiago."

Peter was leaving the decision to her, so she'd better make the right one.

"Maybe I'll contact him and let Carlos help temporarily. If we get a negative reply, he'll just have to stop. I can explain that to him."

Amancia wasn't sure why she was keen to go ahead, but there was something engaging about the boy's enthusiasm and his cleverness. She didn't want to let him go without giving him a try. And she felt sorry about the time he'd lost through his illness.

****

"You have to get close to your subject," she was explaining the next day. "Wait to see if the land will speak to you."

They were standing at the entrance to the dig. Carlos stared at her. "What does that mean? There was nothing about it in any of the books I read."

"No, there wouldn't be, but a good archaeologist has a deep knowledge of his subject. You know a lot about the Romans, don't you?"

"Yeah, I read everything I could find."

"That's great. So now you need to use your imagination, dredge up images and ideas, allow yourself to be influenced by the smells and the sounds and shape of the land. It's not...abstract. The Romans were right here, and basically, you have to see this place through their eyes and apply their thinking to understand what went on."

Bending down, she picked up a handful of earth, raising it to her nose to absorb its smell, allowing it to run through her fingers. Bone dry, it was like fine sand.

"Because?"

"Because that way, you'll read the terrain, get a better idea of what you might find, and where. It means you can work out a plan. Otherwise, you're just digging and maybe wasting time." The frown had returned as he mulled over the information. She continued, "I'll give you an example: it's easy for me to imagine myself in a role, like a soldier or a senator, a street-trader or a slave. I ask myself how each person would've behaved? Ordinary human needs would've affected how the original site was laid out and used, but the status of the owners or users is even more helpful in guiding you to useful conclusions."

Carlos was so quick to understand, drinking in every word, and he'd learned a lot on his own. Amancia was already seeing him as a personal project, a student she'd have a part in launching, and that gave her a particular pleasure.

"My dad was West Indian," she continued. "When we were children, he told us stories of slavery, so I guess that made it easy for me to imagine myself as a slave—although, of course, Roman slaves came in all colors and nationalities. And the slaves were often in the best position to see what went on. I always think it's a pity that so few of them were able to read or write, or we'd have had a lot more information, instead of seeing everything through the eyes of the powerful few, who probably liked to present things in the best light."

It was getting hotter. Amancia wiped her face, and the tissue began to fall apart. She'd get a cloth.

"All right, it's your turn now. Tell me what motivated the Romans. Of course, they were brilliant engineers and had superb organization. Everyone knows that. But what was it for?"

The boy narrowed his eyes, looking out across the rows of vines while he considered her question. "Well, they had this picture of Rome in their heads, like something holy, and it was always there, no matter where they went. They wanted to spread that idea."

"Good. Good, that's exactly right, but that wouldn't have created the massive economic setup including the ports—which is what we hope we have here. All their activity was linked to feeding the Roman

97

army, in order to maintain the peace and extract everything they could from the countries they dominated, to supply Rome."

"*Sí*, okay, I get it. They needed to move around food, wood, silver, all sorts of stuff, in huge amounts."

"That's it. It comes back to supplies. At the heart of the supply chains were the rivers. And the ports."

"Can I start straightaway? *Por favor, señora.*"

"I'll get Chris to sort something out for you. They made a find the other day, and there may be other things where he's working. Try keeping in mind what we've been talking about."

Later, Amancia climbed down into the depression dug by her predecessor. It had already increased in size. The ground within the trench that they'd opened up was now nearly three feet below the current height of the land. She looked around carefully, her back to the river. From here, she could see across the dig and right over the fields of vines, which sloped gently down for some distance and then swept up to the hill she'd climbed the night of the dinner.

She couldn't let go of the idea: an original Roman villa must have been there. She was going back to look as soon as she could arrange it with Max or his mother. But now, she had to think about the inspector who would be arriving soon.

Amancia picked up the tools she'd brought from the store and went to work on the wall of compacted yellow earth.

Chapter 15

The inspector was due at eleven. At five to, Amancia was pacing about, still unsure what he'd require of her so soon after her arrival. She'd started the computer: grids and plans, intended approach, hoped-for outcomes, calendar, health and safety, the on-going work log. He'd probably want to see all this. The most recent log-in was done by Carmen an hour ago, regarding a small object found that morning. It was good to see her team had taken her words seriously and were being meticulous about anything they uncovered.

A vehicle turned into the car park, a dark green 4x4 with the grey logo of the regional historic buildings body. It seemed quite a stretch from historic buildings to an archaeological site that had hardly been explored yet, but perhaps the remit of the organization was wide.

As the driver stepped down from his vehicle, she arrived alongside, and smiling, she introduced herself and offered her hand. He looked at it as if he would much prefer not to touch her, but finally, he gave it a little shake and immediately let it go.

Already, there was nothing she liked about this man, from his bad manners to his too-short, ugly haircut to clothes that looked unsuitable in the heat.

"How can I help you, Señor Barriles? Would you like to start with a tour of the site?"

"Naturally. That is why I have come."

His rudeness annoyed her, but she stopped herself from saying anything that might antagonize him because it was possible that this unpleasant official was a threat to her future. What if he decided things were not up to standard? She didn't want to think about that.

"Would you like me to introduce you to people?"

"That won't be necessary."

"Okay, except you will want to meet Peter who is also in a position of responsibility." He needed to know that this was a properly run site and compliant with the university's requirements.

As they walked, the inspector got out his phone. He set it to record although he didn't do her the courtesy of requesting her permission. Then, he asked innumerable questions, most of which seemed unnecessary. He was a petty little man, pumped up with his own importance.

They came to the store.

"The lock is broken. That doesn't say much for your on-site security."

"We had another attempted break-in last night. We chased them away before they had a chance to get in. Someone is going into the city this afternoon to buy a new lock."

"Have you reported this? Aren't you concerned?"

"Reported to the police and the university, yes. And of course, we are concerned. I don't think there's much more we can do. Either they're petty thieves, in which case, there's nothing here that will interest them if they do succeed in getting in. Or they mean us harm, perhaps are against the idea of a dig here."

He looked up at this. "Maybe you've annoyed a few people with the way you're running things."

"Annoyed them?" What was it with this man? "We

never see anyone and have only one vehicle, which doesn't even go out every day. The road doesn't pass through the village, so there's nothing to annoy anyone with. And we deliberately had a public meeting to which all the locals were invited. All we saw from them was friendly curiosity. You've got that wrong."

His mouth clamped down in a grim line.

In the store, he criticized the logging process, claiming it was open to abuse if more than one person was involved.

"I'm sorry, I don't agree. These students are here to learn, and how can they do that if I do it all? I check frequently, and that's all that's necessary."

She felt her voice rising and deliberately lowered her tone, but she wouldn't accept his ideas because he didn't appear to know anything…about anything.

It was twelve when they finished, and she invited him to lunch out of politeness. The thought of sitting with him and carrying on a conversation was repugnant.

"No, thank you. I don't think that would be appropriate. You'll be receiving my report and possibly a summons to speak before the committee."

What a relief. But not appropriate? What on earth was he talking about? Did that mean he was going to set about criticizing her? She stood still as he stalked off to the car park, and she forced herself to remain calm. Let him go. She certainly wasn't going to trot behind him to see him off the premises. Okay, he could give a damning report, but if he did, she'd fight it. What he'd just indulged in was an exercise in undermining her. He revved the engine and kangarooed forward, almost stalled. He was angry about something. Angry with her. As she was with him.

Then her phone buzzed. How could this day get any worse? It would be James, but she needed to look in case the text was from someone else altogether. I won't read it, she thought, but couldn't help herself.

—*Okay, I get it. You want a bit of freedom. But be careful—you've made mistakes before.*—

Had she? What kind of mistakes did he mean?

—*You can always call on me.*—

He must be talking about when she'd caught a virus after the main pandemic seemed to be over. But she couldn't recall any mistakes, just that she'd lacked energy and spent several weeks mostly curled up on the sofa, thinking maybe she wasn't going to make it out the other end. He was playing games with her mind, working on her, trying to keep control.

While James was constantly pursuing her, she hadn't heard anything from Max. No reason why she should, of course, but she wondered what he was doing in Madrid and when she would see him again.

There was too much going on to fret over the unpleasant visitor or her former boyfriend. Somehow, she had to ditch James, but she wasn't sure how to do it. Maybe she should block his phone number.

She looked up. Clouds were rolling in from the south which would change the weather. That was much more important. She forgot everything else and went in search of Peter.

Chapter 16

On Friday three days later, a thin layer of fine, grey powder lay over everything. Amancia smoothed down her hair, and it was thick with dust. There was dust in her eyes and even her mouth. The wind had started to blow only a few hours earlier, and Peter said they would soon have rain. Not a big storm but heavy rain. It couldn't come soon enough. Provided there wasn't too much, it would clean everything and lay the dust, and perhaps the temperature would come down. But the ground was hard, baked clay, and a heavy downpour could also cause problems.

"We should get back to work," she said. "Before the rain gets here."

She rinsed her cup and placed it on the draining board, grinning at the notice that had appeared over the sink since the evening before: "Wash your mug and stand upside down on the worktop." That was something she hadn't been able to do for years. She turned to those still seated at the tables.

"Come on, everyone. Those clouds are very heavy. When you finish, make sure you put down the covers."

She went out and crossed to where she'd been working, followed by Elena and Chris, who were trailed by Carlos. The flat stone, discovered when she'd first arrived, had turned out to be just a random piece of stone. Two more days of digging at that spot had produced nothing new, and she'd pulled them out to work with her; it made sense to concentrate the effort where there was progress.

"Oh, there's something here," said Elena.

They'd dug farther, and now the corner of a structure was beginning to take shape as it emerged slowly from its tomb of compacted earth. More confirmation they were working along the right lines. There was instant excitement. Everyone always hoped for a decent find, a significant step forward in the excavation. Such a moment was sweet and good for morale, but it would be a while before that happened.

"The temp's gone down. We'll work on a bit this afternoon," said Chris. The young archaeologists were buzzing, desperate to see what lay beneath.

"Well, if it doesn't rain, that would be great."

She wanted to keep them motivated. Sometimes, progress was so slow, infinitesimal, and you never got that exciting sense of achievement.

The earth just here was friable, coming away in large pieces. It needed sifting, but the space they were working in was too confined.

"Could you remove the rubbish?" Chris asked Carlos, indicating a barrow propped against the store. "Tip that out over there in the grid by the fence."

The four of them labored together and revealed another foot of stonework.

Mixed in with the earth were objects, which they would be able to extract later. Probably none intact and none of them very exciting. When they found these tiny bits and pieces, they cleaned off loose earth and stored and labeled them. Maybe they'd turn out to be part of a drinking pot, or there'd be a buckle or a pin. The clay pieces provided hours of reconstruction work when time permitted. Outsiders might think the work slow and unproductive, but such items in this location were significant, rich and promising to the archaeologists.

"You've brought us good luck," said Peter. They were walking slowly around the site a little while later, trying to get an overview of what had been achieved.

"I don't know. Rosalyn already uncovered the top of those blocks. I've taken it farther. But it is exciting."

"How did things go with the inspector?"

"Mmm. I got the feeling he disliked me on sight and was trying to catch me out. It's a pity if I've made an enemy in so short a time."

"Must have another agenda. Maybe he was fed up with being sent out to us. For a non-archaeologist, this historic building must be a bit disappointing."

"That's possible, I suppose. But I hope he doesn't try to make out there's something wrong here."

"He'd better not."

She wished Peter hadn't reminded her about it.

They arrived at the edge of the cliff and watched Chris and Elena working.

Enthusiasm was at a high, now they were beginning to reveal the structure. It wasn't a big discovery, just an old wall. There'd be no mosaic floor or hypocaust such as you would find in a grand house, nothing dramatic. But if they'd got this right, they'd have a functioning stairwell before long, leading from a platform of sorts down to the riverside.

She pictured the wooden jetties constructed at the foot of the steps, with the riverboats tied up alongside, stevedores loading and unloading, all the activity associated with freight carried on the river. In nearly two thousand years, what happened around the docks had hardly changed, not essentially. Since the Roman tripastos, which could even then raise about three hundred pounds weight, things had moved on and cranes now had electronic dials and lifted very many tons. And the operators were no longer slaves. Although maybe they were, depending on how people viewed themselves. The basic principle was the same.

"You can see how this would have worked as a port." Peter obviously was having similar thoughts.

The thick black clouds were now massing.

"Chris, I want you to photograph all the areas where we've been digging, just in case anything gets dislodged by the rain." Chris produced accomplished photos on his phone, as good as anything she'd seen. "We must have a photographic record of what we've done this morning. Then transfer it onto the computer."

What they'd uncovered in the last twenty-four hours confirmed the importance of the site. They were at the upper end of what was likely a flight of broad steps, buttress walls to right and left holding back the bank. Of course, they were going to cover it over against the rain, but photographs were a precaution. She wondered for a moment how much would be left after the afternoon's rainfall.

The first drops came an hour later, large and slow, leaving dark spots on the yellow earth.

"Right, pack up now, and we'll work out how we're going to tackle the next stage."

It was genuinely thrilling but so easy to get carried away, so it made sense to have a logical plan.

The rain was cascading down by the time they'd covered the grids with blue plastic, weighing it down with large stones, leaving little to show for their efforts.

Back in the store, they thrashed out a strategy for working their way down the steps safely, and then went in search of lunch.

Amancia couldn't be bothered to change her damp trousers, instead joining the line of people who were picking up food at the counter. She was hungry and needed time to think through the morning's work, so she looked for a table alone, but two minutes later, Peter left the queue and was scanning the room. He came across and put down his tray, dropping onto the vacant chair opposite her.

"Do you mind?"

She looked up and smiled. "No, of course not."

"So, this is where the fun starts."

Amancia swallowed a mouthful of food, a little irritated about having to be sociable. "I'm sorry? What fun is that?"

There was a lot to consider, and not only archaeology. Max's image floated before her eyes. Damn the man. He'd taken away her peace of mind. And James, with his refusal to back down, just made matters worse; she could do without his interference. She rubbed gritty eyes and suppressed a yawn. If Peter had something on his mind, she needed to listen.

"School party fun," he said. "Thursday next week, we have a group of children visiting."

"What are you talking about? I thought this was the summer holidays."

"Yes, but it's some holiday club. Probably children whose parents both work, and they think culture has to be the answer to child care. Just more school. Kids don't get to run about anymore."

"That's a bit harsh, Peter. Maybe they don't have a choice but to go to work."

He was smiling, but he was irritated by the imposition. "It's just that I want to get on, and a visit like this is going to hold things up."

He was right. They really didn't need this. Time was rushing on, and they were only just getting to the important part of the excavation.

"Can't we say no? Just think how disruptive it's going to be, and we don't want a whole lot of disappointed kids on our hands."

"We can't say no. It's how we get—"

"—our funding. Yeah, I get it. So, how often is this going to happen?"

"No idea, but apparently, we accessed a chunk of money from the Spaniards by agreeing to an education payoff, so I expect there are going to be a few more visits after this one."

"Okay." She thought for a moment. There was no point in fighting it. "Thursday, you said. So, who's the best person to take charge of this, do you think?"

He speared a piece of cold chicken with his fork and popped it into his mouth.

"Let's try Maya," he said eventually and grinned. "She was boasting the other day that she'd been a teaching assistant the year after she finished her degree, while she was trying to decide what to do next. And she seems to speak good Spanish."

"Great idea. We'll get her to join us after lunch and work out how this is all going to be done. Exactly how old are these children, Peter?"

"Oh, nine to twelve, I think. Not that young."

Great. Full of curiosity and unaware of the damage

they could do. If they didn't organize the visit properly, the kids would be everywhere. The headache that she'd been holding at bay over the last few days came sweeping in. She pressed her fingers to her temples. It could be atmospheric pressure. Or lack of sleep.

****

Maya appeared flattered at being picked out but said, "I can't do this."

"Of course you can. You're the only one of us with any experience of children this age, so I'm putting you in charge. Peter and I will help you plan, and on the day, we'll have two of the other students assist you."

That was taking three people away from important sitework, but they'd have to live with that. Good thing she'd agreed to having Carlos on-site. She'd heard nothing from the professor.

"Okay, yes, as long as it's not just me on my own."

"Of course not. Look, maybe you can come up with activities to appeal to ten-year-olds? I don't know—activity sheet, competition, giveaways, that sort of thing." Her friend Katie was a real enthusiast, and she'd told her a lot about how the education section at the museum operated. "They'll be here for two hours."

"Do we have a printer?"

"Yes, in that cupboard by the computers. I've even seen a stack of paper. Why don't you try it out, make sure it's working properly? Sketch out a few ideas as well, and the rest of us can take a look at them later, maybe suggest things. We're not trying to make it all your responsibility."

"Okay, yes. Hey, I could write this in my blog, even publish the worksheets, if that'd be okay."

A blog. That could be a great idea, if handled

properly. What exactly was she putting up, though? Some people were so indiscreet. They didn't seem to realize what effect their revelations might have.

"Give me your blog address before you do that. I'd like to look at what you're posting."

"Well, I...you're not going to stop me, are you?"

"I have no reason to do that, Maya. But I'm interested in how you see things. And maybe the blog could become a useful tool for us as a team."

Chapter 17

It would soon be August. Unusually, after another hot, dry week, warm rain was falling again, large drops that pattered loudly and puddled on the plastic which covered the open areas of the site. On the far side of the river, the ground rose steeply among rocks. The rainfall the week before had woken up whole swathes of brightly colored alpine plants, and a powerful lily smell wafted across to the site. Gorgeous groups of plants with tiny yellow flowers had sprouted around the edges of the buildings. Mum would love this. Amancia took several close-up photos and sent them.

—*Aren't these wonderful? Could you look them up, Mum? Haven't you got that app for identifying plants?*—

After lunch, a noisy group, mixed Spanish and British, pushed three or four tables together in the kitchen and were playing a game, the voices and laughter escaping through the open windows as Amancia walked past.

The rain came down harder, and goose pimples sprang up on her arms as the temperature decreased. She was going for a walk regardless but had a few things to do first. Maya was in the store, preparing for the children's visit, her dark head bent over the table. She'd done a lot of work over the last few days.

"How are you getting on, Maya?"

"I'm creating a worksheet, as you suggested, and I've sorted out quite a few activities for the children. Things to excite them. It would be great if they could leave the dig, wanting to be archaeologists."

She did seem to understand what was necessary. At the far end of the table, Rafa was painstakingly cleaning fragments of pottery, prior to trying a reconstruction. They hadn't really recovered enough pieces yet, but Amancia wasn't going to put him off.

"Rafa, could you give Maya a hand if necessary?"

Dragged from his absorption, Rafa lifted his head and slowly smiled. "I've a lot to do here."

"I can see that. But if she needs help…okay?"

He nodded, and she left them to it. Rain drummed on the corrugated metal roof of the accommodation building, and the atmosphere cooled rapidly. Amancia shrugged on her waterproof, a shapeless garment like a transparent plastic bag. When the rain eased off a little, she walked beyond the boundary and into the vineyard. It felt good to get away.

A workman in the distance was ploughing or clearing or whatever it was they did between the rows of vines, but a mist was rising to obscure everything at the lower level, and he vanished as she walked forward. The rain became lighter, and then it pitter-pattered to a stop and deep silence surrounded her.

Wisps and strands of mist curled upward from the bottom of the fields close to the tree-covered hill. Maybe she'd take a walk in that general direction and see what they were doing down there. She was glad to have some time on her own. Having admitted to herself that she was attracted to Max, she spent half of most nights thinking about him which meant she woke up tired and irritable. It was rebound after James, nothing more, and common sense told her that was dangerous.

Stumbling into a hole, distracted by her thoughts, she landed on her hands and knees. Furious, she got up and stomped on.

She'd thrown everything away to grab this experience. She had to leave with impeccable references, and a list of things accomplished. And Max was getting in the way. Nothing had happened between them, but she knew she could turn that around in an instant. It wasn't all on her side.

He should be back from Madrid now.

Even worse, breaking up with James supposedly set her free to get on with the next stage of her life, but James was still there, causing difficulties. She pounded along and disregarded the mud splashing up the backs of her legs.

She'd sworn to avoid a new relationship, but everything told her she should pursue this, see where it would lead her. But she mustn't. She had to open up to new possibilities, and a part of that was working in archaeology. How long had she waited for this chance? It would never happen if she got distracted.

The clatter of a heavy engine, somewhere to her left, broke through the quiet, but the mist had swirled to within a few feet, and she couldn't see any vehicle. Perhaps this was the man who'd found the gold coin, and she could ask him a few questions. She grinned; that was unlikely if he spoke with the local accent she'd encountered in the village, which had left her completely bewildered.

She moved on down between the rows of vines.

There'd been that conversation with James, just

before leaving Bristol. "You've been seduced by the glamour of the new job, Amancia. You'll come around in the end, and I'll be waiting for you."

She laughed out loud now at the idea of glamour, picturing her tiny room with its shared shower, and the communal kitchen.

But maybe, without even knowing what awaited her, he'd hit on the truth? Seduced?—yeah, probably she was seduced by the work she was doing. It didn't feel like work, more like pure indulgence. For glamour, there was the complex, intriguing, and sexy persona of Max. He'd thrown her into confusion, turned upside down her efforts to become her own woman again, all her plans to search out a teaching post in a British university. Mainly because he filled her thoughts every moment when she wasn't thinking about the dig and the needs of its people. In danger of spoiling this brilliant opportunity because of bloody hormones, she gave a grunt of frustration.

Slowing, she stared into the mist, trying to make out the tractor. Nothing. A wave of guilt swept over her. She hadn't even looked on the net to see if there was anything suitable to apply for. That was something she could put right today, and she would.

She squelched on, down a furrow.

James wouldn't rate Max and probably wouldn't see him as a competitor. A farmer? Not likely. James had a very strong sense of self and of how important he was. "I was up for a major prize, like the Booker, but for journalism. Didn't get it, but next year…"

Amancia had admired him then, but their time together hadn't been good for her, making her play down her own achievements, and soon she'd been asking herself if she was up to university teaching at all. Distance had given her the opportunity to think more objectively about their relationship, and the idea of being with him day after day had shocked her by being so unattractive.

Someone cried out, but straightaway, it went quiet again, while the engine now throbbed gently in the background. The mist distorted sound, and she didn't know if she was still heading toward it.

Her pea-green wellington boots with their silly pink dots splashed in the puddles. A watery, yellow sun broke through the clouds immediately above, and slanting rays of light lit the landscape around, but the vineyard worker remained lost to view. Walking in the mist was a strange experience, cutting her off, turning normal objects into mysterious ethereal forms, especially in the groves of vines. It was cold.

Her phone began to ring, and she fished it out of her bag again.

James.

Maybe she should answer, speak to him instead of replying to messages. Perhaps that would be more effective, and he'd finally understand she meant what she said. But then, a swathe of mist was blown clear by the freshening wind, and she saw a man stretched on the ground. The white curtain closed quickly over him.

She began to run.

The phone was still in her hand. It stopped ringing. Desperately, she tried to recall the Spanish emergency number. One-one-two—but she had no idea how to describe her location. Even trying would slow things down, and a man's life was at stake. She scrolled down to "Max." He should be home.

****

Help was on its way. Amancia crouched beside the farm worker and felt his pulse again. It was thready, his skin cool. He muttered and moaned, but he wasn't conscious. She checked, but there was no blood, no sign of injury. It must be a heart attack or a stroke.

Gently, she eased the man onto his side, into the recovery position. She ought to keep him warm, but her flimsy waterproof was the best she could do. When she turned off the tractor engine, an abrupt silence fell. She sat on one corner of the plastic, in the sea of wet clay, surrounded by the eerie mist, and time passed slowly. For the first time in weeks, it was cold. After a while, she got up and paced back and forth. More mud.

Okay, it was a relief to know James was no longer a part of her life, even though he was bothering her. But she had to get a few things straight about Max.

Her stomach did a treacherous flip. On the plus side—there were lots of plusses: gorgeous hazel eyes and a face with a lot of character, with a nose that called up profiles of the statues of ancient Rome; a good face, despite the ugly scar which, curiously, emphasized the perfection of the rest. How had he come by his uneven gait? A broken leg, badly reset perhaps. Farms were dangerous places.

Then, he had this ability to listen properly, not just waiting all the time to drop his own contribution into the conversation but thinking about what was said and reacting to it. That was a big positive.

She stopped pacing to listen. Distant noises. Maybe people were on their way.

She liked that he didn't come on to her like almost every other man she met. There was something between them—it wasn't all on her side—and yet he held back.

In fact, there was nothing to stop her pursuing some sort of relationship with Señor Maximiliano Dominguez Serrano. Except the thought made her dizzy, and she'd lose control of her destiny, be unable to accomplish the things she'd set out to do.

She did like the name, Max. She grinned. It was another plus. She just shouldn't let it get too serious, if she wanted to retain her independence.

Her smile faded. Really? Not get serious. She was fooling herself, wasn't she? She hadn't felt like this since she was at school and meeting her first boyfriend. Fifteen years of experience had been wiped away, and the butterflies were at work in her stomach as if she were an inexperienced teenager. It was beyond serious. Things had gone much too far.

There was a groan. She checked her patient, but nothing had changed. The temperature continued to drop, and she shivered as she lowered herself again onto the corner of her waterproof and hugged her knees.

Could she let him know how she felt?

No, she couldn't. The last time she'd let her guard down had been with James who'd appeared to be quite a catch. It had taken her a while to understand that a well-educated mixed-race woman might be a suitable acquisition for an ambitious young journalist, going places. He hadn't said it in so many words, but once the early excitement of their relationship had died down, she'd begun to hear another narrative in what he said to people, and to her. And her exotic looks always counted for something. She ticked all the right boxes.

She'd taken a while to see how controlling he was, but the alarm bells had really begun to ring when he'd said, "You've often said you'd like to live down by the floating harbor, and we could afford something really smart down there between us."

The problem was, moving in together did make good sense, if you happened to love each other. But she'd worked it out now. She no longer loved him, and recently, there'd been moments when her feelings verged on the opposite.

She glanced down at her wrist. The bruise had gone, like the one on her jaw, but she couldn't forget it.

****

His head with its arrogant tilt was the first thing she saw. Max was hurrying through the mist, slithering on the wet earth. She put her phone away and gulped air to calm herself as she struggled to stand up in the mud. Then his warm hand clasped her icy fingers, and he hauled her to her feet. She hadn't seen him in a week, and her heart beat an outrageous drum solo that she could do nothing about.

"Thank you," he said, in greeting. "It could have been hours before we realized something was wrong."

"Will the ambulance people know where to come?"

"Pedro's waiting on the road, to guide them here. They'll come as close as they can and then make their way on foot. Thank you for staying with him."

"How could I do otherwise?"

Already, the squelching of boots announced the new arrivals. Accompanied by Pedro, the paramedics appeared, hefting a folding stretcher. The farmhand had tears running down his cheeks.

"*Mi amigo*," he said, rushing forward. "What's happened to my friend?"

"I don't know, *hombre*." Max clapped him on the

shoulder. "But I do know they'll do the best they can for him."

The two paramedics checked their patient and carefully loaded him onto the stretcher, before hurrying off through the mire, clearly anxious to hook him up to the apparatus in the ambulance.

"You go with him, Pedro. I'll find Maria and bring her to the hospital later."

Chapter 18

Max turned back to Amancia with a look of concern, taking hold of her frozen hands and sending a current of electricity shooting through her, before dropping them again.

"You're cold. Come up to the house, and I'll get you a hot drink."

Cold? She wasn't cold. That was fire running through her veins. She couldn't look at him, afraid of what he might read in her face, and instead picked up her muddy waterproof. "What about his wife?"

How awful it would be to deliver the bad news. She'd hate to have to do that.

"I'll fetch her and then pick you up. If you're okay with it, I'll leave her at the hospital, and I can pass by the dig site later to drop you off."

Exhaustion had hit, and she was suddenly relieved she wouldn't have to walk back. "Sure, that's not a problem. Do you think he'll be all right?"

"I don't know. It's probably a heart attack. I think the quicker they get to it, the better the chance of a good result."

They walked up the field, side by side, a space between them. Her legs felt numb, and she wanted to lean on him. Instead, she followed him through the belt of trees near the bottom of the hill, and he held out his hand to guide her onto the road that tracked to the house, quickly letting go when they were on firm ground. The mist was still thick here, but the red pinpricks of the ambulance taillights were just visible as the vehicle disappeared down toward the city, swirling blue flashes silently accompanying it. He led her to the back of the house. A rich smell of coffee and cooking greeted her as they entered the warm kitchen.

"I'll leave you with Catalina. Twenty minutes and I'll be back."

The dampness had soaked into her clothes, and Amancia was chilled. The short, dark-haired woman handed her a towel, and she patted herself dry. Afterward, huddled by an old-fashioned kitchen range, she sipped strong, black coffee into which Catalina had put several sugar lumps, and she began to warm up. It had been a shock finding a man who at first had appeared to be dead, especially as she'd seen him working only half an hour earlier.

Max was back before she'd finished. "I have Juan's wife in the truck. Will you come with us now?"

****

When they'd dropped María off at the hospital, Amancia took the front seat next to Max, and they drove into the center of the city.

"I need a drink. Let's find a bar."

Amancia looked down at their earth-encrusted footwear and sodden, mud-spattered trousers and was about to refuse but couldn't find the energy.

He led her to a small bar where they leaned against the counter and ordered beer. It was early for tapas, but the barman passed across a small tray of some he'd already prepared.

"Try these," said Max, pushing it her way.

"I don't think I'm hungry. I've just had lunch."

"It's five o'clock. You must have eaten hours ago. They're small, and a great accompaniment to the beer."

Cautiously, she picked up a tiny slice of potato omelet and copied the way in which he slid it into his mouth, following it down with a long drink. He was right—it was great with cold beer.

Amancia took another sip, and they talked a little about unimportant matters. She held back, determined to keep things light and friendly, nothing more, but in spite of herself, she was enjoying his company. In the background, the barman busied himself preparing vast trays of tapas for the evening's customers. A delicious warmth stole over her. Max placed his beer on the bar and turned to her.

"I wondered—"

"Yes?"

"Well, I…what's happening on the site at the moment?"

She gathered her wandering thoughts. "Nothing much since we last spoke. Oh, well, there is one thing: a school group is coming to the site." And she told him about the proposed visit the next day.

He smiled. "I think you are not enthusiastic about this…intrusion?"

"You're right. We're making such good progress, and this will hold everything up. And I'm worried about accidents, with that unprotected riverside edge. I often have to warn the students to take care, and I keep thinking how bad it'll be with young children around."

"And you can't refuse to do this?"

"No, it's about funding."

"Ah yes, I understand."

"We'll take care, of course. I wonder if they'll enjoy it. Maya does have lots of ideas to occupy them."

"Maybe I could help."

"You? How?" Realizing this response sounded rude, she added, "Sorry, but what could you do?"

"So, what about something like this: apple juice and cakes in Catalina's kitchen when they've finished at the dig. I remember what it was like to be ten years old, and the best things always involved food. And the juice is made in the vineyard. It's something special."

"Do you really want all those children there? There'll be fifteen of them, I understand."

"You saw the kitchen. It would be no problem to fit them in. I'll talk to María when she's back from the hospital and we know how things are with Juan. She's the world's greatest baker of cakes, and she loves children. Hers are long gone. She's not going to be at the hospital all the time, and it would be good to give her something to keep her busy."

"Do you think she would do it?"

"*Sí.* She and Catalina could work something out together."

It was good of him. He cared about his employees, wanted to make sure they would be all right, and he was being kind to her, too. But she couldn't help but be suspicious of someone who had servants; it was easy to be generous with other people's services. But he'd come up with the perfect ending for the children's visit. Maybe that was all she needed to think about.

"It sounds like that'll leave good memories. Thanks for the suggestion, Max."

"Okay then, when you know the details, tell me when you want me to come over to the site to bring them up to the house. They'll have a minibus, I expect."

"Yes, I'm sure they will. Maya's organizing the visit, and she'll love this. She's so keen, I expect she'll have them filling in a worksheet while they're eating, about what archaeological site owners are like!" She grinned. "And I'm sure you'll get a top rating if you're offering cake. Oh, I've just remembered something she wanted me to ask you, a great idea for the visit."

"Anything I can do to help."

"She wants to use a corner of the field, that part at the top end where it's ploughed, just before the rows of vines begin, to set up grids. They'll mark them out just like the ones we're working in. So, after the kids have had a look at the real thing, they can do some digging themselves, and maybe actually find something. Imagine the thrill."

"No problem. Tell her to arrange it as she wishes." He touched her arm, withdrawing his hand quickly. "Are you okay? It can't have been good sitting out in the field in the mist with a man having a heart attack."

She was suddenly breathless and struggled to hide her reaction. "I'm fine." There was nothing wrong. She just wanted him to put his hand back on her arm. "I'm fine."

****

She'd had far more of the delicious tapas than she'd meant to. When she got back to the site, Amancia no longer wanted anything to eat, but she went into the kitchen that evening to tell everyone about the arrangements she'd made with the landowner and to let Maya know she could create her grids. Then she returned to her room, mobile in hand. It had to be done now, before she found a reason for dodging the obligation. An acid taste filled her mouth.

She opened up the phone and saw yet another text.

—*How can I trust you to deal with things when I've always had to support you—remember last year...*— She scanned down—the text was turning into an essay. —*you've taken on too much, Amancia. You need to come home...*—

Some cruel and hurtful things, wrapped in a blanket of concern. She didn't bother to read farther but instead rang his number. While waiting for him to answer, she decided she'd be calm but make sure he understood that this was their last communication.

"James Talbot."

He always announced himself like that, never looking at the screen to see who it was.

"James, it's Amancia. I'm sorry I didn't call you back straightaway. There was an accident. I had to call an ambulance and—"

"What? On the site? I told you that you shouldn't be doing this."

He managed to make it sound as if it'd been her fault, as if she'd done something silly that she could easily have avoided by listening to him. Determined not to justify herself, she took a breath and waited a moment before saying anything.

"No, it was on a farm. It was chance I was walking past when it happened, but I had to deal with it."

"Oh, I'm sorry." He was silent and then added, "So, are you okay?"

"I'm fine, James."

She had to say it now. What was the point of letting him think they could pick up where they'd left off when she went back to Bristol?

"James, I'm fine, but I'm involved with completely different things now, and it really isn't going to work between us. You're making things difficult for both of us by texting all the time."

That was no good—she was gabbling, and she had to make it clear. "James, I meant what I said before: I'm not coming back to you. In fact, I may not even return to Bristol. I'm applying for jobs all over the country." *Well, she would be soon.* "So, don't concern yourself about me. And you mustn't ring me."

"Take your time, Amancia, and enjoy it," he said finally. "You were cooped up in that museum far too long."

Too right, I was. And you were much too satisfied with that.

She closed her phone then, without saying anything further.

Giving a huge sigh, she slumped down, exhausted. It had gone as expected, just like at home. He was very calm because he didn't accept what she'd said, still thought it would only be a temporary situation.

Or maybe he'd found someone else, hooked up with that girl, Kelly, from the magazine, whom he'd mentioned once or twice? That kind of fitted. She thought about it and found she didn't care.

It meant she could get on with her life.

Chapter 19

Thursday dawned bright, sunny, and already too warm. At seven, two farm workers turned up with wooden posts and wire, saying that Max had told them to erect a fence along the side of the dig that gave onto the river. It was great he'd listened, and she had a warm feeling, knowing he'd understood her concerns. Not worrying about that risk would make a big difference to the day with the children.

They walked along the edge, and she told them how they had to work their way around the top of the stairwell excavation. Sorting this out took time, and she called Elena over to help explain, but by midmorning, the work was finished. She took out her phone, ignoring the flutter at the thought of talking to him again.

"Thank you so much for the safety barrier. It's such a relief."

"It was easy to remedy. We always have fencing materials in the vineyard, part of our basic tools. Do you think it will do what you want it to?"

"Definitely. Of course, I won't be letting the children run around the site unsupervised, but you never know what they might get up to."

"Don't forget to ring when they've finished. See you later."

Something had changed, and he'd sounded more relaxed. Not that it mattered, because all she wanted was a good working relationship. But every contact, every glimpse of the man was drawing her further in.

****

The teams worked on-site as usual, apart from Maya and her two helpers, who were in full organizational mode. Although the young woman seemed capable, Amancia still felt she had to check. "Let's see what you've got for them."

She talked Amancia through her ideas. The girl had done an imaginative job on the worksheets.

"I was sure I could rely on you. Do you have everything else ready?"

"Mateo and Sally have laid out grids, over in the corner where you said. And we've got a bucketful of tools ready, trowels and scrapers and a couple of boxes for anything interesting they find."

"How are you going to ensure they do find something? I'm assuming that's what you intend."

"Yes, I went through the discarded soil heap and picked up a whole lot of broken shards—things we found around the edges of the field, not from the dig site itself. We've mixed them into the top layer of soil and tamped it all down a bit, so the kids can 'find' them. Maybe we'll let them keep any items they unearth as a souvenir, or they can donate them to the dig and feel they've made a genuine contribution."

"So, they all get something out of this."

"Yes, and if they donate their find, we'll record their names." She picked up a pile of A4 sheets of thin cardboard. "Here are the certificates we've designed. I thought we could award a special certificate to anyone who finds an object. Otherwise, they'll get one that says that they came here and dug. We've printed them out, the names blank. Would you mind signing them?"

"Of course, I'll sign. I'm so pleased we chose you to do this job, Maya. You're a natural teacher."

The young woman's face went red. "Thank you. I've been enjoying it so much, I actually think...you know, eventually...maybe instead of sticking with archaeology, I'll apply for..." She stopped, looking embarrassed. "Oh, it's a silly idea."

"Teacher training? There's no reason you can't do both at different times. I think you should look into it—and you'd have much more chance of actually getting a job. I'm keen to see for myself how this visit works out now. I was dreading it and all the disruption it would cause, but you've helped me view it in a positive way."

At lunchtime, Amancia reminded the whole team of what was happening. "Just make sure none of the children wanders into any of our grids. The edge by the river looks a lot safer than it was, but still, keep them away. *Everyone's* on duty, right?"

****

At two o'clock, a dark grey minibus with Hermanos Gonzales printed on its side in bright blue trundled into the car park. A young man, very dark-skinned with floppy black hair, hopped out of the driver's door and then stuck his head back inside, presumably telling the children to stay put. He looked to be in his early twenties. Amancia went up to him.

"*¿Señor Casado? Soy Amancia Harding, directora de este organismo. Amancia.*"

It was all simple language, but she got a thrill from being able to talk to people in Spanish. Still had a long way to go, though.

"*Y yo me llamo Javier.*"

They shook hands.

"*¿Y los niños?* Can I let them out now? They are super excited."

"Of course. I have some of my team here on standby." She introduced Maya and her helpers. "They'll take you around, get everyone involved. And when you've finished, there's a treat up at the house."

"Thank you for allowing us to do this. It's probably not what you imagine. These kids are from the local children's home."

Amancia's heart sank. They'd be all over the place, hyperactive, shouting and screaming. Hopefully, this young man knew how to keep them under control. He'd already opened the side door of the bus, and now the children were tumbling out. All boys. High-pitched voices. There was a lot of pushing and arguing.

"Okay," she said to the boys when he'd got them standing quietly by the bus. "This is Maya and her team. They'll be looking after you. Enjoy the visit."

Amancia meant to continue working on her grid, but the sweat was soon trickling down her face, and the sun sapped her energy. It was as if the unseasonal rain had never been. The shouts of the children came at her from all sides, making it hard to concentrate. Soon, the boys had had enough of walking sedately around the site, absorbing information.

She watched Maya interact with her charges, lining them up and leading them to the special grids that had been organized. She was impressive. Amancia liked children in a general way, but not in these numbers. Teachers came in all types, and Amancia knew she connected well with university students, but teaching primary school was a job she'd never want.

Snatching trowels and buckets, the new archaeologists rushed off in twos to start digging, each pair being allocated a specific part of the grid. They quietened down, and for a while, there was just the clink and scrape of the trowels, and the occasional excited cry when a find was made. They were soon spectacularly muddy.

Javier asked Maya something, and when the girl nodded, he went to the minibus, coming back with a circular object on a stick. It looked like a floor polisher from a distance. Ah, he was a detectorist. He called one of the children across, and having shown him how to operate the metal detector, he caught Amancia's eye and smiled.

"A reward for good behavior, and even then, they only get a few minutes."

"Have you ever found anything with it?"

"Nothing worthwhile. It is single frequency, little more than a toy. It can detect to about twelve centimeters deep, so finding something is—"

There was a shout. The children surrounded the boy with the machine, but Maya asked them to return to what they'd been doing and waited quietly until they did what she said. She told the boy's partner he should help dig at the spot where the detector had reacted.

Finally, metal clanged, and once again the excitement grew, with the children pushing each other out of the way, wanting to see.

"Is this a plant?" Amancia whispered to Maya.

"No, that's quite hard ground where they're digging. We didn't even go down that far with the material we introduced." She turned back to the children. "Be careful, boys. You can damage the artifact, if you're too rough with it. Let's get you help."

Hands went up.

"*Soy yo el descubridor del arte...artefacto.*" The boy was grinning, claiming the word as his own.

But Maya asked the two students to extract the object. It was a rusted metal box, like an old-fashioned tobacco tin. The field would have been ploughed many times, and the tin had probably dropped out of some farmworker's pocket. No Roman coins here.

More finds were being made now, and the boys were invited to keep them since there was nothing of value to the dig.

"What a great idea to bring the detector." Maya smiled at Javier.

He looked embarrassed. "I thought it might go down well."

It was time to ring Max. "They're nearly ready."

"And Catalina and María are ready for them. They've excelled themselves."

"I hope they'll eat it all up."

"They will, I guarantee it."

"Could you take Maya and her helpers with you in your vehicle? They've done a fabulous job, and they deserve a treat, too."

She'd noticed the way in which Javier was looking at Maya. Stunned would probably describe it. If she could give them a chance to get to know one another...What? She really was getting soft.

"Why don't you come over as well?" Max said. "Plenty of room in the truck."

"Ah, thanks. But I'll pass. I've got some clearing up to do here."

****

Max leaned back in his chair as he ended the call. Of course, it was better that she'd said no. He preferred not to meet her at all if it could be helped, but his heart had dropped at her words. It seemed that somewhere in his brain had been the idea that he was going to see her today. And it had buoyed him up.

He looked around on the desk for his keys and rooted around in all the drawers. He had a long search before finding them exactly where he thought he'd placed them, by the keyboard—but mysteriously beneath a sheet of paper. Proof, if he needed it, that he had to concentrate on what he was doing.

Had he got it all wrong, with his lonely, organized life? He wasn't exactly satisfied with it. He functioned. Of course he did. But what if he was about to throw away a precious chance, just because it scared him? How ironic was that? He, the hardened, experienced soldier, who'd placed himself in extreme danger several times over and had the scars to prove it, was afraid to face a situation like this. He knew what it was: he didn't want to see the pity in her eyes. It would pierce his armor, and if ultimately it led to nothing, continuing afterward would be that much more difficult. No, he couldn't let that happen.

He put his head around the door to the barn. "Alejo, I'll be out for about half an hour. I'm going to pick up those kids, okay?"

Anyway, it didn't matter what he felt; keeping out of her way was sensible. He wasn't going to impose himself on anyone. He couldn't do it. And then there were other things. But he was letting his imagination roam again, that was the trouble.

He stood up.

Maybe tonight, he would go and see Vala again, after all. Depended on how he felt.

Chapter 20

Late the following afternoon, Max and Alejo were in the office attached to the winery, for their review of the previous four weeks' work. Used coffee cups were stacked to one side, and the table was spread with data sheets, graphs, and several printouts. Had they made progress? Was it fast enough? Was there anything urgent? Those were the big questions for this critical year, and for the moment, things looked good.

Now, Max spread the long-term weather forecast sheet on top of the other papers, as he brought up the matter that had been giving him sleepless nights. When he wasn't thinking about Amancia, that was. Climate change. It wasn't the distant possibility people seemed to think. In two short years, a lot had changed. It was upon them, and they needed to think hard about dealing with the effects. But there had been so much else to do.

"You really think our grapes will suddenly stop growing. That's not going to happen overnight."

"Overnight, no, but the plants could be long-term damaged, and next year, production could go right down. What concerns me right now is the effect of the heat on the grapes we harvest this year. This is your area of expertise, Alejo. Do you realize that last year, the temperature was over forty-one degrees down in the city in August? It's a little cooler up at this level, but if it goes higher than about thirty-two degrees, the grapes start to spoil. And we're not looking at normal temperatures—they should be dropping, but they're predicting thirty-seven to thirty-nine in the next few weeks."

"It was more than that in 2015. People got through it. It's not as delicately balanced as you suggest."

If the temperature went up much farther, their only resort would be to bring forward the harvest. And that would mean shutting down the archaeology site, and he could only imagine the effect on Amancia. He felt a little sick and resolved to hold off as long as he could. There were other things that could be done.

"*Claro*. I'm still a novice, but you're not filling me with confidence, Alejo, and I'm not just looking to get through it. Look, my friend, there's no point in ignoring what's happening. I hate to admit it, but maybe I made a mistake to try the dry-growth method."

"Much nicer wine. Distinctive."

"Much lower yield, as well, but it is as you say. I think I must consider a standby irrigation system and think long term about how we can collect rainwater, in case we need it. We've had quite a lot of rain, and all that water's gone into the ground—great for now, but what happens later when there's no rain and the temperature continues to rise?"

He didn't know how he was going to handle the water problem, but he wouldn't ignore the obvious. He'd sunk every penny he possessed into the project. "It's your money as well. We have to address it."

Alejo had contributed twenty percent of the set-up costs, from a win on the Thursday draw of the Primitiva, one of the Spanish lotteries. It wasn't a huge amount, but it had been offered on the understanding that he would eventually recoup his stake and make a profit too. But the man wasn't business savvy. His whole interest lay in the making of the wine, and this situation enabled him to do what he loved best. Each day in the winery was a reward, and it was obvious he found the current discussion tedious. Arguably, he should have been the one to bring this up.

"I thought you said you didn't want to do the constant irrigation method."

"I don't. Besides, you haven't listened to what I said. We have to have the water should we need to irrigate—and a means of getting it to the plants if there's a prolonged drought—which comes back to the storage of water. What have we got at the moment?"

"The bowsers. We can get some more."

Max sighed. This wasn't going well.

"Right, but it has to come from somewhere. Last year there was always water in the ponds, but already they're drying up. And there are other things we should be looking at—shelter for the plants, for instance. Come on, man, you brought that up when you came into this, and frankly, we've done nothing about it."

"It was a consideration, something we'd get to eventually."

"Well, eventually is here. We're losing grapes to sunburn and dehydration. So maybe we should consider training the plants in a bush shape so that the grapes are more protected from the sun by the leaves."

"It could help to grow on a trellis, but we can't achieve that overnight."

"No, but it's something to work toward for years to come. You know much more about that than I do, and I want you to look into it, especially some sort of shade cloth for this year. Try and get me some information by the end of next week."

"Okay."

"We have to train the men as well, to spot the problems early, cut out damaged fruit. Our testing regime is going to increase."

Alejo looked at him, alarmed for the first time during the conversation. "You're serious about this?"

"I'm just letting you know I'll be talking to the bank because this is going to cost. I've made an appointment for Saturday morning."

Chapter 21

On the Saturday after the children's visit, Amancia was driving into Zaragoza in the minibus, which the university had loaned to the site for the summer. With the prospect of a leisurely Saturday afternoon, it felt good to be leaving everything behind for a few hours.

Monday would be the first of August, and she'd worked almost nonstop since her arrival in Spain. She needed some free time. It would have been great to visit the city with Max, but still she hesitated to suggest anything. Wasn't it better to keep things on a professional level?

At the top of the list of interesting places to visit was the Forum Museum, which sat on the remains of the original Roman forum. Given she spent her days unearthing Roman artifacts and uncovering ancient walls, this visit was essential. Although she'd seen lots of images of Zaragoza on the city website, nothing was as good as the real thing. It would give a clear idea of how the Romans had built things in this area.

And she wanted to see the modern bridge designed by Zaha Hadid, superstar architect. It couldn't be further in concept from Roman ruins, but the images on the internet were inspiring. That, however, would have to be for a later visit.

She drove carefully, unused to the roads and the vehicle. In internet pictures, Zaragoza looked elegant. It had a Renaissance version of the forum now, but the Roman influence was very much in evidence. Surely, it had to be the most beautiful public space in Spain.

It was hard to imagine such a sophisticated provincial city back in England. Although half of Bristol had been obliterated during the Second World War, rebuilding afterward had suffered from a lack of funding. She loved her city, but she thought it was a little disappointing visually in comparison.

When her phone rang, Amancia didn't answer, and it stopped. The number of houses and shops was increasing, so the center couldn't be far away, and she was looking for a car park. The ringtone came again. It surely couldn't be that urgent.

Then, a van pulled out into the street, right in front of her. Great, she'd found a space. She waited patiently, as far over to the right as she could, while it made several maneuvers. The horn from the vehicle behind blared repeatedly as the driver tried to bully her into leaving the space to him, but she didn't move. She took a deep breath and determined not to lose her cool.

Finally! She slipped in, not daring to position herself to reverse. Ignoring his glare as he swept past, she gathered her things. That was enough stress for a free afternoon.

Recent calls showed her ex-boyfriend had rung twice in the last twenty minutes. That wasn't good.

She texted —*Problem?*— and then wished she'd ignored it. It was harder to break the habit of answering than she'd expected.

—*Just arrived at Zaragoza Airport. Can you come and get me?*—

What was he doing here? And why did he think she

was going to run around after him, when their relationship was over?

—*No, I can't. There's a bus into the city.*—

Now she was relieved she'd responded, even though she felt choked, her heart beating overtime. He was here, and ignoring him would achieve nothing; he wouldn't give up, not after coming over to see her like this. It wouldn't be enough to have the conversation on the phone. She thought for a moment, seeing her precious free time disappearing. But she had to clear this up, so she added —*Find a café in the center and text me the name.*—

With a deep sigh, Amancia got out, locked the vehicle, and set off toward the town center. The sun beat down without mercy, and there were tourists everywhere with their red shoulders and floppy hats. Locals forced into the open at this time of day moved in the shadows the tall buildings created in the narrow streets. Following their example, she turned a corner and saw one end of the big square. She'd arrived.

She wasn't in control of herself, not the way she'd like to be. His arrival brought everything back, and thoughts and memories churned through her mind. It was better to meet in public, where he'd be less likely to lose his temper. He had a hot temper, though most of James's abuse was of the mental kind. It was shocking that she now permitted herself to think of it as abuse. She'd always imagined only weak women allowed a partner to abuse them. She certainly wasn't that, but it had been insidious, happening before she'd noticed.

Almost hyperventilating, she sank down on a bench, seeking a measure of calm. The idea he might show up at the dig was turning her insides to water.

He'd ruin any credibility she had by the way he'd behave toward her. She'd known there were going to be problems breaking up with James. That had been obvious even before leaving England, but she'd never imagined he'd go so far. This level of obsession frightened her.

She switched off her phone, unwilling to extend the text string. Somehow, he was making her feel she was at fault for putting him in this situation, yet he was entirely responsible for his own decisions. But he'd ruined her tranquility, and she couldn't help wondering how it was going to play out.

****

When she switched back on an hour later, she read his text and then quickly turned her phone off again. The small coffee shop he'd named was close to the Forum Museum, but there wouldn't be time for cultural visits this afternoon. Although she wandered in and out of shops, she found scarcely any of the items she'd wanted, nor did she enjoy the experience. Finally, taking a deep breath, she entered the café and immediately saw his dark head in a corner.

He'd chosen a spot where he could see out onto the street, perhaps intending to look out for her, but he was head down over his laptop, typing. James was a true journalist and never wasted an opportunity. He freelanced for quite a few publications and was probably working on a travel report on Zaragoza, taking advantage of being here. The familiar sight softened her for a moment, and then she pushed it behind her. She was almost at the table before he looked up.

He scrambled to his feet. "Hello, darling. It's really good to see you."

Leaning forward, he tried to kiss her, but she ignored the endearment and dropped quickly down onto the chair opposite him.

"I had a few things I needed to do in the city." She'd let him think he'd interrupted her work.

Turning away to the bar, she signaled to the waitress and ordered. A cup of coffee sat untouched beside James, and there was a half-eaten *bocadillo de queso* on a plate. He took it now, removing the pieces of tomato and lettuce, and began to gobble up large bites of cheese and bread.

"Didn't have any lunch." He munched with evident pleasure. "Mmm, this is good."

When he'd finished chomping, he swallowed half of the coffee in one go and wiped his mouth with the back of his hand. She'd forgotten how much his eating habits had irritated her.

"Why did you come, James?"

"I had to see for myself how you were—"

"Okay, and you can see that I'm fine. You don't need to check on me. I wouldn't appreciate it, even if we were still together. But we aren't, not anymore."

"But I must—"

"No, there's nothing you must do, except leave me be. I told you. It's over between us."

"Yeah, but you don't mean it. You just don't realize that. It's all this new freedom and not having any responsibilities."

He was impervious to all arguments. She wanted to scream at him, but instead, she took several breaths and when she spoke, her voice was low. "I do have responsibilities. I manage a large team of people and an archaeological site. You could call that responsibility."

He ignored this and flipped down the lid of his laptop. "Look, I've finished now. Let's go back to your place, so we can talk things through."

And he stood up, just as the server placed her coffee on the table.

She almost laughed at his suggestion of going back to the site with her, thinking how shocked he'd be if he saw her "glamorous" room. But it wasn't going to come to that. Her heart was thudding uncomfortably when she leaned forward to pick up her cup.

"Sit down, James, while I have my coffee!"

He could walk out on her if he wanted to and she wouldn't care, but he did sit, albeit with poor grace. He looked at her, challenging. Then he opened his laptop again.

Chapter 22

"I've researched this farmer guy, you know."

Everything had changed. He was speaking in a colder, more aggressive manner. She recognized the tone, because she'd heard it before, whenever things weren't going the way that he wanted. It was finely calculated to upset her and bring her to order. God, all this was opening her eyes, and one or two things Lizzie had said were beginning to make sense.

"Why would you do that? What does it have to do with you? With me, for that matter?"

"Come on, Amancia. I wanted to check, to see what you were getting yourself into."

"Getting myself into? I don't think I understand. I work for the university, not some random farmer."

He tapped out some words, obviously calling up a website. "He's not what he seems, you know!"

"If you mean the owner of the vineyard, I've hardly met him, so I wouldn't know." She hoped her expression gave nothing away, but she was so angry, she didn't care. She had to stay calm. "Our dig is on the extreme edge of his property, and he is not involved."

Not what he seems. What did he mean by that? What had he found out? But reaching for neutral ground, she said, "I suppose, as a journalist, you just couldn't resist ferreting around, unearthing information you thought could be useful for an article."

"That's right. And it's a good job I had a look."

"What on earth do you mean? Not that it affects anything I'm doing."

"Well, he's not really a farmer. In fact, this evidence suggests he's some sort of soldier. I'm following it through, and then it all goes blank about three years ago. These people keep things hidden. I'd guess he's a mercenary, to be able to afford a huge place like that. Rich pickings in that, I've heard."

It was his family home, she thought, remembering her visit there. But she wasn't going to argue with James about that. It sounded as if he was intent on poisoning things for her. He couldn't possibly have any idea of her feelings about Max, but James had superbly honed instincts. It was why he was such a successful journalist. He would have put the disparate pieces of information together and concluded that she had to have fallen for such a desirable man. Or would soon do so.

Okay, what he'd said was interesting, and his having been a soldier might explain…Anyway, she could see what James was up to, and he couldn't be allowed to continue.

She didn't speak for a moment, letting the information penetrate, although there was no way she could trust what he'd said. He'd chosen a particular interpretation, questioning Max's integrity. Clever journalists knew how to do that. He'd slanted what he'd said to raise her doubts, punching out wildly because he thought he was losing her. Which he was. She tamped down rising fury, forcing herself to stay calm, but the heat in her chest and her whirling thoughts threatened to choke her.

"So, you're on the trail of a story."

"Might be."

"Well, I wish you luck with it. But let me make something clear, James: You're not coming back with me; I'm not giving you any introductions or helping you in any way." She paused, wanting to underline the message. "You've wasted your time coming here. I told you it was over between us. And I meant it."

It had taken a huge effort not to shout. Amancia leaned back in her chair and allowed her gaze to take in what was happening out on the street. Her relaxed pose in no way reflected her feelings, but she wanted him to think that none of this mattered to her. Acid churned in her stomach, and random, unpleasant ideas floated around in her brain. So yes, once again, he'd succeeded in upsetting her. If only she could push it all away.

Sitting upright now, Amancia took a sip of the coffee while James stared across at her as if waiting for some crack in her armor to appear, some sign that he'd got through to her.

She'd leave in a moment. From the corner of her eye, she could see people crossing the road. She watched idly and drank some more coffee. It was strong and fragrant and made her feel a little better. Over at the counter, the usual cacophony of coffee-making buzzed and roared, but a pool of silence surrounded their table.

A movement caught her eye as Max stepped onto the pavement. Despite her misery, her heart gave a little leap, and the blood seemed to run faster in her veins. Max took a step in the direction of the café as James leaned forward and thrust his face right into hers, his bright blue eyes bulging unpleasantly.

"You're not leaving me, Amancia. You're mine. I'll make sure…"

Amancia jerked backward and sprang to her feet, clattering her cup onto the saucer. Out of the corner of her eye, she saw Max freeze for a split second, his gaze on her. Then, as the person behind cannoned into him, he turned to apologize and hurried off down the street.

Her heart was thudding so hard in her chest, she felt it would choke her. How dared James come here and interfere with her life? How dared he try to get between her and anyone she chose to spend time with?

"Don't you threaten me. I don't care for you, James. Go away! I don't want to see you again."

"But you don't understand. I'm here for you—"

"No, you're here for yourself." She kept her tone low. "Find a hotel room and enjoy this beautiful city, before you go back to Bristol tomorrow. I won't be around to see you off. Now, I've got a job to do."

She got up and stalked to the entrance, leaving him to pay for her half-finished coffee. She was beside herself with fury. As she pulled the door closed behind her, she took several deep breaths and pushed her hair behind her shoulders, holding her head high. Her eyes stung, and she could scarcely swallow the lump in her throat. Blindly, she took a few steps, knowing she had to get as far away as possible before tears spilled over; she would not let him have the satisfaction of seeing how much he'd got to her.

As she arrived alongside the window where James had been sitting, she heard footsteps behind her. Had he actually dared to follow? Rage filled her, and she whirled around. She would not allow him to do this.

It was Max. She blinked. Where had he come from?

****

That single moment when he'd looked through the window had been enough for the vicious expression of the man sitting opposite Amancia to imprint itself on Max's brain. He'd glanced behind him on reaching the corner and decided to go back to the café, to make sure there was nothing bad happening to her. Now, here she was suddenly, in the street. A second later, she swung around to face him, glaring. She looked upset, and he caught the glint of tears in her eyes. He hurried toward her.

What had that *bufón* said to her? His face felt too hot, and an uncomfortable feeling began to swell within his breast. He wanted to draw her into his arms and comfort her, smooth the agonized look from her face. And if she gave him half a chance, he'd haul the miserable specimen out of the café and sling him onto that hard marble pavement. A couple of hefty punches would feel good, too.

"Amancia," he said. But her furious expression brought him up short. "Sorry! Maybe I should just go."

"No. No, don't do that."

She flung her arms around his neck and kissed him. This was unexpected, but he needed less than a second before he began to respond.

Finally, he drew back.

"Sorry. I'm sorry," he said, breathing deeply, not letting her go. "I shouldn't have let that happen, but I saw you in there with that man. He looked so aggressive, I thought I'd check with you."

She smiled, but there were unshed tears on her eyelashes. "I can't blame you—he was being aggressive."

Dios, this was wonderful, just wonderful. He

149

tightened his hold, and her heart hammered against his chest, matching the pace of his own. It was intoxicating. In seconds, they'd moved from ultra cool to this intimacy. "Are you all right?"

"I am now. I never want to see him again."

She began to push away from him, probably embarrassed at what had happened, and he forced himself to let go. They were still standing in front of the window, and the man had remained by the table where she'd left him and was now staring out of the window. Here was the chance for a bit of payback. He shouldn't do this, but why not?

"Shall we convince him it's a lost cause?"

He pulled Amancia back into the circle of his arms. His lips were tingling, and if she got any closer, she'd become aware that there were other parts of him reacting to this unexpected situation. Of course, she'd play along for the benefit of that boor in the café. It wouldn't mean anything at all. But it didn't matter. He was happy to assist her.

"Please forgive me," he said again a few moments later. "That was definitely taking advantage, but I never could resist a damsel in distress."

"You shouldn't apologize so much. Thank you for the rescue."

Already she was withdrawing, brushing herself down, preparing to leave.

"Are you really okay?"

They were standing apart now. The experience had left him wanting more, but he couldn't turn himself into the same sort of pest the other man appeared to be. And he had another appointment, this one with Ángel, the final year student who was so usefully combining a degree in IT with marketing. He'd proved helpful in the work he'd done on the website for the vineyard, and Max wanted to test his marketing ideas with him after the bank meeting. He would have a view on ways to go forward. He turned to leave and then decided it could be postponed for a couple of hours. Ángel had said he would be there until late, working on a project.

"Just give me a moment," he said, scrolling down his phone.

****

As they walked toward her vehicle, he said, "Wait for me. I'll be two minutes. I've parked in the next street. I'll follow you to make sure—"

"You don't need to."

"Yes, I do. Please wait. No, it'd be better to come with me, and I'll drop you back here, so you can drive."

She sighed, exhausted. Why didn't he just leave her alone? She didn't want to talk. No one needed to look after her. She was perfectly able to drive back on her own. She gazed with longing at her own vehicle, suddenly a sanctuary.

He'd already offered her a drink, and she'd refused. It was great to feel cared for, but she was wary. If she didn't keep a clear head, she might not understand what was going on. James had been caring like this, at the beginning, in those heady days when they'd first got together. Not that she thought Max was anything like James. How could she believe she could attract two such men? She was hardly the typical victim. But then, who was?

"Max, I just want to go, so I'll say goodbye."

"Of course, you must go. I'm being too pushy."

He was clearly disappointed but was doing his best

151

to accept it gracefully.

"No, it's not that. I've just had enough…of everything. I'm going back to the site." They'd arrived at her van now, and she touched his hand fleetingly. "I'll see you soon."

She got in, shut the door quickly, and set off, heading in the wrong direction. She'd have to turn around in the little square just ahead.

Dabbing at her tears, she swallowed. It would have been good to spend time with Max, but not when she was feeling like this, when she couldn't sort out her feelings. A wave of misery and self-pity engulfed her as she drove away.

What was wrong with James? An attractive man, except when he was shouting into her face, he could easily find another girlfriend. He didn't love her. Love involved giving something up for the other person, being willing to make that extra effort. James had never done that. Instead, he'd taken from her, whittling away at her self-esteem, until she questioned her ability and felt she was losing her sense of self.

It was upsetting that she'd been such a pushover, but her father's death had heavily impacted her, along with the responsibilities she'd taken on. When James had appeared in her life, he'd offered a new direction, and she hadn't asked herself too many questions. But if there'd ever been any chance they could work things out, all that had ended when he'd struck her.

As for today, he'd ruined her afternoon, with his insistence on flying to Zaragoza, and then trying to blacken Max's reputation. Well, maybe he hadn't quite ruined everything, because she had got to kiss Max twice. And that had been…most satisfying. She felt again that rush of feeling he'd engendered, a sort of euphoria. She'd wanted to kiss him for some time. In fact, the thought had been hanging between them ever since she'd arrived. She smiled, recalling exactly how right it had felt as he'd tightened his arms around her.

But really, this was silly. She wasn't going to allow anything to develop. Mmm. She had to concentrate on her future, and any relationship with Max would only complicate things.

Max was dangerous to her.

This thought triggered an excitement which had her punching down on the brake a few seconds later, as she found herself heading far too fast toward the rear of an old red hatchback. She really couldn't allow her memory of Max's lips, salty and sweet at the same time, to affect her driving. To say nothing of enjoying the delicious warmth as he'd held her. She must concentrate for the moment, and later, there'd be time to think about it all.

Except that was no good. She had to banish him from her mind. She was in enough trouble already.

For the next ten minutes, she kept her attention on the road and heaved a sigh of relief when it forked, and she turned left to the old farm gate which marked the entrance to the site. Minutes later, she parked the truck under the trees and headed slowly over to the dormitory block, waving at Peter as she crossed the little square. God, how disparaging James would be if he saw all this. She could hear his outraged voice: "It's a hovel," he'd say. "You've swapped all you had at the museum for this."

She hated what James still succeeded in doing to her, but she knew she'd made the right choice.

There was a pricking at the back of her eyes, and locking the door, she lay down on her bed and gave in to the wave of anguish that assailed her. Tears rolled down her cheeks, and she cried silently until she ached. Nothing had been resolved, but finally, exhausted, she fell asleep.

****

Max couldn't help smiling as he drove along. He soon saw her vehicle, but he left a long distance between them and allowed another car to overtake him. What if the boyfriend took a taxi and followed her? The least he could do was to keep an eye open for her, but she would misinterpret his actions, so it was better that she didn't know he was there.

She'd told him no, so he had to leave her to it, but he needed to know she got back safely.

He wasn't stupid enough to think that her grabbing him like that meant anything under the circumstances. But had he only imagined that she'd reacted positively to his kiss? If she was feeling like he was, she wouldn't be finding it easy to concentrate on the road. He already knew she wasn't a great driver because she'd said so. That should mean she'd keep her attention firmly on what she was doing. He hoped so, because he didn't want her rolling into a ditch or driving into a wall.

The car in front turned off, and without meaning to, he was catching up with her. He eased a little off the accelerator. A lack of sensitivity when driving was one of the problems with his foot. He'd learned a long time ago to make the adjustment and rarely even thought about it, but today he wasn't functioning normally, not by a long way. He rubbed his eyes, trying to maintain the distance while keeping her vehicle in sight.

This woman excited him in so many ways. The chemistry between them was huge, and they'd both been trying to pretend it didn't exist. His breathing quickened. Amancia's lips had been warm and generous, her perfume subtle but strong enough to stir his senses. He ran the tip of his tongue over his upper lip and could still taste her there, a sweetness he felt he could never get enough of. She intoxicated him.

The cars ahead slowed, and Max dropped back again. A glance in the mirror showed an empty road, so the boyfriend hadn't followed. Theoretically, he could leave her now.

She'd felt so right in his arms, her body fitting perfectly against his as if they'd been made for each other. His face twisted into a rueful smile at this idea. No one was made for someone else; he was sure of that. But what was undeniable was that from time to time, a beautiful connection happened between two people. It flared quite suddenly into being and could just as quickly die. This had happened between him and Amancia—the flaring-up part. He ought to snatch the opportunity to make it blossom into something worthwhile. Nothing long-term of course, but they were adults. Surely, they could both enjoy a little time together. Was that impossible?

Seeing Amancia turn off onto the site track, Max pulled to the side of the road. When she'd gone, he turned and headed back into the city, to his appointment with Ángel.

Now he came down from the clouds, landing with a jolt. He had to pursue this, get to know her better, but how was he going to tell her about his leg? He'd forgotten all about that, and he really hated explaining to a girl what had happened. That was one of the reasons he'd given up on the dating scene. There were just too many difficulties. But if the next stage in this fascinating relationship was going to happen, she'd be finding out soon enough, and it would be a shock. His mouth set in a grim line as he contemplated what might happen. But she wouldn't reject him just because she found out he had unsightly scars and half a leg missing. Would she?

He didn't need to worry about that. Maybe she'd agree to go out with him, nothing serious. He'd nearly asked her the day before but chickened out at the last moment. Now, he was going to suggest it. It was the wrong thing to do, but he couldn't stop himself.

Chapter 23

It was early evening when she awoke. Her eyes felt raw and swollen, but her spirit was a little lighter. Perhaps she'd shower first and then have another lie-down. She was beginning to feel the effect of long days working in the hot sun without a break. A proper visit to the city would have helped put that right, but it didn't matter. Even though she had no intention of doing anything about Max, something good had come out of the situation. The point had been made to James in a way that couldn't have been improved on.

Startling her, Max's image floated into her head. How forward she must have appeared to him. Heat rose up her cheeks. She hadn't meant any of what had happened, had gone with it instinctively. The scene played slowly through her mind a dozen times over. James must have seen them. If he had done, that was good. And surely now, he'd leave her alone.

She sat up, feeling suddenly better.

****

Damn, it was off. Amancia turned her phone back on, and it rang straight away.

"Mum, can I ring you back in a little while? I must have a shower. I've had a long day, and it's hot here."

"Okay, when you're ready, love. I just wanted to have a chat."

"Later, Mum, about nine. Is that okay?"

It wasn't good that she'd not rung home recently. Once again, she'd forgotten the important things in life while she obsessed about her job. Then, she smiled. It wasn't just the job she'd been obsessing about, was it? And she'd better stop thinking about him.

She took a deep breath and closed her phone, already beginning to strip, but after a few seconds, it started to ring again. The shower would have to wait. She looked at the screen. Number withheld. Could it be James with a different phone?

"Amancia Harding," she said, unzipping her skirt with one hand.

"Dr. Harding, I'm sorry to ring you at this time, but I've been trying to get hold of you all afternoon."

Oops! She'd been out of contact for hours, ever since agreeing where to meet James, making sure he couldn't get back to her so she could complete her shopping in peace. She sat down, giving up on the zip.

"I'm sorry. How can I help you?"

"I'm Pablo Morales," he said. "I run a film company, and the university has commissioned me to make a short informational film about what you're doing on the site. I hope you'll let me do a preliminary visit tomorrow and maybe give me an hour of your time to go through things. Would that be possible?"

Receiving visitors was the last thing she wanted to do, but on Monday, they were starting a new dig area, as recent calculations suggested the top of the stairwell started even farther back than they'd supposed. She wanted the day free for that, and she had a list of other things she should tackle. So, it looked as if she'd spend tomorrow leading him around the site. Most people had a very narrow view of how an archaeological site operated, and it would need explaining.

"You say the university's commissioned it."

"Yes, that's right."

That could be interesting. "Okay. What time do you want to come?"

"Seeing people at work will help me understand how you do things."

"We start early but have a break around eight thirty, so what about nine o' clock or thereabouts?"

"Thank you. I'll be there."

She'd better let Peter know. She yawned widely. She could just ring him, but perhaps it would be better to talk it through with him, even though it meant she'd have to go out again.

Half an hour later, freshly showered and clothed in a pale green cotton shirt and denim shorts, Amancia knocked on Peter's door. She waited a while, but there was no sound. Maybe he was having his dinner at that little place in the village. She crossed to the kitchen. It was redolent of recently consumed food, which reminded her she'd had nothing but two sips of coffee since breakfast. She went to the fridge and began to put a meal together from the leftovers, making up a simple supper of cold meats and the remains of a potato dish.

On the shelf that ran along from the fridge, there was a book with the title *Las Ruinas Romanas más importantes de España*. That looked interesting, though it would tax her embryonic knowledge of Spanish. Sitting at a table with it propped up in front of her, she was soon deep in the well-researched text and wishing they'd included more photographs. Knowing the subject and recognizing the technical language helped her understanding.

She read on. That place down the coast from Barcelona, Tarragona, looked interesting. She'd have to go there one day, maybe stay overnight.

The door opened, and Peter walked in.

"Ah, just the person I wanted to see." She told him about the man's visit the next day, and the likelihood of a film crew being on-site later in the week. "I know it's a pain in the neck, when we want to concentrate on a new section."

"Ah, well," he said. "It could be interesting."

"That's true. We weren't very happy about the children's visit, but that turned out all right. And I know some of the younger members of the team would love the idea of seeing themselves on film."

They all seemed to be camera savvy, pulling out the phone and clicking away the moment they found something, however inconsequential. She'd tell them in the morning and ask for suggestions as to what it would be best to include.

"What—and who," said Peter, as she shared the thought.

"Yes, I got the impression this producer will want to do a couple of interviews as well. It could be that it'll form part of the introduction to an archaeology course. I haven't much information yet."

"Alexandra is articulate, and very photogenic, with those dark blue eyes and the blond hair."

So, he did notice the females around him. But he clearly knew how to behave appropriately. She met his eyes, to find he was smiling. "I'm not blind, you know—just not interested. I met Janey twenty-five years ago when I was a student, and there's never been anyone else. Not for me, anyway."

This was interesting. Amancia had never met anyone who felt like that, except for her parents, maybe. But closer to her own generation, people either hadn't got around to getting married yet, or were already chasing a divorce. Or, like her, leaving a long-term partner. Unaccountably, her thoughts swiveled around to Max, but she shut them down straightaway.

"If Janey's strayed, I've never seen the evidence."

Amancia smiled and took the last bite of her supper. According to Lizzie's stories, academics were as likely to go off the rails as any other section of society, and contrary to popular belief, it wasn't always their young students they got entangled with.

"I'm happy for you, Peter. I'm still looking for that special person."

"And maybe you've found him, eh?"

"What do you mean?"

"Oh, come on, Amancia. I can't believe you haven't noticed Max and maybe speculated a little. The way I've seen him looking at you, I don't think he'd need much encouragement."

Heat darkened Amancia's cheeks. "Peter..."

"Sorry," he said, looking away. "None of my business. Anyway, what time did you say this guy's coming tomorrow?"

"Around nine. Can you make yourself available for a while? I'd appreciate it. He may have questions I'm unable to answer."

"I don't believe that's likely, but I'll be there when you want me."

Chapter 24

"What exactly are you doing here?" asked Pablo, as they stood at the edge of the area where Amancia had been working, watching three students who were marking out the oblong which would be the focus of their attention for the next few days. They knocked short posts like tent pegs into the ground and ran twine from one to the other to create a boundary.

Amancia was giving him her full attention, but after getting up at five, she'd felt strung out by a sleepless night and the events of the day before. When she'd focused, Peter's words about Max came back to her. Had she been that obvious? She really didn't want everyone on-site paying attention to her personal life. That was a surefire way to undermine her authority.

"Setting up a new grid." Amancia explained now how all the evidence pointed to there being a set of broad steps leading down to the river. "So, we've calculated where they would likely begin. Given these buttresses we've already uncovered, there are a couple of possible places."

"How do you even know where to start?"

"A set of twenty or so steps might start several yards back, measured horizontally from the bottom step, and all sorts of things could affect the position of the top step."

"What, for instance?"

"Well, you have to take into account the possibility of landings."

"Landings?"

"Yes. I don't imagine the Romans had a health and safety policy, but they wouldn't appreciate losing slaves or want to risk themselves on a long flight of steps. They were too logical for that, and slaves were a valuable commodity, as was the merchandise they'd be carrying." She paused, reviewing the minimum amount of information she'd need to give. "This would be a functional structure, not monumental, so they'd probably break a staircase up into flights, the way we do. There's also the height and depth of the steps to consider, and maybe places to accommodate machinery. The Romans had cranes, you know."

"It sounds quite scientific—or at least mathematical."

"Well, decisions like the ones we're taking at the moment require basic math and an ability to visualize."

"So, if you've got the calculations wrong, you could be digging in the wrong place."

"That's right, and it wouldn't be the first time that's happened, but we know enough now on this site to be sure there was something of the kind here. We'll find where they begin eventually. And doing it this way means we can have a second team working at the same time farther back, to move things on more quickly."

"Would you be willing to do a short interview on the subject? I think you'd be very photogenic, and that's important when you're trying to be persuasive."

"I guess." She thought for a moment, and added, "But actually, it would be better for you to talk to Chris. I've been working with him to establish where to put this grid, so he's already looked at the possibilities, and where we're setting up at the moment is his decision. Let's see if he's willing."

The young man was intuitive when it came to reacting to the site. He'd made suggestions which were beginning to bear fruit, and it was certain he'd have interesting things to say. Besides, the younger those who participated in the film, the more useful it would be from the university's point of view. Someone of their own generation demonstrating the necessary skills was always going to be the most effective with potential students. Pablo finished the discussion with Chris a few minutes later and left, promising a list of his questions before the end of the day. Chris appeared at her side as the filmmaker drove off.

"I hope he sticks to the questions. I'm no expert, and the idea of an interview makes me feel nervous."

"You'll be fine, Chris. Besides, this is a film, not a live broadcast. They'll edit it afterward if there's anything that doesn't come out quite right. And I'll insist we're allowed to see it in its entirety before we sign it off. I already made that clear to him."

"Okay, that's a relief."

****

Pablo was a whirlwind of activity. An email arrived after lunch with a long list of what he intended to do, where they would film and for how long, and he followed it up with a couple of questions about time and the level of light. It would take about two days but could be longer.

"I wouldn't have thought there was enough happening on the site to occupy them for longer than that," Peter said.

"Well, I'm no judge. He doesn't know much about archaeology, but I know even less about filmmaking."

Pablo telephoned midafternoon. "Can we meet?"

"Sorry, but I don't have the time. Can't we discuss things now, over the phone?"

"What, you don't even have time to eat?" His American-accented English was excellent. "Look, I'll buy you dinner, and we can go over the details. I promise you it'll result in a better film."

"If you really think it's necessary."

"I do. Say you'll come, just for a couple of hours. It's on me."

"Right, I'll come then. Can you pick me up?"

"About eight, okay? *Hasta la vista.*"

"*Hasta luego.*"

Chapter 25

How charming Pablo was. He combined it with a businesslike approach.

As they ate *tapas* in a quiet restaurant, he went through each stage of what he intended to do, asking searching questions. He was thorough. The result was going to be excellent.

"What brief have you been given? Is the film aimed at general education, or at those thinking of studying archaeology?" A mushroom coquette melted in Amancia's mouth. Mmm…delicious. She followed it up with a sip of red wine.

"Mainly the latter. Would that alter what you would say, or want us to show?"

"It might do, yes. For potential students, we should emphasize the need for a rigorous approach. Maybe I can organize something to illustrate how we go about such things." She smiled and watched him add notes to his phone. "People have romantic ideas about what it is to be an archaeologist, and it's a good idea to clear up any misunderstandings before they sign up to a course."

He snagged up some cured ham on a crunchy bread base. She'd already tried that, so now, she helped herself to a forkful of *patatas bravas*, a glorious fiery explosion in her mouth.

"I've probably got a few misconceptions myself."

"Well, we've all seen *Raiders of the Lost Ark*. It's a

lot of fun, but it really isn't like that, and there aren't many archaeologists who resemble Indiana Jones, more's the pity." She grinned. "Maybe we could look into the forensic side of things as well and talk a little about what happens to artifacts after we unearth them."

"For anything like that, we'd need someone to focus on, especially if there's a lot of information. You have to capture people's attention, you know, and break up the facts to keep them interested. Attention spans are limited among the young."

"I get that. My last post was in a museum, and I remember how it worked when they did some filming for the website." Taking another sip of wine, she thought about whether it would illustrate the point she wanted to make. "I'll give you the link to their website if you want to have a look, because I thought it was done well."

"That would be helpful."

"One of the Spanish students here, Rafa, spends a lot of time on reconstruction. He's passionate about it, so we should probably get him to explain how he goes about things. And I like that we'll have a Spaniard from this university on film."

Amancia was glad now that she'd agreed to meet Pablo, and not only because of the delicious dinner; Spanish food had gone right up in her estimation, but the conversation was interesting and had given rise to quite a few new ideas. And it was exciting to have a hand in forming future generations of students.

Swallowing the last piece of tomato salad, she sat back and relaxed. How lovely it was to be here, great to be doing what she was doing, involved with students and with the university. Having an actual working site was a wonderful bonus. This was exactly the right career for her. If only she could find something similar for next year.

"I lost you there." Pablo was watching her closely.

"Sorry! But I need to spend a bit more time thinking about this. Could I give you a ring if I have any suggestions?"

She was tapping his number into her contacts when a shadow loomed over their table.

"So, it's not enough for you to make a spectacle of yourself kissing people in the street. You've now picked up someone else."

Pablo looked up with a tentative smile, as if he thought a joke were being made, but Amancia knew, with a cold certainty, that there was nothing amusing about this. James had already ripped into her, and it was clear that he hadn't finished.

"I suppose I shouldn't expect anything else from someone with your background."

With a dangerous challenge in her eyes, she stood up. They were facing each other across the table, inches apart, Pablo still seated. Curbing her desire to scream at James, she said quietly, "What exactly do you mean by that?"

"Well, the fancy doctorate can't hide the origins, can it? Where was your father from?—Kingston, wasn't it? Jamaica, that is, not Kingston on Thames. And it seems you're ready to prostitute yourself, just like a lot of other women out there."

As if the vicious, unwarranted words had only just penetrated his consciousness, Pablo sprang to his feet. *"¿Qué ha dicho? ¿Cómo..."*

"¡Déjalo!" Amancia pushed him back down and

turned her back. James's words had lacerated her, had slashed at something deep within her. Her heart began to pound, and she wanted to pitch into him, but nothing would be gained by overreacting and starting a fight. She had to remain calm.

She took a deep breath and turned once again to her dinner companion. "I'm so sorry, Pablo. Do you mind waiting here while I talk to…to this person? Please," she added when the man began to protest. "I'll just be a few minutes."

Her back straight, she walked out through the front of the restaurant and stood on the dark street, shuddering, oblivious to everything around her, waiting for James. Folding her arms across her chest, she tried to contain the anger, but it didn't feel as if it was working, and she swallowed several times to prevent herself from vomiting. He came out a minute later into the weak light cast by a lamp that stood a short distance away. It threw his agonized features into relief.

"You know what, James, you've gone too far. There's no way we can remain friends after this. You just interrupted an important business meeting, not a romantic dinner. But of course, you wouldn't have thought of that because you don't believe I'm capable of having important meetings."

Indoors, he'd worked up a high color, which she'd taken for anger, but now he stared hopelessly at her, seeming incapable of speech. She hadn't finished. "You have no rights over me, and you definitely have no reason to insult me, or tell lies about me in front of other people."

She hadn't liked it, and it was completely unjustified, but it wasn't the implications about her behavior that had cut deepest. That, she could have shrugged off. The racial slur was something else.

"Amancia…"

"What you said there was unforgiveable…just unforgiveable." She paused, waiting for a reaction, but he was silent. "To be honest, James, I can't believe I heard such prejudiced remarks from a notable journalist. You wanted to hurt me. I get that. Okay, you have succeeded."

She said nothing more. Despite the warmth of the night, she was shivering, and she kept her arms clasped tightly around her body, as if it were the only way to hold herself together. A deathly pallor, evident even in the dim glow of the lamp, spread slowly over his face. Tears glistened in the corners of his eyes, and she knew he was wretched; it had been a last desperate attempt to get her back, and it had failed. She was truly sorry for him, but to show any sympathy at this stage would simply prolong the whole cycle.

"I'm going in now. If you come anywhere near me again, I'll inform the police."

He put out his hand when she made to go, and his voice shook as he said, "Amancia, I'm really sorry. I love you."

"I believe you, James." She didn't bother to hide the ice in her voice. "But it is over."

She turned and disappeared inside. The waiter was standing at the table, and Pablo touched his card to the reader as Amancia sank down onto a chair, a weakness invading every part of her being. Eventually the man went away, and Pablo regarded her with interest. She didn't want to talk about what had happened, but she said, "I'm sorry you had to witness that."

"It's unforgiveable, but the man's in love. Anyone can see that."

"Let's just leave it. Please. Do you mind taking me back to the site?"

He was instantly attentive, rising to his feet. "I'm sorry. I can see that this has upset you greatly."

****

Amancia threw herself onto the bed. This was becoming a pattern of exhausting emotions and tears. It was dark, but she didn't put on the light, just lay there, fully clothed. She didn't care. Frustration, anger, and too many other feelings battled within her. What he'd said had stung. She'd never thought of him as racist, nor had he ever given her reason to believe that he was. But maybe there was a streak of racism in most people.

Tears were running down her cheeks now, and she wiped at them ineffectually.

Yeah, that was probably true. Buried deep in the primitive past, where someone just a little different was always a threat. But most intelligent, educated people had worked through that, understood exactly where such thoughts had come from. He'd obviously been pushed just as far as he could take and was so wounded that he had to strike out, searching for the most hurtful thing he could find.

And he had found it.

Maybe he did love her, but it didn't excuse his appalling behavior. Those words could never be unsaid. Even if he were the last person in the world, she wouldn't be able to forgive him. Understand, maybe, but not forgive.

She wanted to run away, put as much distance as possible between herself and everything that had happened, but that didn't make sense; this was her life, and she had to accept it. She didn't have to accept being insulted, though. She was done with men fighting over her. None of them really knew anything about her. Despair threatened, and her mouth twisted. For this to happen just hours after the satisfaction she'd been feeling about being here. It was a reversal so painful she burst once again into tears at the loss, and lay there for a long time, her mind playing over the recent events.

Finally, she sat up. Slowly, she got to her feet, stripped off, and went into the bathroom, surprised at her shaky legs and a dizziness she associated with illness; the awful confrontation had hit hard. She showered and lay down again a few minutes later.

Forcing herself to stop agonizing over James's behavior, she switched to thinking about Max and became calmer. Was there anyone else in his life? She thought not, but if there was, she hoped it wasn't serious. Something was definitely bothering him, and he was holding things back.

She pictured him walking away from the site on that first day, watched the film of it run through her mind several times over. And then it clicked, and she remembered where she'd seen that slightly rolling gait before. She was sure she knew what the problem was.

Gradually, the ugly present receded to the back of her mind, and only the thought of Max remained. She desired him. Now, when she felt diminished by the events that had unfolded, she wanted him to hold her again in his arms. She didn't care if he had hang-ups. She didn't even care if there was no future in it. It was more than twenty-four hours since she'd seen him, and that was twenty-four hours too long. She wanted to kiss him and be kissed in return. If he didn't ring her or come over tomorrow, she would contact him.

She turned onto her other side, the prospect of another sleepless night becoming a reality.

Perhaps he was busy, as she was, so maybe she could suggest a tour of the vineyard. She'd like him to show her how it all worked.

This thought brought her crashing back to her current situation. Of course, with the harvest approaching, she and her team would eventually have to vacate the huts, to accommodate the vineyard crew. If she didn't get herself organized, she'd be unemployed. She couldn't avoid it any longer.

Sighing, she turned on the light and, reaching down to the floor, picked up her laptop.

Maybe she'd have to go after something she didn't particularly want, but she could at least look. She typed into the search engine "university archaeology jobs," and this threw up a list, but a PhD studentship wouldn't be any good, and a quick glance at an assistant professorship advert showed that her lack of recent experience of teaching students would almost certainly disqualify her.

She scrolled down through the list of possibilities, which were farther away from her desired post. The idea of teaching history at Aberdeen University or humanities at Portsmouth held no appeal. She sighed. The trouble was her heart simply wasn't in it. Her heart, that treacherous organ, was completely taken up with Max, and everything else had fallen by the wayside.

She had to get over this, go on stronger than before, because she wasn't going to leave until the very end; she loved her job, and people depended on her.

She'd fight for it.

Nor would she sacrifice her burgeoning relationship with Max. This conviction surprised her. The easiest thing would be to turn her back on all men. Instead, she was linked to him in some way she didn't yet understand. It was still fragile, that connection, but it was worth pursuing, even if it never led to anything. Unlike so many other men, Max did see her, not just appreciate the physical woman. He saw the person inside, and that was important.

Very soon, she turned off the light and lay down again, and now, she did sleep.

Chapter 26

Peter was talking to someone, a woman from the sound of the voice. They must be standing in the square of which the kitchen formed one side, and the low murmur carried in through the window. Amancia had been deep in *Ruinas Romanas* while she drank an after-lunch cup of coffee when the quiet conversation disturbed her. She read on to the bottom of the page and then tuned back in. They were speaking English, and at first, the words had scarcely registered, but who else spoke with that unmistakable Bristolian accent that education had softened but could not remove?

The door opened, and Peter ushered in a pink and perspiring, slightly oversized figure that was dearly familiar to Amancia.

"Lizzie, I don't believe it. How did you get here?" she said, springing to her feet. "How did you even know where to come?"

She flew across the room and crushed her friend in her arms.

"Well, I'll leave you to it," said Peter, grinning at her exuberance. Ignored by both the women, he slipped discreetly out as they sat down.

"This is just wonderful. I'm so pleased to see you."

Amancia made coffee and handed the cup to Lizzie. She raised her own and took a sip, puckering her lips at the bitter taste.

"Sorry, this coffee isn't great."

"It's fine. What do I care about coffee? I'm here because I wanted to see you."

"You happened to be here, you said. That's hard to believe." Someone like Lizzie wouldn't happen to be on a dusty site along the banks of the river Ebro, miles from civilization on a random Monday afternoon.

"True, however. Well, not at the site, specifically. I had to make quite a lot of effort to get here. Jake's been modeling for a series of adverts in Barcelona, a last-minute change of plan, and I persuaded him to take me along as I had some holiday owing. But, honestly, there's a limit to how much time I want to hang about on set with so many large egos. Not Jake, obviously, but even some of the photographers have hissy fits these days and expect the star treatment."

Jake's craggy face featured on so many advertisements in "The Great Outdoors" sections of catalogues and websites. It was coupled with his six foot six body with muscles in all the right places, and this placed him in great demand. As Lizzie said, she loved telling people her boyfriend was a male model.

"They look at me as if to say, 'And how did that happen?' " She laughed at herself. "He claims he wants to go back to his main job as an engineer, but as far as I'm concerned, let's enjoy it while we can."

Modeling in far-flung locations was a large part of his work: the Yukon, Nepal…but Barcelona? How had that come about?

"I know," Lizzie continued. "You're wondering why the big city location. I think they're trying shock tactics. It's certainly not his usual scene, so I had to take advantage of the opportunity. I can't see it coming up again. He'll not be taking me to Alaska, which is his next photo shoot—and I won't be asking to go."

She gave her friend a long look and took a gulp of coffee. "So, let's start talking. What've you been up to? Who is he?"

"What do you mean? I've been too busy to—"

"Come on, sweetheart, I can tell. Either the Spanish sun is just so-o good that it's transformed you, or there's a man on the scene."

Given several nights without sleep and James's horrible visit, this seemed unlikely.

"Okay, I'll talk," said Amancia, caving in immediately. Having Lizzie there in front of her brought home how much she'd missed the chance to discuss things with her. It was exactly what she wanted to do. Needed to do. "I take it you didn't drive here?"

"Train from Barcelona after breakfast, and I've just got off the bus in that village down there, the one below the big house. And then, I walked," she added, looking surprised at her own foolhardiness. "Blisters—bound to be. Had to see where you're working, though. And I do have to go back today."

That explained the pinkness. Lizzie wasn't in the habit of walking anywhere, unless it was to totter from her office in her spiky heels to the café down the street, to pick up lunch. The shoes she favored weren't made for walking. For anything more than a couple of hundred yards, wheels were required, preferably attached to a stylish vehicle.

"Right, I'll let Peter know I'm going to be out this afternoon, and I'll drive us into Zaragoza. It's a lot nicer than here—for a visitor, that is, and we'll be able to get you to the station when you want."

"Don't you have to work?"

"Started at six this morning, but I've finished now for the day. I do have a report to write, which I'm putting off until tomorrow. Let me give you a quick tour of the site, and then we'll go. Come on!"

****

"Well, this is more like it."

They settled comfortably at a table toward the back of the cafeteria, where a large fan turned lazily overhead. The air was laden with the twin aromas of sugar and chocolate. Lizzie sniffed like a truffle hound, and an expression of pure bliss crossed her face when the waitress brought their order. She'd always enjoyed sampling local produce when on holiday, and she'd jumped at the opportunity to treat herself. Now, with a look of delighted expectation, she plucked an icing sugar-coated churro from the mountain on the plate in front of her and thrust it into the bowl of thick, warm chocolate. Then she raised the dripping stick of carbohydrate heaven to her mouth.

"A moment on the lips…" said Amancia, recalling something her grandmother used to say.

"I know." Lizzie patted her generous hips. "I know I should restrict myself, but fortunately, Jake likes me like this."

It did appear to be true. Amancia bit into an almond-flavored *marquesa* and sipped her herbal tea as she regarded her friend. Physically, she and Lizzie were very different, but they'd remained firm friends through many difficult times. She loved so many things about Lizzie, those qualities she didn't possess herself, and probably her friend felt the same about her. They were lucky to have a friendship like that, and here was a chance to nourish it, so she wasn't going to hide things.

"Okay, then. Who is it?"

"Max. You know—the man who interviewed me back home in Bristol."

Saying his name made her heart flutter, and she felt the sudden warmth in her cheeks. She forced herself not to look away. It was all so new that they hadn't actually told each other what they felt. Scared that she might jinx things, she was reluctant to share what she was experiencing. But why shouldn't she?

"Ah!" Lizzie looked almost as satisfied as she had when she'd devoured the first churro. She dipped another, more delicately this time, into the runny chocolate. Now the first rush was over, she seemed prepared to take time to appreciate the fabulous dessert.

"So, you guessed who it was?"

"I hoped it was him. I thought, when I first saw him, that he'd be perfect for you." Lizzie stretched her hand across the table and laid it gently on her friend's arm. "I'm really glad for you, Amancia." She gave a little smile. "I'm so happy with Jake, and all I want is the same for you." She wiped her mouth. "Just to let you know, we're getting married in the spring, and yours will be the first invitation I write."

"That's such a lovely piece of news, Lizzie!" Amancia gave her friend a hug. "Jake is a great person, and I do love his jokes—they're so lame."

They laughed in agreement, and Lizzie said, "Now, are you going to tell me anything, or am I going to have to prize it out of you like a pearl from an oyster?"

"It's nice you consider my information so worthy of retrieval. Maybe I should be like the oyster and keep my shell clamped tight shut."

But then she began to talk, and three hours and two coffees later, the young women were still seated in the corner of the café.

"Oh, my goodness," said Lizzie, catching sight of the clock on the opposite wall. "I absolutely have to be on the next train. I promised Jake. It's his birthday, and we've booked a table. I've got less than half an hour before it leaves."

"It's too far to walk. I'll drive you there."

They paid and ran out of the café to where the van was parked close by, finally arriving at the station with five minutes to spare. Throwing caution to the winds, Amancia found an unmarked space, and they ran to the platform where the train was already waiting. Lizzie hauled herself on board and stood in the doorway.

"Don't forget what we agreed." The buzzer sounded to warn that the doors were about to shut.

"I won't."

A moment later, the train rolled out of the station, and then it was gone. Amancia sighed with pleasure. What a lovely afternoon, downloading her pent-up frustrations, hopes, and fears, and it was just great that Lizzie and Jake were getting married. They were so well suited. She was really looking forward to that.

Now, while Lizzie's big, exuberant presence was being carried away to the coast, Amancia hurried back to her vehicle. Oops! A man in uniform was heading in her direction. She climbed in and left immediately.

Her heart rate slowed down as she reflected on the afternoon. It had been so good to see Lizzie again. They'd exchanged information and supported one another in the past. But it did underline how, after three short weeks, she was out of touch with the city life they'd enjoyed in Bristol. She'd loved that frenzied lifestyle, but today, she'd found Lizzie full on; being with her friend had felt as if she were being zapped from all sides at once.

Had she changed that much since coming to Spain? Or was it just that her experiences had revealed another side to her? These days, she liked being out in the countryside. She wouldn't have believed that could happen a few months ago. It was great to have such a beautiful city close by, but she didn't need to be there all the time.

Her friend's visit had been a lovely surprise and had rescued her from the despair of James's actions. She had to get to work, put all of this to the back of her mind, because the next two or three days were going to be the busiest ever, as the cameras started to roll.

Chapter 27

On Tuesday, Amancia thought through the making of the film as she chewed on something that was supposed to be toast but had the texture of cardboard. Things would be slow at the beginning, Pablo had said. It was only on the third day that the crew would be there at five in the morning to shoot the sequence of a typical day, leaving it to the end because they needed some different equipment to cope with the light levels.

She still hadn't talked to Max. Despite having discussed things at length with Lizzie, Amancia was diffident about chasing after him. What if it was all in her imagination? Those kisses—that had been spur of the moment and didn't necessarily mean anything. She'd leave it for the time being. She was a coward.

It was a pity there'd been another attempted break-in the night before, especially with all this going on. They'd given chase but had failed to catch anyone. Too bad. As she was finishing her breakfast, the yellow van entered the car park. Draining her cup, Amancia got to her feet and urged everyone back to work, before hurrying over to the young filmmaker.

"Do you need any help? I can easily find someone to help move equipment for you."

"No, thanks. If there's a problem, I'll find you."

This suited her. This morning, she wanted to tackle the steps where progress was fast, and they were revealing new things every day, not the sort of thing that would make the news headlines but proof that they were working along the right lines.

There was a lot to do, and the meeting with Lizzie and Jake in Barcelona they'd arranged for the weekend was going to limit her time. She had that report to write, and it must be a professional job. She'd be presenting it to the professor when he returned from Chile. Her employer in Bristol would want a copy, too.

The notes she'd made on her laptop every day since her arrival would form the basis of it, but now she had to analyze them, maybe research a little more, and present some cogent conclusions. This afternoon after lunch, she'd get started.

"Hey, Amancia. Just come and look at this."

Chris was standing on the first landing in the stairwell and now showed her a niche he'd been working on. "I noticed there was a patch in the wall that didn't look like the rest of the stone, so I started scraping, and it all came away quite easily—compacted earth, not stone."

She climbed down the ladder and inspected the aperture and its contents.

"Do you think this could be the remains of a votive statue?" he asked. "In a place like this? Would they have a place of worship in a stairwell at the docks?"

"Who knows, but I'd guess not. It's probably the statue of a god placed there by one of the workers to watch over them, like a lucky charm."

"Okay, that makes sense. Yeah, the Romans loved their gods."

It was a small, crudely fashioned clay figure, not the type of thing you'd find in the *lararium* of a Roman home or in a temple. All that remained was the head, separated from the rest but with recognizable features, the torso, and the right arm. But very small broken pieces of clay littered the floor of the little niche.

"Maybe the person who provided this statue thought if everyone prayed to his god or goddess, they'd be better protected."

"It's a god," said Chris. "Look at the muscles. And no breasts."

He was right. The figure was tiny, but on closer inspection, you wouldn't mistake it for a female.

"I've no idea if all these pieces are part of the same thing, but we can have a go at putting them together. That's great, Chris! Maybe you'll be able to work out which deity it is. Do you want to attempt a reconstruction yourself?"

"Shouldn't we let Rafa do it? He's keen on this sort of thing, and he's already done a few pieces."

"You should push yourself a bit, you know. You ought to develop all the skills that go to make up an archaeologist, even if that's not your favorite thing. Have a go yourself, or at least, work with him."

"Okay."

He picked up a couple of small plastic containers. They had to be careful with artifacts, especially the smallest objects. It wouldn't take much to lose pieces as tiny as this. They worked on, the only sounds being the scrape of the trowel and the tap-tap as one or the other tried to dislodge the hardened earth.

At first, Amancia was totally absorbed, but then, the little niggle at the back of her mind showed itself to be Max-shaped. She'd promised Lizzie to get in touch with him, not just wait for him to contact her. He'd be involved in preparations for the harvest already, so maybe he was busy. She allowed her head to fill with his image while she chipped away at the stone, not consciously seeing what was in front of her.

Nevertheless, she missed nothing; something was resisting her probing. It wasn't good to apply too much force; it was too easy to break fragments which were often so delicate, they only held together because of being compressed into the earth. With rising excitement, she said, "Take a look at this, Chris."

They excavated gently around the object held in the wall, working side by side. It was slow progress, but they kept at it until they recognized a buckle, probably from a military belt.

"Wow! Two things in one morning! What were the chances of that?"

"*¡Hola!*" Pablo was calling them. "Carry on. Davide's coming down there to film. We've already recorded your conversation about the figure you found, and we have visuals as well. But there's more to be done." He pulled up a microphone on the end of a cable. "I don't know how good it'll be, but it was worth a try to get something unrehearsed like that. Obviously, if there's anything you don't like, we can scrub it."

"Oh, f—" said Chris. "I didn't swear, did I?"

"No problem if you did. This equipment is great— we can remove anything we don't like."

Amazing. Neither one of them had been aware of the film technicians. Pablo had warned them he'd try to get conversations on tape, and no one had objected. The ongoing drama of their discoveries gripped them to the exclusion of all else.

The videographer climbed into the stairwell and

positioned his equipment. Amancia and Chris continued scraping, tapping, and brushing. It was a tight squeeze.

"That's perfect," he said, panning in on the trowel work. "I want to show in detail how you go about it."

Pablo remained on the surface, watching. The earth was more friable here, and things were happening quickly. The man seemed excited at their progress, expecting some great footage.

Finally, Amancia stopped work. "We get up very early, so most of us eat at midday and then take time off. What's your plan now?"

"That's perfect for us. We'll do a sequence of the kitchen in action, if that's okay, and then we'd like to film areas where people were working earlier today, while there's no one there. These may be snippets we splice in for the sake of continuity. Is that okay?"

"Yes, no problem."

They cleared away and headed toward lunch, to which the filmmakers had been invited.

"Who's the girl who runs the blog?" Pablo asked. Amancia and Peter were sharing a table with him and the videographer, Davide. "I spent a while studying it last night. It's fascinating."

"Oh, that's Maya."

"It's vivid and full of information about life on a site. She's a natural on the internet. I'd like to interview her as well."

Maya was at the next table and seemed relaxed about it when approached, her enthusiasm for the blog evidently receiving a boost from the request. They'd gone through it together a few days earlier, agreeing on some basic rules, but since then, Amancia hadn't looked. It was important to have confidence in people, once they'd shown they had the right qualities. Still, she'd log on quickly after eating, just to check.

"Don't worry." Maya grinned at her. "I've done exactly what you said."

The first day of filming had gone much better than Amancia expected. The second day would be devoted to interviews, and the third was meant for that early start and the loose ends. It was all very exciting, but it didn't leave any time for her personal life.

"Rafa and Chris will spend this afternoon and tomorrow working on the little figure they found, so you'll need to agree with them when you're going to record the different stages." There were too many tiny pieces of clay for it to be a perfect reconstruction, but something recognizable would emerge.

"Yeah, that's good, but we'll leave Rafa's interview until the end and hope the statue will be finished by then."

She rinsed her plate. Free time was in short supply, but it would be good if she could see Max. It was time she did something about that. As she stacked the dishes on the table, her phone rang.

"*Disculpe*, I have to take this." She walked outside and dragged in a breath on seeing Max's name, trying to stay calm.

"How are things going with the film crew?"

"It's going well. We'll have an excellent film."

"Good to hear. I…er…must be in Zaragoza tomorrow afternoon for a meeting. I wondered if you'd like to grab a drink after, maybe something to eat."

Keep it casual. She took another deep breath, trying to deal with the rush of excitement. "Ah, that would be nice, Max. It's time I got out a bit."

They talked for a little while before hanging up. This was a casual date, not some big romantic deal. And that was all she wanted, wasn't it? Okay, she thought him sexy, and that was great. It was always good to find your date attractive. And she found him very attractive indeed.

Chapter 28

Max's eyes widened as she walked toward him with that confident stride. This was not the demure young woman asking questions about the history of the house with passionate interest, nor the hard-working archaeologist in cotton shorts with dust on her nose, scraping earth from stone in a trench. Here was someone altogether different, and she looked gorgeous. He loved the way the gauzy, zingy red material of her thin, sleeveless dress set off her dark golden skin and strong, slim figure.

He held the car door open, and Amancia got in, a smile playing about her lips. Inside, a faint scent floated around, something very individual. He inhaled, already recognizing it as hers, her essence, and he waited for it to envelop him as he steered toward the gate. Now he had to drive, pay attention to what he was doing. He turned his eyes to the road.

"I thought you had a meeting," she said.

"They rescheduled it for tomorrow."

"Oh."

After the last time they'd met, he'd walked around with a picture of this woman in his head, while he forced himself to carry out the work in the vineyard, as if everything was as usual. The way he saw it, everything was completely different from usual. It was a good thing there was so much to do at this season because it left him little chance to speculate about where this infatuation with Amancia was leading. But a little was all he needed—he couldn't stop thinking about her. He'd even blanked Alejo when he'd said, "I've done some research. Can we talk about the shade cloth?" His head had been somewhere else altogether, and he'd had to go back and ask him what he'd said.

That was no good, if he wanted to keep on top of his business.

Now she was seated beside him. It was just a date with a beautiful woman. He'd better remember that.

The traffic was thickening. He concentrated on driving as they entered the city, then looked around, hoping for a parking space.

All the while, back in the vineyard, as he'd delegated tasks, checked the fermentation, helped Alejo turn the bottles, and carried out the work his unfortunate laborer had been doing when he'd had his heart attack, even waiting on that important telephone call from the bank—Amancia had been there, at the back of his mind. He'd wanted to be with her again. He'd thought her beautiful. And she was, only more than his imagination. More lovely, more intoxicating. And entirely different.

She turned to him now. "I really appreciate this, Max. We've been so busy, I've not had a chance to enjoy this beautiful city. *Me gusta mucho…muchísimo.*"

"It's a pleasure to show it to you." He took a moment to smile at her, continuing in Spanish. "Your Spanish is becoming very good."

"It isn't really, but I have tried not to use English. I practice on the Spanish students. I'm flattered you notice a difference."

"It's impressive."

He hadn't been able to cope with emotions, had tried to cut them out of his life, only allowing himself certain ones—satisfaction at a job well done, love for his mother and cousin, friendship. But where women were concerned, there was only lust, which he satisfied by having sex with suitable females when the opportunity occurred. That way, he could keep it neatly corralled. He had no idea where this was going, but he felt compelled to continue, had to know if this crazy, exhilarating feeling was mutual. And if it was? Well...

They crawled along behind a large truck. Horns sounded, and red lights lit up all around. He put his foot on the brake and relaxed, waiting for the blockage to clear. Everyone was out on this warm evening.

Across the road, a car pulled out from a space in front of a florist's shop, and he slipped his sleek sports model in, causing another flurry of horns as he deftly avoided the van in front. He silenced the throb of the powerful engine, and she turned to him with that beautiful smile that dragged the breath out of him once again. What was happening terrified him; he was losing control of himself. He swallowed and said, "*Espera un momento. It's a busy road. I'll come around.*"

As they walked into the center, he closed his fingers around hers. A spark of pure electricity ran up his arm, and a deep warmth invaded him, coursing through his body, forcing him to acknowledge that this was something special. It felt as if she trembled a little as she leaned into him. Was she feeling the way he was? Excited and hopeful? Or was he imagining the response he wanted to find?

They stopped at a crossing, waiting for a change in

the light. He looked around, trying to push the inconvenient thoughts away. It was tempting to move things quickly on, but he mustn't rush, even though what he wanted was to pull her into his arms, hold her close, and breathe her in like a fine wine. But he couldn't do that.

They started across the Plaza del Pilar. The hard-paved square was filled with the sounds and emotions of the evening: the clack of high heels echoing, the calls to friends, the feeling of expectation, and behind that, the twitter of birds preparing for night. It thronged with people on their way to restaurants and bars, or the theater. Or maybe just going home after a long day.

"Where are we going?"

"A jazz restaurant—that is, a restaurant where they have jazz musicians performing while you enjoy the wonderful stuff on their menu."

"That's my idea of heaven," she said. "Good food *and* music."

He hadn't read her very well at the beginning. He'd had the feeling she wanted to get close, and then it'd all changed. Since then, of course, he'd learned about the boyfriend. It would explain her coolness. He thought fleetingly of Vala—his ex, if you could call her that. The woman had lost all her allure for him, but how much easier that had been, with no obligations, no responsibility, no risk. But now, it wasn't enough.

Even if asking for anything more terrified him.

"I love this square." Amancia waved her arm, encompassing the fine architecture, the lights, and the strolling couples, people hurrying through on their way to some other destination. She moved close beside him, so that her loosened hair tickled against his chin, a tiny breeze ruffling and lifting the black curls as they walked along. "It's unbelievably beautiful."

"This is truly the heart of the city. Just wait until October. You'll be astonished."

She glanced up at him with a frown. "I will probably have left by then, unfortunately."

A future without her looked arid and barren, despite the short time he'd known her. Before October, the arrival of his workers for the harvest would mark the end of the archaeological work on the site for the year. But a lot of things could happen before then.

"Have you a job to go to back in England?"

"I must start the search." She gave him a guilty look. "I've been so busy..."

The thought of her going left him desolate. He wanted to say don't search, don't go...and then he wrenched his mind away from the depressing thoughts.

"In October, there's a festival," he told her instead. "A whole week of celebrations and fireworks...the place is transformed, and it's not just for the tourists; the inhabitants take part as well, everyone. I'd love to show you that. If you're still here, of course."

Chapter 29

They descended a flight of stone steps and went through into a long, low room, bathed in golden light. At the midpoint was a small, raised stage where a trumpeter in a scarlet velvet jacket was playing a solo. The mournful notes sent ripples through Amancia's soul, and she shuddered at how the music stirred her, sharpening her appreciation of everything around. The colors were brighter, carrying nuances of things she had yet to see, cutting through to a deeper layer of emotion.

A waiter appeared and towed them along, threading around seated couples to a squashy leather sofa, heaped with cushions. He pulled a low table in front of it and handed out menus, but after a moment, Amancia turned to Max. "Surprise me with something you like. I don't have enough Spanish to understand most of this, and I eat absolutely everything."

"Everything?"

"We-ell…er…not tripe."

"What is tripe?"

"It's kind of…the insides of a cow's stomach."

He was grinning. "Ah, *callos*. What, you think I am a sadist? I had in mind something a little more agreeable than that."

It had to be a better, more authentic restaurant for not having everything translated—as if they weren't bothered particularly about attracting tourists and just wanted to provide good food for anyone who came in. The smell of various dishes, with an overlay of garlic, intoxicated her. This was going to be a special evening.

He bent toward her, explaining some of the dishes, to make sure she would enjoy what he ordered. She looked up. His lips were just inches away, and this nearness made her want to move even closer. Heat flushed her face, flames searing through her before settling low in her abdomen, their grip tightening. She glanced away, down at the menu, but the words blurred.

The trumpeter finished as their wine arrived. They raised the glasses to their lips and took a sip, and Max said, "It's a Rioja, quite lively, but completely different from my own production. Do you like it?"

"I do. You'll have to make sure they stock your wines here."

"You'll have to try some of mine and tell me if it's good enough."

"I'd like to do that."

"Then we'll make a date for a tasting."

The words resounded in her mind, creating some future she didn't yet recognize.

Now a trio of guitar, bass, and drums took over the performance area. They began playing a soft jazz piece, nothing she recognized. It wasn't a concert. The music was there to create an ambience, and couples all around them were talking in low voices.

"I want to know more about you, Amancia, your family. Tell me about them. Tell me about your home in Bristol. What kind of place is it? I saw so little of the city when I was there, and it looked old...and crowded. Zaragoza must feel very different to you."

"Bristol is a beautiful city as well, and...culturally

very exciting and individual, especially if you like music. But yes, it's quite different from here."

She talked a little about her family. "Of course, I'm proud of Chedza. We all are. She's my youngest sister, just sixteen. She has the most wonderful voice, strong and full of emotion."

She looked at the stage, where a woman was now singing an Ella Fitzgerald number.

"This is the kind of thing she sings, jazz, very smoky and atmospheric. Her voice has so much power, even though she's mostly untrained."

"Does she sing in places like this?"

"Oh, no, my mum says she's still too young to perform in public—to say nothing of preparing for exams over the next two years."

"So, she's clever as well."

"She is. Dad would have been so proud. As he was when I got my university place. I was the first in his family to do that."

Amancia swallowed and dabbed at the tears at the corners of her eyes. She'd been away from home for longer than at any time since being a student.

"I see how much you love and miss them. I can't imagine growing up with sisters or brothers. It's always been my mother and my grandparents."

Her childhood had been rich, despite the lack of money, and each one of them had been so much loved. "I've been lucky, even though we lost Dad much too early. What about your father?"

"We didn't live with him," he said. "Tell me about your other sisters."

She looked up at him. He clearly did not want to talk about his father, so she continued, "I have three

196

more sisters. Mel's married, with a small boy. Back in Bristol, I used to get together with them at least once a week. So you see, I'm an aunt already."

"And so am I. No, not an aunt." He laughed. "I'm a sort of uncle. I'll take you to see my cousin and her daughters. Sofía will want very much to meet you."

Did that mean he'd spoken to his cousin about her? Again, she felt a stirring deep within her, as she recognized a rightness about what was happening between them. It might not lead to anything, but what an idiot she'd be to pass on a relationship with this man.

But what if she was just trying to fill the hole left by James? That would be so unfair to Max. Her emotions were in turmoil, but that was due to James's recent behavior, not because she was in love with him. If she ever had been, it'd ended long ago. She would give this a chance. She wanted to.

The conversation flowed gently along, covering a lot of ground. It was surprising how similarly they thought about things, even the little things like preferring to read real paper books with their distinct smell.

"Even my grandma thinks that's old-fashioned," said Amancia. "She was the first to go electronic, and my sisters just say I'm weird."

This first time together was so special, this process of discovering the coincidences, the places where their tastes and interests overlapped. The feeling of sharing was exciting and a little dangerous. She'd never really experienced it before, had never wanted to let down the barriers. Maybe what she was doing tonight was reckless; he said less, holding something back.

They finished eating, and someone took their

plates. Max's right arm lay loosely across the back of the sofa, and gently, absently it seemed, he stroked her neck. When he'd first laid his hand on her bare shoulder this evening, his touch had carried with it a promise of something to come, maybe only of sex, but she thought there was more. She pictured herself lying naked alongside him and shivered.

She must try to rein it in, but that wasn't easy to do. She stole a glance at him. He was good-looking from where she sat, almost too much so. Probably she preferred his other side, where the livid scar added character. He was listening to the music with intense concentration, as if it carried him to another place. Although they hadn't talked about music in any depth, it was clear it mattered a great deal to him.

When Max turned his head briefly in her direction, there was a smile on his lips, but his eyes were fixed on a scene far away in his mind, and she understood then how the music spoke to him in a profound way, perhaps healing something within him that had been broken. She sensed a fragility; if he let her get close, she could hurt him deeply.

Amancia looked back to the stage and gave herself up to the moment. If this went on forever, then it would still end too soon. At the same time, she couldn't deny the tension between them, the desire to touch and be touched, and she yearned to take the next step. And now, there could be—would be—something to follow. It was like walking a tightrope from which any moment, she could slip, and the situation would erupt into something unpredictable.

The evening wound slowly on; each moment was a delicious experience that left her tense and expectant;

each turning in the conversation became a place where they lingered. But finally, people began to leave.

He held out her bag. "Time for us to go, too."

She tucked her head through the straps and looped it across her chest. On the stone flagstones outside, she stumbled, and he took her hand. A fine rain began to fall as they wandered down the street and over the plaza, to where they'd left the car. It grew heavier, and they took a moment to shelter in an embrasure by the remains of the Roman wall. It offered a space of deep shadows, cut off from the clicking heels and shouts of laughter a few feet away.

She wanted him to kiss her but didn't know how to make it happen. The rough stone pushed through the thin material of her dress as she backed in and he took her in his arms, and her heart pounded, shortening her breath. She raised her hand to his cheek, looking into his eyes. It began tentatively on both parts, their lips just brushing at first, not like last time, when she'd flung herself at him, wretched, her emotions in shreds. The kiss deepened and pushed away the outside world until it was just the two of them, and when they broke apart, she was shaking.

The rain had gone, leaving behind a new freshness. The marble flagstones now shone in the streetlights, but already they were drying.

"Come on," he said, a huskiness in his voice. "Let's go home."

The roads were busy as they exited the car park. Gradually, the lights vanished into the distance, and finally, a velvety darkness embraced them. It would be good to walk on this lovely night, but they both had other things on their minds. They were almost back at the site when he finally spoke.

"Shall I drop you off?"

Here was her choice. Her heartbeat accelerated. "No, I—"

They rounded the last bend and saw the horizon lit up with a flaring golden light.

"*¡Jesús!*" he said and pressed down hard on the accelerator.

Chapter 30

There was no time to assess the situation. Max swung the vehicle through the gate and brought it to a halt, inches from the fence that divided the car park from the site. Even before he'd slammed on the brakes, Amancia jumped out and ran to the tents, ignoring the shouts and screams around her, focused on getting to the problem. He tore past her a moment later.

One tent was ablaze, the flames much too high. With the wind now getting up, the fire could soon be out of control. There had to be some accelerant; what might it have been? Other tents were close by—too many, too close. What if it spread? Max snatched up a spade that someone had left against one of the huts and ran toward the conflagration.

"Check there's no one in them," he shouted to her.

A few students watched the scene, as if they were at some kind of show, not really doing anything. Maybe they didn't know how to help. One lad was trying to remove his belongings from a tent alongside the one that was burning. A puff of wind carried a flurry of sparks to where he was slowly backing out and a few landed on the outer sheet, flaring up momentarily before dying.

"Get back," she screamed at him. "Stand back."

Didn't they understand the danger?

"Pull up the damned guy ropes!" shouted Max.

"We have to get this away from the other tents."

Suddenly animated, several people heaved up the pegs, leaping backward when the fire threatened them. Others were gathering around now, and some were helpful. A moment later, they'd freed all the ropes, and Max shoveled the burning wreckage away from the other tents. The material flapped around, sending out more showers of sparks, while the stink of burning plastic fouled the air, but finally he had it at a safe distance. A couple of students had fetched spades and forks, and now they too helped clear the smoking debris. It was over in a matter of minutes.

Suddenly, a wailing sound cut through the chaos, and Amancia spun around. A group of girls clung together in a tableau of distress, like a Greek chorus.

"But what am I going to do? That's all my stuff, my new T-shirt, even my phone."

Was this the source of the problem? Amancia ground her teeth but kept her tone civil. "Your tent, was it, Mandy? You three, go to the kitchen and wait for me there. We have to talk."

"But what am I going to do?"

Amancia stared at the girl, who lowered her gaze but repeated in a whimper, "I don't know what to do."

"That's not important at the moment. Just go to the kitchen." She turned to one of the other students. "Make sure she gets there and stays. Right, let's get this cleared away. Come on, all of you help, but be careful. You, as well," she said to two boys who still appeared mesmerized by the scene. "Make yourselves useful. Grab the buckets and fill them with the loose soil from those grids we made for the children. That'll put the fire out completely. I don't want to risk it starting up again in the middle of the night." She sniffed. The site stank. "We have to live and work here. I want it all gone, all the debris, everything. We start as normal tomorrow morning."

Her stomach heaved at the smell of burning plastic. They were lucky it wasn't burning flesh. What if someone had been sleeping in one of the nearby tents and she and Max hadn't arrived in time? What if Max hadn't been so quick at shifting the source of the problem? She could hardly bear to think of it.

"Tomorrow, after breakfast, I want all these tents moved, big spaces between them."

"Let's move ours now," Elena said. Soon, others were following her example.

Amancia turned her back on them and went to see the three girls.

****

"Just what did you think you were doing?"

She stood in front of the table where they'd seated themselves, but it was Mandy to whom she'd addressed her question.

"What? I didn't do anything. I've lost all my gear, and you're blaming me."

Amancia felt like swearing. Didn't the silly creature understand anything? Still, she stayed calm. She might have got it wrong—but she'd seen the tiny brass oil lamp, blackened by the fire, that had rolled clear of the debris.

"Amancia, she's really upset." Carmen wrapped her arms around her friend. "Can't we leave this for now?"

"Well, I'm really upset as well, so no, we can't."

The door opened behind her, but she paid no

attention.

"It was your lamp. Was there something you didn't understand when I talked about site safety?"

"It was just a lamp. I got it from a market stall. It was so pretty." Suddenly, Mandy sat upright, an expression of horror on her face. "Oh God, you think I did this? You think I lit it and left it burning?"

"Well, didn't you?"

"No! No, I didn't. I put a pile of stuff including the lamp, still in its box, in front of my tent and went to get a drink, but I got talking to Rafa."

"Then, you're lucky you weren't in the tent when it exploded. Even luckier that no one was hurt."

"Except for Max," said Peter as he joined them.

Amancia whirled around. "Max? He's hurt?"

"It's only a superficial burn, but bad enough that it needs attention straight away. Can you do that, Amancia, or shall I drive him to the hospital? I've told him to come over, but instead, he's tidying up with some of the students. Maybe you could have a look."

"Get him in here quick, Peter."

Now Mandy began to cry. Amancia wasn't having that; a few easy tears would not solve the problem. "Shut up and start thinking about what's happened."

"I didn't mean any harm." Fat tears rolled down her cheeks. "Really, I didn't. Please don't send me away. It could mean the end of my career. My parents…"

She broke into loud sobs. It was all about her.

Disgusted, Amancia said, "Carmen, Vicky, take her into your tent tonight and sort her out somewhere to sleep. I'll decide what's going to happen tomorrow." She turned to Mandy. "You need to think about whether

204

I should allow you to stay. Now, go away, all of you."

Their arms around each other, the young women, reduced to a bunch of silly schoolgirls, seemed welded into a single unit as they left the kitchen. Amancia sighed and immediately forgot about them.

How bad were Max's injuries? The first-aid box was in the cupboard by the sink, conveniently placed in case of kitchen accidents. She was pulling it out as Max entered the room, and Amancia turned on the kitchen tap and filled a deep pan to the brim with cold water.

She looked at the injury. The end of the left sleeve of his jacket and shirt had burned away, and the skin exposed was a raw red color. He'd obviously put the flames out quickly when his jacket caught alight, and now she made him plunge his hand into the water. The burn didn't look too bad. But it would be painful.

"Stay there and let the water cool it," said Amancia. She turned to Peter. "Could you make sure they're all settled? I think we need some calm on the site. We'll decide what we're going to do tomorrow."

A few minutes later, Max was sitting on a kitchen chair, his arm held across his chest.

"I'll try not to hurt you."

"It's okay. It's cold, so I can't feel anything." He cranked out a weak smile. "I could hear you outside. I'm sure those girls will do whatever you say because you terrified me, the way you were speaking to them. The quieter your voice got, the more frightening it was. I'm glad it wasn't me you were talking to."

"I am so angry," she said. "I could have killed that silly little cow. After all the things we've said about site safety! There were reports on the local news about those lamps bursting into flames. We absolutely forbade buying them, tourist tat like that, warned them how dangerous they are. And I'm not sure it was true that she left it outside. Oh Max, I'm so sorry this happened when you were trying to help us."

He was smiling at her. "*No es nada.* I'm okay."

"Well, you're not really. For a start, you're going to have to replace that beautiful jacket," she said, producing a small smile, "and I thought how good it looked on you earlier this evening. What a pity."

"Come here," he said, grabbing her arm with his uninjured hand and pulling her onto his knee.

"Max! What if someone…"

But she allowed herself to sink against him, and they began to kiss.

"Thank God you're safe," she whispered when they were forced to draw a breath. "And thank you for what you did. That could have been a major incident, but you seemed to know what to do."

"I have army training."

"They trained you to put out fires?"

"No, but they did train us to react quickly in an emergency. I have the army to thank for that."

Maybe. But she didn't think that was necessarily the case; he was quick and resourceful, decisive. Amancia liked a man with those qualities. She kissed him again and stood up.

"Come on, let's get your hand cleaned up before it gets infected."

She took antiseptic wipes from the first-aid box and began to clean the skin. Her movements were rapid and deft but gentle at the same time, and soon she was unrolling a bandage, ready to strap a dressing in place. She looked up and found his eyes on her.

"Amancia."

"Pay attention," she said, returning to her task.

"Amancia, I— "

"I'll give you some dressings and show you how to look after this. You'll have to be able to do it yourself, but you should see a doctor as well."

"Right, that's enough," he said, as she packed the first-aid supplies away. He'd followed her across the room and now took her hands in his uninjured one and looked deep into her eyes, wiping away all her good intentions. Again, she wanted to kiss him but felt unaccountably shy.

"I don't suppose there's any chance we can pick up where we left off, and go to my place? You'd be surprised what I can do with only one hand."

She felt the heat rise in her cheeks. How could he? Yes, he definitely could, no question, but she'd got herself together now; she wasn't going to give in to this.

"Tut, tut! No, I'm going to refuse that offer, attractive though it is. Any pressure on that burn will be very painful. It might slow the healing, and you can't afford to have that happen. Besides, I can't leave the site, not after this."

He grinned. "I didn't think you'd be able to, but I had to try."

"It's good to hear you wanted to."

He came close and pulled her back into his arms, so that her face was up against the navy silk of his jacket. She nuzzled close, and her hand crept up his chest. It was involuntary. She'd meant to push him away, but somehow, instead, she was doing the opposite. Her fingers brushed the slubbed linen of his

207

shirt. His skin was warm beneath it, and she breathed in his scent with a mixture of soot and smoke, which made her wrinkle her nose.

He hugged her closer. "Naturally I wanted to."

A flood of warmth coursed through her body. With his good hand, he began stroking her neck, making the fine hairs at the back stand up, and she shivered.

He tightened his hold. "Maybe we can carry on right here."

"You're incorrigible."

"That's not a word I know."

"It means like a naughty boy, unashamed."

"Unashamedly pursuing you, you mean. We say *sinvergüenza.*"

His English really was very good.

"Max, you're going home to bed—alone—to rest and recover as quickly as possible." She tried to push him away.

"Hmm…disappointing." He was suddenly serious. "I do want this to go somewhere, Amancia—us, I mean. Can we try?"

He bent toward her, and she brought her head up to meet his lips. His kiss overwhelmed her. If he didn't go soon…But she couldn't leave the site—that would indeed be irresponsible. She pushed him gently away.

"Yes, we can. I want that, too. Now go. And ring me, Max."

****

He'd finally gone, and Amancia tidied up, every sense heightened, every nerve tingling. It had cost her so much to send him away when she longed to be in his arms. Soon she gave up on the futile attempt to clear the kitchen, switched off the lights, and went outside. There was a low mutter of voices from the tent that was now being shared by the three girls. It didn't sound as if they'd be getting to sleep anytime soon.

The whole site smelled of burning, which kept the awareness of danger on high, so that she checked everything several times over, before reluctantly allowing herself to believe that all was safe. They'd done a good job around the area where the tent had been, and now, a dark mound of earth marked the seat of the fire. Most of those whose tents had been closest to Mandy's had already found a new pitch, and calm had returned to the site. She headed back to her room. So much had happened in such a short time. It was surprising that it was only a few minutes after one, much earlier than she'd imagined.

She probably smelled as bad as the site did, and her hair would be even worse. She stripped off the pretty dress she'd worn on her date and dropped it on the floor. When she'd showered and washed her hair, she rinsed out the dress and hung it up to drip dry. Finally, she lay down. How was she going to handle the problem of the fire the following day?

But inevitably, her thoughts strayed to Max.

It distressed her that he'd been hurt, though she didn't think there'd be any permanent damage. And the fervor of his kisses had demonstrated that his mind was not on his wounds at all. Now she was consumed by longing, a desperation to be with him, which made her wish once more that she hadn't sent him away alone.

But she'd been right to do so. Desiring someone didn't mean you could shirk your responsibilities.

Chapter 31

When Amancia opened her eyes the next morning, it was a quarter to five and she'd been dreaming about the festival in the village, only it was Max who was with her instead of Peter. She rolled onto her side, and her body tingled as she'd just made love. It was a pity that part of the dream had completely vanished, but she kept very still a few moments longer, trying to revive its effects.

****

Breakfast was over. The three girls had shared a table, and during the meal, they'd carried on a low-voiced conversation. Now silent, they remained behind as the last few people trailed out. Amancia pulled over a chair and sat down. All three looked anxious, and Mandy's eyes were rimmed with red. It wasn't such a bad thing if she'd spent a sleepless night considering where her actions might have led.

"I'm sorry. I've been stupid and selfish. Please let me stay."

Amancia looked at her with curiosity. This might be a real change in the girl's attitude, but she'd need proof. "Can you think of a good reason why I should?"

"No…yes," she said, flushing slightly, not meeting her eyes. Then she did look at Amancia. "I really didn't light the lamp; I just left it lying around. Please believe me. I know it was stupid to buy it and stupid to leave it

210

outside my tent. I'm very sorry."

Amancia said nothing.

"Please, you said yourself that I have the right instincts on-site, that I could be a good archaeologist. Give me another chance, and I'll show you how well I can do. If you send me away, my parents won't pay for me to start my third year and I won't be able to afford it myself. They were completely against archaeology. They wanted me to do something practical like accountancy or business studies. But that's not for me."

At least, they could agree on this. It would be hard to imagine anyone less like an accountant than Mandy. She did have good instincts and seemed genuinely to enjoy working on-site.

"I love archaeology. Please let me stay."

If what the girl said was true, they needed to find out how the lighted lamp had ended up inside the tent. Someone must have put it there, but it was hard to think any of the students could be responsible.

"So, if I agree to let you stay, what are you going to do to make it right?"

"We've talked about that." She looked over to her friends for support. "At supper this evening, I'll apologize to everyone, admit how stupid it was, buying it after what you told us, and that I put people's lives in danger. And I'll ask them to forgive me."

This was quite brave and suggested the girl really did want to continue her studies. It wouldn't be a small thing to put herself in that very uncomfortable position, and there was a risk, because maybe others wouldn't accept her apology. Amancia looked into her eyes and could see no trace of insincerity.

"Okay, maybe." She waited.

"And I'll apologize to Max for...his hand." The tears spilled over. "Oh God! What happened to him made me realize how everything could have gone the other way...if...if someone had been sleeping in the next tent and it had caught alight. I feel so bad about it."

Mandy was sobbing now. It was good that she'd realized how dreadful the situation could have been. Even now, Amancia felt sick at the disaster which had so very nearly occurred. She stayed silent for a while, waiting for the crying to subside. It could have gone so wrong—but it hadn't. Should she give this young woman a chance to learn from her mistake?

"Right, let's see if everyone accepts your excuses. This evening at supper, you do what you've said. You three arrange it, and I'll be there to hear you. Shall I ring Max and tell him you want to speak to him?"

"No. His number's on the notice board in the store. I'll...I'll do it myself...now."

Good. She was taking responsibility.

"Just one thing, Mandy, are you on good terms with everyone on-site?"

Mandy stared at her. "You think someone might have done this to get me in trouble?"

"Well, it's not impossible. What do you think?"

She was quiet for a moment. "No, no one here would do that, and we all get on well."

The other two were nodding. "Everyone likes Mandy," said Carmen.

Right, they had to look further afield. She had a horrible idea she knew who might have been responsible. Mandy's tent had backed onto the fence that divided off the car park. How difficult would it be for someone from outside to access it in the dark without being seen? Not very. Maybe they'd waited until they saw her heading into the kitchen. But if she was right, the incident was directed at her, Amancia, not at Mandy, designed to throw the maximum amount of mud at her. She shrugged, dismissing the idea for the moment. That way lay paranoia.

****

A faint smell of charcoal still hung in the air the following morning. Otherwise, except for a black stain on the earth, no trace of the fire remained, and the tents now stood well separated. Amancia stopped at the blackened patch to wipe sweat from her brow. Each time she walked by, she thought of the event which could so easily have turned to tragedy. Handling the situation had been tough, but she believed she'd made the right decision. If only the rain would return, it would clear everything away, and they could put it behind them, but the temperature continued to rise. She had grown accustomed to the heat, but it was still hard to bear.

She caught up with Peter and steered him over to where she'd been working. They hadn't only uncovered the first few steps but had worked quickly downward, and more of the stairwell was visible. Chris's calculations, which had been spot-on, were responsible for a leap forward: a new pit was opening up where he'd placed the possible stair head.

They worked in shifts on this part, two or three at a time, because the spaces were tight, but everyone was keen to keep up the momentum. It was heartening that someone was always willing to continue into the afternoon, despite continued high temperatures. The work was relatively straightforward, but sometimes that could mean people didn't take enough care. She reminded them often about how delicately the excavation needed to be handled, how easy it would be to damage something, how easy to slip and fall.

Amancia was taking photos and making notes on her phone about this stage of the work. It was material for the final report, but she'd also had an idea for a book, one that could support an archaeology unit on a course. Being published was important for an academic.

"It's going well," Peter said, looking down at the steps which descended to the landing. "We'll have a lot more excavated before we vacate the site. I like the idea that when we leave, we'll have achieved something conclusive."

Amancia's heart gave a thud, and she felt the familiar guilt. She hadn't sorted out anything about her future, and more specifically, she hadn't even looked for a post for the autumn term, except for that one night when she'd drawn up the short list of unattractive possibilities. Something would be available if she searched hard enough, but she hadn't because her heart simply wasn't in it. What was she going to do?

"How's Max's hand?" Peter asked.

"I don't know. I haven't had a chance to speak to him." He hadn't rung her.

"Why don't you contact him? The poor man—the least you could do is follow up after the way he saved the situation."

Amancia gave him a smile. "He said he was going to be busy, but you're right—that's exactly what I should do."

She'd desperately wanted to contact him but didn't want to appear needy, preferred to let him show he meant what he'd said about taking things onto the next stage. This was so uncharacteristic, but she couldn't risk that she'd got it wrong, that maybe he didn't want her as he'd seemed to. This time it mattered too much. It had seemed really positive, but if so, why hadn't he been in touch? He must know how worried she'd be.

On the other hand, maybe he was wondering why she hadn't rung.

He'd accepted Mandy's apology, she'd said. When Amancia discussed the situation with Peter, he'd been reluctant to let the girl stay, which had surprised her. She'd thought he'd be more liberal, more than her, anyway, but that turned out not to be true. They'd gone back and forth, trying to see what was best.

"She's very young, Peter, young for her age even. I think we have to give her a chance. It's not as if she's likely to do the same thing again."

"No, but something equally stupid, perhaps—and dangerous. But it's your decision, Amancia."

Okay, that was scary, that the responsibility would be all hers. But Amancia was cautiously optimistic about her, so finally, she told the girl she could stay but was on probation; the slightest reason for concern and she'd be on the next flight home. Already, she appeared a changed person, working hard and contributing in ways she hadn't done before. Maybe something positive could come out of the incident.

"Oh, I just remembered I took a phone call from Pablo," said Peter now. "He tried you first."

Her phone had rung while she was talking to Chris. A glance had shown her it wasn't Max, so she'd continued her conversation.

"He and his people will be back this afternoon to

film this part of the dig, here where we've uncovered more steps. I think they're pretty excited that they can include this. We got it done just in time."

"Yes, and Wednesday afternoon next week is scheduled for the preliminary screening. Everyone's going to want to see that."

"There's a lot going on, but is there any chance I can take time off late Sunday to Wednesday? My wife's managed to get away for a few days, and I thought it would be good to head to the coast. I'll be back in time for the screening of the film."

He'd barely left the site since her arrival.

"Okay. Remember I'm out this Friday evening, and all day on Saturday." Her phone rang, and her heart rate jumped on seeing the name. "Sorry, I'll need to take this." She walked away with a little wave to Peter and stopped where she could look down onto the river, the water swirling below her. He'd rung after all.

"How are you, Max?" She took a deep breath to calm herself. "I was worried when you didn't ring."

He laughed. "I'm sorry I didn't contact you, but I wasn't very well this morning. I'm better now."

"Oh, if I'd known—"

"You could have done nothing at all, *querida*. Anyway, I am much better. Will you come out with me on Saturday? I've got a backlog of work, so I'm very busy until then."

"Oh, Max, I really want to, but I'm going to Barcelona tomorrow afternoon to spend some time with Lizzie and her partner, Jake. It's all agreed, and they'll be leaving Spain on Saturday, so I can't back out."

It was just a date. They could meet at another time, but it felt as if she were turning down something tremendously important, and she desperately wanted him to understand.

"You will be returning here on Saturday evening?"

"Yes, but it'll be quite late."

"Let me know your train time, and I'll meet you at the station. We can eat in town, and then we'll go to my place, if you'd like to."

"It will be great to see you on Saturday, but I'll be on duty from Sunday lunchtime."

"Even so, that's good. Text me the details, and I'll meet you at the station."

She really wanted to see Lizzie and Jake. She was very keen to visit Barcelona. But just for a moment, she felt like canceling.

Chapter 32

This city was fabulous: noisy, colorful, like no other place Amancia had visited. Her friends had grown to love Barcelona in the short time they'd been there, which was becoming clear as they lingered over lunch of *pulpo a la gallega*. The dark red dish was heavy on paprika but delicious, and a big contrast to the simple fare on-site. She was falling in love with Barcelona too.

"Park Güell and the Sagrada Familia have to be the most amazing," said Jake, who'd become a great fan after photo-shoots in Gaudi's famous park and outside the cathedral. "He was a crazy artist—"

"Architect," said Lizzie.

"A crazy artist *and* architect who was wonderful."

Later, they stood on the far side of the road for ages, gazing up at the white building that was the Casa Milà. "And it's like being inside some kind of mad fairyland in there. You've absolutely got to come back when you have time. In fact, we've enjoyed it so much that Lizzie and I are going to visit again."

He was so well-traveled, he sometimes appeared jaded, and this instant love affair with the city impressed Amancia.

"Yes, but I think you'd probably appreciate the Templo de Augusto and the archaeology museum as well," said Lizzie, familiar with her friend's interests. "Next time I come, I'm going to do the cooking experience. I didn't find out about it until yesterday, or it would have been top of my list."

"A cooking experience? What on earth is that?"

"You sign up for this mini cookery course, just an afternoon. You learn how to make paella and then eat the results. Fabulous."

"I can see I've got to visit again before I leave."

"Oh, you must. You're living in Spain, but you're not experiencing it."

But she was. What could be more Spanish than Max? And Zaragoza was a quiet gem, just different, more restrained and well-mannered when compared with the exuberance of Barcelona.

"Just remember, you're not going to be leaving anytime soon. You'll have plenty of opportunities." Lizzie gave her a meaningful look, which was a bit irritating. It really wasn't necessary to keep on doing that.

In the afternoon, Amancia, Lizzie, and Jake wandered along La Rambla and the surrounding streets in the hot sunshine. With the backdrop of chattering starlings, day slid almost imperceptibly into night. Even Lizzie seemed to have forgotten her aversion to walking, and they strolled for a long time in the velvety black evening shot through with brilliant colors. Light streamed out of windows and doorways, cutting bright oblongs and squares through the shadows on the famous street, the ruby, emerald, and white of the lamps shining like gems, while the air carried relaxed conversation and laughter.

The jewel-like light set against the background of deep darkness epitomized the beautiful city. What a pity she hadn't fitted in a visit before. It wasn't far from where she was working, but she'd been too busy.

Much later, they went back to the hotel and spent some time in the bar, a very relaxed catching up with friends. It was after eleven when they said goodnight in the corridor.

Amancia had been up at six and worked five hours before catching the train, but there was no way she'd be able to sleep. She took a leisurely shower and wrapped herself in the thick, toweling dressing gown the hotel provided, wishing it was Saturday night. How wonderful it would be to have Max beside her now, because finally, they would spend the night together—only not this night. She wanted to make love to him, have him love her.

Tomorrow.

She sighed, thinking of their kisses in the shadow of the Roman Wall, and goose pimples swept across her skin as she recalled how they'd pressed up against each other, the way his hands had caressed her neck, the warmth of his fragrant skin through his shirt when she laid her cheek against his shoulder. And she imagined the deep pleasure of his fingers kneading her shoulders, straightening out the knots and kinks in her muscles, his hands working their way down her body, and hers smoothing over his hips…

The thought made her nipples harden under the rough material of the gown. She crossed her arms and grasped her breasts, flattening them with open palms, trying to make the sensation go away, determined not to spend the night in this state of arousal. But the effort was less than successful.

In bed, she watched the occasional headlights flicker across the ceiling. But thinking about sleep was never going to make it happen. She shivered suddenly at the thought of what being with him was going to feel like, goose pimples once more roughening her skin. Then, she gave another sigh. It was only twenty-four hours away. Determined, she closed her eyes.

Twenty minutes later, she got up. She'd brought her laptop, and with less than two months to go on-site, doing the outline of her report and organizing the material for the first few weeks was an urgent obligation. She could work at the table by the open window. A requirement of her current job, the report would also be an important document in her search for the sort of post she wanted. Resolutely, she pushed other thoughts away and got down to work. Midnight chimed from the little church tower down the street, a cascade of musical notes, and then came silence. By one, she could have the bulk of the work done.

Occasionally, she looked down on the darkened street. Over to her left behind the trees, the moon appeared. Heat and dust were forgotten. The Catalonian night had taken over, and there was an enchantment in the air. Even the name, *Catalunya*, cast its spell, its pronunciation liquid and beguiling, speaking of things that were strange, of infinite possibilities. Muted sounds drifted upward. That same air was balmy and had acquired from somewhere a strong floral scent she tried to identify but couldn't. Turning back to her laptop, she typed her introduction. Soon, she was lost in the task.

As Amancia analyzed her material and made decisions about presentation and emphasis, cars came and went in front of the hotel. She paid them scant attention. It was going to be a long night, but for the moment, the work held her attention.

Chapter 33

Amancia's phone gave a low buzz. Who could be calling her this late? As she crossed to the bedside table to answer, she had a little flicker of alarm, that maybe something was wrong at home. And then her heart gave a leap. Max. Who else was going to ring her at one in the morning?

"Still awake?"

"I couldn't sleep."

"That's good because I'm downstairs. I was about to get a room. Or, er…may I come up?"

"Downstairs! In the hotel? How did you know where to come?"

"Something you said when you were telling me about your friends, so I phoned a couple of places and struck lucky."

"You could have rung me."

God, this was unbelievable. She breathed deeply. It was no time to lose her cool.

"I could have, but I enjoyed the detective work. And it would have ruined the surprise. Is it okay if I come up? I can get a room, no problem."

"No, you can't. It's room five six two."

How could he be here? The lift had been quick when they'd come up earlier, and there'd be no one around now, so…Before she got any further, there was a gentle tap on the door. When she opened it, Max stepped in and dropped his bag, pulling her straight into his arms. He pushed the door shut and held her tight, and she felt the wild beating of his heart match her own.

"You sure it's all right for me to be here?"

"I can't imagine anything I want more. But how is it you're in Barcelona?"

"I want to be with you, *querida*. I didn't want to wait any longer. And I hoped you'd feel the same way." He nuzzled her ear.

"Oh, I do."

He began to kiss her, and her hands crept up around his neck, pulling him close, responding as he deepened the kiss. The arousal she'd experienced earlier swept through her again, doubling, overtaking rational thought, and leaving her desperate and wanting. It scared her that she was so needy, that in a few moments their relationship had moved so far on. Finally, he let her go, took off his jacket, and threw it onto a chair. They were both breathing hard, more than ready to take things to the next stage, but he grasped her hand and walked her over to the bed. He sat and pulled her down beside him, his arm around her, cradling her.

"Before we go any further with this, I have to tell you something."

"No, please. You don't have to tell me anything." She kissed his mouth. "I really don't want you to stop."

But he pulled back. "I must."

Amancia thought she knew what was coming. She laid her hand on his. "Is it about your leg, Max?"

He looked surprised. "You know? Did...¿*Alguien te lo ha dicho?*" he asked, his English suddenly deserting him. Then he repeated, "Did someone tell you?"

223

"No, no one has said anything. It's the way you walk, even though it's almost perfect." She raised her hand to stroke his cheek. "No one else would notice, but I have experience of this. My uncle was a soldier. He lost his leg to an IED in Afghanistan, and he lived in our house during recovery, learning to walk again, learning to cope with the mental scars. I was still at school then, and I saw him every day for at least two years. I wouldn't have guessed otherwise."

She could see from the anxiety in his eyes that this moment meant a great deal to him, that her reaction was important. She had to reassure him.

"It doesn't matter, Max. It does to you, of course it does, but it doesn't affect our relationship. Why should it change how I feel about you?"

"Amancia, I want you, God knows I do, but I couldn't have a relationship with someone who…pitied me."

She laughed. "Pity!"

He winced and started to speak, but she laid a finger over his lips.

"Max, you're the least pitiful person I can think of. I don't know how this happened to you, but whatever the reason, you've overcome the problem. You're running a successful business—and it's physically demanding work." She grinned. "Running a successful business and still finding the time to drive hapless academics wild with desire. What's pitiful about that? And I think the chivalrous thing right now would be to kiss me again."

She pushed up against him, seeking his lips, and whispered, "To say nothing of impersonating professors and inviting people to dinner under false pretenses."

Then she said slowly and carefully, searching for the right words, "*Escúchame, Max. Te quiero tal cual como eres.* Exactly as you are—I meant what I said."

His face broke into a wide smile. "*Muy bien.* I see you have been practicing your Spanish."

She was smiling as well now. "Of course. Did you believe I wouldn't think about what's happening between us? Kiss me, Max. Don't leave me in this pathetic state."

He tightened his hold and put everything into it, and it was a while before they disengaged.

"I've had a long drive. I need to use the bathroom." He got up, grabbed his bag, and went through.

It was hard to think straight. Left alone in the room, she extinguished the last lamp, and moonlight picked out various objects in the room, a faint reflection from a mirror.

She took off the dressing gown and lay down on the bed, pulling up the thin coverlet, even though it was warm in the room, and she wasn't shy about revealing her body. A little modesty, though—it was always worth retaining that.

He was taking his time. But she'd have to be patient. She needed him to lie down beside her, didn't want to wait any longer. She'd never known this intoxicating combination of the physical wanting and what was going on in her head. Such desire.

How would it feel when he ran his fingers along her neck and down her spine again, not over her clothes this time, but when she was naked? It had driven her a little crazy the first time.

The door opened, and Max stepped out into the room, carrying the bag. The blinds were open, and the moonlight fell onto his naked body. He quickly turned his back to the window, but she caught the faint sheen from the prosthesis which replaced the missing part of his leg. She remained quite still, though she longed to hold him in her arms. She'd told him it changed nothing and meant it, but that didn't necessarily mean he believed her.

Max sat on the bed. He stretched out a hand and stroked her arm. "Give me a moment."

He bent forward, and the muscles of his back rippled. She'd never thought how sexy that was. Now, she wanted to run her fingers across the smooth skin, white like alabaster in the silvery light, like the marble of those Roman statues that the shape of his head had recalled at their first meeting. Passionate as she was about all things Roman, it acted on her like an erotic charge, and she drew in a sharp breath.

He was undoing the contraption that was strapped to the end of his limb. The knee was intact, and the remains of his leg sat in a sort of cup. How painful must that be at the end of a long day's work? He must often feel pain. Amancia tried to imagine the world from his point of view, and a deep surge of desire for him swept through her. If he allowed her to, she could take away some of that suffering.

Finally, he discarded the prosthesis.

Still, she waited while he unwrapped a condom and placed it on the table by the bed. Then he lay down beside her, and when he reached for her, they turned to face one another and lay there for a few seconds, looking deep into each other's eyes.

"*Mi querida. Mi amor.*"

He leaned over and feathered kisses over her eyes,

her cheeks, her chin, her mouth.

"I never knew lips could taste this sweet. *Eres tan bella, perfecta.*"

She groaned. "Oh, I wish that were true, but I'm not—look at what happened with James. That's got to be my fault."

"The fault is his. He wants to own you, and no one can do that."

She was trembling, hopeful, wanting to believe him and absolve herself of blame.

It was good to hear that he didn't hold her responsible, even though she'd failed to understand what James was about, but no matter. The thoughts faded away. What was happening now was more than enough to fill her mind. She would do better this time.

"Anyway, you told me you'd already broken up by the time you came to Spain, *¿verdad?*"

"That's true. For my part, our relationship had died a long time before…ah…"

How hadn't she noticed what he was doing? Somehow, his lips were now on her nipple. He sucked and teased until it burned. She moved, unable to stand any more stimulation, but he wasn't going to allow her to escape so easily. She groaned as he insisted. Something was building deep within her, and now, she was seeking release, but he didn't stop, instead transferring his attention to the other side.

"I want you, Amancia, everything you can give."

"Is this what you mean?"

She moaned and fell onto her back, pulling him down on top of her, swiveling her hips to invite him to explore, cupping her hands around his buttocks to bring him in closer. His whole body hardened against her with a fierce heat, and he pushed her legs apart.

"It's a good start."

"Start? I'm already desperate. It needs to be now...now, Max."

She was making little, stuttering moaning sounds, breathing more and more deeply.

"No, it doesn't. You can wait longer, I promise you. Give it a little time, and it'll be so much sweeter."

"But I can't...control it."

"Maybe you can't, but I can."

How much longer? Oh God, how much longer? It was almost too much, but still not enough. Then, he thrust deep inside her, and the world erupted.

And now, they lay entwined on top of the sheet, their bodies slowly cooling.

"*Nunca lo imaginé.*" His voice was husky. "I never thought I'd have this again. After what happened, I couldn't bear to see myself as others might see me, and I thought it was all over."

He traced her high cheekbones, the curve of her lips, with his fingertips. "But then I saw you, and I knew I had to stop running away, and face up to life as it is now." He bent his head again.

"I'm so glad you did," she whispered and returned his kiss.

Everything about this felt different. There were emotions at play here that she'd not experienced before. It would take some getting used to, this willingness to sacrifice for the other, the profound desire to make someone else happy. And she sensed the same in him, a need to be honest about what he was feeling, a lightening of the spirit.

It was a whole week since their date on the night of

the fire, and every day, she'd tried to imagine this moment. But she could never have conjured up the tsunami of sensation that had just swept her away—or the whirlwind of conflicting emotions that now engulfed her.

She sighed deeply, and Max was instantly alert. He raised his head and looked down at her, his eyes searching hers.

"Regrets?" he asked.

"Never. I'm trying to understand how I got to be thirty, without ever experiencing anything like this. Max, I don't know how to say it in any other way, and I wish I did because it's inadequate, but…"

"But?"

"But you really turn me on."

"Well, that was my whole intention, and it's great to know I've succeeded. Now, it's still early. Let's try something different."

Once again, he parted her legs, but this time, he went to work with his tongue.

Chapter 34

Jake and Lizzie were leaving. They stood by the taxi which would take the two of them to the airport at Girona. Lizzie was very excited by the conclusions she'd drawn from Max's impromptu arrival in the city.

"This is so romantic," she whispered, as she kissed her friend. The two men stood a little distance away, talking about Jake's proposed visit to Alaska as they waited for the women to take leave of one another. "He came for you. He couldn't even wait a few hours for you to come back. He's just lovely. Don't let this one go, Mancie."

The earnest way she spoke made Amancia smile.

"I've no intention of doing that. If we break up, it won't be because of me."

"So, what could go wrong?—he quite obviously adores you."

"There are other things, Lizzie. Don't be obtuse. Have you forgotten I'm Black?"

"No, but I don't ever think about it."

"Well, sadly, I'm forced to, and even if Max doesn't care about it, there's his family. He comes from an ultratraditional family. How easily are they going to accept me?"

"Why should it matter? What about Prince Harry and his Megan? You can't get much more traditional than that family."

"And look how difficult it's been for them."

"They haven't exactly made it easy, have they, spreading themselves all over the internet. That's my opinion, anyway. And not everyone reacts like that."

"True, and his mother's lovely."

"The queen? She was his grandm—"

"No, silly. Max's mother."

"There you are, then. Just don't back down—on anything, okay? And don't start obsessing about not having a job. I know what you're like. It's not a good reason for accepting something a thousand miles away and disappearing out of this man's life. You do know that, don't you?"

"Yes, I'll try to avoid that," she said. She would try, but there was no guarantee she could find something nearer. "But I don't know how serious this is for him. He finds me attractive, but that doesn't make it a life partnership."

"Are you blind, Mancie? The guy's head over heels in love."

"Maybe, but I don't think he knows that. He's fighting it. He says he can't commit to anything long term. He has things he must sort out."

That had hurt, after the wonderful lovemaking they'd experienced. But he'd been honest, and she preferred that.

"So, just go with the flow. Enjoy it."

"Okay. We'll see. Now, have a safe journey."

****

Max grasped her hand, and they meandered around the city center, finally sitting under a huge, spreading plane tree.

"So, tell me about your leg."

"You don't want to hear this."

He didn't want to talk. They'd made love, but he was still a stranger. Sex could be very good, but alone, it couldn't sustain a relationship, not the one she wanted with him. If that was all, it would be very shallow, but with Lizzie's comments in mind, she knew she had to go deeper. "I do. I need to know you a little more."

He was silent for a minute, gathering his thoughts, the struggle he was having written clearly on his face. "All right, it happened because I joined the army."

"Why did you?"

"Why did I join the army?"

He was repeating things, putting off the moment when he had to talk about it.

"Yes. Why did you?"

"It's traditional in the family, but these days, it's considered by some people as a very controversial thing to do. Grandad served in the army of the Generalissimo, like a lot of the wealthy Madrileños at the time. They had money in those days. I joined a different, modern army, one that was entwined with the European Union. I had to get away from Madrid, from my grandparents. My lovely grandparents. They'd brought me up, sent me to university to study languages. But I was living at home. I had to change that, become truly independent."

"The language studies—that explains why your English is so good."

"Yes." The fact that he didn't come back with a witty comment told her how hard this was for him. "Well, when I'd finished at the university, I needed to change a few things. My grandfather could be very dictatorial, although he's mellowed now. Living at home, I felt pressure to conform to the family rules. I love them, but they're not my parents, and their views are…a little old-fashioned. So, I left.

"But after a few years, I felt I should go back. My mother's health was deteriorating, and I wanted to spend some time with her, in case what she had was terminal. That was just over four years ago." He turned to look at her. "Look, is this really necessary?"

"It is. Go on."

He wiped both hands down his face, giving him such a look of vulnerability, her heart felt as if it melted within her, but she forced herself to show no sign of her feelings. He gave a deep sigh. "Okay, I'd had quite a successful career in the army and served well over the minimum term. I could have stayed in the service and worked my way up the hierarchy."

He was silent for a long time.

"Couldn't you have asked for a posting closer to home, so you could see your mother more often?"

"Probably, but I didn't have the army mindset. It was very structured, not much different from living with *los abuelos*, so I didn't want to spend the rest of my life being a soldier."

Amancia was listening carefully. Every item of information was important because, although she was gradually getting to know this man, it was rather as if she had a jigsaw and some of the most important pieces were missing. This part was completely new to her. She had to fit it into the puzzle.

"I think growing grapes is in my blood. It was something I had to do, though I didn't know how I was going to make it work. At first, I thought I'd buy a few hectares, an abandoned farm maybe, and start something entirely new. My father was still alive at the time and living at the vineyard, but he and I could never have worked together.

"Then, before I could decide to leave, I was seconded to the UN and sent to…*Ucrania.*"

"Ukraine?"

"Ukraine. I could have refused, but they put on a lot of pressure and pointed out that, as the only Spaniard in the group, I'd be representing my country. And of course, it was a peace-keeping mission. There's a sort of nobility to that idea which appealed to me."

"So, there shouldn't have been any danger."

"Well, you can't ever be sure of that, but it's rare with the UN forces. I guess I was very unlucky. It was an IED, like with your uncle. We were driving along, the front jeep in a convoy, when it exploded. I was thrown clear. The last thing I remember was running back toward the vehicle where my sergeant was trapped at the wheel. They said I saved his life, but then a second explosion occurred—and that did for me. I have no memory of any of it. Nothing at all."

He stopped talking, and Amancia thought about what he'd said.

"And you don't understand why you did it?" she said eventually, earning a curious look from him.

"No, I don't. It was such a stupid thing to do and the wildest pure chance that it succeeded. They gave me a medal, but I don't deserve it. I've thought it over and over, and I came to the conclusion that it was because Micky had a lovely wife and a couple of children. He was worth saving."

"And you didn't think you were?"

"In comparison with him? No, not really. Not until I met you. Now, I feel differently. *Mi querida,* you've given me hope."

Amancia reached out now and squeezed his hand, wanting him to know how she felt for him. Maybe he'd tell her one day why he'd considered himself so worthless, but it wouldn't be today.

Tears were running down her face now. The UN soldiers had gone to Ukraine to maintain peace, and along with the civilian groups, they seemed to do a good job. Then a couple of years later, the Russians began a full-scale attack, which was still going on. To her, it looked like it had all been for nothing.

Max leaned across and wiped her cheeks. "Don't cry for me, *querida*. I am much better."

****

She loved the car in which she was sitting a little while later, its sleek beauty and the feeling of controlled power. When they'd driven into Zaragoza the previous week, the journey had been brief, and she'd been so taken up with the driver that she hadn't paid attention to the car. She only managed to drive safely if she concentrated very hard, so to her, it was a machine that was in equal parts beautiful and terrifying.

"Enjoy it while you can. I'm selling it."

"Oh, what a pity. Why?"

"There are very few of these in existence, and it's worth a lot of money—which I need for the vineyard. I've had it nearly ten years, but it already has vintage status, and with some cars, age only increases the value. When I set up a business, I didn't know all the things I'd have to do to make it work, and the hot summer is taking its toll, burning the grapes. We have to protect the crop from the sun, and it's going to cost a lot, so I'm selling."

They'd been on the road to Zaragoza for about an hour when Max's telephone rang.

"I'll leave it."

The ringing stopped, but it niggled with Amancia that they'd received the call and not responded. It was something she found very hard to do. Of course, he wanted them to have this time together, just the two of them, just as she did.

They drove on and passed very few other vehicles. The route took them along the A2, and they circled around the city of Lleida, coming now into Soses, and there was the AP2. It wouldn't be long before they were back in Zaragoza. The ringing began again. Max sighed and said, "Okay, maybe I should…"

He flicked a switch on the dashboard.

"*Sí. ¿Qué pasa?* Catalina."

The woman's voice sounded high-pitched and panicked. Amancia listened carefully, but she could scarcely understand anything of the quick-fire conversation that followed. But there was a rise in tension as Max reacted to the information he was given. He ended the call. "I have to go straight to Zaragoza."

"What's happened, Max?"

"My mother—she's been taken to hospital. She collapsed, and Catalina called the ambulance."

"Oh, I'm sorry, I—"

"I'm going to ring the hospital now and find out what the situation is."

He signaled and pulled onto the side of the road and then spent a couple of minutes searching for the correct number. When he finally got through, there followed a lengthy conversation, during which he asked a number of questions. Finally, he ended the call.

"How is she, Max?"

"She's come round. They're checking everything, but she hit her head when she fell, and they're worried that may have caused damage. She's fragile." He was quiet for a moment, thinking things through, and she didn't attempt to disturb him. "Listen, you need to get back. I don't know how long I'll be there, but once we get to the hospital, why don't you take the car and drive back to the site?"

Amancia didn't want to drive that beautiful, dangerous beast through the dark night. As they turned back onto the road, she said, "I have a better idea. I know you want to be there, but couldn't you drop me off at the site on your way? It won't add more than ten minutes to the journey. And then you'll have your car when you need it."

He considered this for a moment. "You're right. That's what we should do."

The powerful vehicle was eating up the miles now, the dark boles of ancient trees that lined the stretch of road flashing by.

"This is not how I wanted to bring this day to an end. I'm sorry."

"I understand. I hope you find it's not too serious." But she knew, after what he'd told her earlier, that it might well be very serious. "Just keep in touch."

****

Seeing Max drive off into the night was a little strange. Like on the night of the fire, she'd been cheated of the expected outcome. But this time, she had the memory of the night before. Her own affairs were of little importance; Max would be worried, and she should stop feeling sorry for herself.

She wondered about this family with which she now found herself involved. She liked Max's mother very much but had quickly realized there was a story she hadn't yet heard. There was some mystery, something he was keeping to himself. And before their relationship went much further, she would have to find out what it was.

Chapter 35

When Max called Amancia on Sunday morning, it was with good news.

"She'll be allowed home on Wednesday or Thursday and confined to bed for a while, very bored, I expect. Especially as I'm not going to be around much. We have some issues in the vineyard."

"Maybe I can visit her. Peter will be back by then."

"She would love that." Their conversation grew more intimate as they recalled how much they'd enjoyed Barcelona. "I have to see you. Why don't you come over on Thursday? We can look around the vineyard too, if you'd like to."

"I'd really like that." Apparently, he'd modernized everything when he took it over; it would be very different from the French *vignoble* she'd worked in when she was seventeen.

"Good. Late afternoon, there's usually a quiet time. Perhaps you could visit my mother first. She wants you to look around the basement to see if you can find evidence of old foundations. I think she was quite inspired by the idea."

"That's good—so was I."

"*Hasta jueves, querida.*"

"See you on Thursday."

She closed her phone, thinking through their conversation. He'd call her *querida* several times. It was an endearment and had sounded quite natural, but despite the night they'd spent together, she couldn't relax completely, couldn't quite believe what was happening, not least the change in her own attitude, and she wanted to pursue things with him as far as she could take it. But Max was not there yet, and maybe he never would be. He was a wonderful lover, so what was she complaining about? Whether there was any commitment or not, she found herself quite unable to hold him at a distance.

****

Everything was calm at the dig, but there was her report to finish, which she'd abandoned on Max's arrival at the hotel. After lunch, the site fell into a deep silence, disturbed only by the bees buzzing in the remaining patches of flowers. The sun beat down, steadily baking the terrain. Unless it rained again, those flowers would soon disappear.

She sat at the computer, and seeing an email waiting unopened, she froze. It was from the organization for historic buildings and had been cc'd to the Professor of Archaeology at the university. The list of findings the inspector had promised was attached.

It glared at her from the screen, a threat to her peace of mind, and she did not want to open it. It felt like a lethal weapon that was going to blow up in her face. He'd been an unpleasant man, the inspector. He did not wish her well. Swallowing down the bile that'd risen to her throat, she forced herself to click on it and then open the attachment. As she began to read, her heart started to race. It was every bit as bad as she'd feared. Worse.

After a short description of the site, location, and

its purpose, several things were highlighted: a worrying disregard for site security, evident from the fact that there'd been many break-ins and they'd never managed to catch anyone. It didn't mention that nothing was stolen, nor that the police had been out to visit and could suggest nothing better than buying a bigger lock.

The report then alluded to a failure to control the students resulting in a dangerous fire which had put people at risk. *How did he know about the fire?* He must be keeping a close watch over the site. Or was her earlier suspicion that his activities might extend beyond checking on historic buildings not as paranoid as it had seemed? She couldn't imagine any of the students were broadcasting that information. However, people did stupid things on social media, unaware of the effect.

Complaints from the public were mentioned. The link he provided to the local newspaper showed this article had appeared long before the public meeting, indeed before Amancia's arrival, and those had been innocuous comments from locals who simply wanted to know what was going on. They'd all been resolved now, after their meeting in the village.

The most bewildering point was the comment about poor progress, that virtually nothing had been passed through to the university. Was it a suggestion that they weren't working hard enough? This was archaeology, and you couldn't just conjure objects out of the ground if they weren't there. It was nonsense.

There were some lesser points, contributing to a dim view of what was happening on-site, and the report concluded that the site manager had been appointed to a post beyond her abilities. The site manager. Her. It made a recommendation to relieve her of her duties immediately, citing a poor grasp of Spanish with the consequence of a possible breakdown in communication.

So, maybe she was not completely incompetent, and it was the language to blame—how magnanimous of him. He'd hit just about every point possible, however tangentially.

There was more along the same lines, but by the time she'd reached this stage, Amancia had stopped wanting to cry and was trying to control her anger. Now, she was sure of something she'd already suspected: she was being set up. The question was who had done it. And why? She turned to the end of the document and studied the almost illegible signature: Barriles. Had this report been seen by anyone else in the organization?

She couldn't leave the matter there. She was going to investigate him, find out what this meant. Peter was away. The professor had finally been located but was still in Chile and unavailable. She went to look for one of the older students and found both Chris and Maya in the kitchen.

"Okay," Maya was saying as Amancia walked in. "I'll include that in the blog."

They looked up, and the girl immediately picked up on her state of mind. "What's wrong, Amancia?"

"Come over to the store. I've something I want to show you both."

****

"It's been four days since the last attempt to break in," said Chris, when they'd discussed the implications of the report. "You know, it's weird—these people keep on coming back, but they're not trying hard enough."

"What do you mean, not trying?"

"Well, if they really wanted to steal something, they would. It's as if they just want us to know they've been here."

"Maybe that's it. It's a threat, designed to upset things," said Maya. "And just so you know, I did not put anything about the fire on the blog."

"Listen, I've got an idea," said Chris. "We've never seen anyone around the site before midnight. I reckon we can arrange a guard for a couple of days, from about half eleven onward. A lot of the guys will be up for this. That's got to be our starting point."

"You think you could get people to help?"

"Definitely. We can't let him do this to you, Amancia. We'll have a bit of fun. Leave it to me."

****

It was good to know her students didn't think badly of her, but she wasn't as confident as they were; this was her future on the line. It was horrible the way all her old insecurities were coming back to haunt her; she'd only just got away from James's constant digging at her, and now, here was someone else having a go. Or wait…could James be involved? She hadn't seen or heard anything to suggest that he'd continued his harassment.

She glared at her laptop, paralyzed for a moment. That email would be sitting in the professor's inbox. She had to be able to refute every point that'd been made before he got the chance to read it. And the best way to do that was to work on her own report. It wouldn't impress anyone if she wasn't up to date with that. She got down to work.

****

The following afternoon she sat on her bed and began a proper search for work. She'd been here since the second week in July and had done nothing yet to sort out that problem. All these weeks she'd been here and still she had nothing. There were possibilities, even one in an archaeology department in the north of England. She understood Lizzie's views, but there was nothing cool about hanging around in Zaragoza without a job in the hope that something more permanent would develop with Max, so she had to do this.

It was a long way from her home in Bristol and a long way from Spain—she'd looked up the distance: 1207.9 miles, and every point-one of a mile would take her that little bit farther away. But it was a proper archaeology post which could help move her career forward. If they didn't offer it to her, the fault would be entirely hers for leaving the application so late.

She was so unsettled; she sprang up and began walking around in the restricted space, desperate to get something arranged.

How would things work out if she ended up in that northern city? Of course, there were trains, and the nearest airport was barely an hour away. But it felt distant, psychologically. And why would a busy man like Max stick with a girlfriend who lived that far away? You had to have a strong relationship to do distance successfully. But she didn't have the option of doing nothing.

Just out of interest, she looked up universities in Northern Spain, and even in Southern France, which sounded so much closer than anywhere in England. But she found nothing of interest. And she had to remember the language problem. Sure, she was working at her

Spanish, but unless she could find somewhere which permitted her to teach in English, no one would be interested in taking her on. There wasn't a single suitable post advertised.

Her spirits had hit a new low by the time she pulled up her CV and began to update it. It sounded pretty good, actually, and she felt a little pride as she read what she'd achieved. It would be surprising if it didn't produce a couple of interviews, even if not in the places she would prefer.

Hours later, she closed the laptop and stood up, yawning widely. She'd fired off half a dozen applications, and feeling slightly better after that, she'd rechecked the interim version of her report, attached a few photographs and emailed it to the professor. Today, two important things had been accomplished.

She stood up, turning her attention to the Roman villa she was sure had been at the top of the hill, wondering if she could find evidence of its existence. She'd get a better idea later in the week.

Chapter 36

There was a buzz in the kitchen while they were eating the following evening, as everyone discussed the plan to grab the intruder.

"Just be careful," said Amancia when Chris sat down at her table. "We can't take the law into our own hands. We need to catch them, but we mustn't do any harm. And I don't want any of you hurt, either."

"Don't worry, I have a black belt in judo. And so does Carmen. We can look after ourselves."

"Even so. Just keep in mind what I say."

She'd got the impression that some of the young men were looking forward to a fight. It was scary how you could scratch the surface, and those basic instincts came to the fore. What if things got out of hand? But they had to find out what was going on, so she repeated her warnings and hoped there wouldn't be a problem.

By eleven, the site was quiet. Sebastian and Carmen had chosen to keep watch for the first hour of the rota they'd drawn up, followed by Chris and Rafa.

Waiting in her room, Amancia lay on her bed, fully dressed. It was a pity Peter was away today, so she couldn't discuss it with him. Had she been right to allow them to do this? What if things did go wrong? That inspector and his bloody report had pushed her into action that maybe she shouldn't be taking. The intruder might be armed. None of them had thought of that, but if he was, people could get hurt.

Unable to lie still a moment longer, she got up and walked about and then stared out the window onto blackness. She was probably going to lose her job. It nagged away at her, threatening her whole future. And it wasn't just about her. She cared about the students. She gave a wavering sigh that could easily turn into a sob if she let it. Why were things always so hard?

She could have forbidden them to go forward with this plan, but hazardous though it might be, it was a good idea, and she could see no other way of arriving at the truth. Thoughts whirled round and round in her head, giving no clear answers.

Max was so busy this week, catching up on missed work. She shouldn't...

It was coming up to midnight when she rang him.

"Did I wake you?"

"No. I wasn't asleep. I was thinking about you."

A rush of warmth spread through her. Their time together meant something to him. He cared about her.

"I...me too." She paused a moment, thinking how it was going to sound to him. "Max, can I tell you what's going on here at the dig?"

"What is it? Has something happened?"

She went through the inspector's visit and the arrival of the report.

"That's completely wrong. How can the man say such things?"

Amancia took a moment to reply, getting her thoughts in order. "I've had time to consider all of this. I actually thought at first that it was James, trying to undermine me by making things go wrong. It's not hard to imagine him doing it, and honestly, that would have been easier to accept. So anyway, to make sure, I rang Lizzie, and she said she'd seen him around in Bristol."

"Maybe he has hired someone, do you think?"

"I can't imagine that. He doesn't know anyone over here. It doesn't feel right. So, I looked again at the report. It's signed by the man who did the inspection. He was really unpleasant to me when he was here. It's an assassination of me, Max. Either he's working for someone who's opposed to what we're doing here…or he personally wants me off the site."

"Which means he wants your job."

It was so simple. Why hadn't she thought of that for herself?

"I…yes, I think it has to be something like that, but who would possibly want my job?"

"Someone who applied and was turned down, maybe at the same time as your predecessor."

"I suppose it's possible."

Shouts and running footsteps invaded the quiet.

"Wait, something's going on. I have to go."

"Be careful. I'm coming over."

****

Amancia slipped out of her room and hugged the wall as she headed toward the sounds. A scuffle was taking place, the clap and thud of punches reverberating around the site, then quiet. There was a flicker of movement, just a black shape against black, and she smelled the farmyard, maybe cows or pigs, and then something sharp punctured the skin of her forehead, at the same time as a heavy object cannoned into her, driving the breath from her body. She fell to the ground. She couldn't see anything but heard her assailant grunt. Then pounding footsteps hurried away.

She tried to pull herself into a sitting position. Warm liquid ran down into her eyes. Blood everywhere. She felt her forehead and found the source. He must have had some weapon in his hand. She slumped back as she lost consciousness.

****

Max ran to his truck and was on the road two minutes after he'd closed his phone. The headlights picked out a bright tunnel through the darkness. He should keep a lookout, might see the intruder running away down the road. What if Amancia was in danger? He couldn't bear the thought of that, and anxiety made him drive faster than he should.

She'd been concerned for the students, but he was beginning to know her; she was a determined woman, and he didn't trust her to keep away from a fight.

He turned into the car park and slammed on the brakes. His mouth was set in a grim smile as he remembered the night of the fire. Emergencies like this shouldn't be happening. A moment later, he was running toward the arcing torch beams and shouts.

A man lay face down, a student sitting on his legs, and another on his back, but as Max approached, they got up and pulled him around. It was just a boy, maybe only sixteen or seventeen, wiry, filthy, his face bruised and bloody. There'd been a fight.

Where was Amancia?

"We're going to call the police," said the tall guy with the ponytail. He was flushed, breathing deeply.

"Just a minute." Max turned to Maya. "Go and see if you can find Amancia. Please. I want to know nothing's happened to her." Then he watched as their captive was hauled to his feet. "Maybe he'll talk to us.

If we want information, it's better we ask before handing him over to the police."

The boy's mulish expression didn't promise much.

"Get off me." The lad shrugged out of their grip and gave Max a defiant glare.

"What were you doing here, on my land, in the middle of the night?"

"Nothing. I was just…looking."

"You'll be better off telling us. Otherwise, we'll take you down to the police in Zaragoza. It's no problem. I have my truck right here. Then you'd have to explain why you were here, stealing…"

"No, nada de policía. Y no estaba robando nada— papá me mataría."

"You're lucky *we* didn't kill you, never mind your dad," said Sebastian. The boy was speaking a rough country Spanish, but Sebastian didn't seem to have any problem understanding him.

"All he told me to do was break the lock, make sure you lot knew I'd been here."

"What for?" asked Chris.

"Dunno. He was in the bar where I drink. And he paid, so I did it. Two hundred euro up front, and he said another hundred when it was all finished."

"All what," said Max.

"Dunno. Five visits, that's all I know. And I did that so he can pay me now."

"Describe him."

"Describe?"

"What's he like. Big man, was he?"

"Nah, smaller'n me. Glasses, red beard."

There was a ripple of laughter, and someone said, "Sounds like a disguise, Seb. We'll never get him."

"Maybe we will." Leaning on Maya's arm, Amancia staggered into the circle, phone in her hand.

"Oh God, what's happened? He hit you?"

Max hurried across to her, but Amancia held him off. "No, no. Never mind me. I've got this!"

She opened up her phone and then the app which allowed her to listen to recordings, and she turned to the boy. "Do you recognize this voice?"

She played the last few seconds of the site tour she'd taken with Barriles. She'd been so incensed by the fact that he was recording her without asking permission and had grown increasingly angry at his unwarranted aggression. When his attention was on taking photographs, she'd grabbed the opportunity to set her own device to run. The setup was simple; she'd used it for a thousand things around the site before.

The boy didn't hesitate. "Yeah, that's him. That's the man I met in the bar."

"And did you set the fire for him?"

"*¿Un incendio? ¿Qué incendio?* I never. Told you what I did."

****

They let him go, once they had the details of the next meeting in the bar, which was to be in three days. It would give the opportunity to set a trap.

"I don't think he should be allowed to collect that money," said Amancia. But she was overruled. They'd all be hoping to catch the inspector red-handed.

"You trust that idiot not to give the game away?"

"Not really," said Max. "That's why I told him if he let on about what happened this evening, I'd make sure he'd never got the money. And he knows I know who he is, and I could still hand him over to the police.

I think it's enough to make him do what we want."

As the group broke up, Max turned to Amancia, who was holding a medicated pad to her forehead. "Are you feeling well enough to walk a little?"

She smiled at him and tucked her hand into the crook of his arm. "Thanks for coming, Max."

"What?—you thought I was just going to leave you to it? You really don't know me very well, do you?"

They were out of sight of the students now, and he kissed her. He studied her face and traced the outside of the cut with his finger. "How did this happen?"

"An accident. He didn't hit me deliberately. He came around the corner where I was hiding and had something in his hand."

"Yeah, bolt cutters. Probably planned to break open the lock. You sure you're going to be okay?"

"I'm fine. The cut bled a lot, but it's not serious. I'll clean up in a minute. How will we handle this?"

"I'll get in touch with Andrés, the professor, and tell him what's happened."

"And the bar?"

"I know a man in the police. We'll sort it out."

The knot in Amancia's stomach began to loosen. If Max could help, it would make all the difference.

Chapter 37

Amancia was increasingly impressed as she watched the film on Wednesday afternoon. She should be giving it her full attention, but thoughts of the inspection report wouldn't let her relax. At some stage, the professor was going to read it, perhaps already had. It came from an official body. A cold feeling washed over her. What if he took it at face value and didn't allow her to explain? This could derail her whole future. She had to explain that there was more than one way to interpret events.

And then, there was Max. How would he react when she told him where she might be getting a job back in the UK? Perhaps he would feel that she wasn't interested enough in him to stay around. That would be so wrong. But making no effort to secure a post would also be wrong.

She forced herself to pay attention to what was happening on screen. The photographer was excellent, but Pablo was clearly a brilliant editor too, and the people he'd interviewed presented well. Chris came across as serious and committed, which he was, of course. Rafa's genuine enthusiasm for reconstructing the artifacts from tiny fragments of pottery shone through, and the obsessive nature of the work soon became evident. Both these men were young enough for students to be able to imagine themselves in those roles. Alexandra was just as effective as Peter had suggested she would be. A few shorter snippets added to the feeling that everybody's contribution was important. Even Maya's blog was referenced.

She frowned as she watched and listened. She had to bring a critical mind to this because her input could be significant, but when they started the discussion later, she suggested only one or two minor changes which they could implement without difficulty.

"I'm very impressed, Pablo. Honestly, I didn't think something of this standard could be achieved."

What had Alexandra and Sebastian made of it? They'd been tasked with looking at it purely from the point of view of a student trying to decide whether the archaeology course was for them. A lively discussion broke out between them and Pablo as she headed for the door, responding to a phone call.

"Max?"

"Have you finished with the film?"

"Just this minute. Pablo's clearing up now, but they're still talking."

"Come across now if you can. Let's bring the tour of the vineyard forward. I have a little free time."

"So you thought of me."

"I did, *querida*. Who else?"

The caress in his voice made her shiver.

"I won't be long." She went back to the store where they'd shown the film. "Pablo, I have to go, but as far as I'm concerned, it's fabulous."

"Thank you. I hoped you'd say that."

She changed her shoes and left the site via the field, crunching into dry soil. The grapes were ripe now, fat and juicy. They looked ready for picking already. How did they know when it was exactly the right moment to do it?

As she crested the rise through the trees, she saw Max on the road below walking toward the house. The bandage had gone from his hand.

He came to a halt, and as she descended the bank, he stretched out the undamaged hand to prevent her from sliding down the last few feet. "Perfect timing." He put his arms around her and kissed her. It was lovely to be held close to him. She drew in the warmth emanating from his skin, that carried the woody notes of his own particular perfume.

"Let me show you around," he said, turning back toward the farm buildings, "and then we can have coffee with my mother."

He took her hand, and they entered a smart, modern barn, a cathedral to wine. A central aisle split the building in half, with massive steel barrels to right and left, and one area where smaller oak barrels on wooden stands remained. Were these left from the original process of winemaking at the vineyard? The floor was concrete, with channels running to drains on both sides. Everything gleamed, and it smelled clean, but in the background was the nutty aroma of wine.

"This is fabulous. It all looks scientific and nothing like the vineyard I worked on in France as a teenager."

"Things have moved on. And it's mostly new because everything here had been neglected for a long time, so we had to start again with the equipment. This will be our first full harvest, though we're still clearing land and rehabilitating old vines. Let me introduce my head man and partner, Alejo. We were just discussing how to welcome group visits."

"Groups? You mean people will come round…like tourists on holiday?"

"Yes, that's the marketing advice I've had. We've not done wine tasting for visitors before, so we've been trying to learn what people would expect to be offered."

They rounded a corner and came on a balding man in a white lab coat, engaged with what looked like laboratory equipment. They shook hands.

"A laboratory is exactly what it is," he said, when Amancia commented. "Would you like to taste?"

"Very much. Is it only red wine?"

"We have both red and white," said Max, "but it's mainly red. Many of the vines we would use to produce white wine perished. We've replaced them, but it will be some time before we get any wine. Have you ever done a wine tasting?"

"No, I haven't. Is there a special way to taste?"

The bald man chuckled. "Definitely, or Max and I would be drunk when we did the tasting which we have to do from time to time."

He placed glasses on the top of a long wooden table and picked up a couple of bottles of wine, one each of red and white. "The first thing to note is that you sip, not gulp. And don't swallow, hold it in your mouth so that the flavors come through the nose."

He poured a small amount of red wine into each of the large wineglasses. Max's hand brushed Amancia's as he handed one over, and heat pulsed through her body, as if she were getting drunk before she'd even begun the tasting. He smiled down at her. "We use large glasses so we can swirl the wine a little like this."

"What exactly am I looking for?"

"Ah, how nice to have an intelligent question," said

Alejo. "You want to note the body and warmth, the smell, the sweetness or bitterness, the tannins and acidity. And, of course, the taste."

"That's a lot to remember. Plus, I'm not sure what all of it is. And you mentioned warmth." She touched the bottle. "But this is quite cool."

"True. But a residual warmth in your mouth will indicate high alcohol and probably a provenance from a warm climate."

"I'm going to make a mess of this," she said to Max, but Alejo hadn't finished. "Gradually, you learn to keep the list in your head and work through it, one item at a time. Now take a sip and hold the wine in your mouth." He wrote down the list of words. "Only when you've considered each of those points do you swallow, so take your time. Then you can judge the warmth left in the mouth afterward."

Carefully following his instructions, Amancia finally swallowed the wine. "It's delicious!"

"Excellent," said Max. "So, what conclusions have you come to?"

"Oh, that's unfair. I really don't know what I'm talking about."

"Nonsense. I want to know what you think."

She thought for a moment, looking down at the list. "Okay. It smells like heaven, quite fruity and er...heady. It's a dark color and has body, if that means it's not a thin wine. I don't find it acidic, but it's not too sweet either."

"Very good. Go on."

She wrinkled her nose, thinking. "Definitely a cherry flavor, and something that could be vanilla. Is that possible?"

"Oh, I think we'll turn you into a professional wine-taster. You've pretty much picked out the things that make our wine special. Can you still taste it?"

"Yes, the flavors are still in my mouth. What does that tell you?"

"It's called the finish. The longer it lasts, the higher the quality."

"So, in theory, the better the finish, the less wine you'd need to drink to get the effect?"

"That is a theory," said Alejo, "I guess, because it tends to mean it's more alcoholic, but I don't think it works like that with most people. They just like it more and drink more."

They went through the process once again with the white wine, and then, as Alejo moved away, Max poured out two glasses of red.

"Oh, I can't have any more. I feel drunk already!"

His eyes crinkled at the corners, and he looked at her. "I don't think you can be, Amancia, at least not on two small sips of wine. It must be something else. Here's to us." His eyes had darkened, and he'd moved closer. She wanted to melt into his arms, but Alejo was just a few feet away.

Instead, she gazed at him and held out her glass. "To us. And to your vineyard."

She sipped, holding the liquid against her tongue, and he smiled. "You can drink it properly now."

"This is delicious. You must want to drink it with every meal."

"It's not a good idea to get too keen on your own produce, particularly when it's alcoholic. I tend to be sparing and save drinking for special occasions." He looked again into her eyes and held her gaze. "But then, that's what this is," he added.

Putting down his glass a few minutes later, he placed his hand on the small of her back and steered her around to the barn door.

Chapter 38

Amancia had promised to return in time for supper. "I'll drive you back."

They climbed into Max's truck and got on the way.

"It's been great to see what you do here, but there's one thing I don't understand about the vines. There's no irrigation. I noticed there are no pipes or anything like that, yet they look healthy. And those grapes you showed me were plump and luscious looking. How do you do it?"

"We grow them dry. These are mostly old vines, and their roots reach far down into the soil. If you water constantly, the roots stay near the surface and then you're caught in an irrigation cycle because the vines will die if you stop. We can do emergency watering from bowsers if the season is exceptionally dry, but so far, I haven't had to do that."

"Sounds weird that anyone bothers to water in the first place."

"It's about the yield. We have a smaller yield than the big commercial vineyards, but the grapes are much sweeter with a more intense flavor, as you noticed a little while ago. And watering to produce those huge crops—ultimately, you deplete the soil, and then you're into fertilizers in a big way." He maneuvered through the gate into the car park by the dig and stopped the engine. He didn't move, staring out the windscreen.

"What is it? Max?"

"I have something important to tell you. I'm sorry, but you're not going to like it."

Her heart gave a thud. What did he mean? Hadn't there been enough trouble?

"Remember I mentioned we had a few problems in the vineyard?"

"Yes, I should have asked, but I was too wrapped up in my own affairs."

After a moment, he explained that the prolonged high temperature was damaging the grapes.

"I thought that's what grapes need—heat and sun."

"Not temperatures like these. The grapes get sunburned, and it changes everything: acidity, flavor, alcohol content, the nature of the wine we produce."

"What is it you have to tell me?"

"I have to bring forward the harvest by two weeks. That means—"

"That we have to vacate the site two weeks early."

It was only the middle of August, and he was telling her they'd have to wrap things up. Her anger and disappointment made her want to hit out. How could this happen now? All that stress about the inspection, and now this. "When did you decide this, Max? Couldn't you have told me earlier?" She hated herself. She was casting around for someone to blame for the situation, and Max was right there. She gripped the door handle, her knuckles showing white through the skin of her hand.

She took a deep breath and slowly relaxed her fingers, as he continued. "I hoped it wasn't going to be necessary and held off, but last night I had to decide. I'm sorry. I know it's hard to accept, but this is my livelihood. I cannot risk a failed harvest if there's any chance that I can do something about it."

This was entirely reasonable. Of course it was. She swallowed, in control of herself now. "How will you get the workers to come early?"

"Some will be available, but there will be a problem. You're right."

"It's a shock. Leave me to think about how I'm going to manage this with the team, all right?"

"Yeah, talk to me please, Amancia. Don't be angry on your own. When shall I see you again?"

"When I've had a chance to speak to the team, and we've got a plan."

She got out before he could come round to open her door. "It's okay, Max. I'll ring you when I've worked out what we're going to do."

The rush of anger, the sense of unfairness had surprised her with their intensity, even though it didn't make sense to think like that because there was no point in being angry with the climate. All the pleasure of the wine-tasting had gone from the afternoon. And she hated that she'd reacted badly. Though she'd said little, she knew he'd picked up on it.

Now she had to tell the students they'd be wrapping up early, a completely different topic from the one she'd intended. She waited until everyone had eaten, which only made her feel worse because it gave her time to imagine their disappointment.

Sebastian was the first to react. "*¡Qué lástima!* But it means I can fit in an extra holiday before term starts."

Others seemed philosophical, too. They soon found a positive side and went off to their laptops to change travel reservations.

"What about you, Peter? Max has said you and I can keep our rooms for a while if fewer workers come. Will you stay on?"

"Just long enough to help you shut down the site. Then I'll get back."

With the students, the news seemed to draw a line under their stay. Six elected to remain as long as they'd be allowed on-site, including Chris, Maya, and Rafa. Among the younger ones, to her surprise, were Mandy and Carmen. And the last was Carlos, the boy from the village. Those remaining made up a good group. Maybe it would be possible to get a little more sitework done.

"You said that not all the workers will be able to make the earlier date. What if we helped out?" said Rafa. "I've always fancied the idea of bringing in the grape harvest."

Surprised the suggestion came from Rafa, Amancia said, "I'll pass it on to Max. Are you all agreed?"

"Yeah," said Carmen. "Great way to end things."

Amancia was baffled for the moment. Was she the only one who wanted to continue digging? Somewhat disillusioned, she reminded herself that they were young and would see things differently. And working for a living hadn't started yet for them. This had been a nice summer break, and now they'd go back to their families and their studies.

****

Max was working through a batch of emails to people who usually made up his harvest workforce and had already received several refusals, when the phone rang. He'd wanted to talk to Amancia, but she'd told him to wait until she'd spoken to everyone, and he'd understood her need to do that. "Are you all right?"

"Not great, Max—but I understand why you've had to do it. Anyway, we may be able to help you."

"What are you proposing?"

"Look, I've got six students who want to work for you, to help collect the grapes. Is that of interest?"

So, she hadn't completely given up on him.

"That's wonderful news, *querida*. And the answer's yes, I'd really appreciate the extra help. Please don't take this so hard."

"How can I not, Max? Do you know how much this means to me?"

He was beginning to understand that. It was so sad that he had to be the one to inflict this wound on her.

"I never expected to finish the dig, but we haven't even tackled all the possibilities we've uncovered. And now, I'll have to leave, and I'll never get the chance."

"Listen, *querida,* try to understand how important it is for the vineyard to get the harvest in. I absolutely would not do this otherwise. And you and a couple of others can carry on working, although once your students have left, I don't think you should live alone on-site. The seasonal workers can be a rough bunch."

"Okay. I'm being such a diva, I'd almost forgotten you said we could work on for a while. I'm sorry. I'll get over it."

****

August was nearly at an end, and Max's days now stretched into the late evening as he approached the harvest period. Amancia worked every day until it was too dark to see. It was hard that she couldn't spend time with him, but when she finally made it into bed, intent on thinking about him, she fell very quickly into a dreamless sleep, only waking up to the sound of her alarm.

For several days, the whole team had been working extended hours on the various grids, ignoring the heat, keen to move things on as far as they could before everything shut down.

Amancia, Chris, and Maya continued digging downward, and Carlos progressed beyond being the wheelbarrow man, hard physical work they now all shared, hauling buckets of earth up out of the stairwell, and then carting it across to the tip. She needed a break, though work was a good antidote to all the things that were worrying her, allowing her to escape into a different world.

Max had told her he'd contacted the professor about the inspector, but he'd had no reply. He, Chris, and Sebastian had gone to the bar where Tomás, the intruder, was due to receive his money, but the man who'd hired him had not turned up. Tomás was furious, convinced it was Max's doing, and they were very disappointed not to unmask the man who'd set it up.

"I think Tomás has forgotten that what he was doing was illegal," Max said. "And also, that there's no reason why the man would pay out now. That wasn't a very intelligent arrangement he agreed to. Unfortunately, we have no way to find this man."

The good progress on-site went some way to stopping Amancia's endless mulling over the conversation she'd had with Max a few days earlier. She flushed at the thought that she had shown so little understanding. How selfish she'd been. They were talking every day on the phone, although neither had the time to meet. But she was going to make it up to him.

Chapter 39

Amancia watched her team at work. Six days had brought about a transformation of the riverside grid. It was great they'd now uncovered enough of the site to show its importance. When information filtered out, there would be many visits from interested parties and approaches from media. Though she had little experience of this, she knew how it worked. As she climbed out of the trench, her phone rang.

"*Doctora Harding, buenas tardes. Soy la secretaria del profesor Hernández.*"

She felt a spike of fear. He must have returned, and he'd have read the report and would now want to discuss it, and the work on-site. He'd be angry and disappointed. Adrenaline flooded her system, and already, she was thinking through the evidence to defend herself against what he might have to say. It wasn't only that she'd let herself down. What was much worse was that she'd failed Max as well, because he'd been the one to take her on. That was a painful thought.

"Could you come to the university? The professor had an accident while working in Chile, and he finds it difficult to travel at the moment."

"Of course. When would be convenient? *Mi colega está ausente. Soy la única responsable aquí.*"

Amancia held on while the secretary spoke with her boss, who said he was happy for her to leave the site unsupervised for the afternoon. She took a deep breath to calm her nerves. Finally, she was going to meet the real professor.

****

A flight of shallow stone steps led up into the modern building where Professor Hernández had his office. Doors opened automatically as Amancia approached, and a few moments later, she was ushered into his presence by the young woman with whom she'd spoken.

A dark-haired man with an aquiline nose was seated on a couch, his foot resting on a stool. Amancia was relieved when he greeted her with a smile. She smiled back and went over to shake hands.

"I fell down a waterhole we uncovered on the site in Chile. Or rather, my fall uncovered the hole. This was very embarrassing for me," he said ruefully, "since part of my work there was advising on-site safety. But maybe it served to illustrate the point I was making."

He laughed, and the tiny lines at the corners of his eyes crinkled. Although he must be ten years older than Max, Amancia saw how the two men might get on well.

"Tell me about the site. I've read your report and looked at the photos—very good ones, by the way—but I'd like to hear what you think."

"Did you, er…did you read the report from the historical society?"

"I did. Please don't distress yourself, Doctora Harding. There are a lot of reasons why I should discount it, the main one being the name of the writer." He smiled, clearly wanting to put her at ease. "He worked for this department, but we let him go after an unfortunate incident. I can't go into more detail, but I advise you to put it behind you. The report will have no impact on you." But of course, it already had.

He smiled at her again. "I was much more interested in reading what you had to say."

She couldn't believe how differently that made her feel. It had been right to get her report to him early, but she still needed his approval. "I'm so relieved, *señor*. Do you want to ask me any questions about it?"

For the next hour, they talked through what had been done, the approach she had taken, and how successful she believed it to have been. She was surprised at how probing his questions were and decided it must be because of the inspection report. He had to make his own assessment. But this didn't worry her. She knew exactly why she'd taken certain decisions and where she hoped they'd lead.

"We've got to a really exciting point, but I'm not sure how much farther we'll be able to take it. It's such a pity that we are having to shut down early—another fortnight or three weeks, and I feel we'd have been so much further on. There's quite a lot of disappointment."

"For you, too, I'm sure."

"Yes, very much so. I've talked it through with Max, but I agree we can't allow it to impact on his business. He's been more than generous with his support." The professor was nodding, allowing her to tell him more. "I can't see any way to keep the site going this year. Of course, next summer, I'm sure there'll be many people who'll want to get involved. In Europe, so many sites have been dug out that a find like this is truly exciting."

"Indeed, it is, and this is something I'd like to discuss with you."

That was a surprise. What did he have in mind?

"May I ask your plans for the coming year?"

Amancia felt the heat rise in her cheeks.

"I'm afraid I…I got rather carried away with the site and only recently began making applications, so I have nothing definite yet. You are aware I'm not attached to any university at the moment?"

"Yes, that's what interested me—why someone with your qualifications and obvious passion for the subject, has not been snapped up."

"Thank you," she said, flushing again. Then she found herself giving him a shortened version of how she'd arrived at this point. "But you're right. I am passionate about it."

"I wonder, could I prevail upon you to stay? I'm keen to keep the work moving forward on the site. You'll have noticed we are trying to attract high-quality students with the film that's just been made. This is all good for the prestige of the university, and if we can add to our website that there's an active site just a few kilometers away—well, I can see that working well for recruitment. We newer universities have to think about these things, or our students are disadvantaged."

"Yes, I heard about El Forau de la Tuta."

The discovery of what was possibly an entire Roman city just a few miles away had put the main Zaragoza University way out in front when it came to taking on students of archaeology. La Nueva Universidad was playing catch up. "But what we have here changes everything."

Could she persuade him to offer her paid work? This could help her in the short term.

"Please tell me more about what you intend."

"There'll be at least another month, maybe two, during which work can be done on-site before winter sets in. I can't offer you a full-time post, but we need someone involved with the excavation throughout the year. A twenty-five percent salary to cover everything you might do linked to the site may be possible, and then I could try to assign you a couple of classes, to make it up to fifty percent. I'm sure other opportunities will present themselves during the year."

Amancia was tempted, but how could she live on a half salary or even less if he didn't find any classes for her? Academics weren't that highly paid, particularly at the lower end of the hierarchy, and she'd done no research at all on the costs of accommodation. Her mouth was so dry she didn't think she could speak, but before she allowed herself to get carried away by the possibilities, she said, "There is one problem, *señor*. My Spanish isn't good enough to teach a class."

They'd spoken in English right from the start. He wouldn't be considering it if he'd heard her faltering Spanish.

"My secretary said she was very impressed by your Spanish, particularly as you were speaking on the telephone at the time, but don't worry, I'm not relying on her assessment. All our students have to raise their level of English. We advertise this as an advantage of doing our courses. And, to achieve that, we teach a percentage of many subject classes in English. In fact, we often struggle to find Spanish archaeologists whose English is good enough."

That had not occurred to her.

"This is so much the sort of post I was looking for, mixing site work with teaching in my prime subject area. But I'm not sure I could find somewhere affordable to live on a half salary."

The professor smiled.

"Well, we might be able to sort something out for you. I have a young colleague who's gone to the US for six months. Unfortunately, we've already taken someone on to cover his work, but his flat is still available." He handed her a sheet of paper. Below the photograph of an attractive building, there was an estate agent's description of the flat. "I know it's short term, but I'm sure we could come to some agreement with him. I think he might accept a lower rent to have someone take care of it."

"Do you really think he would?"

"They got him to bring forward his start date to take part in a project, so he's already left for the States and didn't have time to find a tenant. It's in a good area. While you take a moment to think about it, I'll ask Juliana if she'll bring us some coffee."

He hauled himself to his feet with a grunt and limped out of the room on crutches, leaving Amancia to consider the opportunities the post offered. She didn't want to work in the north of England, which would mean weeks of being separated from Max. She didn't like the idea of frequent flights, and…well, there wasn't anything attractive about that post. Would they even offer it to her? It probably wasn't sensible but…

"I'll take it," she said when he came back. Juliana brought the coffee. She took a huge gulp and spluttered as the hot liquid burned the back of her throat.

"You've made the right decision, Doctora Harding." He shook her hand.

"Sorry." She wiped tears from her eyes and smiled.

"I do believe I have."

"I'll email you information about the work. Talk to my secretary about a formal acceptance of the post and the accommodation."

"Thank you, Professor. If that's all, I should go. I have a lot of work to do over the next few days."

"Of course."

She stood up to leave. As she reached the door, he said, "How did you get on with my friend, Max?"

"Very well," she said, keeping a straight face. "He's been so helpful, very charming."

He smiled. "Good to hear. He can be difficult to get to know."

Amancia wore a wide grin as she walked away down the corridor. Her whole life had turned around. She almost skipped as she headed for the foyer. The next few months were going to be very interesting.

Chapter 40

Two weeks seemed to pass in moments. The days were frenetic as they began to clear the site. Despite working until late every evening, Max remembered to send over workmen to erect a small shed for equipment. Amancia hadn't yet told him about the job. She wanted to do it face-to-face, but there was no time to meet. To free up the common room, she made numerous trips into the city, the university minibus bulging with boxes.

At the farewell party, she went in search of Maya. "I wanted to catch up before you leave."

"You'll be pleased to know I've submitted my thesis, *and* I applied for teacher training. My mum says I got the acceptance this morning."

"Congratulations, Maya! I think it's a good decision. You had a real rapport with those children. I'd say they recognized the teacher in you straight away. You must be very happy."

"I am, but I'll be apart from Javier."

Amancia had completely forgotten about the romance which had started during the children's visit. She sipped her cola, considering. "That's going to be tough. Is he trying to get a job in England?"

"He's started applying. Fingers crossed."

Elena joined them. "What about you, Amancia? Are you going back to Bristol?"

"No, I've got a post at the university here. I may

even get the chance to work a little more on the site."

"Oh, I'm so envious."

Peter approached. "Just a reminder you may need to drive us into the city tomorrow, Amancia. A bus is ordered, but a lot of us will be getting on that plane, and we may have to lean on you." He was leaving at seven the next day with most of the students. He gave her a hug. "It's been a pleasure working with you. We've got on very well together."

"A pleasure for me, as well. I'll make sure to look you up when I'm back in Bristol."

A few toasts and then, still early, the festivities broke up. The next afternoon, the first harvest workers would move in.

In the morning, a black minibus arrived to take all the departing travelers, letting her off the hook, and by midmorning, a team of cleaners was on-site.

Everything was transformed. Work had already begun on the harvest, and the once-silent countryside reverberated with the engines of trucks pulling the first trailers filled with the hand-picked grapes. Power tools whirred and clanged. It was hard to throw off the feeling of anticlimax.

Amancia was not going to work on the harvest. Trowel in hand, she stood looking down at the excavation. Instead of dry soil and mounds of earth, she saw the students hard at work, the boys who had visited with Javier, Pablo and the filmmakers consulting their light meters and calculating shots. This deep quiet brought tears to her eyes, but she had no reason to be sad. She was here in Spain for the next few months, and she was close to Max.

"What about me, Amancia? What would you like

me to do?'"

She'd forgotten that Carlos wasn't yet strong enough to do the heavy manual work of the harvest; taking the wheelbarrow to the tip had pushed him to his limits. "You'll be working with me now."

Her phone rang. "Doctora Harding?"

It was the professor's secretary. "I have the keys to the flat. Would you like to pick them up?"

The minibus was still at her disposal. Her excitement at this next stage chased away the feelings of disappointment about the closure. Anyway, it wasn't really closing.

"Right, Carlos. I have to go into Zaragoza. You're in charge now."

****

With that lovely feeling of expectation that accompanies not quite knowing what the next step is going to be like, Amancia clutched the keys in her pocket as she left the university. She walked to the desirable old town area of Zaragoza where the apartment was located, passing the central market and various entrances to buildings with residential floors above street level. Flanked by venerable five-story apartment blocks dating from two centuries earlier, her target was a narrow Art Deco infill. The apartment was on the fourth floor, and there was no lift.

The building entrance was gorgeous, an austere, pale polished stone, very impressive. She keyed in the code to open the stylish outer doors, which had panes of glass set in brass, everything gleaming, with sunlight reflecting off the beveled edges, throwing a rainbow of colors across the floor of the lofty hall. She entered. A powerful scent of magnolia suggested the cleaners had made a recent visit.

To the left, a door led to an undercroft where tenants kept buggies and bicycles. A secondhand bike could be useful for getting around.

When she arrived on the top landing outside a set of double doors painted a smart dark blue, she was breathing only slightly harder than usual. She entered directly into a narrow sitting room. The only window was in the ceiling, though there was plenty of natural light. She frowned at the realization; having a view of the outside was important to her.

The room was simply furnished, and with good taste: grey sofa, low table, a couple of bookcases, half occupied with the owner's books, a rug in an abstract design of red and blue. It worked rather well. A huge TV screen was mounted on the wall over the only other piece of furniture, a shallow drawer unit you'd usually find in a hallway, a clever way to make the room look bigger. She moved on to the kitchen.

Cupboards, predominantly dark grey, were crammed into every available space. It was all a bit masculine for her taste, but smart, and a couple of houseplants would soon soften the effect.

In the large bedroom, she sat on the huge bed. There was room for a desk and chair. She'd be able to do more work in this quiet room than in the claustrophobic office at the university. Here the roof was exposed, with beams starting just above the bedhead and rising to twelve feet or more at the apex. And a narrow floor-to-ceiling window opened onto the parapet. She gazed at the street leading away from her building. The view was great, down between blocks of apartments to trees and a city square in the distance.

A minimalist shower room completed the tour. There were white tiles, silver edges everywhere, and a showerhead big enough to suggest the pressure was good. It was all very, very clean, essential as far as she was concerned. She walked around taking photos and then rang Hernández's secretary.

"I'd like to take it, Juliana."

"Great. So, hang on to those keys. Could you sign some papers tomorrow? At about ten?"

"I'll be there."

She rang her mother. "I've accepted a job here in Spain, Mum. And I'm in my new apartment right now."

"Have you any pictures I can look at?" Her mother sounded excited at the news.

"Hang on." She placed her phone on the loudspeaker, and still talking, took a few photos. Then she sent them, and they chatted for a while, catching up.

"What's made you stay, Amancia, apart from continuing to work on the site, that is? That must have been a big attraction."

Her mum was so transparent. Amancia had known she wouldn't be able to resist asking. Mum knew her better than anyone else in the family. They'd grown so close after the death of her father.

"Well, that is a huge incentive. But I think you've guessed that I've met someone. It feels good when we're together, but I'm so selfish, I'm lucky he's still bothering with me." She told her mother about bringing forward the harvest, and the way she'd reacted.

"Well, it doesn't sound as if that's a problem, as you're still talking to each other. You've always been very focused, Amancia. It's a good quality, but maybe sometimes, you should think about moderating it."

"I will, I promise. And I'll make sure you get to meet him soon."

A little reassured, Amancia brought the conversation to a close. It did feel good. And over the next few weeks, once she'd settled in here in the city, and the harvest was over at the vineyard, they'd have a chance to get to know each other better.

It had happened so fast, this relationship. She probably hadn't been ready, but equally, she hadn't been able to fight the attraction, something she'd recognized the moment she met him. A few weeks ago, she'd still been thinking in terms of flirting, then maybe sex—definitely sex. She'd shied away from anything more. But as soon as they'd had sex, she'd wanted commitment, and that made this relationship very different. She'd changed, and Max had, too.

She rang him late in the evening, and they talked for a long time, arranging for her to visit the house. And to see each other. The harvest was now in full swing, but he'd free up some time on Friday evening.

She gave Lizzie a ring but had to leave her friend a message. It would have been great to stay the night in her new flat, but there were still students living on-site. She needed to be there.

Chapter 41

Amancia ran her fingers along the stonework just above floor level. It was interesting the way it cut across the basement, bedded in modern concrete. It didn't mean the house hadn't been constructed on a part of ancient Roman foundations, but there was nothing specific to support the theory. She stepped back, a little disappointed because she'd built up her hopes.

As she skirted a pile of stacked, broken chairs, a movement, just glimpsed, startled her. What had she seen? When she focused, her own image stared back at her from an enormous, dust-covered mirror with a beautiful gold-painted frame, the glass badly spotted by damp. It dated back a couple of hundred years, at a guess. She wanted so much to see something to support the idea that this house stood on Roman foundations, and now she smiled ruefully—an image in a mirror wasn't going to do that, even if it had frightened the life out of her. She was much too fanciful.

What a pity the floor was concrete. Breaking open a corner would be useful, to see if it was just a thin layer covering the old Roman tiles she longed to find. In truth, the floor could have been covered with different materials many times over the centuries. That such a floor existed was a real possibility, but she would need permission to do an investigation like that. It would have to wait.

"*Señorita.*"

Lost in speculation, she jumped at the voice and found herself face-to-face with the young man, Fer. Max said he had an office in the main house and worked on the estate accounts. However, he seemed to carry out many other functions as well, one of which was to assist Consuela.

"*Señorita, por favor. La señora le invita a usted a tomar café con ella.*"

She smiled and thanked him. A cup of coffee would be welcome, and they could catch up. She followed him up the stairs and into the sitting room.

"Tell me more about the basement," Consuela said, after Amancia had enquired about her health. Amancia shared her thoughts, but the older woman knew nothing of what might be underneath the concrete. She poured coffee and offered a delicate pastry that oozed chocolate. "You'll need this after your hard work."

Amancia hadn't really worked hard, but she wasn't going to turn down Maria's exquisite concoction. It reminded her of the woman's husband.

"He's back home recovering now, but Maria still finds the time to bake."

"Oh, what will he do now?"

"Max had a talk with him to see if he wants to go back to his old job. They're trying to find something that's less strenuous because it will be a while before he's back on form. He's only forty-three, so he won't want to retire, and anyway, I don't think they could manage without his wage. I'm sure we'll find something for him as the vineyard expands, but I think we'll also have to take someone on."

It was good to hear that Max was trying to fix

something for him.

"So," she said, laying down her plate a while later and licking the last of the chocolate off her fingers, "I wonder if I could have a look outside now?"

"Go ahead. Go anywhere you want. Max knows you're here, and he said he'll finish work in about an hour. You'll wait for him, won't you?"

Her heart gave a little flip. She would be there.

****

Sometimes, Amancia had to wait until she slotted into the right mental groove. Or something would alert her to a shape or the placing of an object or a structure that sent her digging into her store of knowledge about Roman construction, things she might not even notice on another occasion.

Outside, she found herself seeing things differently from when she'd arrived two hours earlier. She walked around, scrutinizing the wall surrounding the courtyard. Knee-high, it was composed of stone blocks that were brick-shaped but with the square end facing forward into the space. If this were a piece of Roman wall, the other end of each block would be narrower, tapering so that the stone keyed neatly and securely into place.

On the far side of the entrance, a small section of wall had fallen, maybe knocked over by a vehicle. She examined one of the blocks, noting how it narrowed slightly from front to back, and she felt a surge of anticipation; the stone in her hands held the distinctive marks of Roman workmanship. She checked two more of the blocks, examining them from all angles, her excitement mounting.

She wanted to rush down the hill to the barns and tell Max. But instead, she sat on the wall among the

281

lengthening shadows with a block on her knee and tried to work out how it fitted in with the house.

"What have you found, Amancia? You look completely lost in thought." Consuela wheeled herself out onto the raised apron that fronted the house, and intent on joining her guest, she descended the ramp they'd created at one end. "I can see you're onto something. We should have thought about investigating this building a long time ago."

"There was no reason why you should. It's only the discovery of the site by the river that's made me consider these possibilities. But I found this." She showed her the heavy piece of stone and explained about Roman construction methods. "There are two others just like this lying loose over there. I do truly believe there could have been a Roman villa here."

They talked a while longer, and then Consuela, excited by Amancia's enthusiasm, went back into the house. "I'll do some more research among my husband's papers."

As Amancia returned to the wall, a text arrived.

—*Going to be visiting Javier.*— This was followed by a clutch of pink hearts. —*Okay if I drop in to see you in a few days?*—

—*Let me know when you're coming.*—

It would be good to catch up with Maya. It sounded as if things were progressing with her boyfriend. Smiling, she put her phone away. Caught up in her own affairs, Amancia had paid little attention to the young woman's romance with the Spanish teacher. Now as Max drove into the courtyard, she forgot the girl again.

She'd reacted so selfishly when he'd told her they'd have to bring the harvest forward. By the time the truck came to a stop, she was hurrying across to him, and the moment he got out, she threw her arms around his neck. Her heart was beating so fast, it felt as if it would burst out of her chest. He pulled her close, and they kissed. "You've forgiven me," he murmured, his lips in her hair.

"I'm the one who needs to be forgiven. I'm so ashamed of myself. You couldn't do anything different about the harvest."

"You were disappointed."

"Yes, and I acted like a spoiled child. I am sorry."

He kissed her again and chased away her fears. The strength in his arms, the warmth of his body, the sweet persuasiveness of his lips easily triumphed over the excitement of her discovery. But eventually, they drew apart, and hand in hand, they went to sit by the pile of stones. The sun was going down, and the air had grown a little cooler.

"Max, I've found out something about the house."

"Tell me what you've discovered."

Her enthusiasm bubbled over as she explained. "This wall has got to be of Roman origin. I don't think anyone would transport that sort of material here from elsewhere just to construct a garden wall. You know the history of the house, Max. Is it a possibility?—that someone just collected stones that were lying around the site to construct this wall? I'm trying to read the signs. Oh, I wish I could look down on it all. The land so often reveals things which have lain buried for centuries, but you'd need to see it from the air to get a true impression of what was here."

"Let's go and look at my house. What you've said is making me think of the way it's constructed."

"Your house, Max. I thought…"

"You thought I lived here, but I don't. Come on, I'll show you."

He took her arm and guided her through the metal gate where the garden wall met the trees. As they walked along, there were more signs of long-ago construction, lumps of stone pushing up through the earth in relatively straight lines. Foundations—these were the foundations of several buildings. She was dizzy with the possibilities.

They emerged from the trees, and she caught her breath; how enchanting this was. What a lovely place to come at the end of a long, hot day. The stretch of water, a swimming pool, was a vast, oblong basin, lined with a subtle mosaic that avoided the obligatory blue. Even that chimed in with Roman design.

"This pool is magnificent."

"And twentieth century, I assure you."

A long, single-story pavilion with four columns, that supported an over-sized and elaborate triangular pediment, stood to the right of the pool. The building itself was small, extending to either side of the portico, each part containing a single window.

"I don't believe it. It's…it's like a fairy tale."

"I hoped you'd like it. It's certainly not Roman, and it needs restoration. An ancestor enjoyed creating this a couple of centuries ago, when garden buildings like this were popular."

"Oh yes, a folly. There are lots in England. Is it fit to live in?"

"Someone installed a bathroom and kitchen about fifty years ago, at the same time as the pool was constructed, but it's not been improved since."

"Do you think they might have built on the foundations of an older building?"

"Possibly, yes, but I know nothing about it. It's up to you to find the evidence, my sweet searcher after the truth." He bent his head to kiss her. "My traveler into the distant past."

She laughed. "That'll be easy to achieve then."

"If there's something here, I'm sure you'll find it." They'd arrived at a bench placed close to the water. "Would you like a drink?"

"Maybe some white wine. Yours, of course."

"Sit here, and I'll bring it out."

Amancia took the glass he held out to her a few moments later, and as he sat down, she said, "I need to tell you something."

"What is it?"

"I guess I'm concerned about what you might think about this. We haven't discussed things—"

"I know, I know—we have to work something out. I really don't want you to walk out of my life, but bringing the harvest forward has taken up all my time. You do know I care for you very much, Amancia, don't you?" He landed a soft kiss on her lips. "I've missed you over the past weeks. I can't just let you go. I hope you haven't accepted some post back in the UK. It'll be so hard for us if you do that. Of course, I know you have to be able to work, but—"

"But that's just what I wanted to talk about, Max. I have accepted a post, but I'm not going back to the UK."

"To the US? Please don't say that."

"No, of course not." She smiled and took a sip of wine, playing with him a little now. "I've agonized over

285

the possibilities—which aren't many, believe me, because I've left things so late. Anyway, I've found something in Zaragoza."

He was silent for a moment, taking in the information. "You did say Zaragoza? You mean you're staying?"

The look of relief on his face made her heart leap.

"Professor Hernández has offered me a post."

"Andrés!"

His surprise was genuine. The two men couldn't possibly have discussed it. She'd got the work on her own merits, and that was so good. After the inspector's report, she had needed to prove to herself that she could do the job well.

"I've signed a contract but it's not great—only fifty percent of a post. But it means I'll continue to run the site, and I'll have a small teaching timetable."

He pulled her hard against him and kissed her.

"This is the most wonderful news, just wonderful. I've been dreading the moment when you told me where you were going."

"Max, I've got a small flat as well, right in the center of the city. I already have the keys and am about to move in."

For a long time, they talked, until it was completely dark, sitting by the glimmering water while they drank the estate's chilled white wine.

They grew silent. Amancia laid her head on his shoulder, wanting to kiss him, to hold him and be held. They shared a long look.

Then he took her hand. "Come."

He led her up the steps, between the magnificent stone columns, into his tiny home.

Chapter 42

A few days later, well after night had fallen, Max walked down to his office in the winery to finish a task he'd begun before the harvest started. Alejo had left for the day, having worked three sixteen-hour shifts in a row. Even with the help of the students, they were short of people. But finally, everything was quiet, and his boots rang on the concrete floor as he crossed over to the office side of the room and sat at the computer.

He pulled up the information they'd collated on visiting groups and sent it to print. This had been neglected for far too long, but it was still worth getting something up on the website.

With the sheets in his hand, he went back to his worktable and forced himself to continue, making a plan and a timetable, comparing with what he had onscreen. It was Ángel who would put this together for him and create the pages on the website. A modern agribusiness needed something special to draw in the tourists. Diversification, they called it. Doing wine tours was very, very popular.

Powering down the computer an hour later, he stretched, allowing his mind to fill with Amancia's image. It was sad the boyfriend had made things so difficult, but Max himself was hardly an example of how to behave. She accepted him as he was, which was wonderful. That determination to speak Spanish, her sense of humor, the scent she wore—he couldn't have said what it was, but he could smell it, even in his imagination—all these things drew him so powerfully.

He leaned forward and rubbed his leg above where it sat in the cup of the prosthesis. There was an insistent throb after so many hours on the go. He'd need to apply some cream tonight.

He was glad now that he hadn't said anything to Andrés about a job, that she'd done it on her own. It was great she had an apartment in the city too. She'd be nearby, and it would allow them time to grow together.

He pulled the sheet of calculations toward him and scanned the figures again. Ángel's suggestions were grand, but all this was going to cost even more money. The bank did seem willing to extend him a loan. Hopefully, it would cover all these initiatives.

He put the sheet down, and his mind wandered back to Amancia. He wanted to be with her, because the alternative was unthinkable. Momentarily, that bleak future stretched out before him. But being with her was going to bring so many complications. He didn't know how he'd handle things…never mind, he'd work something out when the time came. Right now, he didn't need to think about it, just enjoy the moment.

Anyway, no way he'd apply pressure, not after her experience with James. When she'd eventually told him about the man's behavior the evening she'd met the filmmaker, Max had felt such a rage that he'd suddenly understood the phrase "seeing red."

"*¡Qué cabrón! Le voy a romper la cara.*" He'd slammed his fist on the table. "*¡Perdona!*" he added when he'd calmed a little, ashamed of his language.

When she'd recounted the incident, it had made

him want to rush out and fight the man, beat him into the ground. His anger had shocked him later, but it hadn't changed his feelings.

"Leave it, Max. I don't want you or anyone to hurt him. Besides, he's no longer in Spain."

"And you think that would stop me? I'll search him out, and I'll tear him apart."

She grinned at him. "You're behaving like an unreconstructed caveman, Max. I'm a little flattered, but I absolutely do not want you doing anything of the sort. It would put me off you forever."

"Sorry, but I can't stand people like that, or the fact that he made you feel so bad. *Me sulfuré*."

She kissed him and convinced him that the course of action he'd outlined was inappropriate.

"I don't know how you can be so calm about it."

Amancia was quiet for a moment. "What he said really hurt me at first, but I am mixed race. I can choose to believe I have the best of both worlds, or not. I decided a long time ago it had to be the best, that I'd inherited all the good genes from both my parents—and I have great parents. That way, I'm strong, and I can show I'm just as good as anyone else, ignore people's ignorant attitudes. They are the ones who don't know any better, not me."

"That doesn't sound just."

"Maybe it isn't, but this is the life we have, and I believe we have to make the best of it."

It was great the way she could do that, deflecting him from his more destructive impulses. And all of this had pulled them closer together, hadn't it? He couldn't help remembering their night in Barcelona, and the brief couple of hours they'd spent together after she'd discovered the Roman stones around his house. Hopefully, there'd be more opportunities. He smiled to himself. He was indeed an unreconstructed male of the species; she was absolutely right.

But he didn't think she'd want it any other way. She'd shown quite enough passion of her own. Talk about him turning her on. What did she think she did to him? Damn, he was getting aroused, just thinking about her. He got up again to walk around, wincing when he put his weight on his right leg. There was nothing like that to bring him back down to earth.

A few minutes later, Max opened the gate in the wall and headed through the trees. The pool was enticing in the silvery light of the waning moon. Swimming would be a good idea. One of the doctors had recommended it as regular exercise, but he didn't use the pool nearly enough—too much work, too tired. He was going to change that, now he had a reason to keep himself in shape. He'd said he didn't want pity, so he'd make sure he wasn't pitiful.

He stripped and removed the prosthesis and slid gratefully into the water. After days of uninterrupted sunlight, the water was wonderful, silky and warm on his sore stump. Why didn't he do this every day? It wouldn't be that difficult to make it part of his routine. Batting a few leaves out of the way, he turned onto his back and paddled along with his hands, gradually relaxing. Then he swam a hundred lengths. He felt tired at the end of it, but good at the same time.

After a shower, he climbed into bed and straightaway imagined Amancia by his side. He really wanted her there now. Okay, he wasn't going to rush things, but that didn't mean he couldn't speak to her.

"I'm sorry to ring so late, *cariña*. I just wanted to hear your voice."

"It's not late. And anyway, I was awake. I like to hear your voice, too."

"I was thinking about you, *mi amor*."

"I was thinking about you, too—most of the time." She laughed. "But I have to confess, I'm really excited about the flat, so I've spent some time thinking about that as well."

"When will you move?"

"I'm moving in this weekend. Max, it's tiny, and the only window in the sitting room is in the roof, but it's perfect for me. After these months on-site, it's a palace. Having my own shower room is absolute bliss. And a proper kitchen. You cannot imagine how liberating that is."

"You realize I'll expect an invitation to dinner, don't you, *querida*?"

"Of course. I can't wait to see you here, darling."

"I like it better when you say it in your beautiful Spanish."

"Say what?"

"Darling."

"*Querida*. You see, I do know—"

"No, that really won't do."

"Oh no, I'm an idiot. It's *querido*."

"Say it again."

"*Querido*," she repeated, emphasizing the *o* at the end to make it masculine.

"And again."

"Max!"

"I just want to hear you say it—over and over again."

Amancia laughed. "*Sinvergüenza*. You are shameless. I said so before, and it's true."

"But did you mean it?"

"I did—*querido*." She was silent for a moment. "Anyway, I want to cook something for you. Special Caribbean recipes. Oh, I just love cooking, fried plantains—if I can get hold of any—bean salad, codfish fritters. And I'm going to learn some Spanish dishes, too, I promise you."

When they ended the conversation, he got up and went to the kitchen. Talking about food had reminded him he hadn't eaten since morning.

Chapter 43

On the first Monday of September, the morning was muggy indoors, and Amancia needed some air. They'd sent her the information necessary for her to prepare her first lectures, but there was plenty of time to sort that out. She closed her computer. A few minutes later, she bought fuel for the van and set out toward the dig. It was great to have several hours of freedom ahead of her.

Enough rain had fallen for the water to have soaked into the very dry, compacted earth. That could be a good thing. When she arrived, she hauled a short ladder into the stairwell and descended to see if the weather had caused any problems. A little more earth had broken away, nothing substantial. Everything was wet.

She returned to the minibus to get wellingtons and a small bucket of tools and was soon working on the next section, oblivious to what was going on around her. It was very satisfying to move things forward on-site. At half past one, she carted a sheet of thick, blue plastic from the hut, spread it onto the ground, and sat down. Feeling good about being outside looking down over the very beautiful river, she sandwiched a piece of omelet between slices of bread and studied her phone while she ate.

A twig snapped, and she swung around. "Maya, what a surprise."

"Good thing you told me where your flat was. There was no one there, so I guessed you'd be here and got the bus."

"You can share my lunch. There's more than enough for two. You didn't ring me or leave a message."

"No, it was a sudden decision to come today, and I didn't want to talk to you on the phone."

Amancia poured steaming coffee from the thermos and handed her the outer cup, pushing the foil-wrapped food toward her. "Help yourself. How are you, Maya?"

The girl's face looked white beneath the tan, and her eyes were rimmed with red. "Not good, really."

"I thought you'd have begun your course by now, trying to work out whether you wanted to be a teacher after all."

"We've only just started, but we're having a week where we're supposed to be studying before going into the classroom, so I came to see Javier for a few days. His mother invited me."

"Well, that sounds positive."

"She wanted to inspect me, to ensure I'm suitable."

"But surely…"

"She's Muslim, Amancia. As is Javier. He warned me she would be like that. She just wants the best for him. And she was charming. But…"

"But what?"

Tears appeared in the corners of Maya's eyes. "I was there for three days, and I saw how they lived. His father is dead, so they live with his uncle and his family in a large house in Cádiz where they have two rooms. It's all beautifully kept—but they share all their meals, and everyone contributes. It was like a…a commune.

I…it was too claustrophobic."

"It was only a visit, Maya. You and Javier will have your own place."

"I'm not sure anymore. It's a whole different lifestyle. While he was working up here at the children's home, I got the impression he'd lapsed from his religion, but when he's with his family, he prays several times a day. Religion is such a big thing for them. And now she's talking as if we're going to be living in the same house, saying the uncle could free up another room. But you're right—Javier and I had discussed getting a flat together in England."

The tears were now rolling down her cheeks.

"What does he have to say about all this? I thought you were getting on really well when I saw you last."

"He's more subdued when his mother's there. She has huge influence over him, Amancia, as does his uncle. And then yesterday, he said maybe I could get a job in Cádiz, that they always want teachers. But I'm training in England. I'd probably have to train again or become a classroom assistant like before, downgrading what I can do. We'd agreed!" she wailed.

Amancia patted her arm but could find nothing useful to say.

"He seems different. I was there for three days, and I felt stifled. I'm an only child of a single parent, Amancia. It was too much. I do love him, but I can't be that close to people all the time. I need my space."

"Have you told him how you feel?"

"I tried, but like I told you, he's different. I don't think he understands."

"It sounds like a big change."

"It is. I'm on my way home. I left a day early

because I decided I wanted to see you before leaving Spain." She was silent.

"And?"

Maya burst into sobs.

Amancia put her arms around the girl and held her while she cried, thinking about parallels with her own situation—different in many ways, but depending on how her relationship with Max developed, she too would have to fit into a new family with their own particular ways—and maybe prejudices as well. Of course, she'd met his mother, and she really liked her. The wider family was another matter. It was going to be tough for her too, but a strong flame burned within her. She was older, and experience had shown her who she was. Poor Maya. Her heart ached for her. She searched her bag for a clean tissue and offered it. "I think it was good to come away early. Have you anywhere to stay?"

"Not at the moment."

"Okay, you can sleep on my sofa, while you rearrange your travel, and we'll go out to eat tonight and take some time to talk through things. If that's what you'd like."

"I would. Thank you, Amancia. I do appreciate it."

Amancia's phone rang. Max. They talked for a couple of minutes, and then he said, "I'm going to text you Maite's number." Maite, Maria Teresa, was the professor's wife, whom she'd met the previous week. "Can you get some time off on Thursday? She'll take you shopping for the dress for the dance."

"That's great. I can be free all day. I'll call her."

The prospect of the shopping trip was so exciting. And she knew exactly the dress she wanted for the festival—wearing fancy dress was the one requirement to follow the procession of the Virgen, the Pilar, and she had every intention of doing that.

"Yes, that's good. Shall I see you this evening?"

"No, I'm sorry, *querido*, but I can't see you today," she said, as they finished. "I have an unexpected visitor, Maya, you remember?"

Neither was free the next day.

"*A miércoles, entonces.*"

She closed her phone.

"Your relationship with Max is so uncomplicated."

"Believe me, it's not. But maybe we're more similar to each other than you and your Javier."

Chapter 44

It was Wednesday, and they were well into September. Amancia had been looking forward to the evening all day. She finished studying the archaeology course offered, working out what her input was, and a surge of anticipation coursed through her. Max would be here at six. They were invited to dinner by his cousin, Sofía, and her husband, Ricardo.

"You'll be able to meet her daughter, Marisol. She's so charming."

It was obvious that he had a lot of affection for the child, and that made her think of her nephew, Robert, and how much she'd missed him. The little boy would have changed so much in the months she'd been away.

****

Amancia left the university and returned to her flat, where she had a shower. She was a little nervous, but the way Max had talked about his cousin reassured her. Still there was the question of how she should dress. She always took care with her appearance but more so this time; except for his mother, this was the first time she'd be meeting a member of Max's family, so she wanted to impress but not look too formal. She'd had to buy a couple of items of clothing since moving into the city, but she was going back to Bristol soon, to say goodbye to her sister, Anna, off on a world tour with her boyfriend, and she'd pick up the rest of her clothes while she was there.

Now she chose a blue, mid-calf dress. She held it up against her and looked in the mirror. The simplicity of the design looked good on her. She'd also invested in new lingerie—white cotton knickers and sports-style bras were ideal for working on-site, but it could hardly be called sexy underwear. She ran her fingers now over the oyster silk and lace she'd selected for this evening. It was good to get back into something pretty.

She wandered around, deciding between her two pairs of city shoes, nothing much on her mind, enjoying the freedom of having her own place. Imagine, she could've ended up with some tiny studio or even one room with a shared bathroom, given the amount she was earning. Working on-site, it hadn't bothered her, but now she needed her private space. And of course, she could have Max come here, with no one to object.

She was still wearing her shabby red and orange Chinese silk dressing gown. The caress of the heavy silk on her skin was a sensual pleasure, to be prolonged whenever possible. She'd change into her dress in a minute. But suddenly, there was a knock, and she opened the door.

Max stared at her for a moment, clutching a huge bunch of pink-tipped lilies, a bottle in his hand, his eyes raking over her unexpected garb.

"You look wonderful in that, Amancia." He pushed the door shut, placed the bottle on the floor, and slung the arm he'd freed around her. They kissed. Then he pushed her away a little, looking her up and down, smiling. "You intend going out in that? It's okay by me, but Sofía may find it a bit odd."

"Let me get dressed. Do you want a drink?"

He laid the flowers carefully on the coffee table and then ran his hands slowly down her silk-clad arms. His eyes were like dark pools as he drank in every nuance of her expression, every curve of her body.

"No, I don't think I do. Shall we occupy ourselves a little? There's plenty of time, and I haven't seen you for days. Do you know how hard that's been for me?"

He was nudging her gently toward the open door of the bedroom, and she felt his heart thudding against her breasts through the silk. Something lurched inside her, reminding her just how much she wanted him.

"Well, if you put it like that…"

"I do."

A moment later, he was untying the belt of her gown. She tugged open the last button of his shirt, and he shrugged it off his shoulders, the rest of his clothing following seconds later. Then, he pulled her up against him, cupping his hands around her buttocks, squeezing, kneading. Oh God, he'd got her fired up in seconds, and she simply had no defense against him. She had her arms linked behind his neck, pulling him close, and now he was walking her backward toward the bed, and with every step, her heart rate increased. It had been too long. She wanted him now.

"This is a very good…way to end the working day." She almost purred, responding to the hardening of his body against hers. His masculine scent with the hint of sandalwood fired her up—as if she needed any further stimulation. The desire to feel his weight on top of her, to feel him inside her, was overwhelming, but she forced herself to hold back. Pushing him away slightly, she brought her hands slowly down his body, just skating over the muscles of his chest, and she felt him tremble. She took her time, allowing her fingertips to wander here and there, until she just touched his penis. There was a sharp intake of breath.

Now, he lifted her onto the bed.

"Damn, where did I put—"

"Here." She retrieved the small, silver-wrapped package he had dropped onto the bedside table.

"Not very romantic."

"But sensible. It's okay, Max."

He slid on top of her, and when he entered her moments later, it happened so quickly, she squealed.

"I didn't hurt you, did I?"

"No, not that. I just didn't expect it to be so…quick."

He grinned down at her. "You must have been ready then, because I didn't have to try very hard."

"Yeah, I think that's just possible."

She hadn't even noticed the prosthesis until now. Somehow, there hadn't been enough time to deal with it. He lay back, a film of sweat covering his chest. A little while later, he sat up and swiveled, pulling his leg over the side of the bed.

"It looks like we christened your flat, *querida*."

"Mmm, that was a better method than the traditional champagne."

"Yeah, but I did think of that as well. Somehow, I forgot to put it in the fridge. I'd better do that before it begins to warm up."

"I need to shower again."

When he came to join her under the water, he was hopping, and it was good that he was relaxed enough to do that in front of her.

Chapter 45

"Let's drink to your new home." Max raised his glass and clinked it against hers, looking into her eyes. "You are pleased you stayed in Spain, aren't you?"

"Of course. How can you doubt that? I want to be with you, Max, to get to know you better, and that takes time. Are you glad I stayed?"

"Let me show you how much."

He put his hands to her head and ran his fingers through her hair, sending little trails of electrical impulses across her scalp, so that she shivered as he pulled her into his kiss.

Eventually, he backed away.

"Now, we'd better go to Sofía's. We can walk. It's not far, just beyond the center." He eyed the elegant high heels. "If you can do it in those shoes?"

****

Marisol climbed back up onto Max. He'd taken off his jacket, rolled up his shirt sleeves, and was lying on his stomach, but as soon as she was on top of him, he began to lift himself onto his knees. The rough and tumble had been going on for at least ten minutes, and Max's dark hair now flopped damply on his forehead. The little girl was indefatigable.

"¡Caballito, caballito!" she screeched, falling straight off again.

"Enough of playing horses," said Sofía, coming

back into the room. "Thanks for keeping her occupied, Max. I'm going to feed the girls now, and then they're going to bed, to give the grown-ups some peace."

Ignoring Marisol's sulky pout, she led her daughter toward the kitchen. On her way, the child turned and gave the visitors a brilliant smile. Then Sofia closed the door, and Max dropped back onto the sofa.

"Phew! I'm exhausted."

"After a hard day's work…and other things."

"Exactly."

They sat side by side, quietly talking, mainly about how the harvest was progressing.

"I haven't had any spare time. I'm out among the vines most of the time, and then I try to put an hour in at the office right at the end of every day. Wine making never stops—while one lot is fermenting, we're already looking to the following year." He took out a handkerchief and wiped his forehead. "I have to force myself to squeeze in office time, or there are certain things that would never get done. If our wine sells well, I'll be able to employ others to do some of this, but for the moment, it's up to me. But I promise I'll make it up to you when the rush dies down."

She leaned across and kissed him. "Of course, you haven't had time. And anyway, I've spent so many hours familiarizing myself with the course, I haven't exactly been lazing around myself. I didn't want to do anything less than a first-class job."

"I can't imagine you'd have a problem. And you seem very confident handling young people, from what I could see on-site."

She gave a lopsided smile. "Well, I'll admit to being very nervous. It's going to be different from the bit of teaching I did as a PhD student. But I expect I'll soon get the hang of it."

The house was quiet now. The occasional murmur came from the kitchen, then the click of the front door.

"There's Ricardo."

He stood up and held out his hand to her.

"Come on. Let me introduce you."

****

It was a good evening. The food was delicious, and it was great the way they made her feel so welcome, his cousin and her husband. She couldn't mistake the warmth they felt toward Max.

They'd talked about a whole lot of things, swapping from Spanish to English and back again. She thought this had been harder on Ricardo than the other two. His grasp of English seemed rather shaky, while Sofía and Max switched effortlessly, and Amancia tried hard to do the same.

"She's making huge progress with the language," Max had said at one point, showing her off a little.

"Yes, I am." She gave him a sly smile. "I'm even beginning to work out the difference between the masculine and feminine endings, aren't I, *querido*?"

Later, they walked across the city. It was like being back home in Bristol, which was about the same size, with everything in easy reach, no time wasted on traveling. This was what Amancia loved about city living, what she'd grown up with. Would she really be prepared to give it up long term? Yes, if she and Max could be together.

"Are you coming back to mine?"

"If you don't mind that I don't stay long. I have a heavy day tomorrow, and it starts early."

They climbed to the fourth floor, and Amancia let them in.

"Coffee or more champagne?"

"Coffee, please. I'm too old to work with a hangover," he said, "and I need to be sharp tomorrow."

In the kitchen, she set the super coffee machine going for the first time since she'd moved in. She'd soon find out if she'd understood how it worked. She returned with a tray on which were two cups and a little bowl of the brown sugar lumps he liked to sweeten his coffee with.

"I had such a lovely time this evening." She placed the coffee on the table and sat down beside him. "What a nice cousin you have, Max. Ricardo, too. And Marisol is gorgeous. She reminds me of my sister when she was little—so charming, but manipulative as well." She took a tiny sip, testing the temperature. "I can see you love her."

"Yes, I do. That's partly because I'm very close to Sofía since I had no siblings. We've always had a good relationship, and when she married my friend, it just made things better. But I do love Marisol—it's that artless innocence. I expect she'll be a little monster later, the way everyone spoils her."

"Yes, I noticed the face she pulled at her mother when she made her go and eat. And the lovely smile she gave us."

"Oh, I think Sofía knows how to handle her. She won't let her get all her own way."

They drank some more coffee, holding hands, enjoying the closeness.

"Do you want to have children eventually, Max?"

Max turned and stared at her for a moment. She

looked at him, curious about the expression that had suddenly appeared on his face. What was going on?

"What?" He passed his hand over his eyes, shutting her out. His heart was pounding. Here was his greatest fear materializing. He didn't want to see her face, to see her reaction. "Oh...oh no, I wouldn't want children of my own."

God, he'd known this would come up sooner or later. But he hadn't prepared for it because he'd been enjoying these last few weeks so much, loved being with her, sharing thoughts and ideas. And with all the work of the harvest, it'd been easy to push away the moment when he'd have to deal with it. He hadn't wanted to think about how saying these few words might alter their relationship...might bring it to an end. Why did she have to ask him that?

"No," he repeated, his mouth suddenly dry. He swallowed. "No children."

Amancia stared at him. She looked bewildered. She looked hurt. He stiffened, fixed his gaze on the opposite wall so he didn't have to look at her.

"But you're a natural father, Max. I saw how much you enjoyed playing—"

"I said no!" Springing to his feet, he almost tumbled over when his leg muscle spasmed and gave way. He lurched to the wall to help himself stay upright as the moment passed.

"I'm sorry, it's not possible. I don't want to talk about this, do you understand?" His voice was harsh, with a note that sounded close to panic. His phone rang, and he snatched it out of his pocket and looked down. "I'd better go."

She was on her feet now, about to remonstrate, but

he turned his back on her.

"I'm sorry," he repeated. "I'll let myself out."

He snatched up his discarded jacket and strode to the door. A moment later, it slammed shut, and his feet pounded on the stairs.

Chapter 46

Max clattered down to the hall, stabbed at the green button, and shoved out through the glass doors. People were still on the streets strolling along, enjoying the mild evening, just as he and Amancia had been doing half an hour earlier. Car doors slammed, and lights were beginning to be extinguished, but wrapped in his misery, Max saw none of it.

"*¡Mierda, mierda, mierda!*"

What a complete idiot he was. What the hell was he doing, behaving like that when he had criticized James for his behavior? Why hadn't he worked all this out, got his ideas sorted, been able to explain?

Because it hurt him too deeply, that's why. He hadn't wanted to acknowledge it—that he was still running away. Oh, God.

He dragged in a couple of deep breaths, trying to calm himself, but it had no effect. This was it—she'd never want to speak to him again. And he could never face her again. He cringed with embarrassment, and an enormous sense of loss threatened to engulf him. He scrubbed at the dampness welling up in the corners of his eyes.

"*¡Idiota! ¡Hijo de puta!*"

The army had provided him with a whole lexicon of swear words, but none of them were bad enough to express the way he thought about himself.

He stomped along, hot arrows of pain lancing up his right leg with each step, and it was a while before he realized that people were watching him warily and giving him a wide berth, but he didn't stop; he was in self-destruct mode, intent on getting the job of destroying himself done. He didn't come to a halt until he stumbled over something sticking out from a darkened doorway.

With the way blocked, Max looked down and tried to make out what had stopped him. A homeless man was laying out his sleeping bag, preparing to settle down for the night. El Calvo, that was his name, wasn't it? He'd seen the bald man several times and recognized him as ex-military. He'd usually bought him a coffee or a sandwich. People fell on hard times, and the army didn't do a good enough job of caring for its veterans, many of whom were damaged by their experiences.

"*¡Cabrón!* What's got into you?" said Calvo, rubbing his leg where Max had kicked it. "Not everyone's as forgivin' as me, 'specially this time o' night. You gotta watch out. There's some peculiar people around."

Dragged from the depths of his despair, Max suddenly focused. The man was skinny and unshaven, and it was obvious that these last few weeks on the streets had done him no favors at all. At the beginning he'd always made an effort to be tidy and clean, but no longer. And it could only get worse with the coming winter. Grateful to be presented with a problem he might actually be able to solve, Max said, "Sorry. Buy you something to eat, Calvo? Come on."

The homeless man strapped his sleeping bag back

onto his military kitbag. He looked in a bad way and followed as if every step cost him. "Not here," he said when they came to a small bar that sold food. "They won't let me in these days."

They walked on and found a place with tables out on the pavement, and Max went inside to order, adding a black coffee for himself.

"It'll be a few minutes. Might as well get yourself cleaned up," he said when he came back from the bar.

The meal and Calvo arrived at the table at the same time. A wedge of omelet and a heap of left-over tapas, the last of the evening, went down at an alarming rate. The man swallowed almost without chewing, tearing at the bread, as if someone were going to snatch it out of his hand. Max let him get on with it, until the last juices were soaked up and the plate was wiped clean.

"Want anything more?"

"No, that's enough. *¡Me voy a estallar! Gracias.* Maybe something for tomorrow?"

"Got a better idea. Might be able to offer you a job, hombre."

Max had been thinking while the soldier was eating. Bringing in the fruit was almost done now, and the *obreros* who'd come to handpick the grapes were already leaving, but there were dozens of jobs that had to be done postharvest, weeks of work to ensure the vines were in good condition for the following year. Juan wouldn't be back at work for some time. He could easily find tasks for Calvo, somewhere to sleep, food. He scrutinized him carefully. Any addiction would be a big negative. He didn't show the signs, although if he had to live on the streets much longer, that might change. Why was he here? There must be some reason.

"It's a real job," he said. "You have to work hard."

"Anything, anything, I don't mind. I need someone to give me a chance."

"PTSD," Max said. "Is that the problem?"

"Yeah, I'm not a hundred percent, see, have days when I can't do nothing. Monsters in the night, can't get back to sleep, and then, I'm laid up. Got thrown out o' my lodgings because of the screaming."

Right, he knew what that was about—horrible scenes that made no sense, waking up with no idea of where he was, flashbacks. For Max, the flashbacks even came during the day sometimes. He'd been through it all. And after a short time, the therapy he'd been offered appeared to be useless, and he'd stopped going. Just a week earlier, he'd woken covered in sweat at three in the morning, from a nightmare that seemed so real, he'd been screaming in terror, and it'd taken several minutes before he worked out that he was at home, in his bed.

Since he and Amancia had got together, the frequency of those episodes had diminished, but not significantly. He cringed; he'd just wrecked that relationship. What a complete blockhead he was.

Calvo licked his lips and in one go downed half a cup of *café con leche* the reluctant bar manager had made. Who drank anything other than black coffee or a *cortado* at this time of the evening? But Max had wanted to feed him, and milky coffee would help.

"You give me a chance, *hombre*, and I'll not let you down."

"Okay, it's going to be like this: the vineyard's located about fifteen clicks outside the city," he said, dropping into military jargon. "I can take you there tonight. You start at 0700, and this time of year, you'll be working at least nine hours a day, hard physical work. Short breaks, all food provided, showers, somewhere to sleep, basic wage. How does that sound?"

"Fucking fantastic."

"Right, but I'm not a charity. I'm trying to make a go of this, and I have to be able to rely on you—you're there every day, however you're feeling, or you're out."

"Got it…sir," the man said, responding to the officer tone.

"You've got a problem. It'll be better if you sleep on your own, because if you have an episode, everyone will be affected. I had a couple of extra berths installed in a barn. You'll be okay there, and you can walk over to the kitchen in the main house for your meals. If you're ill, you come and find me or my foreman straightaway. We'll see how it goes at the beginning, take it day by day." He looked at his watch. "Wait here. I'll pick you up in twenty minutes. Got to get the car."

As he hurried along, he thought again about what he'd said to Amancia, and he felt like crying. But he had no tears. Instead, a deep despair invaded his being. He was so messed up. How was he going to cope?

Coffee with a down-and-out at a squalid bar was a great way to end a romantic evening. He grinned mirthlessly. It was no more than he deserved.

His soon-to-be-former car was parked a few streets away. It was a pity he hadn't brought the farm truck— the guy stank, despite the clean-up, but he didn't want to leave him on the streets another night. He found a blanket in the boot and covered the passenger seat. Then he got in and, smoothing his fingers over the beautiful walnut dashboard, he inhaled the leather scent—it could be an ironic last journey together, depending on when the buyer closed on the deal.

****

Amancia slumped onto the sofa. What had just happened? Had she said something she shouldn't? One minute they were making love, trying to please each other, knowing that whatever they did next would move their relationship forward. They'd come so far, and then…well, what *had* happened?

She'd asked him if he wanted children, and he'd suddenly turned on her as if she were the devil in the flesh. How could he do that? A deep sob escaped her, and her tears spilled over and coursed down her cheeks. What had she said, exactly?—that he seemed a natural father. Could he really be offended by that? It was a compliment, for Heaven's sake!

Leaning back against the cushions, she cried quietly as she saw all her dreams of a future that might possibly contain Max dissolve before her eyes. He'd called her confident, but that confidence was fragile, wiped away in an instant. A few minutes went by. Then, exhausted, she sat up.

She didn't know what she was going to do, but she was due at the university tomorrow for an induction, and she had to project the right image: calm, organized, confident. For that, she needed a good night's sleep.

But it was not easy to achieve. In bed, the bed in which they'd made love just a few hours earlier, she smelled his scent, and her sobs redoubled. Her mind continued to work overtime, and she couldn't relax. She sighed. A whole lot of painful thoughts chased around, and oblivion would be slow in coming. She turned over for at least the tenth time.

****

It was seven in the morning. Two twenty-nine a.m. was the last time she'd looked at the clock, so she must have slept, but it didn't feel like it. She showered and dressed smartly but comfortably in black trousers and a cream top with a stylish, bronze-colored tweed jacket, the clothes jacking up her self-assurance. She gathered her things and walked in, arriving a few minutes before nine at the university.

She wanted to think about how to approach Max. She'd be free after lunch with some of her new colleagues. Maybe she could try to see him then. It was tempting, but it didn't feel like the right time to go to the vineyard. He'd be busy—people arriving on-site, organizing the work, whatever. He certainly wouldn't be open to an approach from her. What they had to say to each other was not for public consumption, and she wouldn't risk making the situation more difficult by being insensitive.

She mulled it over again and again and finally decided she should contact him in the evening. In the meantime, she had to put up with the idea that her life was falling apart, and she could do nothing to stop it. She made a herculean effort and pushed all thoughts of him to the back of her mind.

It was good to meet some of the people she'd be working with. Afterward, she bought a coffee and sat on a bench in the gardens. Max had a problem, that was obvious, and he didn't know how to deal with it. Was he infertile? Did he have some awful, inherited disease? Maybe he was concerned about overpopulation. A surprising number of people of their generation had decided not to have children. But this didn't sit right with the way he'd reacted to her words. It had hurt him deeply to say what he did. She thought about his relationship with his mother—loving, and fiercely protective. So, maybe something had happened to them. She had to discover what it was.

Unaware that she'd got to her feet, she found herself staring at fat goldfish swimming in the basin of the fountain, while she probed mentally at the Gordian knot. Like Alexander the Great, she had to unravel the strands to achieve her goal, and only bold action would enable her to do this. What that action might be, she had no idea. The answer had to lie in Max's past, possibly a long way back in his past. Of one thing she was sure—he didn't know how to lower his defenses, how to trust others. He still didn't trust her.

But that had to change. And unless he confronted the problem and determined to solve it, there could be no future together.

She folded her arms and then dropped them to her sides, refolded them, ready to jump up at the slightest excuse and tackle the problem.

What if she just rang him? Forcing herself to remain seated, she thought about this for a while. It wasn't such a bad idea. She could say she was sorry that she'd upset him, that she hadn't meant to, and could they meet and talk it through? But accepting the blame for something that wasn't her fault was a poor way to build a strong relationship. She'd tried that before. There had to be another possibility.

An hour later, hyped up on caffeine, she came to a decision: she would not let this happen. He wasn't going to walk out on her as if he didn't care. Because he did care. And he was suffering as much as she was. This evening, she'd drive to the site and check on things, and then make her way through the vineyard to catch him at his office. And if he wasn't there? Well, she'd just have to think again.

In the meantime, he'd have time to cool down and get over his upset.

Chapter 47

It was very late when Max finally got Calvo settled in. Then he went to his office. He'd been here two, maybe three hours now, and accomplished nothing. How had he imagined he could work, after all that had happened? The computer screen went dark, and he leaned back in his office chair. He'd picked a beer out of the minifridge a few minutes ago, and now he opened it. Maybe it would lubricate the thinking process. It was time that he sorted out his thoughts—not about work. Amancia.

There'd been no talk of marriage between them, but he hadn't failed to hear the subtext behind her question, either. And that had led to the realization that having children or not would have a major impact on her life if they stayed together. A meaningful relationship for Amancia would have to include the possibility. She was an educated woman, and he guessed that if they couldn't have children, she'd accept it. But to rule it out unequivocally without explanation?—no, that could not happen. Her reaction to Sofía's daughters was much the same as his; she'd been fully engaged, enjoying the children, responsive. And she'd mentioned a little nephew she loved.

Maybe he could say he was infertile. But that would mean their relationship was based on a lie, and he couldn't do that. Tears came into Max's eyes, and he thought about having children of his own. He took a drink and replaced the bottle on the desk.

There was one clear message here: for her, children were a normal part of any couple's life, and he knew that in other circumstances, that would be true for him, too. But it went further for her. She'd already allowed her career to be impacted by the needs of her mother and younger sisters. Family.

The love she felt was evident every time she spoke of them, and despite the responsibility she'd taken on at the death of her father, there was no resentment at what it had cost her. She'd recognized they had to come first, and she wouldn't be abandoning them anytime soon. Wherever she lived in the world, they would remain an integral part of her life.

He'd not really thought about this family she cared for so much, but now he was doing so, and it took him into different territory. With sudden clarity, he knew he loved her. "I love you" was something people said sometimes without thought of commitment, but at some time over the last few days, he'd recognized he wanted to share his life with her. Sharing her life would mean becoming a member of her family.

He raised the bottle and saw that it was already empty. Dumping it in the waste bin, he picked a second beer out of the fridge. This broke all his self-imposed rules, but just now, he needed it. He sat down again.

Much of his adult life had been spent in other countries, among other cultures, working with people of different races and religions. There had never been any problem with that. The sergeant for whom he'd risked his life had been Black, of Caribbean origin. But that was work. It couldn't compare with joining Amancia's extended family, and it was naïve to think it could. Although her skin was relatively pale, Amancia was classed as Black in the modern world. Such classifications were totally bewildering to him, and a waste of time. She was just Amancia.

But other people didn't necessarily think like that. She had a Black family—apart from her mother. They would enter his life, maybe eventually become his relatives. He forced himself to consider that. It was different, but was it a problem? A slow smile curved his lips, and for a few seconds, he allowed himself to dwell on what could be and would be, if he got himself together and pursued what he wanted. No, it certainly wasn't a problem.

He stood up and went to the window. Taking a sip of beer, he stared up at the big house and thought of his mother. She had warmed to Amancia immediately, had really enjoyed talking to her, two intelligent women, relishing the exchange of ideas. But then, Consuela was pragmatic—his happiness was paramount, and she'd fretted over him since he'd lost the lower part of his leg. If he'd fallen in love with Amancia, and Amancia felt the same way, then that was fine with her. The easy relationship between the two women was a definite bonus, but there was much more to be considered. Like his ultraconservative family in Madrid. Could they handle his having a mixed-race wife?

But all this avoided the issue of children. If he couldn't sort that out, nothing else mattered because there wouldn't be a relationship anymore.

He stood up. What if she refused to see him, sent him away without allowing him to explain? It gave him a jolt, how much he wanted to explain, underlining how important she'd become to him. He gave a half sob and pushed it down with another swallow of beer; he could not lose her.

A dreadful thought entered his head: she'd been so sad and angry at James's crass words. What if she'd misinterpreted his rejection of having children with her as some peculiar form of racism? A dislike of the idea that his children would also be Black?

Oh God, please don't let her think that.

He took another gulp of the beer. He had to see her as soon as possible.

****

The first fingers of dawn pushed through the windows. Somehow, in the uncomfortable office chair, his head pillowed on his arms across the desk, Max had fallen asleep. And now, fiery pains were stabbing him in the neck. He must have been crazy, staying out here. He stood up and stretched, noting every aching muscle.

He hurried back to his house, showered, and changed. Coffee, that's what he needed. Lots of it. While they'd brought in the harvest, he'd eaten all his meals in the kitchen of the big house, and he hadn't yet reverted to cooking for himself. In Catalina's kitchen, the aroma of coffee made him dizzy, and he gulped down a large cup while explaining to her about Calvo. He chewed a last piece of bread and helped himself to an apple on his way out.

In the barn, Pedro was talking with the newcomer. This morning, the man looked better, cleaned up in borrowed clothes, while he put his own through the washing machine. He'd made a start, but reintegrating into the world of work was not going to be easy for him.

"You stay with Pedro, learn what needs to be done, Calvo. Give us a moment, could you?" He walked out of earshot with the foreman. "Let me know right away if there are any problems. Don't put up with anything, but it will be difficult for him for a while, so keep a close eye on him."

He left them, ticking another item off his mental list of things to do.

Back up at the house, he spoke to Catalina. "Can you tell the *señora* I won't be able to join her today? I'm wanted elsewhere."

An inspection of the accommodation was due. The tents were long gone, and the last few itinerant laborers were beginning to pack up. He provided good accommodation but had no illusions about the behavior of the average seasonal worker.

Max shoved thoughts of his personal unhappiness right to the back of his mind and took a small amount of comfort from the way things were progressing in the vineyard. The machinery in the main shed hummed. This was a critical year for him, and hopefully, they'd saved the wine by bringing the harvest forward. As he crossed the yard, he looked up. Clouds had appeared in the otherwise bright blue sky, far over to the west. They didn't look too threatening, but he'd watch them, although the time-critical work had moved indoors.

Things weren't too bad at the accommodation huts, though as always, there were a few items needing repair. Maybe Pedro could take Calvo along to help him, a way to ease him into work. Good idea.

As he locked the store, he heard a scuffle over by the archaeological site. He scanned along the fence, but everything looked exactly as it should. The division between the accommodation and the dig site had been reinforced, and no one'd had permission to be on the site...apart from Amancia.

What if it was her? He could apologize, try to sort things out with her.

A stab of panic at the possible consequences of such a conversation set the adrenaline rushing through him, but of course, the minibus wasn't in the car park. She was meeting new colleagues this morning.

The shame of the way he'd left Amancia the previous evening was excruciating. He was running away, trying to bury himself in a long list of tasks, but he couldn't run far or fast enough. He'd hurt her. How could he have done that?

Cursing his stupidity, he swung himself over the fence, sprawling a little as he landed. He'd been in special forces, highly trained, but he no longer had that agility, and an awkward landing could leave him in pain for days. Gingerly, he put his artificial foot to the ground. Okay, no pain around his stump. He'd been lucky. But it was luck that he didn't deserve.

He headed for the new shed. The lock hung off the hasp, and the door opened to his touch. Someone had been along, and all the tools were gone. Maybe the boy from the village had been brazen enough to come back on his own account to steal. But he didn't think so. This place was always going to be a target for petty thieves.

He looked down at the dig site at the newly revealed steps. The scale of Amancia's achievement was impressive, and it would be good to tell her that, give her credit for the effort she'd put in, the expertise she clearly possessed. There was no sign that an intruder had been anywhere other than the shed.

Max sat on a low wall. After the intense activity, it was dull here. Everything was dull without her. He stared vacantly into the distance. It had been mad to speak the way he had, but it was even more crazy to think that he couldn't go around to her flat to apologize and explain.

Calm now, his thoughts cleared, and he understood it was about pride, that he didn't want to admit to being in the wrong. And fear. Making any explanation would hurt him and would mean allowing her into his inner self, that part of him he'd kept for so long inviolate, maybe almost the whole of his life. And it would give her the opportunity to say definitively that she didn't want him anymore.

That had to change.

Of course, he could see her, though there was no excuse for what he'd done. He gave a jagged sigh. In a moment, he'd be crying his eyes out. *¡Dios!* Why did this have to be so painful?

He'd go into town this evening, go to her flat and talk to her. He'd get off early. Things were running pretty smoothly now, here on the vineyard, and they could do without him for a while.

****

At half past five, work was still in full swing. He wouldn't be missed. He checked with Pedro, telling him he was going into the city. Calvo's first day had gone well, which was good. If the man shaped up, Max had the beginnings of a plan for him.

Now, he armed himself with a bottle of red from his own *bodega,* just in case. Of what, he didn't know, and maybe he shouldn't bother. She wasn't going to invite him back to the flat. It was a long time since he'd felt as bad as this. Maybe he'd end up chugging it down his throat in his car when she refused to speak to him.

Leaving the vineyard behind him, he drove toward Zaragoza.

****

Amancia wasn't likely to do much work on-site this evening; her mind was too full of Max and the situation that had suddenly erupted between them. Nevertheless, she would drive to the site to check on things and later go over to Max's office. Hadn't he said he often stayed on in the office after the working day finished?

A few minutes later, she steered carefully through the campus gates, taking the road that meandered out of the city, parallel to the river Ebro. A minor road, it cut the distance to the site by a third. She'd driven along it a couple of times and had come to enjoy the drive. The route was secluded, but she'd got used to the minibus and thought it easier to control than most private cars. Being squat and heavy, it made her feel safe.

If not for the forthcoming confrontation, Amancia would have been quite relaxed. Instead, her heart was thudding uncomfortably, reminding her she was about to see him, that the meeting could be crucial, could be the end of everything she'd thought they shared. Tears gathered, and she brushed them quickly away. It would not be the end of their relationship. It would not. This was too important to let go.

She should be there in half an hour.

But as if to contradict this thought, the engine began to emit a series of knocking sounds. Vehicles were not supposed to do this when she was driving, because she was hopeless at dealing with car problems.

She'd checked the fuel and the lights before she set out. A careful driver, she always did the things you were supposed to do before leaving. She glanced down, but no oil light was flashing, and the tank was half full. So, what could it be? But her knowledge didn't extend any further. Whatever was going on, it was serious.

The vehicle was bucking, and she'd have to stop. Right, a layby was coming up. She steered toward it, tucking her tail end within the line before the engine stopped working. She put the gear in neutral, pulled up the handbrake, and sat there in the sudden silence, dismayed. It was too quiet. Getting out, she took a good look around. The last golden rays of the sun glimmered through the trees, but the shadows were already lengthening. There was no traffic. She was stuck here, and she had no way to help herself.

Why was she so useless with vehicles? She wouldn't let anything else defeat her like this. Flooded with self-disgust, she suddenly remembered a card the university office had given her for roadside services from a local garage. That was it. Okay, yes, she did have her phone with her, which was something. But what if they didn't understand her? She lifted her chin. Nonsense, her Spanish was good enough for this simple task. How did you say breakdown? Averi...something? She'd seen it somewhere but wasn't sure. She could say "the car is not going well, and I am at the side of the road." She got back in and rehearsed the sentences she'd need several times over. *El coche*...yes, that was right, now she could do it.

But there was no reply. That felt like a big setback, as she'd psyched herself up.

A couple of cars whooshed past, and the minibus

rocked. When she looked around again, her eyes searched among the ominous shadows that had replaced the last of the sunlight. On the one hand, it would be good if someone stopped. On the other, she was dead scared, because it could be anyone, some predator even. But that was ridiculous, and she had to stop thinking like that. If only she could ring Max. She shook her head. No, she'd find some other way. It was horrible to be so dependent.

She tried again, with no response, and then again, this time getting the engaged tone. Which meant someone was now there. She got out and walked about. There were still no cars. A few minutes passed, and dusk was well advanced, especially at this side of the tree-lined road, in the middle of nowhere. This stretch was gloomy and dark and getting blacker by the minute. She'd try that number one last time, and if there was no answer, maybe she would have to ring Max, even if it went against her principles. Or the police? Yes, that was always a possibility.

She rang the garage again and hung on. Suddenly, someone picked up. Chewing noises at the other end of the line. Yes, they would come. Voices in the background. The clink of cutlery. Yes, they understood where she was, and they'd be thirty minutes. Or had he said fifty? "*¿Cincuenta o treinta?*" she asked, but he'd already hung up. When she thought about it, that wasn't good—fifty minutes? Young woman by the side of the road in the dark? No way this was safe. She had another walk around.

She was thinking of phoning the police when a smart-looking vehicle signaled from the other side and pulled across, coming to a halt in front of her. Blinded by its lights, she had no idea what it was, and with her heart hammering off the scale, she darted back into the minibus and locked it, relieved to find the central lock was working. She lowered the window half an inch, just enough to be able to speak. It was almost too dark to see now, but a figure was coming toward her.

"Damsels in Distress, Special Service."

"Oh Max, how could you scare me like that? I was so frightened."

"What? I didn't do anything. It was only when you rushed back inside that I realized it was you. I thought it was some poor, benighted traveler."

"I am a poor, benighted traveler."

"Get down from there."

She was shaking when she released the locks and slid back the door. She jumped down, straight into his arms. "Thank God you've come. You can't believe how scary it is waiting at the side of the road in the dark."

"Oh, you were really afraid," he said, tightening his arms around her. "I can feel your heart fluttering. You poor thing."

"Okay," she said from the comforting safety of his embrace, "if I admit just this once to being a little, tiny bit scared when you came across, will you help me? I know you're not officially talking to me, but this has to be a special occasion."

"It's the special occasion on which I grovel for your forgiveness. I'm so sorry, Amancia, so sorry for last night, sorry to have caused you pain." He held her close, cradling her in his arms. "I mean it, but I can't forgive myself for it. Please allow me to explain. I was on my way to see you, to do just that."

"And I was coming to see you. Only I was

pretending it was just a visit to the site."

"I was there earlier, and I can tell you, it has been burgled. They've taken all the tools."

She giggled, nerves getting the better of her. "Oh, if that's all, I don't care! That seems like nothing, after what I've been suffering here."

They stood together, his arms tight around her, her head buried in his chest, and all her terrors receded. He lifted her chin and started to kiss her. "Told you I couldn't resist a damsel in distress."

She pushed him away. "You don't get to do that until you've explained yourself."

"Okay, here they are, finally," he said, as the swirling, orange lights appeared at the bend in the road.

Chapter 48

Amancia sipped her wine and then poked at the prawn on her plate. Serving it with the shell on required her to grasp it with her fingers. She'd stink of fish at the end of the meal. It wasn't that she didn't like fish, but this was a different thing altogether. She prodded it again with her fork. Those little white legs and the shiny black button eyes made her feel queasy.

"Here, let me."

Max efficiently stripped it, using his fingers, licking the juices afterward with every appearance of enjoyment. "Now, dip it in the sauce," he said a moment later. "It's delicious."

She followed his instructions. Actually, it was delicious. "So, what was the problem yesterday?"

She still felt aggrieved and had wanted to say, "What did I do?" but it hadn't been personal to her, however badly she'd felt.

He took a deep swallow of his wine and set his glass down, his long fingers flexing around the slender stem. "There's a part of this story I haven't told anyone, not even my mother, whom it concerns."

"Okay." She laid her hand on his and pressed gently. "I'm listening, Max."

Again, there was silence.

"When I was four, I saw my father push my mother down the stairs. She fell from the top to the bottom."

He was no longer looking at her, and the faraway expression in his eyes told her he was reliving the scene. "It's probably the first memory I have, except that I know I'd seen him hit her before that. The atmosphere of violence had been with us a long time."

"What happened then?"

"My father ran down the stairs. He was shouting that there'd been an accident, that she'd fallen and needed help. Catalina came running into the hall. She was already working for my parents and was devoted to my mother. That has never changed. I think now that she was aware of what was going on and had probably stayed to support her. Because I'm sure no one would have put up with my father and his frequent rage otherwise. Maybe she even suspected he'd pushed her.

"It all played out then, flashing blue lights, ambulance, raised voices, crying. My father crying, long-drawn-out howls, like an animal in distress." He glanced at her and then away again. "That's strange—I only just remembered that."

"What about you?"

"Good question. Nobody thought about me. I'd been lying in the upper corridor, playing with a toy car, when they shot out of the bedroom, him shouting, her terrified. He was pushing her along the landing, and I remember her saying, 'No, no, no…' "

He fell silent.

"Catalina came for me and took me to the kitchen. She sat me on her knee and held me a long time."

"You were lucky to have someone like her."

"Yes, she was very good to me."

"So, this is why your mother is in a wheelchair."

"The fall damaged her spine. It could have killed

330

her, but somehow, she survived."

Amancia's heart was breaking as she watched the emotions flit across Max's face. He took another drink, replaced the glass, and folded his arms across his chest. His shoulders were raised, his right hand rubbing the top of his left shoulder, a look of deep vulnerability replacing his usual strength and assurance.

"The next day, my grandparents arrived and took me to Madrid, and Catalina came with us. I think my grandmother thought that would be good for me, but I don't believe Catalina would've let me go otherwise. She was very protective. They'd been to the hospital and got the story from my mother, who I learned later was drifting in and out of consciousness and probably not making a lot of sense. But they weren't taking any chances with their grandson.

"I never set foot in the house again, not until my father died three years ago. He spent many years trying to get me back while I was a child, but they feared he'd turn the violence on me, and the courts repeatedly upheld my mother's claim, that he was unfit to care for a child. So, I was brought up by my maternal grandparents while my mother slowly recovered, as far as that was possible. My other grandparents had been killed in a plane crash two years before."

Such a horrifying series of events must have had a profound effect on a small child. Amancia hardly knew what to say.

"Max, that's a terrible story. Maybe I've missed something, but I don't see what it has to do with not having children."

He picked up his glass and took a long swallow, before placing it carefully back on the table. He fixed his eyes on hers, searching for something.

"Don't you see? He was a violent, cruel man." He looked down before continuing. "What if I've inherited it? It's a kind of insanity, the violence, isn't it? It came out of nowhere, and maybe one day, I'll start to behave like that. What if I'm as evil as he was? What if I pass it on to a child?" He raised his eyes. "To our child?"

Amancia was quiet for a while. There was a shift in their relationship, but she ignored that, more concerned at the agony imprinted on his face. She had to help him to see things differently.

"That's a lot of what ifs, Max. It doesn't work like that. I don't accept the idea that anyone is inherently evil. Really, I don't. I think it's much more about how you're brought up. Maybe you can inherit a tendency to act violently, but I haven't seen much evidence of it in you." She was quiet for a long moment and then added, "Why did you join the army? For the chance to fight?"

Max raised his eyebrows at this change of subject, his eyes questing, trying to understand what she was getting at. "No. I…er…I hated what I'd seen that day. It never left me. I don't know how to explain it, but it made me feel worthless. Whenever I allowed myself to think about my life, which I did as little as possible, I couldn't see the point of it. The army? I suppose I thought it was a chance to serve my country, maybe be useful to others."

"You weren't attracted by the potential for killing and violence, were you? The opposite, by the sound of it." She dealt with another prawn, copying what he'd done with the first one, and ate slowly, which gave her thinking time. "And anyway, when you're aware that there could be a problem, it makes a big difference.

You can take measures to avoid the consequences."

"How can I run the risk? It would be wrong."

"You're not your father, Max."

"How would you feel if our child's grandfather was a murderer?"

"But he didn't kill—"

"He was tried for attempted murder and served three years in a mental institution. They claimed the balance of his mind was disturbed. When he returned here, he started proceedings to get me back, and when he failed, he drank the profit from any wine they managed to produce over the years."

Max's eyes swam with tears. It was a horrible story for any family to deal with, but he was still looking at it the wrong way around; it shouldn't be about his father but about who he was, and how he chose to live his life.

"It's so sad."

They sat in silence for a while, and then he said again, "How could I possibly take the risk?"

"There are never any guarantees," she said gently. "All you can do is your best."

Amancia didn't know what to do. He was deeply traumatized, but there had to be some way of moving him on, getting him to look at it in a different way.

"Are you really prepared to do this to yourself, Max? Your father has already been punished for the crime, and your mother still suffers. Is your life going to be ruined, too?"

"Can't we leave it, Amancia?"

"No. I don't think we should. You need to talk about it. And I need to know."

He stared at her for a long moment and then said, "It's not only my father. I can't trust myself either, but it has nothing to do with my genes. I have PTSD, a bad case. It makes me…unpredictable, and knowing what I do about him, I'm terrified of how that might develop."

He lowered his head into his hands, and after a moment, his shoulders heaved. Amancia slid along the bench and pulled him toward her, and he laid his head on her breast. "I don't know what to do." His voice broke. "I don't know where I should go from here."

Now her tears spilled over. When she looked up, the restaurant proprietor was heading in their direction, but she shook her head, and he turned away.

Max pulled himself upright, wiping his eyes with the back of his hand. "I'm so sorry…about how I've hurt you…about everything."

"You've had a lot to cope with, Max. It's hard, but you have to resolve this. This is your life we're talking about—and potentially, mine as well," she added, looking directly at him. What they had was no longer just a light-hearted romance. There was what he'd said about "our child." There was the way she felt about him. There was the way he surely felt about her. These things could not be pushed aside and ignored. "I think your mother would be horrified if she knew how you viewed this."

He took time to consider the idea and then said, "You're right. I can't go on like this. I was…I was coping, everything neat and organized, but since we met, that hasn't worked. You've made me think about my life—and I don't like what I see."

"I care for you, Max. That's why I'm pushing you to do something. I'll back off if you don't want me…involving myself in this. But I don't see how we can go on in that case."

It cost her so much to suggest they needed to part. She didn't even know if she could do it, but he had to confront the problem and begin to deal with it. The decision had to be his.

"No…no, please don't abandon me. I need you."

The pain in his eyes was unbearable.

"Aren't there practical steps you can take? What about PTSD? People do have treatment, don't they?"

It took him a while to reply, but he said suddenly, "I could go back to therapy."

"You already tried it?"

"Yeah, my grandparents insisted, set aside the money for the fees when I left the army. That was three, nearly four years ago, but I didn't believe in it, and nothing seemed to change. There were too many drugs involved, and I was already taking things to stabilize me physically after the amputation, so I gave up. Maybe I didn't give it enough time. I thought I'd got on top of things. And it didn't seem to matter."

"But now it does?"

"Now it does. It matters a lot."

They sat in silence after that, thinking about the next step while they finished off the wine. Finally, he said, "It's late, and I didn't really sleep last night." He grabbed her hand. "Please don't give up on me, Amancia. I don't want to lose you."

"You won't lose me unless you push me away. I want to help, and I don't want to lose you either." She had to drive him to take action, whatever the risk. "Until I know you've done something about it, we can't meet."

This was so hard, forcing him to tackle the issues head on. But if he wanted her, that's what he was going to have to do.

He was silent for a long time. Then he whispered, "I know."

A few moments later, they left the restaurant.

"I'll walk you back now, and then I'm going home. I'm going to sort this out. I'll ring tomorrow and tell you what's happening."

****

He had to see his mother, talk to her about what had happened all those years ago. He felt sick after the realization that he'd almost lost Amancia. She was still there, but he knew he must earn her trust, be the partner she deserved. She was encouraging him to sort this out, and doing so was the only way he could get her back.

"I have to work now, but I'll be here at eleven to have coffee with you, Mamá," he said the next morning when he poked his head around the sitting room door.

The thought of Amancia not being a part of his life made him view everything differently, and he realized they'd always pushed everything away, he and his mother. It was just too painful for both of them. But by suppressing those events, he'd done great damage to himself. It was time to face up to the past.

****

"Amancia means everything to me. I can't let her go if there's anything at all that I can do to make things right. So, we need to talk about…about what happened that night when you fell…when he pushed you down the stairs. I have to know if there's some madness in me that could affect my children. I have to know."

He'd talked for a long time, and she'd listened in silence, hearing the depth of his despair. She was responsible for this. She'd caused his suffering by

336

refusing to confront the issues herself, to accept her role in what had happened. She laid her hand on his arm.

"Listen to me, Max—there's no madness, just greed and selfishness and bad behavior. And not just on the part of your father."

"What do you mean?"

"I have to accept the blame for it."

She covered her face with her hands, ashamed that the great love she had for her son still hadn't shown her how damaging her silence was. She'd convinced herself it was better not to talk about it. Even now, it was painful to reopen the wounds. She took a deep breath. "I had an affair after we married. I guess I married too young, dazzled by a handsome, older man. I was sixteen, half Amancia's age. Maybe he saw me as a suitable mother for the son he desperately wanted."

Now she'd started talking, she felt a growing calm; at last, she could unburden her troubled conscience.

"Or maybe he just wanted our money. Because we had the vineyard, you see. It was ours, and it passed immediately into his hands when we married. Even my parents were taken in, flattered in a way that their daughter had been chosen by this *hidalgo*. But he was a nobleman without land and money—and, as it turned out, without nobility. But it's easy to gloss over that when everything seems to be going well.

"The moment I gave birth to you, he disappeared off to the capital, to his mistress, and he spent our money. Gambled it and lost. Drained the estate. Gradually, the vineyard began to go downhill through lack of care. Women, racing, drugs. The old story. But there are lots of men like that. That's not insanity.

"I struggled for a long time, trying to understand

why he treated me like that, still innocent in a way. Then, one day, a friend introduced me to her brother, and we became friends and then lovers for a brief period. I learned what it really feels like to be loved."

"He found out?"

"Yes, and two months later, my lover died in a mysterious one-car crash on a local road." She gave a hiccough that was more of a sob. "I'm even responsible for his death. Nothing showed up in investigations, but there was speculation among people who knew him that your father had killed him.

"After he found out, we argued about it constantly. He was determined to make me suffer for the blow to his pride. The evening of the fall, I told him I was leaving him. Of course he couldn't allow that. So he pushed me down the stairs.

"I was his possession, and I'd fought back. He couldn't accept that."

****

Max had phoned. Staying away from him would be the toughest thing she'd had to do, much worse than not being able to pursue the archaeology post she'd been offered just before her father died, which before had ranked high in her list of losses. She was to be deprived of his company, and it was entirely her own fault.

On her own, she cried again, but there was a scintilla of hope. When she'd heard his mother's story, she'd felt so sad that the intention to shield her son had led to so much suffering and that the actions of the young woman, deprived of love and affection, had set the whole thing in chain.

"I do understand," Max had said, "but it's a lot to take in. I've spent my whole life believing something that wasn't true."

"Don't let it change your relationship with your mother. She was young and inexperienced—and suffering."

"That won't happen."

The therapy to tackle his PTSD was to begin the next day.

She wanted to support him, but she accepted that he had to do this for himself, though it broke her heart. A whole month, they decided, during which they would not meet. She insisted they talk several times a week.

Closing her phone, she had to deal with the feeling of being abandoned. But she had set all of this in motion. And she didn't need to hide away in her flat moping. She had plenty to occupy her. The first and most important was to organize her classes. She made an appointment to see the professor.

Chapter 49

Had she done enough preparation?

Amancia glanced at her notes once again. She had prepared well but couldn't help feeling nervous.

While continuing to work on-site, she'd also spent some of the previous week reading through the curriculum and discussing teaching methods in Spanish universities with her new colleagues. Carmela and Juan had recent memories of their first teaching attempts as lecturers and were helpful. She'd even managed half an hour with the professor. He'd looked through her plans.

"These seem fine to me. Remember, the students want to be here, want to learn."

"Yes, but I also remember being a student, and honestly, some of the cleverest lecturers were hopeless at teaching, so boring. A lot of people didn't bother to turn up for their classes. I don't want that to be me."

He laughed.

"Okay, I'll grant you that, but you don't have to worry. You project your voice well, which is one problem solved already. Too many people mutter and lose their students in the first five minutes, even if they have something interesting to say. You'll be all right," he added, in his own rich, mellifluous tones.

She had to settle for that, and her first day, in just over a week, would show her how true it was. She had two days of teaching a week: Tuesdays and

Wednesdays. And a fair amount of time on those days was supposed to be for preparing future classes.

As she was about to leave, the professor asked how she was getting on with the dance club. "Maite's excited to have you in the dance team."

"I'm feeling anxious about that as well. I've never danced in my life."

"They're just ordinary women who decided that this year, they would take part in the festival instead of being onlookers, so don't worry. I think they're curious to get to know you, as well."

She'd hardly reached the bottom of the stairs when her phone rang.

"*Hola*, Maite. *¿Qué tal?*"

The woman had taken her under her wing, helped her choose the beautiful dress and the heavy black leather shoes with their high chunky heels that flamenco dancers wore. The distinctive part of the shoe was the metal plate fixed beneath the wooden heel and the toes so that the dancer could make the classic drumming noise. She felt honored that the little flamenco club was ready to let her dance at the festival with them.

At first, she'd been resistant.

"Maite, I can't. I've never danced. I don't even know how to start."

"Just come to our meeting tonight and see what you think."

She'd been enchanted. They'd drawn her in and made her practice a few steps, and she'd shown an aptitude for a first timer that had surprised the group. Amancia lost herself in the intricate movements, suddenly understanding the passion, the despair, the joy, and the love they expressed. Each dance told a story, and each dancer expressed that differently.

When she donned the dark amber dress with its black trimmed flounces and slipped on the heavy shoes, she entered a different world. As the music started up, her heart picked up the rhythm, and her body expressed the emotion that had built up over the last few weeks.

And now she knew that she wouldn't be experiencing the festival with Max, it had become important to do this.

"Don't forget about our final rehearsal on Friday."

"I'll be there."

Chapter 50

October twenty-first was her birthday. Thirty-one. Her life was rushing on so quickly.

But all sorts of good things were happening, and she'd had such fun during festival week: the flower pyramid was unbelievable—sixteen thousand flowers had gone to make it up. And she'd been overwhelmed by the procession with singing and music, the colors of the dresses and of the exaggerated street decorations: pink and purple paper balls hung overhead in one street, green and blue umbrellas in another, nets with balloons or flags. Individual shops displayed their own decorations. It had all added up to a wonderful frenzy. And then in the evenings, there'd been theater and so many concerts, from baroque music to rap, in every conceivable venue.

She'd danced with the club before an audience in a tiny venue, and they'd received a standing ovation. If only Max could have been there. But she'd promised to allow him this time, and she'd scarcely mentioned it to him, though she longed to do so.

She'd even gone to a bullfight with two of her new colleagues. Zaragoza had a magnificent bullring, the current building dating back to the eighteenth century. People said the bullfight wasn't for tourists, but although she felt queasy at the idea of the killing, she couldn't help but be affected by the magnificent spectacle it was, and the cries of the crowd. Still, she wasn't sure she'd go again.

The yellow brick museum of origami had been entrancing. Following that visit, she'd wandered alone through the craft fairs, choosing presents for her mother and sisters, wishing she were hand in hand with Max, listening to his suggestions.

"You'll be carrying all this back to Bristol," he'd said when she'd told him her intentions the evening before, "so don't get anything too big."

In the end, she'd chosen scarves and typical Spanish sweetmeats that were often given at Christmas and were already available at the stalls, so the tourists could stock up: *turrón* and *mantecadas*, *polvorón*; many of them used almonds in some form or other, whether in the making or to decorate afterward. And the packaging was exquisite, so typical of what she had seen of the Spaniards. Already in October, these things were offered at the stalls.

"You have to try *turron*," he'd said.

So, she'd bought some and opened a packet while they were still speaking on the phone, biting into a large piece. It was wonderful, but it was so intense, like fudge times a hundred. Just one bite was enough.

"I imagined you eating it. Did you leave any for me? In my mind, there was a tiny piece of *turrón* on your lip, and I licked it away." A flame of desire flashed through her, and sitting on her bed with the phone in her hand, she found herself unconsciously lifting her head to allow him to do so. "Of course, the most important sweet for a Spaniard is the *roscón de reyes*. You do know that, don't you?"

"I think I've heard of it—a sort of pastry ring with

jewels in it?"

"Yes. It'll be on sale soon, the commercially made type, but you can watch it being made in some bakeries. Mainly that doesn't happen until the beginning of January, in time for the Day of the Three Kings on the sixth, so maybe we can do that together."

"Yes, please! What about Santa Claus?"

"Yeah, some people celebrate that as well, but the sixth of January is still more important, and the day when children receive presents."

It was astonishing how much time people spent making sure everything was perfect for each festival. Attention to detail was everything. There was so much for her to learn, and she wanted to embrace it, become a part of this society. But uppermost in her mind was the question of when this self-imposed agony of separation was going to end.

****

Max was picking her up at half past eight. More than a month had gone by since they'd been together, and she could hardly contain herself with excitement and desire. When she'd asked where they were going, he'd said, "I'm not telling you. It's a surprise."

"So how do I even know what to wear?"

"Okay, valid point. Only it doesn't really matter. Maybe something practical, with a warm coat."

And that was all he was prepared to say.

She picked out smart, skin-tight, black jeans with boots and a loose sweater with a huge neck. It didn't look too bad. Maybe the brown leather jacket as well, the one with the quilted lining.

She rinsed her breakfast cup and tidied the flat, which took all of five minutes. It was far too early, but she so longed to see him. Where were they going? He'd kept that information very quiet. It could be somewhere like Pamplona, which would be interesting. But was it the right time of the year for it? That was the place where the bulls ran free in the streets. Only not all of the time, of course. People weren't that stupid— although allowing yourself to be chased through the streets of the city by bulls, even on one day of the year, sounded idiotic. They said someone was always killed, but it didn't seem to put people off.

Her doorbell buzzed. When she opened the street door, Max stood there, and they stared at one another for a long moment. She was overcome, wanted to cry. Then they flung their arms around each other and kissed, only stopping when a neighbor needed to gain entry. A few minutes later, she was climbing into Max's elegant car. It was bright and cold outside, but he had the top down. They kissed again, and then with trembling fingers, she took a scarf from her bag to cover her hair because a tangled mess wouldn't look good at all, would it? He picked up on her thought.

"You look perfect this morning, and the weather is just right, no cloud. *Buen cumpleaños, querida.*"

What was that comment about the weather?

"*Gracias.* Where are we going, Max?"

"This is your birthday present, *querida*. You must wait to find out."

They passed through the old town with the huge Moorish palace looming over them, the Palacio de la Aljaferia. How extraordinary, the way it brooded over the city. Then they drove a short distance along the banks of the Ebro, and still she had no idea of their destination.

"You still have your car."

"The buyer's abroad until Wednesday. The sale goes through at the end of the week."

The road looped sharply around, losing sight of the river. They were heading west, according to the dashboard compass. She sat straighter as they approached the airport, surprised when the main entrance flashed by. Almost immediately after that turning, they slowed. An open barrier led into a field at the far side of the aviation hub.

They swung in, and he nursed the beautiful vehicle along a gravel track, crunching around potholes. In the distance, a group of huts appeared and grew larger until she could make them out clearly, along with a couple of small planes. The stink of aviation fuel was everywhere. When they pulled into a roughly marked parking bay at the side of the first hangar, the propeller of one of the planes was rotating and the noise from the engine filled her ears. A man in a grey flying overall came toward them as soon as they got out of the car.

Amancia glanced at Max but said nothing. He clapped the man on the shoulder by way of a greeting and shouted to her, "Let me introduce you to my friend, Felipe. He's our pilot for this morning." She shook hands with him, and they moved into the hangar. It was relatively quiet, and they could now hear themselves speak. A tall, thin Asian approached. "And this is the photographer, Jesús Maria Li."

"Just call me Li." They shook hands.

"Right, if you're ready, let's go," said Felipe, glancing at his watch. "I'm going to run through general safety instructions, so listen carefully."

They approached the plane.

"Is this safe, Max? It looks like a toy."

"Safe enough," said the pilot, catching her murmured aside. "I'm out at least once a day, and we do make sure it's kept in tip-top condition." He smiled. "Don't worry—I wouldn't want a problem to develop."

A few moments later, they were strapped into their seats, and they bumped along a track and onto something that was recognizable as a runway. Her heart was thudding in her chest. She was okay with flying, but this machine didn't give her any confidence. The pilot got clearance, and then they took off. Amancia had grabbed Max's arm and now found that she'd been holding her breath as well. But they were in the air, and nothing bad had happened.

"Max, what a wonderful idea," she said, squeezing his arm and giving him a quick kiss.

"I thought we could fly over the vineyard and get Li to take a few photos. You tell him what you want."

"It would help if you could talk me through it," the man said through the noise. "I've done a lot of aerial photography, but usually for people wanting a picture of their house. This sounded a bit more interesting when Felipe invited me."

Tamping down her excitement, Amancia explained that they were looking for foundations and walls which might have the shape of a very large house, like a floor plan. "But it's likely to be overgrown in places with trees and bushes and may also be built on."

"No problem," said Li. "This camera is state of the art and will take very good photographs, and some video as well, yes? If it's there, we'll see it."

"Here we are," said Max, interrupting suddenly. "Look, the house is just ahead."

They'd been following the river, but now, the dig swung into view. They went down low and crossed it twice, and Amancia took her own pictures with her phone. Whether they'd be any good was another matter, but she had to have a go. She was thinking about the book she would write about their work on the site, and such photos would be an invaluable resource.

"Head for the main house, please."

It took a moment to focus, to ignore the modern buildings and read the shapes on the land, but as they made several passes over the house, she began to see the pattern of walls, the huge footprint of a villa with the current house perched on one side of it, covering about a third of the original. Low walls that were broken up in places by trees and bushes disappeared and then reappeared and ended at the pavilion that was now Max's house. How wonderful. She could hardly contain her jubilation.

There was a media story here, but Max wouldn't want journalists crawling over his property, disrupting work at the vineyard. It would take careful handling.

Again and again, she pointed out what she wanted Li to photograph. Later, they were back in the hangar, drinking coffee with Li, while he worked with Amancia on what she wanted from the photos.

"I can send you a link," he said, "so you can view all the photos and ask for enlargements of some of them—and they'll always be available to you."

They took their leave, and Amancia clutched Max's arm. "This is the most wonderful birthday present I've ever had. Thank you for thinking up such a brilliant idea."

He kissed her. "I love it that your best-ever present

is something for work."

"But I love my work. It's always interesting to me. I'm worried though. You couldn't afford to do this when you need money for the business."

"They're friends of mine, Amancia. They charged me very little, just covering costs, so don't worry."

They walked back to the car.

"And now," he said, "we have the rest of the day together, if that's what you like."

She made it abundantly clear that it was exactly what she'd like.

Chapter 51

It was great to be part of this lovely group of people. Four days after the birthday flight, they were in the professor's home. Einaudi played in the background, and glasses clinked above the hum of conversation. The last four or five weeks had given Amancia the chance to make friends, and her new colleagues had welcomed her.

Across the room, Max seemed a changed person, almost light-hearted, as he talked to another guest. After their conversation on that first night, he'd chosen a different therapist to start tackling his PTSD and was attending weekly sessions, paid for by his grandparents' original fund.

"You can pay them back," Amancia had said when he told her he couldn't possibly accept this. "You need every penny of your money for the vineyard, and you told me they're well-off. Don't be stubborn, Max. If they care for you, they'll be very hurt if you don't ask for their help."

"How do you know that's true?"

"Oh, Max, it's common sense." She sighed. "Sometimes high principles and pigheadedness are not such good qualities."

"Well, when you put it like that…" he'd said with a faint smile.

He was doing something called CBT—trauma-focused cognitive behavioral therapy. Amancia understood little about it, but it meant he could avoid the use of drugs. He'd been carrying the burden of his parents' story as well as trying to come to terms with losing his leg for a long time, and it would not be cured overnight. But as he tackled the problems of PTSD, he was beginning to see everything in a different light.

One thing, however, had changed completely: with his mother's confession came a realization for Max that his father's actions had little to do with a tainted heritage but instead were a result of immense pride and a sense of entitlement that came from his upbringing.

"I love you, Amancia, and I need you to believe that what I said about having children is no longer true. I want you. And I want your children if we can possibly make it happen. I want our children."

He'd told her this on her birthday. It had been wonderful to hear, and she couldn't doubt his sincerity.

"Congratulations on the site work, Amancia."

Staring unseeing across the room, Amancia startled at the sound of her colleague's voice. She swung around. Magdalena taught history, but she'd been interested in Amancia's work from the first.

"*Gracias*, Magda. Would you like to come out and see how far we've got? I'll be on-site with Sebastián and Martí tomorrow for most of the morning."

"I'm not free until eleven. How about I drive over after that?"

"Okay. We'll take a break when you arrive. But I have to leave at one, at the latest."

Amancia was going home for a short time. She turned away to speak to another colleague and caught Max's eye across the room. She loved his gaze on her;

something she had greatly missed, it was almost a physical thing, as if he caressed her, and a lovely, warm feeling coursed through her body. She gave him a tiny wave, turning to the professor who was approaching.

"It looks as if you've settled in well, Amancia."

"I have. Everyone has been really kind, your wife in particular. I'm enjoying what I'm doing so much."

He'd been very supportive, too.

"Professor, I'd better let you know I'm going away tomorrow to England for a few days. The students are doing practicals in various subjects, so there are no classes for me this coming week."

"You've been here quite a while. Will you be seeing your family?"

"Yes—and I have to pick up my cold season wardrobe unless I want to freeze over the winter. It's been more than three months since I was there, but I'll be back before the classes restart."

"*¡Buen viaje! ¡Qué te diviertas!*" He smiled and moved on.

She would have a good time. It was great to be going home, although it was sad that Max couldn't come with her, but it was the time of year when all the preparations in the vineyard were made for the following year. He and Alejo were trying to put in place a robust scheme for tackling the effects of climate change. She looked across at him again. He was now deep in conversation with Ángel, who'd been invited with a group of other final-year students. They'd be discussing the next addition to his website.

It wouldn't hurt to do her own thing, even though all she wanted was to be with him. Their relationship had certainly been tested. Hmm! A colleague from the

English department made a beeline for him. Maybe a different sort of test was going to happen, and sooner than she'd expected.

Carla sidled up to Max, a delighted smile on her face. Amancia disliked her bright red lipstick and vampish appearance, but the overuse of eye makeup and the figure-hugging dress was eye-catching. Experience suggested that Max wouldn't be interested in advances from other women, but who knew what might happen when two very attractive people were in proximity? And she certainly was a good-looking woman, while she whom he professed to love would soon be a thousand miles away, with a channel of water twenty-six miles wide and the whole of France between them. This thought was very depressing.

"She's the determined type, isn't she? You'll have to watch out."

Núria, who divided her time between teaching forensic science and offering her expertise to the state, was watching Carla and grinning. Aware she was only teasing, Amancia still couldn't help bristling as she saw Max turn to greet Carla, the spike of jealousy catching her by surprise. What on earth could the woman have to say to him when he wasn't even a colleague? Carla reached up and placed a hand on Max's shoulder, pulling him down to her level. Suddenly, Amancia felt large and ungainly, compared with the dainty person by his side. She forced herself to turn away.

****

"You were getting on well with Carla," she said as they walked to her flat a little while later. "It looked as if she was making some proposal. Interesting, was it?"

Today was the first time they'd met since her

birthday four days earlier. When she got back from England, this was going to change. A desperate longing had invaded her, every part of her responding to his nearness. She wanted to reach out and draw him close, and she couldn't bear the thought he might leave her at the street door and not go up to her flat.

She continued walking. She hadn't quite kept the acid note out of her voice, and now, Max stopped and pulled her to him, running his finger down her cheek, sending a shiver right through her.

"You're not jealous, are you, Amancia?"

"Of course not—well, only a little. After all, I am going to be away."

He gathered her in and kissed her, persisting until she responded. "That's better. You're going to have to trust me, *mi amor*. Her partner's involved with the archaeological site they've discovered at El Forau, and she wondered if I'd heard about it. Believe me, she has no interest in me, nor I in her."

"I'd like to think that's true."

"It is true." He tightened his arms around her, and she pushed up against him, inviting his kiss. The packing could wait until morning.

Now, they'd arrived at the street entrance. She put in the code, and the doors swung open. "Come on up."

Chapter 52

It was weird being back among her family: noisy, intense, with little time on her own. She'd forgotten how their big house had always been full of people when she was a schoolgirl. Nothing had changed. Of course, people knew she was back home and dropped around. She got that. But when the mortgage repayments had ended two years ago, she'd got a flat of her own, and she'd got out of the habit. Suddenly, she needed time to herself.

"We're doing a pork roast on Saturday," her mother had said when she arrived. "Can you help me with the organization?"

Amancia sighed. In her family, it was like the return of the prodigal son. Or in this case, daughter. Pork roast parties equaled "welcome home," using any excuse, which she'd now provided. The news filtered out to family, friends, and neighbors, and magically, people would appear on the appointed day.

They had a large walled garden, ideal for the event in summer, but if it was cold and misty November weather on Saturday morning, the whole thing would move indoors to the huge basement kitchen.

"You go to Herbert's to pick up the rolls and order…let's see…another sixty, Amancia."

Okay, so there was no getting out of it. Truth to tell, this forced immersion in family life was enjoyable.

She wouldn't change them for anything.

Early that morning, she jogged along Picton Street and was waiting outside the bakery by seven o'clock, picking up the white rolls and warning them she'd be back for more. The baker smiled. "We'll get another batch on after the morning rush. Come back after twelve." Over the years, Herbert's had got used to the ways of the Harding family.

By the time she arrived home, Uncle Dan was there, getting the barbecue started. His craggy face creased in a wide smile, he came over to give her a hug. "It's good to see you. You finished over there in sunny Spain?"

"It's just a flying visit, Nunc. But I'm glad to see you all as well."

There was a ritual about the barbecue as far as her uncle was concerned. He liked to get it right, starting long before any cooking took place. He used a Jamaican-style oil-drum barbecue and wouldn't be seen cooking with anything less than the genuine article. Although traditionally, Jamaicans cooked jerk chicken or beef on the barbecue, he'd add vegetable and beef burgers and sausages. This was the twenty-first century, and people had different requirements. He even knew Jamaicans who were vegetarians these days. He didn't approve of this betrayal of tradition, as he'd often told his nieces, but in the end, he'd make sure everyone got what they wanted.

They talked for a minute or so, before she said, "Got to go, Nunc. They're waiting for these."

The heavenly smell of roast meat that had greeted her out on the street did not come from Uncle Dan's efforts. Two magnificent pork roasts now occupied the middle of the kitchen table. Juices leaked into the channel around the boards on which they stood, and they were covered in crackling. She couldn't help taking a piece.

"Leave that," said Anna, her next sister down, who was beginning to slice the other joint. Amancia slipped a piece into her mouth and snatched her hand away.

Her youngest sister, Chedza, stood at another table in a huddle with a group of school friends, boys and girls. Shrieking with laughter, they were chopping salad ingredients and filling an assortment of bowls with different kinds of pickles, sage and onion stuffing, and apple sauce. A skinny boy with red hair and an undernourished look stood beside Chedza. Her little sister was growing up. The lad was interested in her. In fact, it was a sure bet he was in love. Not that Chedza appeared to notice. Who wouldn't be in love with her beautiful and talented sister? She turned away, smiling, and began to cut the rolls.

"Don't fill them yet. Wait till people come to the table and leave them open so they can pile on the salad and pickles." Melanie shooed away her two-year-old, who was trying to help himself from the table. "Have you forgotten, Amancia? You bin gone too long, girl," she added, dropping into the patois they sometimes used at home.

Sisters! There was truly something special about the relationship. They'd all changed in small ways that probably only she noticed because she'd been away. Each of her sisters contributed something different to the family, but time passed so quickly, and everyone was changing. Yet she felt the strength of their love and bathed in its warmth.

But now there was another love and other good times to come, and her sisters were not the only ones who were changing. It would have been great if he'd been able to come with her.

People began to arrive, and a queue formed, as if a mysterious message had been transmitted.

Someone removed the Rolling Stones album, and now, one of Chedza's friends took over and put on some drum and bass, nothing Amancia could identify, but it did do something for the atmosphere. Her mother told them to turn it down, and she smiled to herself—how many times had she heard that in her teens?

When they began to serve lunch, everyone wanted to talk to her about what she'd been doing, where she'd been, whether she was home for good. Then some hungry person behind in the queue would prod them to move on, and she was spared further conversation.

"Zaragoss? Where zat to?" asked an elderly man who lived alone but always turned up at a pork roast. "Sounds forrin ter me."

Glad to escape for a few minutes, Amancia went to fetch more of the soft, floury rolls from the bakers, and by one o'clock, the queue was snaking around into the garden. It was great to see so many friends. She'd had reservations about a party, but now, she was enjoying herself. Max would have liked this, too. She gave a regretful little sigh; it wouldn't be long before she returned to Spain, and then she'd see him again. She had to be patient. She went into the house with her purchase and resumed her place behind the table.

"Ca-an't eat this, me luvver. It doan' agree wi' me, pork."

"Okay, Mrs. Evans, Uncle Dan's outside with the

barbecue and beef or veggie, if that's any better."

Finally, there were just a few people in the line. When Amancia looked up, her mum caught her eye on the far side of the room and mimed a cup of tea. Amancia nodded. There was beer and pop in plenty and lots of other drinks people had brought along, including the homemade scrumpy cider, contributed by Mike-next-door-but-one. Exceedingly alcoholic. But none of it appealed to her, especially not the cider. Her mother filled the kettle and switched it on.

She was looking tired, and there was a slight stoop to her tall, angular frame, but her lovely English rose complexion had scarcely changed. It wouldn't be a bad thing to look as good as that, once she passed fifty. Amancia went across and gave her a hug.

"I'll make the tea, Mum. You sit down and have a rest. You've been on the go since four this morning."

The doorbell chimed. Who was bothering to ring the bell? Anyone who'd come to this party knew they should go through the side gate into the back garden.

"I'll go." Chedza rushed past and vanished into the corridor.

****

"Someone for you, Amancia." Chedza was back and giving her a curious look. "I've put him in the sitting room."

Him.

Amancia left the kitchen, her heartbeat picking up as she took the stairs two at a time. No...it couldn't be...could it?

She waited a moment to get her breath back, preparing herself, because she knew. She pushed open the door. The room was in semidarkness, but he'd pulled one of the wooden shutters a little way open and was gazing out of the window, like that first time she'd seen him in the university. She recognized every line of his head, the slope of his broad shoulders, the way he stood when thinking, his head slightly to one side. He turned, and as she met his eyes, the muscles tightened low down in her abdomen, and she flushed. She ran to him and flung her arms around his neck.

"Max! Oh, Max. I can hardly believe it."

"Hey, you're going to knock me over," he said, wrapping his arms around her and taking possession of her mouth. She didn't care. He was here, and everything was perfect. After a long moment, she drew back to look at him, and then they kissed again.

"What made you come? I thought you had so much to do, that you couldn't be spared."

"I lasted two days, and then I was useless. I couldn't do anything without you there, so I had to see you. I needed you."

"But your work…?"

"You're more important than work. I cleared up any problems and left Alejo in charge."

She laid her head on his chest and just wanted to stand there in the circle of his arms. As they kissed yet again, a crash of breaking glass reached her ears, and she grabbed his hand.

"Come on. I'm going to introduce you to my mum and the rest of the family. Pretty much everyone I know is here. Lizzie and Jake arrived about half an hour ago."

"Let's do that," he said.

****

Max was speaking to her mother, who was assessing this newcomer in her daughter's life.

Amancia saw cautious approval. But Max could be very charming, and it would be hard to disapprove of him under these circumstances.

"Amancia, the room next to yours is free now that Christina's not living at home. While I'm talking to Max, why don't you make up the bed and let him leave his things there?"

Of course, Mum was laying down the rules; with her youngest daughter still at home, she wasn't going to suggest the two of them share a room. They were still talking when she returned. Lizzie caught her eye and mouthed something that looked like "very good."

Later, he met each of her sisters. Scenting romance in the air, the four of them looked about as excited as she could ever remember. They were too polite to say anything about what they were thinking, but there would be an interrogation in the not-too-distant future, that was for sure.

It was just great that he'd come, and now she wanted to be alone with him. She scraped food off plates, carried a stack to the dishwasher, and returned for another pile. Despite doling out the rolls almost the whole day, she'd hardly eaten a thing, and lack of food was beginning to make her feel dizzy. She leaned across to pick something from among the remains on the table and found Max at her side.

"You're tired. Can you leave this? Can we get away for a while, maybe find somewhere to eat?"

"You read my mind." Her favorite restaurant was just around the corner on Zetland Road. "We could go to the Saigon Kitchen. Lots of lovely Vietnamese dishes, and you can order as much or as little as you like. Would that do? I could ring them."

"Perfect."

"Okay, give me a few minutes. I need to finish clearing in here. Then I'll change."

"Go now. Leave me to do this."

She raised an eyebrow.

"You? In the kitchen?"

"I do know my way around a kitchen, you know." He was grinning at her obvious astonishment. "I even cook. When we get back home, I'll prepare you a meal. You'll see what I can do."

"I'm surprised Catalina lets you anywhere near her wonderful kitchen."

"She doesn't. I'm talking about *my* kitchen."

Amancia looked at him quizzically. "I don't remember seeing—"

"No, we weren't there for eating, I seem to remember. But we soldiers are very practical, and food is high on the list of necessities, so I do have a kitchen, and I know how to use it."

She hurried up to her room. The little restaurant was very popular, and it was quite late, but Trung was a friend. She managed to get a cancellation. Then she studied her reflection critically in the mirror. She wanted to look her best, but wild hair, old jeans, and a crumpled, blue shirt with a red ketchup stain on the pocket didn't come anywhere near. She'd gone for practical for the party. Now, she needed a little allure.

Quickly, she stripped off, laid out fresh underwear, and showered. Then she opened the wardrobe and flicked through the dresses hanging there, finally deciding on a long sheath of fine, plum-colored wool with a huge roll collar and a narrow leather belt of the same color. Yes, that would work, especially with the boots she'd unearthed the other day. Now, what was missing? Lipstick, that was it. She didn't have many of them, because it was something she almost never wore, but that coppery shade always looked good. She leaned forward and stared hard into the mirror. Okay, it was quite a transformation. She'd achieved a lot.

She checked the mirror again. Was it possible she was trying to compete with Carla, with the lipstick and clingy dress? She smiled at her reflection. And if she were, why not? Now she'd identified her man, she wasn't going to sit back and allow others to take him over. She transferred things to another handbag and threw her long, brown winter coat over her arm. It would be cold outside by now.

Downstairs, the kitchen had been cleared. A low hum came from the dishwasher, and voices floated in from the darkened garden. Sitting with his back to the stairs, Max was deep in conversation with her uncle Dan, who'd finally abandoned his barbecue. As she came down the stairs, Nunc gave a bark of laughter and clapped his hand on Max's shoulder. They were sharing some military reminiscence, by the look of it, both men clearly enjoying the moment. It was great Max had found a way to connect, wonderful that, already, he seemed relaxed with her family. Amancia left them to it and went to find her mother.

****

It had worried him, the idea of talking to Amancia's uncle, raking up what had happened to them both, but the older man was very relaxed. "It was sheer bad luck," he said, having described how he'd lost his leg. "And I was a complete mess when I came home."

He talked about his time in Afghanistan, after

hearing Max's account of what had happened to him, and Max said, "I know what you mean. I'm not proud of the way I've behaved. Frankly, I'm not out of it yet."

"Yeah, but honestly, I was ready to kill myself, and so unpleasant—bad-tempered, difficult, not helping myself, blaming everyone else. I wasn't married, so my brother made me come and live here. I didn't want to, and I'm lucky he didn't throw me out. I wouldn't have got through it otherwise. I feel sorry when I look back and think how hard it must have been for all of them."

This was a fresh glimpse into the family dynamics.

"At the time, I'd have done anything rather than face up to what had happened, but they cared for me."

At the moment, the treatment Max was undergoing was bringing positive results. He hadn't had a nightmare in the last ten days. They'd hardly broached the horror that was his family's past, but somehow, having talked to his mother, he no longer felt the same way about it. But neither did he have any illusions; it was going to be a long haul.

Curious as to how things had worked with Dan, he said, "I can see they got you back to being yourself. Did you do any therapy?"

"Yeah. Didn't believe it would work, but every time I wanted to quit, Amancia wouldn't let me. She was a little angel, but...even then, she was tough, you know. She wouldn't give up."

Max smiled. "I have noticed how determined she can be."

"Eleven years old, but she knew how to get a laugh out of me. I think, mainly, I didn't want to disappoint her, you know, and somehow, being positive got to be a way of life. I'll never forget how important that was to me. Three months in, and I started to feel different." He was quiet for a moment. "Listen, a lot of guys give up on it. If you get the chance for treatment, take it. And stay with it."

****

Amancia didn't have to look far to find her mother. Ensconced in the sitting room upstairs, she was pouring yet another cup of tea. In this house, the world turned on cups of tea. Without asking, she handed a cup to her daughter, who sat down and took a couple of sips.

"Mum, we're going out for a while."

"Make sure you've got your key then. And don't forget to lock the door when you get back."

It was strange, when she came home, how it felt as if she were a child again. "Yes, Mum."

They talked for a few minutes. When she got up to leave, she bent to kiss her. "It's been a great day, a lovely party. Thanks. Now you get some rest."

"I've rarely been at a party where the person it was given for did as much work as you did today. Thank you, Amancia. I have missed you, you know. Now, don't keep him waiting."

"We're going back to Spain tomorrow, Mum."

"I know. Just don't leave it so long next time."

Chapter 53

Why did they have to go to Madrid? As she climbed aboard the plane in Zaragoza airport two weeks later, there was a sour taste in Amancia's mouth and a weight like a stone in her stomach.

This was a bad idea. There couldn't be a bigger difference than the one between her large, ramshackle family in the house back in Bristol, with its doors open to all comers, and his starchy, aristocratic relatives. A grandfather who'd joined the army and fought, albeit for a very short time, on General Franco's side. A tyrant who had people tortured, for God's sake! Not his grandfather, of course, but even that connection wasn't acceptable. She didn't want anything to do with them.

The plane was only half full, and they had a row of seats to themselves. "He was only nineteen at the time," said Max as they settled in. "And he's not starchy. I care a lot for him, and anyway, it was his father who pushed him into joining up. He's a monarchist if you talk politics with him these days. It's my grandmother that you need to watch. Now, she can be scary."

He was grinning as he spoke, trying to lighten the moment, but the image of a supercilious, horse-faced grande dame slid into Amancia's mind and wouldn't be dislodged. She was not reassured. "They'll look down on me. A Black girl from the ghetto."

"You are being overdramatic. You know that, don't

367

you? First, you've had more education than the whole of my family put together. Not a single one of them has been anywhere near a university. They do read a lot, I'll give them that, but my grandfather restricts himself to biographies, and my *abuela* reads romantic novels, although she claims they're of a superior quality."

"There's nothing wrong with romantic novels."

Her mother was much the same. She was a busy woman, but it must have been so difficult to fill the time after Dad's death, all those hours when she used to share things with him, and suddenly…a void.

Max continued, "You said that you were the first to go to university in your family; well, so was I. The only difference is, they've got some money, but a lot less than they used to have."

"Money of which you refused to accept a single euro, you said."

"What I used for my business was my own. I spent almost nothing while I was in the army and invested well. I had to make a go of things, prove to myself that I could. That was important to me, and it still is. That's why the car had to go. And I will pay back the fees for the therapist as soon as the vineyard starts to make a profit." Suddenly, he turned and hugged her. "Thank you, Amancia, for making me talk to my mother…give the therapy another try. All this has changed my life. You've changed my life."

His words seemed to penetrate her skin and then her heart. A glow began within, and she clutched at him, never wanting to let go. "I can tell how different you feel now. It's such a relief. I was really worried about you."

"It's shown me how to look at things in another

way, how to stop being so…self-centered."

"I don't think it was surprising you felt like that, given what happened to you." She gave him another hug and then settled back on her seat. "It's sad about your beautiful car."

"True, but it's just a car. The vineyard will be successful, I'm determined. Then I'll be able to get another one. Anyway, don't change the subject. My grandparents won't be critical. More likely, they'll be terrified of you. And secondly, they love me and want the best for me, *entonces…*"

"How do you know that'll make any difference?"

"It'll be enough, *querida,* believe me."

"Well, I—"

"Amancia, I don't like this 'Black girl' business, as if it's something to be ashamed of. It doesn't matter where you come from or what your background is. How's that important? It's what you are that I care about. And you're lucky in having a wonderful family, so warm and welcoming. And talented. There's nothing to be ashamed of, and by talking like that, you're making it seem that there is."

He squeezed her hand. "Listen, *querida*, there's no other way. I'd spare you if I could, but if we're going to be together, you have to meet my family, not just once but many times over. They matter to me. They're part of who I am."

"Oh, Max." She kissed him. "I'm sorry. But my family isn't composed of wealthy aristocrats with an image to live up to. Your people go back a long way, and they're going to be much more resistant to the idea of…of us."

"You're looking at this wrongly. Everybody's

people go back a long way. There won't be anything like that."

She was quiet for a moment, thinking it through. He was right. Then she remembered what Maya had told her. This was not as difficult as it was for her.

"You took the risk and turned up at my home, and they loved you. Mum asks me every day when I'm bringing you back to Bristol with me. I'm just being silly. I know I have to do the same."

"And you know what? I was scared. It's part of the reason I came over. I had to see how things were."

"You were scared?"

"I was. I thought many times, what if they don't like me? What if they think I'm the same inside as I look on the outside?"

"And what's that then?" she asked, batting her eyelids. "Gorgeous? Sexy?"

"That, of course." He dropped a kiss on her head. "But you know—arrogant. Sadly, this could be."

Her cheeks darkened a little, as she remembered her own first impression of him, and she turned her head in case he noticed. What had been her thought? Full marks for arrogance? Ouf!

"Is he looking down on us from the top of his nose?" he said, giving the expression his own twist. "He looks scary with that scar. What's he doing with our dear, beloved Amancia?" He squeezed her hand. "I know what I look like to some people, but no one can help their looks. And talking of looks, I feel I should say this, because I'm not sure I have, but you are the most beautiful woman I have ever met. Ever." Now he pulled her to him and kissed her hard. "I adore you, Amancia, and I want to be with you always."

Her heart beat faster, as she understood what his words meant.

She said in a small, choked voice, "You never told me you liked the way I looked before, never once."

"Perhaps not. But it's not because it's not true. I just thought you probably got enough of that. I see the way other men look at you. Men sit up and pay attention when they see you, and their eyes light up. Even that charming old professor back in Bristol was being…er…extra-charming when you walked in. It must get on your nerves sometimes, as if they don't really see you, the person, just the exterior."

He did understand.

"You're right. I do feel like that. But you do know that all women like being told they look good, by the right person, of course, don't you?"

"I'll try to remember that. It won't be difficult."

She took his hand and held it tightly. He'd come so far in the last few weeks. And so had she.

They landed and now sped away from the airport in a taxi. But as they entered the city, they slowed down, and she began to absorb the details of the capital, a city marooned high up on a plateau.

She'd found her milieu easily enough among the academics in Zaragoza, enjoyed working with them, and never gave a moment's thought to what impression they had of her. It was brains that mattered, and she hadn't even questioned whether she matched up, knowing that she did. But this would be a whole different scene.

They passed through some outlying districts and were heading for the flat where his grandparents lived, on the avenue between Plaza de Colón and Plaza de

371

Castilla. He said they'd had to sell their property in the country, but as they drove down the avenue of luxury apartments, the reduced circumstances he'd mentioned looked opulent to Amancia.

As they closed in on the Plaza de Colón, she took her eyes off the discreetly expensive blocks that lined the wide avenue.

"What is that fantastic monument?" The sculpture was huge, the head of a girl in white marble.

"You're looking at Julia." He pronounced it as if the *J* were an *H*—Hoolia. "She's caused quite a bit of trouble one way or another, quite divisive."

"Don't people like it?"

"A lot of younger people now believe a statue of Colón—Columbus, for whom the square is named—is not…how do you say 'políticamente correcta'?"

"Politically correct, it's the same in English."

"Right. So, they prefer this. But many people are shocked, horrified even, and see it as an attack on tradition and on the respect always accorded to him. People love Colón."

"It reminds me of the Black Lives Matter protest in Bristol, when they threw the statue of Colston into the river because he profited from slavery, even though his activities had done so much for Bristol. It was quite shocking. What do you think about all that, Max?"

"Did you feel insulted by the statue of Colston?"

"No, but I'm not political. I'm basically a historian, and it is history. What sort of historian tries to hide away inconvenient facts? Bringing down the statue was supposed to help Black people, but it's more like pushing all that away, so people don't have to confront it. Maybe instead they should just alter the descriptions that accompany these statues, explain the change in attitudes, and why. That would be good, I think, more educational. A French friend told me they've done that in Bordeaux, which was just as involved in the slave trade as Bristol."

"Yeah, I think we Spaniards are a bit too keen on tradition. But sometimes, change is necessary. Besides, this is a great work of art."

Amancia gazed up at the statue as they approached. "She's beautiful, and her eyes are closed. So maybe it's meant to show she's not making any judgments."

"You're lucky to see her. It's a temporary installation, so she'll be taken away in a few weeks."

But now, Amancia was no longer paying attention. The car was slowing. Seconds later, the driver made a turn, and they drew up at the foot of a flight of steps leading to an imposing entrance.

Inside the wide foyer, Max called a small, private lift which stood alongside the main ones. Reality hit her. She was about to meet his family. This was truly the moment when her life would change.

He darted an anxious glance at her, saw how nervous she was, and drew her into his arms. "I love you, Amancia, and I want you to marry me. Say you will, *mi amor*."

A gentle sound emanated from the lift shaft, and the doors swished open, but neither went to get in.

"I love you too, but I don't know about m—"

"Good, then, it's settled," he said, kissing her quickly. "Come on. We mustn't keep them waiting."

The lift carried them up to the eighth floor. Max's arm was around her waist, holding her firmly, making her feel safe. But she was troubled, too. Pondering his words, Amancia looked at the floor as they rose through the building. When the lift came to a silent stop, she lifted her head. The door slid back to reveal an elegant hallway, with light everywhere, high ceilings, gleaming wooden floorboards, silk rugs. But she hardly took in her surroundings because Max's grandparents were coming toward them.

She took a deep breath. The way her thudding heart was threatening to choke her, she couldn't speak.

Max introduced his grandparents. His *abuela* was exquisitely dressed in fine, pale blue wool and cream silk, her faded blond hair in a French pleat. Kind eyes. No trace of horse features. His grandfather had the military bearing of one who had been in the army. Dark eyes she couldn't read, black hair turning to silver, an impressive man who was only a little shorter than Max. His smile was welcoming. Amancia shook hands with them both, and Max embraced and kissed them. His grandmother held him in a long hug, and that was the beginning of a thaw in Amancia's feelings toward her. She cared about her grandson.

They answered questions about the journey while coats and gloves were being removed, and now they were sitting in front of a truly panoramic view. The French windows looked onto a wide terrace and from there, onto Plaza Colón. Over to the left, Amancia caught a glimpse of Julia, symbol of a new attitude. Twelve meters high, Max had said.

Nothing occurred to make her feel uncomfortable, but the atmosphere wasn't easy. Then she thought, *It's not them. It's no different from when you meet anyone for the first time.* She had to make an effort as well.

Maria, his grandmother, said in her impeccable

English, "Amancia—may I call you that?"

"Of course, please do."

"What about tea? Could you help me with that?"

The woman was reaching out. And maybe she wanted to leave the two men together to talk. It was a long time since Max had visited.

"I'd love to. Everyone in my family drinks tea."

"That's quite an English thing, isn't it? I expect there are lots of different traditions."

"A few. But I wouldn't call myself an expert."

They went on toward the kitchen discussing whether they preferred tea or coffee.

"You speak wonderful English, María."

"I spent a year in England, with cousins in Derbyshire. Not long enough to understand everything about the English, but I did pick up on your best traditions, and tea is one of them."

They put things together on a tray and boiled water. She took out an old-fashioned English china teapot and placed an array of tiny pastries on a plate. Her hostess must use this kitchen for times when she wanted to prepare tea or coffee, not for real cooking.

"Max looks well, so happy. It must be due to you."

Amancia flushed. "I haven't done anything to—"

"We have worried so much about him since he returned from Ukraine. He has been sad, and for a long time, it was difficult to get through to him. I feared he was a lost cause, alone, unhappy. But I can see he has changed. He must care a great deal about you."

"I hope that's true," she said, "because I care a lot about him."

Chapter 54

"Let's go for a walk."

They'd had a long, slow lunch which began late and finished around five. It was amazing how much they'd talked. Amancia hadn't noticed the time passing, but now fresh air beckoned. The sun was descending fast toward the horizon. The air was cold, and it would soon be dark.

"I thought you said the weather would be mild in Madrid," Amancia said a few minutes later. The sun had just set, and a mist was beginning to rise.

"You cannot be sure at this time of year. But you are warm, ¿*verdad?*"

"Oh yes!" She was wearing a fur scarf his grandmother had pressed on her as they left the apartment. She patted it now and said, "I know all the reasons why we shouldn't wear fur, but my goodness, this is great."

They turned through tall gates into El Retiro. The park was deserted, and the last of the leaves crunched beneath their feet in the growing darkness, as they strolled past a pale sheet of water that gleamed in the mist. It was impossible to see to the other side of the lake, and soon they left it behind.

"Max."

"What is it, querida?"

"You know I won't hold you to what you said."

"What? What did I say?"

"About getting married. I know you wanted to make me feel good, so I could face your grandparents—and it worked. Actually, they're great. And I really like your terrifying grandma because she cares so much about you. But also, she's just very nice."

Max stopped walking and turned to face her. "Amancia, you're talking nonsense—or at least that part about getting married. I have no intention of letting you go again. Haven't you understood that? And I didn't ask you at that precise moment to help you face my grandparents, although I'm glad if it had that effect. No, I wanted you to know that I'm committed to spending my life with you, to creating our own family. Whatever my grandparents' reaction might have been, you are more important to me. Even if they were negative, it's you I would stay with. And we'd work to change their minds. But they love you already."

He caught her hand, pulled her hard against his chest, and kissed her. It took some time, and when he released her, he said, "*Y eso es solo para empezar*—that is only for starting."

Sometimes, when he was feeling emotional, his almost perfect English slipped a little. She gave a little smile. It endeared him even more to her. But his declaration had stirred her. Weak and a little trembly, she clung onto his arm.

"I couldn't have given up my family, not even for you, Max," she said in a small voice.

"Nor could I give up mine. No one should ask that of anyone. But I would have gone against their wishes, even if that made them give up on me, and that's what I wanted you to know."

Holding tightly onto each other, they walked on a little. The massive black trunks of trees, whose tops were now invisible, loomed up out of the thickening mist. The fuzzy glow of lights in the distance shed no illumination here, and they were only just able to see their way. In this environment, nature dominated and screened them from others.

He grinned at her now. "You know, if it weren't for the fact that the temperature is two degrees and the mercury's still heading downward, I'd drag you off into those bushes and have my wicked way with you."

"That sounds good," she said. "Where did you get an expression like that?"

"I don't know, but I hope it conveys how much I desire you."

"Oh, I think so." She kissed him. "Just so you know, you wouldn't have to drag me. I'd probably push you along, even try to get there first, but..."

"But you don't like the cold."

"Or the damp, so that's out."

"Good, very good, because instead, I'm going to ensure this agreement that we have is—"

"What agreement is that?"

"That this agreement is...*vinculante*—binding. In case you try to escape from it. What time is it?"

"About seven—five to."

"Come on, then. They'll be closing soon."

Grabbing her hand, he set off running toward the shopping streets that bounded the park. As they hurried along, their breath huffed out and hung in the damp air.

"What are we doing? Where are we going?"

But he said nothing, continuing to pull her along. They ran past the Fuente de Neptuno, where they crossed to the other side of the road. A few moments later, he halted in front of a shop in the Calle de Serrano, a curiously understated little place painted pale grey, with small windows artfully lit.

"Max."

"Come. I got the impression that you…what's that expression you use?…that you're quite fond of me."

"I don't use it about you, Max. It seems rather inadequate for the way I feel about you. But yes, I am…very fond of you."

"So, I hoped, if I asked you all over again now, properly, that you might agree to marry me and mean it this time. Proposing in the foyer really lacked style."

He turned her to face him. "*Amancia, mi amor. Te quiero desde el fondo de mi corazón.* I want to marry you and for us to have children together. *¿Quieres casarte conmigo, querida?*"

Almost overcome by the violent surge of emotion that swept through her, Amancia took a deep breath. "*Te amo también, Max.* And yes, I do want to marry you."

"*Mi querida.*" He spread fervent kisses over her throat, her cheeks, her lips. "You have made me so happy. Come on in. Why are you hesitating?"

"These things are worth a fortune, Max, and you have no money to spare. You can't—"

"I can. Stop looking at the prices and—"

"There aren't any prices. That's why I'm hesitating. It's so expensive here that most pieces are not even on display. But anyone can see what stones like these will be worth. A lot, too much for—"

"I know you're concerned about the cost but—"

"I don't want you to spend money that's vital for

the vineyard. I have simple tastes, Max. I can do with so much less."

"The stone is a family possession and belonged to my great-grandmother, who was just a little fiery like you. I think she'd appreciate your having her ring. It looks very old-fashioned, so I'm getting them to mount it in a modern setting. It is costing me very little."

"You really mean that?"

"Amancia, I wouldn't risk the vineyard. This is separate, I promise you. Come inside now and stop prevaricating."

They entered the shop, hand in hand. A small man with a bald head and an impeccable suit approached.

"*Señor. Señorita. ¿En qué puedo servirle?*"

They talked a little, and Max took out the ring, a beautiful diamond, still in the original setting. The stone was quite large, but the simple oblong design was bold, very much her style. He reached for her left hand. "In Spain, you wear it—"

"On the middle finger."

"On the middle finger." He slipped it on and kissed her. "Now we are *novios*."

The jeweler looked on, impassive. Now he took the ring and measured Amancia's middle finger, before inviting them to study the proposed design.

"It's really beautiful."

Max arranged payment. "It's a pity we can't take it now, but they'll deliver. It won't be long."

Outside, it was completely dark. They crossed back into the park and sat on a damp bench.

"I saw you, you know. Dancing."

How was that possible? The venue had been tiny. Then she remembered how dark it had been.

"I was sitting with Andreas in an alcove. When you finished, I left. I knew how involved you'd become, wanted to support you."

"What…what did you think?"

"It was the moment I truly knew that I'd fallen in love. That dance…I imagined everything was for me, selfish brute that I am. I love you, Amancia."

She took a deep breath. "I love you, too, Max. And, yes, it was for you, in my mind…"

She trailed off and began to kiss him, felt him respond, knew how much he wanted her. "You excite me, Max. But you also make me feel…cherished, that you will always take care of me. And maybe even allow me to take care of you. That is such a wonderful combination. You give me so much."

"And you have given me back a reason to live. I knew, from the first moment I saw you, that something special was happening to us, but I tried hard to resist."

"You did?" She leaned back now, a teasing smile curving her lips. "Because you were terrified of me?"

"Yes, that day when you grabbed me in the street and kissed me, you put a spell on me, *mi pequeña bruja*, and I tried to run away. I should have known better."

"*Pequeña*—little?" she said. "Are you sure you have the right woman?"

"Ah, I know I have." He kissed her again. Never had she felt so small and delicate, so protected. "How could I imagine I could escape?"

"That was foolish of you. I never intended to let you go. Oh, Max, I'm so happy. I can't believe we've sorted everything out. I never thought about being engaged. It's a big statement to everyone. I don't know what to say."

"As long as you haven't changed your mind in the last two minutes, there is nothing to say."

A while later, hands tightly clasped, they turned in the direction of the flat.

A word about the author...

Mary Georgina de Grey lives on the beautiful English Riviera in the UK with her artist husband. Having lived and worked in several countries in Europe and South America, she sets out to infuse her books with the language, culture, and atmosphere of the country in which the story is set.

A prolific reader in a variety of genres, Mary Georgina has interests that range from European cooking to designing and making haute couture clothing, so there are plenty of sources for ideas.

Mary Georgina swims every day and often walks on the dramatic cliffs of this stunning coast.

Visit Mary Georgina at

Facebook:
https://www.facebook.com/profile.php?id=100086424 198194

Instagram:
www.instagram.com/marygeorginadegreyauthor/